T0194269

Finding Favor and the Secret of Rainbow Moor

Yvette S.M. Debeau

authorHOUSE®

AuthorHouse™
1663 Liberty Drive
Bloomington, IN 47403
www.authorhouse.com
Phone: 1 (800) 839-8640

Published by AuthorHouse 11/08/2016

ISBN: 978-1-5246-1369-3 (sc)
ISBN: 978-1-5246-1370-9 (hc)
ISBN: 978-1-5246-1371-6 (e)

Library of Congress Control Number: 2016909489

Print information available on the last page.

Dedication

This book is dedicated to my two sons, Troy Shane and Shiloh Dante'. They have given me immeasurable joy and pride as I watched them grow from little boys into happy, responsible adults with families of their own. I am very proud of them and their accomplishments.

Epigraph

"Life is not measured by the number of breaths we take,
but the moments that take our breath away."
--Unknown

"Life isn't about how to survive,
but how to dance in a rain storm."
--Unknown

Preface

My passion and fascination for writing stemmed from early childhood. I was most content when putting pen to paper, often turning my work into oral presentations, which lead me to take a number of Public Speaking classes both in High School and College.

We all have childhood dreams. Some dreams fade away, but others never fade. Instead, they lie sleeping within waiting to be awakened. And then one day you realize that passion is still there and suddenly you feel more alive than ever before.

When I entered a new world of imagination, be it another author's book or my own writings, I happily became part of a new world, place, time or adventure and remained as long as possible. For a while, like many, I'd relish in that world as it became more real to me than the actual world around me. It was a marvel to feel each and every character's emotions and cry, smile and laughed with them. When fear gripped their hearts it gripped mine as well. Their emotions became real. Their grief became my own. Amazingly I experienced their pain, anger, hurt, fear, joy, laughter and happiness.

I wrote this book many years before, but with the passing of time, raising a family, the relentless push to survive, eventually becoming a single parent, and the daily demands with its many expectations led me farther and farther away from the world of writing that I loved, leaving in its place a void.

The inspiration for this book came from two separate but very profound personal experiences that occurred several years apart from the other. The first was a mysterious caller who watched me for over two years. I never found out who he was.

The second was when I visited the house that became the main setting and focus of this book. Putting them together I created the story you are about to read. It is about everyday people who live simple, ordinary, day to day lives, but whose lives, aroused by the unexpected, become the extraordinary.

I chose to give the main character of this book the name of Favor (French for Approval), her French sir name, Durand, is a derivative of Durandus. I chose this name for its meaning of "everlasting".

In late 2012 I almost destroyed this book, but a few words of confidence from a friend encouraged me to find my passion again, and finally led me to pick up my old manuscript and revive the dingy faded words, bringing life back into the patiently waiting pages of my sleeping manuscript.

That friendship made me mindful that life is astonishing and wonderful. Our lives become intertwined with others. Friendships come and go. Each friendship is a privilege and an important part of life's journey. We never know how another person can or will affect our lives and that they may only be there for a season. We cross paths with some that, even if only for a short time, somehow become a very important part of our lives. Some friendships are forever friendships, while others are but a stepping stone or a stopping off point where we stay but for a while. Sometimes these friendships though unexpected, for one reason or another, have a profound impact on our lives.

One particular friendship made a profound, "forever" impression on my life. The connection was unique, extraordinary and exceptional. This individual's sense of humor and uncanny ability to make me laugh unwittingly helped me get in touch with my inner self and helped me truly believe in my creative ability. The result of many long conversations coupled with the laughter, taught me to be true to myself, first and foremost. A hard lesson to learn, and one I still struggle with, but from which I found fortitude and the staying power to complete the book I had written on a typewriter many years before.

Acknowledgment

M any sincere thanks to my family and many friends, too numerous to mention, for the support and encouragement I received when I set out to complete this book. Their belief in me has been unbelievably inspiring.

I'd also like to thank Keith Carter former owner of Rainbow Moor, and his wife Virginia Thissell-Carter, both longtime friends and former colleagues, for sharing some interesting history of Rainbow Moor with me and the house that inspired the setting for this book.

The land where the house stands had been owned by the Roth family and traded for some other land to Major Wallace C. and Inez Clapp. Major Clapp served in both World War I and World War II and suffered Delayed Stress Syndrome due to his time in the military. His desire to live a secluded, simple life away from crowds made the property an ideal place to build his home. He built the two story 3 bedroom home and gave it the name of Rainbow Moor. Both Wallace and Inez Clapp were teachers and bore one son. Their son had to ride a tall draft horse down the mountain to attend school in the Bridgeville School District. The Clapp's requested permission to home school their son after he fell off the tall horse on his way to school. The request was denied by the school district so Inez packed up and left with her son to return to Texas where she had grown up. Major Clapp stayed behind and continued to live in their California Mountain home.

Major Clapp even built a crypt in a portion of the home which was large enough for one single casket to fit into. Upon Inez insistence he installed a "bathroom" which at that time consisted of only a toilet. Around 1954 or 1955 the Clapp's sold the 600 acre property to the Carter family which was later split between four siblings. A larger lake above the property is called Sweasy Lake. I am told the small lake outside the house at Rainbow Moor has pretty much been taken over by peat moss.

Keith gave me the name of the current owner of the land where the house stands. It was my desire to return to the house on Rainbow Moor that inspired the setting for this book, to touch the worn stair railings, to look out to the lake area where the grape arbor stood, to feel the serenity and peacefulness of that mysterious mountain home, but unfortunately the current owner was reluctant. I know that seeing Rainbow Moor again would have been ideal, but alas fate did not allow it. I found myself having to rely on the memories of that majestic house and the setting on the moor for my inspiration to bring new life and meaning to the pages of this book. After speaking with the Carter's I was thrilled to find that my memories of the home and the surrounding moor was pleasingly and relatively accurate.

Last but not least, I'd like to thank Author House Publishing for their direction, support staff and for the opportunity to work with them on my first publishing adventure.

Now I invite you to tiptoe quietly off to your favorite hiding place, be it a quiet corner of your house, a wooded grove, a sandy beach or river bar, your own mountain top, wherever you are, relax and get lost for a little while in the cryptic life of Favor Durand.

Chapter 1

Late afternoon and the suns glow cast a soft shimmer on Favor's cheeks as she rested her elbow on the slightly weathered wooden railing of her deck. Brushing back a wisp of hair as it strayed across her forehead her gaze wandered contentedly over the peaceful countryside and the nearby Eel River meandering along its banks. The fresh air smelled of honeysuckle and roses. With her eyes slightly closed and her head tilted slightly backwards she took in a deep breath, letting the sweet spring air fill her lungs. Then slowly she exhaled as a soothing breeze caressed her face like an invisible creature daring to touch the soft wholesomeness of her skin. Feeling invigorated as a slight tingle swept over her, a wave of contentment made her smile. The sweet smell of the honeysuckle growing along the nearby fence engulfed her as it trailed aimlessly up the pergola creating a shady haven for the little meditation garden below. Tams and junipers and shiny-leafed caramel creeper, with its sage blue blossoms, lined the driveway leading up to her modest split-level home. The long, slim, leafy branches of a nearby willow caught the soft, early June breeze, blowing gracefully like long locks of hair.

Immersed in subconscious thoughts and unaware of an approaching figure, she hummed softly as she ambled aimlessly along the length of her deck. Startled back to awareness by the sound of deep hearty laughter, she leaned precariously over the railing edge.

"Adam, how long have you been standing there?"

"Let's just say long enough. I tried calling you earlier, but you must not have been home or you didn't hear the phone. So what daydream were you so lost in that you didn't even notice a handsome cuss like me?" Favor

just smiled, ignoring the question. "Since I've interrupted your secret little world, how about coming over to my place for a while? Most of the gang is there and we're getting ready to barbecue up some burgers. We thought we'd watch a movie or play some games after dinner."

About to reply her phone rang, "Come on up," she called over her shoulder as she disappeared through the open deck door. Tall, thin and lanky, Adam Jennings took the steps two at a time as he bounded up the stairs and entered the front door. Comfortable in her little bungalow style house, he knew Favor didn't mind his intrusion and he waited quietly as she answered the call.

"Hello." Her cheerful voice greeted the caller at the other end of the line. There was silence for a moment. "I've told you before when you talk to me like that I'll hang up. You can't be talking to me in that manner. You won't tell me who you are so why do you keep calling? Aren't you getting bored? Maybe you need to think about getting a life?"

Adam stood listening to her conversation and noticed that her last remark was spoken in more of a teasing almost flirtatious manner. It troubled him because it didn't seem like her nature to be speaking to a perfect stranger in that way. It also sparked a strange feeling of jealousy in him which took him by surprise.

There was silence as Favor listened to the anonymous caller. "I can't stop calling you. I want and need you. And, Favor," the caller hesitated a moment and then concluded, "I will have you one day," then he hung up. His words sent a chill down her spine and made her cringe just a little. This call was different and there was something strange in the tone of his voice. She couldn't describe it. It was more of a feeling she couldn't quite wrap her mind around. Standing there staring at the receiver in her hand she slowly put it down as she turned around with a puzzled and a little concerned look on her face. She had all but forgotten that Adam had come in and was startled when he spoke. The look on his face made her suddenly feel self-conscious.

"It was that guy again, wasn't it? Why don't you just change your number?"

Favor didn't like the look on Adams's face. It was her business and she didn't want to talk about it. "I don't know, stubborn I guess," she said shrugging with a matter-of- fact attitude. "It's no big deal. Sometimes he's actually nice to talk to."

She thought about the mysterious caller and his secretive voice that for some reason intrigued her. Yet for some reason the call tonight seemed different than his usual calls. The call and maybe the fact that Adam was standing there listening had frustrated her. "Sooner or later he'll find a girlfriend and quit calling me. He really does have a terribly sexy voice," she teased, then promptly changed the subject. "I thought we were going over to your house. Do you want me to bring anything?"

"We were, but now that I'm alone with you I think I'd rather stay here." Adam's eyes took in the soft willowy lines of Favor Durand's sleek body. She wore a pale blue, hooded sweat-shirt over a tiny white camisole, with matching blue shorts. Her subtle skin had turned a golden tan from the summer sun, adding vitality to her already healthy radiance. Favor had long, dark hair as black as a raven. It enveloped her face like it was wrapped in black velvet, cascading softly down her shoulders and back. But even more alluring was the intensity of her deeply mesmerizing brown eyes. Her mother often said she had bedroom eyes. Whatever that meant. It was a comment that intrigued Favor and made her feel daring and confident which didn't set well with her mother who held a deep jealousy of Favor's beauty and would rather have locked her away so no one could see the delicate, yet strong mortal that she was.

Favor laughed in a playful way at the expression on Adam's face. "Come on, let's go before someone comes looking for us," as she whisked passed him she quickly grabbed his hand.

Adam knowingly gave a good humored shrug as he followed her out the door. "Well, you can't blame a guy for trying." Favor hesitated a moment as she pulled the door closed, looking back towards the phone, still thinking about the caller's words, a slight frown creased her brow and another peculiar unexpected chill crept up her spine. His words still echoing in her mind gave her an unsettled feeling.

Cindy, Favor's closest friend, greeted her with a welcome hug as she and Adam came through the door of Adam's house. A bubbly little blond, she didn't have the spark and intrigue that Favor had, but was pretty in her own right. "When Adam said he was going to get you, I didn't expect you back so soon. I figured we'd end up having to send out the troops," she teased.

"Cindy, don't be silly. There's nothing between Adam and me. We have a completely platonic relationship."

"Oh sure, I've noticed how he looks at you. He's crazy about you! I really think you should take him more seriously. All the other girls envy your relationship with him, even if it isn't as you say, intimate."

Looking at Cindy for a moment with a puzzled look on her face, she seemed to be letting Cindy's words sink in. Peering around Cindy she looked over at Adam Jennings. He was about five feet ten inches tall, muscular build, sandy blond hair and skin deep bronze from long hours in the sun. His features were strong, but gentle. Funny she'd never allowed herself to think of him as any more than a friend. There were rumors that he'd had a relationship in the past that had ended on a bad note that he didn't want to talk about. She admittedly knew other girls had spoken enviously about their friendship, but she had never thought to be so presumptuous as to think he could be more seriously interested. From what she had heard he was a confirmed bachelor and simply enjoyed a special friendship with him. While growing up they had attended the same high school. Now, years later, they had both returned to their home town, and had surprisingly purchased homes on adjoining properties, becoming close friends. It all seemed a lifetime ago.

Her thoughts were interrupted when Houston, Adam's roommate and best friend, came over to greet the two girls. Houston Olsen was a rather large, burly sort of guy who was a little rough around the edges, but the big teddy bear type. He had played football in high school and college and later took up bull riding at the local rodeos. Though very attractive to women, he never seemed to have anyone steady in his life and didn't seem to date much. They often teased him about having a secret lover hidden away somewhere. He would jokingly go along with the teasing and say, "Yeah, I have to keep her away from your influences."

Adam called him over to the barbecue. He leaned over and gave each of the girls a kiss on the cheek saying, "Don't go away. I'll be back. He can't keep me away from two beautiful women like you for long."

"Hey, don't be kissing my girls and get over here."

"Your girls, huh, who says they're your girls?" They all laughed as Houston headed over to where Adam was busy getting burgers ready to cook. Favor caught Adam's eye and she blushed at the way he looked at her. He winked and she smiled, turning away so he could not see her flushed cheeks.

"Favor, see what I mean, you're blushing!"

"I am not!" she chided, much too quickly to be convincing. "Speaking about men, Houston wouldn't be a bad catch for you," she spoke out bluntly, then laughed at Cindy's obvious embarrassment. "Now look who's blushing. So do I detect something? Do you have a thing for him?" Cindy didn't answer, but her blushing red cheeks were a dead give-away. They looked at each other and both broke out laughing, neither confirming the other's assumption. Their outburst caused everyone to turn to see what they were laughing about. Turning, they both walked off to get something to drink, still laughing. "Come on, let's go over and make sure they don't burn the burgers," Favor concluded.

Adam and Houston had been watching the girls with interest. "Ok, ol' man when are you going to tell Favor how you feel about her," Houston urged. "You snooze, you lose."

"You've got a lot of room to talk. You think I don't know you're interested in Cindy? What are *you* waiting for?"

"Shucks, she'd never want to be with a big oversized oaf like me." They saw the girls approaching and abruptly stopped talking. "So what were you two laughing about over there, or should I dare ask?"

"Dare if you want, but you won't get an answer?" Cindy chided.

"Hey, I've got an idea. Let's play a game of touch football." Favor, always spontaneous and exuberant, eyes that glistened like a shiny mirror, never afraid to take the initiative, stood there with a childlike grin and an expectant look. How could anyone say no? Never over-bearing, strong and enthusiastic she drew people in and captivated their hearts. A sheepish twinkle in her eyes and you were hooked. Before long she had everyone out onto the lawn to choose up sides. One just couldn't resist her play-fullness.

"What about the burgers?" Adam yelled after them.

"The burgers can wait, unless you two want to keep on cooking. Up to you." she teased. She gave him a challenging look. He knew that look, so play they did. It was one of those late spring days when the weather was so perfect that you could hardly describe it because it was more of a feeling. Their laughter and cheers resounded out onto the early evening air. The warm breeze was energizing. Paul threw a pass and Favor jumped to catch it, falling backwards into Adam's arms. They stood there in the street laughing when an emerald green 4x4 truck came down the road. "We'd better move before we get run over." Adam said as he pulled Favor off the road back into the grass.

Favor noticed the driver and said, "Uh, he's a cute one," just to tease Adam and make him a little jealous. As the evening shadows lengthened and it became more difficult to see, players began drifting back to the house. Of course there were a few faithful die-hards who had to give it one more shot. Adam headed back to the barbecue while Houston went to get them a beer. Favor was still playing and he noticed Cindy was now relaxing as she watched the final challenge. When Houston returned with the drinks, Adam nodded in Cindy's direction. "No time like the present ol' man. There's no one else around."

Houston wandered over to Cindy and asked if he could get her something to drink. Smiling she said yes, but that she'd go with him. Wandering out onto the front porch, Cindy noticed the same truck that had passed earlier was parked down the street and commented that it looked like someone was sitting in the truck. Houston shrugged it off saying it was probably someone smoking a joint.

The smell of burgers cooking drew them to the back patio. The football game had given them a hearty appetite. There's nothing like the taste of food cooked over the barbecue. Somehow it seemed to taste better. Add a few good friends, some drinks, and you have the recipe for the perfect evening.

While everyone was settling down to eat, Adam and Favor found them-selves alone in the kitchen. "Houston seems to be spending quite a bit of time with Cindy this evening," Favor commented, hoping to get a response. "Haven't you noticed how good they look together? I think they make a really nice couple, don't you?"

"The only one I've noticed is you." leaning in closer to her. She could feel his warm breath as she turned to face him. Adam leaned in closer and she felt his tender lips as his mouth sought hers. She pulled back shyly,

but he reached out to her and drew her close to his warm body. Again she resisted.

"What are you doing? You've never acted this way before!"

"I'm sorry, I don't know what got into me," he lied. The tone of his voice suddenly made her aware of her own attraction to him. Their eyes met and they seemed to be drawn to each other by some invisible force. Once again he drew her close and this time she didn't draw back. She felt her heart pounding. And then he was kissing her. She responded eagerly.

"Oops! Sorry, ol' boy didn't mean to intrude. I was just coming after a couple of beers." It was Dave, one of Adam's long time childhood friends. Favor blushed at the intrusion and quickly left the kitchen hoping to avoid any further embarrassment. Adam followed. He was pleasantly amused and content to watch the blushing young woman from across the room. Before long Adam was actively engaged in a sports debate while others of the group listened in or got lost in their own quiet conversations. Favor, leaned back contentedly in an easy-chair, and smiled with contentment at the pleasant warmth of her friends. She was keenly aware of Adam's repeated glances in her direction and she wondered just how much of his mind was really on the sports conversation. Something inside her stirred and she realized she wanted to feel him close to her again.

Her thoughts drifted back a few years to a very different life before she had come back to her home town of Fortuna. The quiet, slow pace of the town was a far cry from the life she'd lived in the city. Here she'd found peace, contentment and the realization of who she was. The city was only a few hours away if she cared to go, but she found herself less and less interested in leaving her safe haven. Life here was simple, less complicated. People enjoyed the outdoors and a slower pace.

The fresh country air was sweet smelling, unlike the stale odors of the city. Her three years here had been a time of healing and growing, a time to build her self-confidence. She was no longer self-conscious of her own beauty and self-worth. Unlike the stifling city, life here was intoxicating.

The sun had begun to set. The first stars of the night were becoming visible as the evening shadows stretched across the horizon. At the end of the private lane the occupant inside the green truck had been intently watching the group.

Chapter 2

Just out of college and having landed a very desirable job with a large interior design company, Favor had met Conrad Durand. His firm had hired her company to do the interior design for his new offices. Her whirl-wind marriage to the young corporate tycoon had been nothing short of a carefully orchestrated plan. By choice she had not dated while attending college so she could concentrate on completing her education and pursuing her career. She had been swept off her feet by the handsome young executive. At the age of twenty five he had already been made a partner in his father's firm and was quickly headed for the top. The corporate world she found herself in was overwhelming for a simple girl from the country.

Conrad, who was keenly aware of Favor's beauty and talent, had decided she was the perfect match for him, the "icing on the cake", so to speak, in his climb up the "ladder of success". She was the doting wife, always at his side. They were the perfect couple and the perfect example of how a successful couple should live, act and breathe. Everything in their lives was put in its proper place and perspective. She was the perfect, gracious hostess at the never ending stream of dinner parties and charity events. Conrad insisted she have only the finest and most expensive possessions, always dressed in the latest fashion, and the envy of every woman that she came in contact with, young and old. He adored her and loved "showing her off". When they made love it was always passionate and in the most romantic of settings. He knew how to excite her and took great pleasure in their love making. But the marriage was lacking to say the least. She supposed Conrad loved her in the best way he knew, but her life was not her own. Her "friends" were carefully chosen for her and she was sent to her own job each day in a limousine. She found this embarrassing. Conrad "allowed" her to work. It was not that she needed to work. They were one of the wealthiest and by far the youngest of the rich in Conrad's world. Conrad grew increasingly obsessed with his work and she grew more and more lonely. Her only avenue of sanity was her design work.

He enjoyed watching her work on the designs, and seemed genuinely proud of her, frequently directing clients to the company she worked for. It pleased him to no end to see their pleasure at the result of her designs. But Conrad was so engrossed in his own priorities that he didn't seem to notice she needed more. She needed time alone with him, to visit with him. She wanted to be able to take a walk in the park, hold hands and talk to him with no one else around. She needed more time for intimacy and time for "love". Conrad was on a roller coaster and didn't know any other way.

His work took him away a great deal of the time. When she was not working on a deadline, he would insist she travel with him. On occasion her own work would take her away. Conrad would usually be busy with some other business dealing so he would not be able to accompany her. But he would arrange all of her lodging and travel needs and when she arrived there would always be a lovely bouquet of flowers to remind her, as he would jokingly say, that she belonged to him. Shortly after her arrival she would get a call from him to be sure she had arrived safely and all her accommodations were acceptable.

It was on one of these trips that she had by chance run into Adam Jennings, an old school friend from many years back. She had all but forgotten her old friends and her old way of life. In talking to him she began to realize she didn't really know herself and missed the quiet, simple life she had grown up in. Somewhere along the way her individuality had gotten lost and she realized what she really wanted was to be herself. But she wasn't sure who she really was now. Her life was not structured around who she was, but instead around who Conrad was.

Several months had passed since her chance meeting with Adam. Conrad had been especially preoccupied with work and upcoming holiday get-togethers. Favor had tried, on several occasions, to get him to spend some time with her so they could talk. She needed to tell him how she felt. But he always had something else he simply must do first. She pressed him for some time alone only to have him say, "Soon my sweet, as soon as I finish with the arrangements for this project." But then there would be another project or another function and the months kept slipping by. He was never rude, harsh or impatient with her. He would always sound truly apologetic, but the time finally came when she met him at the door with her suitcases.

It was only then that he realized how alone she felt. He promised to change and be the man she wanted and needed, but Favor knew he was who he was and would always be that way. Her parting was bitter sweet, but they remained friends. He insisted on providing her with a handsome monthly income and helped her to get settled in her new home. True to his word, he called every week and flew out to see her once a month where they would spend quality time "getting to know each other." She looked forward to his visits and he was finally learning to relax. For the first time in their marriage they were both happy. He shared his work with her and she shared her work with him, finding they actually enjoyed talking about and sharing their work with each other. He began making time to travel with her when her job required it. They were even talking about starting a family.

And then one day she got the call that changed her destiny forever. After a remarkable, wonderful weekend with Conrad she got a call from Conrad's father. Conrad's plane had crashed and he was in serious condition. He had internal injuries and they needed to operate. They sent a private plane to pick her up and she rushed to be with him, arriving just moments before they were to take him into surgery.

"Hold on, Conrad. I'm here. You have to get well. I'll be waiting just outside the door. Remember we still have a family to plan. I love you." She squeezed his hand and kissed him gently. It was the longest five hours of her life. The doctor finally came out of surgery to let her know the surgery went well and his chances looked good.

Conrad spent the next few weeks in the hospital recovering. Each day he seemed to improve a little more. Favor stayed by his side every moment she could, talking or reading to him. Sometimes she just held his hand or stroked his hair. One day while she was taking care of some business Conrad called in his attorney and arranged to have Favor made a full partner in his company. He wanted to be sure that if anything happened to him now or in the future, she would not have anything to worry about. He knew she wouldn't like that he had done all this so he instructed his attorney not to say anything unless something went wrong. He needed to have the reassurance she would not have any worries.

One day Conrad took a turn for the worst. The doctors were discussing another surgery. How could this happen? The decision was finally made to perform the surgery the following day. The doctors were optimistic. Conrad was in the right state of mind and he was prepared to undergo the second surgery. It seemed he was resting well that night.

The sun was peeking over the eastern ridge. It was a warm spring morning. Conrad opened his eyes and looked into Favor's adoring face. "Hey beautiful, put your arms around me. I'm a little bit cold."

"Do you want me to get you another blanket?"

"No. I just need your warmth. We can watch the sun come up together." She gently wrapped her arms around him as the warm sun rose into the morning sky. "Favor, I want you to know you will never want for anything. I put your name on the company and I've taken care of everything. Thank you for standing by me and giving us the chance to be happy together. I will always love you, my angel."

"Why are you talking like this? You're going to be fine."

"I just want you to be happy. Promise you'll do that for me." They were his last words to her. A few moments later Conrad died in her arms. As the warmth from his body slowly slipped away she felt her heart was breaking.

Conrad had already instructed his attorney as to what his last wishes were. Funeral preparations had already been made. Standing at the graveside, watching as they lowered his body into the ground, grief enveloped her. Why had this happened when they were doing so well and had fallen so much in love. There were so many people there but she had suddenly felt completely alone.

Chapter 3

Favor's thoughts were suddenly interrupted by a burst of laughter from those sitting in the room. A small glimmer of light rested on the edge of the horizon as the summer sun slipped slowly away, giving way to the soft evening and the sound of crickets as darkness approached. "Did you say something?" was her startled reaction.

"Earth to Favor! Where the heck were you?" Paul was saying. "We've been trying to get your attention. You looked like you were a million miles away." Favor realized everyone was staring at her. "Could you flick on the light behind you?"

"Oh, I'm sorry," she mumbled as she blushingly reached back to turn on the lamp. "I hadn't realized how late it is. I guess I must be a little tired." She rose gracefully from the comfort of the chair on which she had been sitting. Adam's feelings were aroused as he watched the soft lines of her delicate figure. She made her way to the door, saying her goodbyes as she went. Adam rose to follow, stopping her as she stepped out onto the porch.

"Hold on. Are you really leaving? Why don't you let me walk you home?"

"Adam, it's only a short walk down the lane."

"You're not upset about what happened in the kitchen tonight are you? I'm not going to say I'm sorry because I've wanted to kiss you for a long time. Tonight every time I looked at you I wanted to touch you. By the look in your eyes I think you felt the same way. I saw it in your eyes and I felt the excitement in your body when you were in my arms."

"You're right, but maybe we just got lost in the moment. We've known each other a long time. We've been friends since we were kids. I didn't realize you had feelings for me and that my feelings were growing for you. I just don't know how to handle this."

"Favor, all we need to do is continue to enjoy what we already have together and take our relationship to another level. I'm not trying to push you, I just want to spend more time with you and I don't want to pretend my feelings are no more than friendship. Do you have any plans for tomorrow? I really want to do something together." His eyes met hers with a plea that made her melt.

She smiled. "I understand what you are saying and I have to admit I liked the way it felt to be close to you, but I need to take this slow. I hope you understand. I want to do this right."

"What do you mean? Is that a no? As many years as we've been friends I think we know each other better than anyone else does."

"Adam, I didn't say no. In fact I'd love to spend the day with you tomorrow. Call me around nine." She started to walk away, but turned and with a flirtatious smile and said, "Better yet, how about you just come over at nine and I'll fix you breakfast."

"Now that's an offer I can't refuse. Nine it is. Not a minute later. Now are you sure you won't stay awhile longer or let me walk you home?" He had pulled her close again and was holding her tight. She smiled and gently pulled away kissing him lightly, then turning she headed down the steps. She felt as though her feet had wings. It had been such a long time since she'd felt so alive. When Conrad had died she had thrown herself into her work denying any feelings that she might have for anyone and just surviving from day to day. She smiled as she walked briskly down the lane to her home, her thoughts drifting back to when she and Adam had first resumed their old friendship.

It had been about six months after Conrad's death that she was going through some of her clothes she hadn't worn in a while, checking the pockets before sending them for cleaning, she had reached into a pocket and withdrawn a small slip of paper. On it was written Adam's address and phone number. She remembered how seeing Adam had triggered her need to be in control of her life and she had moved back to Fortuna shortly after. But then she and Conrad had grown close and even though she did not miss the hectic life she used to lead, she missed the Conrad she had known before the end.

It was on that very day she found the slip of paper that she had decided to give Adam a call. She smiled to herself as she walk down the lane, remembering how she had frozen when she heard his voice on the other end of the line. She had hesitated long enough that he had thought it was a prank call and had hung up the phone. It had taken her several days to finally call him back again. She had no idea what she would say. Maybe he had someone special in his life or maybe he didn't really mean for her to contact him. But she finally made the call. When he answered she spoke as casually and with as cheerful a voice as she could, hoping he wouldn't hear the insecurity or nervousness she was feeling. She said who she was and before she could finish the sentence he blurted out, "I've been thinking about you. I didn't think you would ever call me, but I haven't been able to get you out of my mind." She had been so shocked that she didn't say a word. "Hello! Favor, are you still there?" She had stammered out a 'yes'. From then as the conversation progressed and after an hour on the phone she had hung up with plans to get together for dinner the following week. Not long after they met up with each other the adjoining property came up for sale and to the surprise of Favor, Adam purchased it. From then on their friendship grew.

The moonlit May evening was studded with stars like tiny creatures watching the earth. Their twinkling fascinated Favor as she looked up at them and thought of them as tiny eyes blinking, watching the silly people of earth going about their daily lives. She almost skipped her way home and the crisp night air filled her with energy. Turning up her driveway she realized she felt happier than she had felt in a very long time. It made her feel giddy like an adolescent school girl, and she felt like singing and acting stupid. She thought of what she would cook for breakfast. It would be perfect to have their meal out on the deck where they could enjoy the morning sun and the sounds of the birds.

Completely unaware of the dark green truck now parked next to her drive she ran briskly up the stairs not even stopping to turn on the living-room light as she entered. The brightness from the moon outside made it easy to see. Instead she headed straight for her bedroom to draw a bubble-bath and soak for a while before going to bed.

She didn't notice the quiet figure sitting in her living-room easy chair in a nearby corner of the room. Upon reaching the door leading into the master bed-room a voice spoke her name. A feeling of panic replaced the feelings of happiness she had felt only a moment before. Heart pounding fiercely in her chest she whirled around to see the figure of a man rise from the corner chair. Seeing the movement she had only a moment to decide if she could make it back to the front door and run or if she should try to get to the bedroom and lock herself in. Her heart was in her throat. Finding her voice and trying to act brave and assertive she choked out in a loud stammer. "Who are you and what are you doing in my house?"

Reaching over he turned on a nearby lamp. The light flooded the corner as he stood there looking at her. Amazed at how strikingly handsome he was she froze in place. His hair was as black as her own, with eyes bluer than any she had ever seen before. For a moment she was awed at his handsome physic and then shocked at her own thoughts and reaction for even noticing his features. Her mind was racing, but her body wouldn't move. Mesmerized she felt anger growing inside herself as she tried to get her mind and body to work together. "What is the matter with me? I need to do something."

"You don't remember me. You don't know who I am, do you?" She didn't respond. "You should, you know," confidently taking a step towards her. Stepping away she tried to figure out who he was and what she should do. There was something about the voice. What was it? Lost in confusion and emotions she didn't notice he had advanced closer to her. He was about six foot tall with broad shoulders and was speaking again as he closed in on her. Startled into action when she realized he had advanced toward her, she bolted, trying to make it to the front door. He had anticipated her move, quickly blocking her path. She screamed as she darted first in one direction, then another, in an effort to escape. Ready for whatever move she made he chided, "Check mate!" mocking as she tried to get past him. Grabbing a nearby lamp, she hurled it at him. As he reached up to block the lamp, she rushed past him. Reaching for the door knob, his hand came down on her arm, hurling her body back against him, his arms quickly encircled her. Struggling blindly to free herself she knocked over several objects in the room. Her attempt failed. Anger welled up inside her. How dare he touch her? Men think they can have a woman just for the taking? Continuing to struggle, her anger gave way to renewed strength. Only a few moments had passed but it seemed like it was an eternity. Tired from the struggle she began to weaken. Unexpectedly she lost her balance and felt herself falling to the floor, and then he was on top of her holding her down. Tears began to burn her eyes as she continued to struggle, breathing hard and trying to avoid looking in his eyes.

"I'm not going to hurt you or take advantage of you so stop struggling! You're taking a little trip with me."

Panic set in as their eyes met. Glaring at him angrily, "I don't know who you are or who you think you are, but I am not going anywhere with you!"

"Yes you are." his masterful voice was firm with calm control that angered her more.

"You can't make me!" Angry and vulnerable her words sounded stupidly hollow and she was acutely aware of his body pressing down on her. Unable to move under his weight she felt the pounding of his heart against her chest and the softness of his breath on her face. He relaxed his hold on her wrists only slightly as he began kissing her neck. Knowing she'd start to fight again he was careful not to relax too much. His eyes softened confusing her and making her even more afraid. Moving slightly he slid his right leg in between her legs. His eyes were fixed on hers as he pressed down against her.

She blinked to keep back the tears that filled her eyes. "You said you wouldn't hurt me."

"I won't. At least I'm trying not to, but you're not cooperating." His matter of fact words conveyed a strange gentleness making her feel even more vulnerable. What was it about him?

And then she knew where she'd heard his voice. The man on the phone! He was the one who had been calling her for nearly two years. Her eyes widened with fear. "Dear God, you're the guy who's been calling me." She began to shake uncontrollably under the weight of his body. "Please don't do this. I don't want to go with you. Please just go away and I won't tell anyone you were here."

"Oh, sure. And how are you going to explain the mess."

"Nobody needs to know! I'll clean it up."

"That's right they don't need to know. I've been planning this day for a long time. Wait till you see your new home. You'll love how beautiful it is. We're going to be happy together. You'll see. I told you on the phone I wanted you and I'd have you. So do you believe me now?"

"You're going to kill me aren't you?"

"Why would you think that when I've gone through so much to show you I love you? I want to make you happy. I've made a lot of plans and arrangements for us. Everything is finally ready to bring you home. It's all part of a bigger plan and part of your destiny.

"You're crazy! You're insane! You can't force someone to go with you just because you want them! It's wrong! I won't go anywhere with you! Now let me go!" He pressed himself tight against her, holding her down as she struggled to free herself.

"I was hoping I wouldn't have to do this, Favor, but you leave me no choice." He managed to pull out a neatly folded handkerchief from his pocket. "Take a good look around, because you won't be coming back here again."

She stopped struggling and looked at him with terrified eyes. "Please, I don't want to die. Please, I'm begging you."

"I'm sorry. I think this is the best way," he was saying as he held the cloth over her mouth and nose. She struggled harder, trying to hold her breath. Then her body went limp. Lifting her into his arms he took one last look around then carried her out the door.

Chapter 4

Adam woke up the next morning and smiled to himself at the thought of his day with Favor. Knowing she was an early riser she'd be up getting things ready, wanting everything to be perfect. He took a leisurely shower, shaved and dressed. When finished he sat down to have a cup of coffee before he headed over to her place. She said to come over at nine, so he finished the cup of coffee and headed over to her house which was less than a 10 minute walk away.

As he was leaving Houston emerged from his room yawning and rubbing his eyes. "Hey, Bro, what's got you all spiffed up and smelling all 'pretty' on a Saturday morning?"

"Breakfast with Favor."

"Heard from Dave you were kissing her last night. 'Bout time," he walked nonchalantly into the bathroom and Adam heard him give out a hearty laugh.

"Big mouth. News sure travels fast around here. That's ok! You're next ol' man!" Adam yelled after him.

Arriving at Favor's house about eight forty-five he noticed the front door was slightly ajar. Maybe she'd seen him coming and had opened it for him, but called out to her so as not to startle her. "Hey, Beautiful, your prince charming is here." There was no answer so he pushed open the door. The sight that greeted his eyes was not only one of shock, but fear mixed with anger to think he had actually let her go home alone the night before. He began to move cautiously throughout the house being careful not to move or disturb anything. He was afraid of what he might find, but still hoping he'd find her alive. He checked everywhere, and finding it empty he decided to call Houston.

Houston answered. With a shaky voice Adam told Houston, "You'd better come over to Favor's house right away. She's missing and the place is a mess. It looks like she put up quite a struggle. I'm going to call the police but I could really use a friend."

"Say no more, I'm on my way."

Within five minutes Houston had arrived, with the police only moments behind. They wanted to know if he had touched anything since he had come in. "No, the door was open. I was real careful. I may have touched a doorknob or two looking to see if she was somewhere else in the house, but I was careful not to pick up or move anything. I touched the phone to call you guys."

Adam watched as the police moved about the house, taking pictures and making notes as they studied the room in its state of disarray. It soon became clear that the only room disturbed was the living room. "Doesn't look like there was any forced entry," one of the cops was saying. "She must have known whoever it was. Looks like she put up quite a struggle. When was the last time you saw her, and where were you last night?" The officer turned and looked at Adam and Houston. "Why were you here this morning?"

Adam glared at the officer. "We both saw her last night at my house which is the next property over. Houston rooms with me. I had a little get together last night with about fifteen friends. We played some touch football, barbecued and then sat around talking and watching some movies. Favor left about ten p.m. I tried to get her to let me walk her home, but she insisted it wasn't necessary. Before she left we made plans to spend the day together starting with breakfast this morning."

"How were you able to get in to her house?"

"I just told you the door was wide open."

"So you did. My mistake." Adam noticed a sarcastic tone in the officer's voice.

"Most of us don't lock our doors during the day. There's never been any need to. We're pretty out of the way and somewhat secluded. It's always been a safe quiet place to live."

"Sorry, I have to ask these questions. You'd be surprised at the so called respectable people who do some pretty horrible things to people they had close relationships with. Everyone is a suspect until we rule you out. I'll need the names and phone numbers of everyone who was at your house last night, especially those who were still there when she left. Do you know of anyone who may have had a grudge against her?"

"No! She's one of the best friends anyone could want. We're all pretty close. Several of us grew up together, including Houston and me."

"What about old boyfriends, ex-husbands, a co-worker with a grudge?"

"You make her sound cheep the way you say that, and no there were no old boyfriends!"

"Hit a soft spot, eh?" the officer taunted Adam when he saw how agitated he was becoming with the line of questioning. Continuing the officer heckled Adam, "You didn't answer my question about ex-husbands and her work."

"She's a widow. Her husband died from injuries after a plane crash. She's an interior designer for a major company out of LA and Chicago and she has ownership in her husband's company."

"We'll need the name of those companies."

Houston had been pretty quiet, thinking about what could have happened. He suddenly stood up and stiffened. "Adam, what about that guy who's been calling her? You don't suppose there is a chance it was him do you?"

"Some guy has been calling her and she didn't report it or change her number?"

"We tried to convince her to change it but she always shrugged it off as if it was nothing. Favor seemed to think it was just some lonely guy needing to talk to someone and said he was perfectly harmless. You don't think there's a possibility of it being him do you?"

The officer looked concerned. "We can't rule out anyone, or any possibility. Have you noticed any change in her behavior or anyone unusual hanging around lately?"

Houston had a pale look on his face. Adam looked at him with concern. "Hey, what's going on with you? You look like you've seen a ghost."

"I have a gut feeling, but it's probably nothing. Yesterday Cindy and I were out on the front porch deck talking and she noticed a dark colored truck parked down the lane from your place. Looked dark green or black. There may have been someone sitting inside and Cindy made a comment about it. I told her it was probably some kid smoking pot. I joked around about going down and inviting him to join us."

"I'll need to talk to this Cindy."

"You won't have to wait long," was Houston's reply. "She's Favor's best friend and I called her after Adam called me. She'd just gotten out of the shower and said she'd meet me here. Speaking of which, she just pulled up outside." Houston excused himself and went to meet her. Cindy was asking, "Is she really gone, Houston?"

"It appears so. The cops want to talk to everyone who was at Adam's house last night. I told him about the truck we saw parked down the lane. I probably shouldn't have said anything, but, it just came out." Tears were welling up in Cindy's eyes and Houston had taken her in his arms and was holding her tight. "It's going to be ok. We'll find her somehow. You'll see. In the mean time you're not to go anywhere at night without me and you're to keep your doors locked from now on. We don't know what or who we're dealing with and I am not taking any chances of losing you, too. Is that clear?"

Cindy looked up at him through teary eyes, with shock. "Don't be silly. Nobody would bother me, but I'll still be careful like you said."

Together they walked up to the house and entered. Cindy's bloodshot eyes became wide with shock as she looked around the room at the broken lamp and other items scattered around. Her mind began to race as she visualized how Favor must have fought. She knew there was no way she would have given in easily. As she stood there she felt overwhelmed. Had she lost her dearest friend forever? Is she still alive, wondering if she would stay alive? Was she cold or hungry or even conscious? How terrified she must be. But Cindy knew Favor would do everything in her power just to survive.

Cindy felt like she needed to pinch or slap herself to wake up from what simply had to be a bad dream when she realizing one of the police detectives was talking to her. What was he asking? "Offhand do you know if he ever threatened her?"

She shook as if startled back to reality, "What were you saying? Who threatened her?"

The detective repeated, "I was asking you what you knew about the anonymous caller. Did you ever hear his voice, and did he ever threaten her. What can you tell me about the calls?"

For some reason the questions only annoyed her. "No he never threatened her. Actually most of the time he was nice. I think it sort of amused Favor. She never took it seriously. At least she didn't seem to until recently. I was here a few times when he called. She put the phone on speaker so I could hear him. She talked about changing her number but never did."

"Why do you think she changed her mind? What sort of things did he say?"

"He would say he wanted her, but a couple of nights ago we had just come in from a swim down at the river when the phone rang and it was him. He said he had seen her in town earlier that day and she looked really pretty. She asked him where he saw her, thinking he was just trying to trick her. He said he'd seen her walking past the bank and then described what she was wearing. That really spooked her, but what really bothered her is when he said he would always be watching her." Cindy noticed the look on Adam's face. He looked hurt and angry.

In an accusing way said, "Why didn't she tell me about this?"

"Hey, don't get mad at me, Adam. You know as well as I do she doesn't like to be told what she should do or worry anyone. She asked me not to say anything to anyone because she didn't want everyone making a big deal about it. She was planning on doing something about it, but if this guy knew what she looked like and was watching her, then it wouldn't do any good to change her number."

"I'm sorry. It's just that…" Favor's phone was ringing. They turned to the officers.

One of them spoke to Cindy. "Do you think you could answer it and not let on there's a problem here? We don't want to cause any alarm." Cindy nodded. "Use the speaker phone if you know how."

"Hello, Favor's residence." She managed to sound convincingly cheerful and she switched on the speaker phone as the voice of a man spoke.

"Is Favor there?" the voice on the other end questioned. Cindy stammered that she was not available to come to the phone just now."

The man on the other end then asked, "Is this Cindy?" She did not recognize the voice and somehow felt strangely intimidated.

"Who wants to know?"

He laughed and then in a peculiar sounding voice said, "Of course she's not available, that's because she's with me. You can tell all her friends and the police that she is doing well. She's ok and won't be harmed in any way. Tell them not to look for her because you won't find us. We're getting married soon. We're planning a new life together. I knew you would be concerned so I called to let you know she is ok and happy. Sorry about the mess we left. We got to playing around and a few things got broken. In case Adam's listening, I didn't appreciate him kissing and touching her yesterday, and he will not get that opportunity again. This is the last you'll hear from us." She started to speak, but the phone went dead as he hung up. There was only the oppressive sound of the dial tone as they stood in silence staring at each other. Cindy's heart was beating so fast and loudly that she thought for sure they could all hear it pounding. She could feel the color in her face changing as it went from flushed pink to pale white.

The silence was broken when the head detective began to speak in a calm, but authoritative way, "Clearly we know now that she has been abducted. This guy sounds intelligent, but he also sounds delusional. There's something about his voice that sounds like he is very reassured and authoritative, yet there is something else very different sounding in his voice. We'll get a trace on the call and see if we can find out where the call came from. But most likely he will have called from a disposable cell phone."

Cindy found her voice. "Favor used to say he sounded mysterious and intriguing. She even said he sounded sexy and gentle but frightening at the same time. I think that's why Favor hadn't changed her number. I think she really enjoyed the mystery and intrigue of talking to him and part of her really was hoping he would let her know who he was. It was like a game they were both playing. Sometimes they would just sit and talk about their day. If he even started to talk inappropriately she would tell him she was a lady and didn't appreciate it and then hang up on him. He'd always call back a day or two later and apologize and then they would talk some more. I'm sure she never expected anything like this. I'm really scared for her."

The detective began to speak again. "Everyone leaves behind a calling card no matter how careful they think they are. We will find him one way or another." "Mike," he said turning to one of the other detectives, "I want you to start with her phone records back to when she first moved here. We're going to check everything and look for a pattern as well as using the process of elimination. Let's get this narrowed down so we can find out who this guy is and where the calls came from. I want a 24 hour guard on the property and I want every inch of this room swept for prints or anything that might lead to who he is and let's put taps on each of your phones just in case he decides to make contact again, but doesn't want to call this phone. Sooner or later he will give us some sort of ransom demand. We need to be prepared and hopefully by then we will have an idea of who he is and he'll lead us to her."

"It gives me the creeps to think of him touching her." Cindy had begun to cry again. "She has to be terrified."

"I need you to be prepared for the fact that even if he makes a ransom request she may not even be alive or if she is alive now he may not let her continue to live. In most cases the abductor has already killed the victim and disposed of the body when they contact someone."

"Hey! Adam had been sitting with his head in his hands. "I don't want to hear anyone say anything like that again. She is not dead and we're going to find her. She's going to be alright! Do you hear me!?" Adam's anger shocked everyone. He turned and stormed out of the house.

Cindy watched with concern, "What in the world has gotten into him?"

"Don't let it bother you. Last night he finally told her how much he cares about her and made plans for a romantic day together, then he loses her before the day even began. He's feeling extremely guilty because he feels he should have insisted on walking her home."

"Whoever took her has been watching her for some time and made sure she was alone. He would have waited or worse yet, might have done something to Adam if he had been with her. He was probably watching her when she left Adam's house. He saw them on the porch when she left so he had to know she was walking home alone. He knew what he was doing and executed his plan just as he planned it."

Chapter 5

Favor opened her eyes, her mind in a fog as she tried to focus on her surroundings. Dazed and disoriented, it took her a few minutes to figure out she was in a truck driving along a gravel road. Looking out the window into the darkness, hoping to recognize some part of the landscape she wondered how long they had been driving and how long had she'd been sleeping. Where were they and where were they going? A hand on her arm startled her and she felt her body jump as she drew her arm away and cringed close to the door. Turning her head to see who had touched her in the dim light she recognized the man who had been in her house.

Focus! Focus, her mind kept saying. He watched her with interest but didn't speak as she looked around the cab of the truck. The truck bounced roughly and she could hear the crunch of gravel under the tires. As her mind cleared and she was becoming more aware of her predicament she began trying to figure out a way out of the vehicle. She groped around in the darkness for the door handle. He had anticipated her every movement. Figuring she might try to get out of the truck he had locked the door for the passenger side from his side.

He broke the silence. "I control the locks for the doors from my side," he said in a matter-of-fact way. Favor turned and looked at him scornfully.

"Who are you and what do you want with me?" He seemingly ignored her and just kept on driving. She became angry and started hitting him and screaming at him. The truck swerved and he brought it to a jerky halt as she continued hitting him.

"Stop it!" he bellowed. She stopped hitting him and her body froze as she stared at him. He switched on the dome light and stared at her. His eyes were mesmerizing and powerful, not harsh or angry. He was very controlled. Drawing back against the door she kept her eyes fixed on his. She stared at him with angry eyes trying to anticipate what he might say or do next. But he said nothing. His eyes softened. Acutely aware of her own heart pounding and the rise and fall of her own chest she cringed back in her seat leaning close against the truck door. Breaking their stare she followed the movement of his hand as he slowly reached over to turn the ignition back on. She thought about grabbing the keys out of the ignition, but knew that wouldn't do her any good. She was so angry that she just wanted to do something, anything to vent her anger.

"I have to stay calm," she thought. "I can't give him any reason to hurt me." She watched intently, but when he turned his eyes back to her she dropped her gaze. She couldn't stand his piercing blue eyes. Hot tears stung her eyes. "I won't let him see me cry," she resolved with determination. "I won't!"

As if reading her thoughts he said, "Go ahead. Cry if you want to. It will do you good," He then reached up and turned the dome light off as if to give her some privacy.

Swallowing hard, she softly choked out the words, "Where are you taking me?" as a tear slowly rolled down her cheek.

"I'm taking you home. I've been waiting for this day a long time. Ever since the first time I saw you and heard your name, I knew you were the one. I was drawn to you and haven't been able to get you out of my mind. There are greater forces involved in the fate and purpose of our lives. You've become part of mine." Then more to himself than to her he continued talking. "So many years of planning. I had to be absolutely sure everything was perfect and I had no doubts before bringing her home." Turning to look at her he continued, "I studied everything about you, what you liked and didn't like, your style preferences, clothes, furniture, colors, books and music. Everything I could possibly think of helped me prepare to bring you home. I know it will take some getting used to, but you'll love everything. We're finally going to be together."

"What is your problem? If you wanted to know me, why didn't you just introduce yourself and talk to me? That's what normal people do."

"I tried to talk to you. It was years ago when you were married to Conrad Durand. It was at one of those big fancy business affairs. You were radiant and so different from everyone else. I could tell you didn't belong with those people, yet you were completely gracious and adoring to everyone, especially him. When you moved you seemed to float, catching everyone's eye. You conducted yourself like royalty but not at all like you thought you were better than anyone else, which totally took my breath away. I needed you then and have needed you ever since."

Favor sat with her mouth open, her eyes wide with shock. She couldn't believe what she had just heard. Finally finding her voice. "You mean to tell me you've been watching me all these years and even followed me to where I live today? How dare you!!"

"Well, pretty much. At first when I asked about you I was told not to even think about it. You were totally dedicated to Conrad. When you two separated I figured it was looking good for me, but then he came all the time to see you and you stayed married and seemed to be getting closer instead of farther apart. I knew as long as you were married I didn't have a chance."

"Did you have anything to do with his plane crash?" she yelled.

Once again the truck came to a screeching halt, the dome light came on and this time it was him with the look of shock and anger on his face. "I am not a sadist and didn't hurt anyone to get you! I wouldn't do anything like that especially seeing how devastated you were when he died. You have no idea how much I wanted to go to you then, but knew it wasn't the right time. I could never have lived with myself if I had been the cause of your pain."

"If you knew I was happy, why did you continue following and watching me?"

"I didn't followed you all the time, but I did keep track of where you were. I had to be absolutely certain you were the one so I attended as many of the events you and Conrad hosted or attended as possible and had to force myself to stay away from you and watch from a distance. Every time I saw you the feelings got stronger. When I heard about Conrad's death I put my plan into motion and that's when I started calling you. You liked talking to me. You know you did. We had a thing going and you liked it as much as I did. Admit it!"

"No! And what about what I want?" Anger flared from her eyes. "You can't do this to me! You have no right!" Hesitating a moment she screamed, "You're an insane, crazy idiot! That's what you are!" Even as she screamed at him she was awed by his handsomeness. She wanted to kick herself and was shocked at herself for even thinking such a thing.

He looked a little sad for a moment, then in a calm voice said, "Favor, this is not like you to speak so harshly, but I understand you're upset."

"Oh, don't speak to me in that patronizing tone." Ignoring he comment he started the engine and drove off in silence.

Favor tried to peer through the darkness in hopes of seeing some landmark or building that she could store in her memory but there simply wasn't anything, no homes or buildings, no lights, or structures of any kind. She kept hoping she'd see the lights of a house or cabin. But, they seemed to be completely alone on a moonless inky black night. The sky was clear as it glistened with thousands of twinkling stars. She found herself naming the stars and constellation to herself, wondering if there was someone out there watching what was happening to her and following her path. They were silly thoughts, the type a little girl might dream up, but in her vulnerable state they somehow seemed comforting. By the sound of the truck and the feel of the road she figured they were climbing higher in elevation.

The lights of the truck reflected back at them. At first there were a lot of trees but then the landscape seemed to be rolling hills, possibly fields. An occasional rock formation would catch the glow of the headlights and just as quickly be gone. The road was rough and presently they turned off onto an even more rugged road as they climbed higher. It was some ten or fifteen minutes later, that they stopped in front of a locked gate. He stopped and turned off the engine taking the keys out of the ignition, leaving the headlights on. A slight hesitation and he spoke, "Don't try anything. There are mountain lions in this area," he said as he headed towards the locked gate. He moved slowly trying to keep an eye on the truck and his captive. The moment he turned to fit the key in the lock she bounded out of his door and began running down the gravel road. He shoved the gate wide open. She was a good runner, but it was hard to see in the dim light. She heard him holler as he set off in pursuit. Hearing his long strides coming closer she looked for some place to get off the road and possibly hide. It was just too dark. About 100 yards down the road she tripped and fell. Before she could get to her feet, he had overtaken her. "Damn it, Favor, I told you to stay put."

She yelled back at him, "Damn you!" There was a burning on her left knee and hand where the rough gravel had caused an abrasion on her skin. A small trickle of blood oozed down her leg. He said nothing as he pulled her up. Trying to jerk away from him, he held tight to her arm as he led her back, struggling as he tried to get her back into the truck.

"I'll put you back to sleep if you don't knock it off." His voice revealed he was tired and testy. She finally slid onto the seat as he pulled a small rope from behind the seat and proceeded to tie her hands and ankles.

"I didn't want to do this, but you didn't give me a choice. I'm tired and I just want to get home and get some rest." They drove past the gate where he stopped and again got out to close and lock the gate behind them. Continuing on they reached another gate. Getting out he repeated the ritual of unlocking and locking the gate. A ways up the road brought them to yet another gate, but this one was open. The lights of the truck illuminated large posts bordering the gate and a beautiful sign above it read "Rainbow Moor". Just past the gate he stopped and exited the truck to lock the gate. Back in the truck he drove up a slight gradual rise in the road, around another bend and then into an open area. Against the clear night sky she could see the silhouette of a large house. As they approached she saw rows of solar lights lining the pathway. At the side of the house he stopped the truck, and turned off the engine. For a moment he rested his head against the back of the seat, eyes closed. Letting out a long sigh he got out of the truck and made his way around to the side where Favor sat. Opening the door he leaned in to untie the rope around her feet and hands, then offered her his hand. Refusing she glared at him defiantly. Taking hold of her arm he pulled her out of the truck.

Favor had no idea how long they had been driving before arriving at the big house. Though Favor had been asleep a good portion of the first part of the ride, he in turn had not had any sleep and was feeling somewhat irritable and wanted desperately to rest. Noticing he was tired she determined to make it hard for him to get any rest. She'd make him wish he hadn't followed through with this ridiculous idea. He thought she was so perfect, just what he needed. Well he had another thing coming.

She'd show him just how imperfect she was so he'd want to take her back. Then she thought again. That could back fire. He might kill her instead so she could never tell. Her thoughts switched back and forth, not even realizing he was talking to her again. "Think all you want, it won't do you any good. You forget, I know the real you. That's the reason why you're here. So put on a good act, it will get old soon enough." He turned and headed up the porch steps. "Are you coming? It's cold out here and I'm tired. I'd like to get some rest before daybreak." He turned to unlock the door.

"Oh, boy," she thought, "he's so tired he's losing his grip. Not too smart on his part." She turned and began to run. Halfway down the lane she turned to see if he was pursuing her. A light was now on and she could see him standing in the open front doorway. He didn't move or make any attempt to follow. She hesitated. This didn't look good. Something just didn't feel right. Just then she heard a low whistle. From out of the darkness came a huge white dog. Turning she began to run faster, but it was impossible to out run the dog as it overtook her blocking her way and growling a menacing warning. She froze and glared at the dog, her defiance was now giving way to fear. "Make him go away!" she screamed.

"Just turn around and walk back here and he won't bother you. I'm going inside."

"Don't leave me out here alone with this beast." He didn't pay any attention, instead turned and went into the house.

The dog followed close on her heels as she started to walk slowly back. "So you're just as much of a bad-ass as he is. He should teach you more respect for a lady." She seemed to perceive the large animal to be less ominous when she talked out loud to him. Reaching the steps she stopped for a moment looking at the outside of the big house as if to get a feel for what to expect inside. Above the porch was another beautifully scrolled sign with the words "Rainbow Moor". There was something about the house that was comforting and inviting. There seemed to be an aura and warmth that intrigued her. The dog growled again. "Alright you big dope, I'm going. Give me a break." She didn't dare turn and look at him. She reached the door, hesitated and looked back just for a moment. The dog seemed quite content that she was about to enter and lay down on the porch. In the light she noticed he was quite magnificent with wolf like features, but he was completely white. For a brief moment she wished she could pet him. When she entered the open door her abductor was standing in front of a stone fireplace putting wood inside. The big house was cold and she found herself beginning to shake uncontrollably.

He looked at her as she entered, then walked over to where she stood. Looking down at her their eyes met. She was intrigued by the softness in his eyes. "Are you alright?" She didn't reply, but nodded. Calling the dog inside, he closed the door. Stepping away she looked at the dog and then back at him. "It's late. We need to get some rest. Come with me!" He turned and started up a staircase to the second level of the house. Hesitating for a brief moment she turned and faced the dog, but when he started to growl she realized it was best to follow the man. The dog followed close on her heels.

The banisters leading up the stairs were oak and at the top was a landing that split in two directions with oak railings on three sides. Facing the stairs, across and directly ahead was a windowed door with two windows on either side of the door that led out onto a balcony above the front porch. There was a door on each side of the railing and hallway and one straight ahead at the top of the staircase. You could walk clear around the railing in a square area. He turned to the right and led her passed to the door on that side of the hallway, stopped, opened it and turned on the light, stepping aside to let her enter. She began shaking again. What now? Did he expect her to sleep in the same room with him? Retreating backward, their eyes met. He held her gaze a moment as if trying to read her thoughts and emotions. What would she do if he made a move toward her? Scream? As if that would do her any good. Who would hear her?

"I think you'll find everything you need. I put in a small bathroom for you. It's through that door on the right. We'll talk tomorrow after breakfast and then I'll show you around. He reached out to touch her cheek but she shrunk back, cringing. His eyes suddenly looked sad and the look puzzled her. Why did he look that way? He hesitated a moment searching her face, then said in a soft voice "Good night, Favor." Turning to the dog he gave the command to stay as he walked away across to the other side where he opened the door to another bedroom. The dog quietly lay down outside the entrance to the bedroom door.

Favor quickly closed the door, noticing there was no way to lock it from the inside. Before her was a simple yet tastefully decorated room about sixteen foot by twelve foot. It looked and smelled freshly painted all in white with a large old fashioned metal framed bed straight ahead. Neatly placed on the bed was a long white bathrobe and a long pink night gown with spaghetti straps. At the foot of the bed was a bench style settee upholstered in a white fabric, with a fluffy rose colored throw blanket neatly folded on it and a pair of soft white slippers on the floor in front. To the far right was an open door leading to a private bathroom. The room was not heated and she shivered from the cold, or was it just her nerves? Feeling very alone and tired she noticed a small loveseat upholstered in a rose patterned fabric.

Without getting undressed she grabbed the throw, slipped off her shoes and curled up on the loveseat. Tears clouded her vision and burned her eyes as she started to cry. The earlier events of the day flooded her brain. It would be daybreak soon. Adam would be coming to her house expecting to enjoy a wonderful breakfast and a beautiful day with her. He had just told her he loved her. Emotional exhaustion began to overtake her tired brain and her thoughts became foggy as she fell into a fitful sleep.

Chapter 6

The disappearance of Favor Durand had the town of Fortuna and surrounding areas buzzing with the news as the police continued to investigate. Yellow tape was stretched across Favor's house as a barricade. No one except the team of investigators was allowed near the property. Houston showed them where the truck had been parked. The ground yielded no clues. The house was thoroughly checked for traces of blood that might have been wiped away as well as prints. Everyone who had attended Adam's barbecue was called in for questioning and all of their finger prints taken, explaining it was to rule out known friends from any strangers who might have been in Favor's house. Each one was questioned. How well did they know her, how close were they, what did they remembered about when she left and if they remembered seeing the vehicle that had passed by. Few remembered the vehicle passing by, and those who did were not sure if it was black, blue or dark green, Ford, Chevy, GMC or Dodge. The questioning was relentless, but to no avail.

Adam became irritated with the line of questioning. They asked if Favor had many men visitors, if she went out much, what kind of neighbor was she, did she do a lot of partying. Adam explained some of them had known her all of their lives. Most had attended both grammar and high school together. Some moved away to attend college, like Favor. Some moved and came back. Some never left, and some came and stayed because they like it here. The fact was they were a close group who spent a lot of time together. Since her husband death she hadn't dated anyone. "I'd say she pretty much has an equal number of both male and female friends." Adam was saying, his voice edgy. The officer noted he thought he was too defensive. "Hey, put yourself in my shoes. How would you feel if you had been the one who let her walk home all alone? If I had insisted, maybe this wouldn't have happened. I feel like hell and damn guilty. It's eating me up inside!" Adam's voice had escalated and he was almost shouting. The officer tried to calm him down. Adam put his head in his hands. For the first time since he was a little boy, he wanted to cry.

"Look, I know you're really upset. But, it's my job to ask these questions. We have to check out everyone no matter what. We want to find her just as much as you do."

Adam looked up at the officer. "No, not as much as I do! You can't possibly understand. Yesterday, for the first time, I told her I love her. Then I lost her that very night. You have no idea how I feel. I waited too long, and now she's gone because I took our friendship for granted, feeling too comfortable with the everyday things. I just want her back."

The officer looked at Adam's blood shot eyes and realized the pain Adam was feeling. "I'm sorry. I had no idea. You can go. We'll keep you informed on even the smallest details."

As Adam rose to leave he turned to the officer and said, "Don't waste a day by not saying I love you to the people who are special in your life. I was stupid and now look where I am. Go home today and tell your family you care. In fact call them now. There's no time like the present. They may know you love them, but they still need to hear it, believe me." With that he turned and walked away.

Adam's house was filled with friends waiting and hoping for some news. No one wanted to leave. Their need to be together, coupled with their need for answers kept them together like a vigil. Adam's gut felt like it was twisting inside out as he wrestled with his emotions. Though tired and irritable he was still glad to have his friends waiting when he got home.

"How did it go, Adam?" Cindy was saying.

"I blew my cool. The questions made me mad. They were making it sound as if she was some sort of slut." Slamming his fist down on the table he yelled, "I feel so damn guilty."

"We all do, but you can't lose control! It won't do Favor any good if you end up in jail."

"If you really care about someone you should tell them. I saw how you two were with each other last night. If you two really care about each other then don't let another day go by without saying it." Cindy and Houston looked at each other. Turning to the rest of the group he finished with, "And that goes for the rest of you," then he walked out onto the deck leaving them to think about it.

"He's right you know. Yesterday Adam and I were giving each other a hard time about being stupid bachelor's when the very women we care about were right under our noses."

"Now isn't the time for us to be thinking about ourselves."

"Yes it is. We need each other especially at a time like this. We all need each other, and I need you. I'm in love with you. I don't want you to say you love me. I just want you to know how I feel. Maybe when this is all over we can talk about us." Houston blurted it out without taking a breath, leaned down, quickly kissed her and walked away leaving Cindy standing there with her eyes wide with shock and mouth open. She was sure she saw the former bull riding, football player wipe a tear away.

Several days went by. Each day that passed Adam became more cross and edgy. His friends became increasingly aware of how deep his feelings were and that he wasn't dealing with just guilt but dealing with the loss of the woman he loved. Through the coming months he would become more and more obsessed with his need to find her.

The police finished dusting for prints matching all of the prints with friends who had been to her house one time or another. They suspected the kidnapper wore gloves.

Adam was relieved when they finally left. Both Conrad and Favor's family were there and at the family's request, it was arranged to have Cindy move into Favor's house to take care of her things. The income from Favor's part of the partnership paid what few bills she had.

Silly as it seemed those close to Favor felt by making sure her home was cared for she would find a way home again. It was somehow comforting. Though gone she'd left them with the gift of each other and an extended family with a strong bond that changed their lives.

Adam was pulling away and no matter how hard they tried he pushed them away with unseen hands and closed his heart to the people who could help him the most. He rejected their support and as the weeks passed became more and more withdrawn. Houston spent more and more time with Cindy at Favor's house and the group of friends moved their weekly gatherings there. Sometimes Adam came but more and more he stayed away. They only hoped he would find healing and forgive himself.

Chapter 7

Early morning, the sun coming up streamed into the bedroom. Favor woke to feel its warmth on her face. Forgetting for a moment where she was she listened to the sweet sounds of birds singing in the crisp morning air. The events of the previous day began coming back to her. Reality set in when she remembered she wasn't at home. Her body ached from sleeping on the tiny love seat. Slowly she walked to the window draped in sheer curtains. In the distance a long row of trees blocked the view to what was beyond the bend in the road leading to the house. There was a large expanse of pasture land and closer to the house she could see flower beds and lawn. Looking around the room she discovered a freshly arranged vase of white roses on one of the night stands. She hadn't noticed them the night before. An envelope was attached with her name on it. Hesitating she opened it. "Welcome to your new home. Hope you slept well. I'm sure you will find everything you need. Breakfast is at eight. I'll come for you then. Please be dressed and ready." The signature was just a squiggle and unlike the rest of the note, completely illegible. Then below was a post script which read, "May I suggest the white cotton sundress laid out in the dressing room."

"What? Now he thinks he can dictate what clothes I should wear? Like hell! If he thinks I'm going to wear what he suggests he's got another thing coming." She looked at the tiny clock on the far nightstand. It read six am, two hours till he expected her to be ready. "What would he think if I refuse to be ready? He can't make me!" Looking toward the open door she walked into the room he had referred to as the dressing room. To the left she saw the white dress draped over a chair at a small vanity table. It was simple with eyelet lace in the bodice. To the right was the closet. Her curiosity got the better of her and she looked inside. She had the feeling it had been added on because it was a fairly large closet not customary for the age of the old ranch house. To her surprise it held a large assortment of clothing, shoes, and accessories all in her size.

An uncomfortable feeling made her step back away from the closet realizing he had been planning this for a long time. He knew her style. In a nearby dresser drawer she found under garments and every personal need possible including her brand of tampons. Angry she began to hyperventilate, feeling completely violated. How many times had he been in her house?

The large tub was inviting. She needed a bath. Eyeing it and thinking how a nice long soak would ease her tense tired muscles she decided to draw some bath water hoping he wouldn't come up before she was done. While the tub was filling up she looked through an assortment of bubble baths including her favorite peach. There were lotions, bath salts and her favorite Lemon Verbena fragrance. Even her brand of makeup and all her skin care products, lip and eye colors. This was just too much.

Turning off the water she stormed back into the bedroom. "Who the hell did he think he was?" Heading to the door she swung it open intent on storming her way out. She'd forgotten about the dog when he jumped up and stood growling at her. Frozen to the spot she glared at the dog. "I'm not afraid of you. Let's see how tuff you really are." Trying to be brave she attempted to get up the courage to go past him. "Ok, big boy, it's just you and me. You wouldn't hurt a nice girl like me would you? Now why don't you be a good boy and let me go by?" As she tried to move passed him his growl became more ominous and he blocked her path. "Ok, ok, I'll go back inside, but you and I are going to have to work out some sort of understanding." She stepped back into the room, but stood for a moment with the door open. The dog settled back down and stopped growling. A second attempt to step out into the hall was met with more growls. "Damn you! He's got you trained. Time will take care of that. You just wait. Two can play at this."

Retreating to the interior of the room she stood a moment looking at him. Speaking softly she sat down on the floor just inside with the door open. Looking straight at the dog she began to talk to him in a soft low voice knowing getting him to trust her would not be an easy accomplishment if she could accomplish it at all. But she was determined to try. For about fifteen minutes she sat quietly talking in soothing tones. It occurred to her that it was somehow comforting for her to talk to the dog. His head turned back and forth at an angle with a look of curiosity as if he was trying to figure out what she was saying. Favor had to smile at his curious look. Fearing the kidnapper might come and see her talking to the dog, she slowly rose as she continued to speak. Backing up slowly she quietly said goodbye and softly closed the door. A feeling of pride tickled her insides as she mused to herself.

The little clock was slowly ticking away the minutes. Now what was she going to do? "Should I bathe or just wait and see what he has to say. I really hate to give him the upper hand. Nope I'm just going to sit here." There wasn't anything else to do, so she curled back up on the loves-seat pulling the blanket up around her shoulders where she soon fell back to sleep.

Promptly at eight o'clock there was a soft knock on the door. Favor was fast asleep and didn't hear him enter the room. He saw her sleeping. Looking around he saw the card and envelope open on the bed and realized she had read it and knew what he'd expected her to do. Crossing over to the dressing room he noticed the open closet door, apparent she'd been looking at the clothes. Returning to where she was sleeping, he touched her shoulder. Startled she woke and jumped up, eyes wide as she stared at him.

"Did you sleep well?" His tone was edgy with a slight sarcasm.

"Did you really expect me to? When are you taking me home?" She returned the sarcasm.

Ignoring her questions he went on, "I see you got my message about the dress and breakfast. You've been in the dressing room but you're not dressed. I heard the bath water running earlier, but it doesn't appear that you have taken a bath after-all. That was just after six. I'm sure two hours is ample time for you to get ready for breakfast. I'm disappointed that you didn't find the bed comfortable enough to sleep in. Do you want to explain why you haven't gotten ready?"

Continuing to stare at her he waited. "Well, I'd like an answer."

"I guess I fell back to sleep."

"Oh, Favor, I assume you can do better than that. You call that a good explanation?"

"You assume too much. I assume you got my message, I assume you saw the clothes." she mimicked. "You assume I want to wear your stupid dress or any of those clothes. You assume I will be happy here. You assume you can do whatever you please and I will just accept it. Well, think again!" Her voice had escalated to yelling at him before finally taking a breath.

"Are you done shouting?"

"Quite done!"

"Good. Now seeing you're not ready for breakfast I hope you will be ready when lunch time comes." He turned to walk out the door.

"Hey, where are you going and what do you mean by that?"

"I mean just what it sounds like. I'll be back at noon to see if you're ready then."

"You mean I have to just sit here and I don't get any food till noon? What are you a self-appointed dictator? You make me sick." She rushed at him with her fists clenched and began pounding on his back. He whirled around and grabbed hold of both her wrists.

"Stop it." he shouted. Their eyes met. Seeing her anger his look softened and again she saw that look of disappointment and the mysterious sadness. His eyes seemed to penetrate right through her. Staring into her eyes again he relaxed his grip and she turned her eyes away to keep from crying. Why did he make her feel this way? What was it about him that intrigued her and made her so angry all at the same time? Slowly he released her wrists and she stepped back. He turned and walked out the door without saying another word. She watched as the door closed quietly behind him.

"Wait," she shouted, "I need to talk to you."

The door swung open again. "If you wanted to talk you should have done so instead of shouting and pounding on my back, and you should have been dressed and ready for breakfast. So if you want to talk be dressed and ready at lunch time." Turning away he thought at least she wanted to talk to him. Yes, that was a start. He felt lonely. Even with her shouting at him he at least didn't feel so alone. He had no choice but to continue to be patient.

"You don't understand," she pleaded, "I have responsibilities, and a job. I really can't stay here. Even if I wanted to I couldn't. Look, the clothes are nice. You had to have spent a small fortune on them. Why would you want to do that when you don't know me? I'm sure there are a lot of nice girls who would be thrilled to have them and would love being here. You can't just force someone. If you just take me back we could get to know each other. We could go out on a date or something. I just need you to take me home. We can forget this ever happened."

He acted as if he hadn't heard a word she was saying and said as he was turning to leave, "Why don't you have a nice soak in the tub and wash that blood off your knee, put on some nice new clothes and I will see you at lunch time."

Anger flared. "Forget it! This is crazy! You're nuts. I'm not putting on any of them."

He turned abruptly to face her. "Oh yes you will." His eyes sparked like fire, but strangely controlled. With a firm, direct, calm voice, his eyes intense and resolute, he said, "Don't make me have to dress you myself."

Favor stiffened her eyes wide, but her expression soon changed and she was back to challenging him. "You wouldn't!" Her tone was daring. Why did she keep doing that? If she kept pushing and testing him she might cause him to explode. She knew nothing about him, not even his name. "Probably be an alias anyway," she thought. Though on the brink of tears crying was not an option. Instead she put on a tough exterior and challenged him not really caring how he would react. Again he surprised her.

"See for yourself." Turning he left the room. She'd expected and wanted to get into a shouting match. The next half hour she sat looking around the room or gazing out the window. Her anger subsided, turning to despondency. The handsome mysterious man with no name overwhelmed her. For some unknown reason she wasn't afraid of him as she thought she should be. He was strangely intriguing and this fascinated Favor. Extremely good looking and sexy in a most alluring way and well groomed, she smiled to herself, amused that she could find something positive in the situation. Favor was not about to be bullied though. Instead of getting dressed she decided to stand her ground, knowing she was pushing his buttons, but angry and defiant enough not to care. How far would he go to get his way? The hours on the clock ticked by slowly and as the noon hour drew near she began to question her decision. Maybe she was going about this all the wrong way. She had just decided she should take a bath when the door of the room opened.

"I see after all this time you still haven't made any attempt to get ready for lunch either."

"Well I guess I'm not hungry then!" What was she thinking? The words coming out of her own mouth surprised her. How long was this going to go on? Everyone has their breaking point, and she was doing her best to get to his. Like playing a game of roulette she kept forcing his hand. It wasn't like her. The person inside her was a stranger.

"I'm going to wait outside this door for five minutes and if you're not dressed when I come back in then I'll be dressing you myself."

"I don't thinks so!"

"Just try me," he said as he waited for Favor's next remark. Instead she glared defiantly at him, challenging him to carry out his threat. "You're wasting time," he said as he stepped back out into the hallway.

She walked to the window fuming. Two, three, four minutes passes. Exactly five minutes later he opened the door walking briskly toward her. Retreating from his advance he grabbed her and started pulling at her clothes. Favor struggled to free herself and angrily kicked at him and bit his arm. If he wanted a fight, a fight he would get. He yelled as she bit harder. They both let go at the same time.

"You didn't have to do that!" He stood back looking disappointed and unsure.

"Oh yes I did!" she yelled, infuriated.

Again she saw the strange look in his eyes. Motionless looking at each other, for a brief moment she felt a strange desire for him. Entranced by his blue eyes, confused by her feelings and thoughts she couldn't look away. He felt the emotion as they both looked at each other with an unspoken desire.

"Why do you have to keep pushing and testing me? I just want to have a decent meal with you. It seems like you'd be tired of just sitting up here alone. I wanted to show you around. If this is what you want then have it your way." He felt a burning sensation on his arm where she'd bit him. His eyes never left hers as he backed out of the room closing the door behind him.

She stared at the door waiting to see if he would come back in. The quiet was deafening. Opting for a quick shower instead of a bath she selected a pair of jeans and a short sleeved pink western blouse. Dabbing on a little makeup she then sat down to wait thinking he'd be back in a little while.

But he didn't come. The afternoon hours slipped by slowly as she listened and waited. Peeking out of the door she saw the dog obediently standing watch. Two bowls of dog food and water were nearby. Listening intently she didn't hear any sounds. The evening shadows began to lengthen and she figured he'd be coming up to get her for dinner since she'd now had no breakfast or lunch. But the dinner hour passed by as well with no sign of him and not a sound. She listened intently for some stirring about, but heard only the deafening silence. The darkness drew near as she listened to the birds outside calling good night to each other. The room grew dark as she sat waiting and wondering.

"I guess I really made him mad." Her stomach grumbled as it cried out for food. The clock read nine so she finally slipped out of the clothes she had been wearing and found some soft teddy style sleep wear to put on. Slipping between the soft sheets loneliness enveloped her as she began to weep. Why had she been so mean? At least she wouldn't be lying here with her stomach tied up with hunger pains. Tomorrow she'd get up early, have a nice bath and be dressed by eight. Overwhelmingly lonely she cried herself into another fitful sleep.

Favor's dreams took her to distant places. Familiar mixed with unfamiliar, faces of loved ones changed to faces of unknown people. Familiar voices were lost in the unfamiliar faces and their words seemed to drift off into an empty void with no meaning. When she tried to speak to them her voice seemed to be muffled and her words did not come out sounding like what she was saying. The faces looked at her with questioning, concerned looks as they seemed to be trying to understand her. Then the faces turned blank and she could only make out sounds coming from them which seemed to grow more and more distant.

Suddenly she woke from one of the dreams. The room was dark save but a thin stream of moonlight coming in through the windows. The clock on the night stand read two am. Shivering she pulled the covers up tightly around her, the dreams still swirled around in her mind. What made people dream such weird things? Though still tired she didn't want to go back to sleep for fear of having more nightmares. Trying to fight back the need for sleep, she eventually drifted off again into the mysterious realm and the strangers within.

It was the second morning in her unknown surroundings and again the sound of birds woke her as the sun crept softly in the window. Relieved to see the sun after the long night of restless wanderings, she pulled back the covers and stepped lightly onto the soft carpet. Wandering aimlessly to the window she looked out at the rising sun, hoping to see something familiar. Instead the wide open prairie grasses stretched out to the distant tree line leaving a question as to what lay beyond the trees.

Turning toward the bathroom a long sad sigh escaped her lips as she drew a tub of warm bathwater. Pouring in a generous amount of bubble bath she watched as the bubbles billowed up. Slowly sinking into the warmth of the water the bubbles surrounded her aching body. The abrasion on her leg stung slightly for a few minutes but soon subsided as the warmth eased over her. Relaxing in the sweet aroma of the bubbles with her head laid back she drifted off to sleep.

Sometime later she woke. The water in the tub had turned cold and the bubbles were nearly gone. Shivering she stepped out of the bath and wrapped in a soft oversized towel. The aching had gone and there was a strong desire to crawl back into the warm bed, but she thought better of it. Wandering over to the dressing room closet she looked over the wide selection of clothes, shoes, boots and more. The white dress was still where he had placed it. Decidedly she would not wear the dress as it represented his control over her which made her resentful of the dress. Instead she rehung it in the closet. It would be her decision what she would wear even though everything in the closet were his choices. A comfortable pair of blue jeans and a simple mint green T-top with a scoop neck would do and a comfortable pair of tennis shoes. After her bath, the crisp newness of the clothes felt good against her skin and the fit was surprisingly perfect. A small amount of make-up helped to make her feel better. "He didn't miss a thing. Even knows my brand of makeup and the right shade," she mused out loud. Her own voice sounded ironically like that of a stranger. Pulling her hair softly on top of her head she sat waiting expectedly.

The clock on the nightstand read seven forty-five am. "Well I'm clean, dressed and ready for breakfast. That should make him happy." The clock on the nightstand ticked away the minutes. She watched as the hands moved into the eight o'clock position. Due to his earlier punctuality she looked expectantly at the door waiting for him to enter. The intrusive quiet scream at her. The door didn't open. She listened intently for the sound of approaching steps or even the sound of the dog. But all was quiet. Her stomach suddenly growled loudly, startling her. "Wow that was loud." Still no sign of the man. A half hour passed, then an hour. Not a sound could be heard within the house. The loneliness and silence began to close in on her and the hunger pains became more intense as tears burned her eyes. In the bathroom she found a glass and drank several glasses of water hoping to ease the pain in her stomach. Curling up on the bed in a fetal position she held her stomach as she cried herself to sleep.

The hours wore on as she woke to an eerie stillness. Afternoon came and went and the waning light of the afternoon sun made the room darken as the evening drew near and the shadows lengthened. Still all was quiet. Not a sound could be heard from anywhere in the house. Could something have happened? Should she dare to try and leave the room to see what might have become of him, and what about the dog? He couldn't still be outside the door. Opening the door slightly she looked out. The hall was dimly lit and the dog was nowhere to be seen. Closing the door quietly she decided to think about it and plan some sort of strategy, just in case. "Just in case of what?"

She hadn't eaten for two days and the hunger pains were getting even more intense. If she went out quietly he might not hear her and she could maybe escape. Knowing dogs have acute hearing and smell could be a problem. If only she knew where the animal was, she could avoid going that way. Then again even if she made it to the outside what's to say the dog wouldn't be waiting there to stop her. She could stay there and continue to be hungry or she could attempt to do something about it.

Again she opened the door and tip toed out. Slowly she proceeded down the hall. At the top of the stairs she hesitated. Her body began shaking as she took one step, then another down the stairs. She wished she would stop shaking, but the combination of nervousness and lack of food made it impossible. As she descended she began to feel light headed. Everything was beginning to spin. The dizzy feeling slowly subsided, but she felt nauseated. Carefully holding tight to the railing she continued, finally reaching the bottom of the stairs. Still no sound could be heard. Steadying herself she moved towards the door, but the need for food suddenly became overwhelming. Looking around she hesitated. Not having paid attention to her surroundings the first night except for the fireplace, she found it somewhat impressive, clean and organized. Though there was no fire going she could still feel warmth from an earlier fire as she drew near.

To her right facing the front door was the living room area. It was an inviting ranch style with overstuffed chair and couch. A more delicately styled loveseat filled the far corner. A few plants were placed about the room. The living room and dining room area were combined into one room across the entire front of the house. Trying to take it all in the dizzy feeling returned. She tried to focus on which way led to the kitchen and the hope of food. To her left was an arched opening that led into the kitchen. Also to her left was a large old dining table. On the table sat a bowl filled with fresh fruit. With a shaky hand she reached out to take a shiny green apple from it, but hesitated. She drew her hand back and stood looking longingly at the fruit. Would it be considered steeling? Why did she feel she needed permission before taking it?

As she stood there unsteadily, trying to decide if she should take a piece of fruit she heard his voice behind her saying, "Go ahead. You've got to be damn hungry by now."

Startled, she turned quickly and in her haste she felt the dizziness and the nausea return. He saw the startled look on her face as she turned suddenly pale. Their eyes met for a moment as he realized she was going to pass out. The weakness overtook her as she felt herself falling. He was too far away and he felt sickened as he heard the hard thud of her body as she hit the floor.

When Favor came to she was laying on the soft living-room couch with a throw cover over her and a cool wash cloth draped over her forehead. She opened her eyes to see him sitting beside her, his mesmerizing blue eyes filled with concern and fixed intently on her.

"I'm sorry. You hit the floor before I could reach you or do anything to stop your fall. Are you hurt anywhere?"

Babbling like a silly teenager he almost made her laugh but then she felt the throbbing in her head. Putting her hand to her head she held it over the cool cloth. Reaching up he gently put his hand on hers. For a moment she let him hold it there, then slowly slid her hand out from under his. For some reason she couldn't draw her eyes away from his. He was handsome beyond words and she unexpectedly felt drawn to him. The two were transfixed on each other. To her surprise it was him who broke the gaze and slowly pulled away.

"I'll get you something for the pain and then we'd better get something in your stomach."

"I don't really need anything except something to eat."

"Don't try to get up. I'll fix you something and bring it in here. Are you warm enough?

"Yes, I think so." She thought kidnappers were supposed to be mean and abusive. This guy was the complete opposite, at least so far.

Leaning back she closed her eyes and tried to forget about the pain in her head. Drifting off to sleep she dreamed of soft music playing and a crystal blue pool of water. Looking down into the pool she saw those incredible blue eyes looking back at her and she was drawn deeper and deeper into the pool until she was engulfed in the music and the blue water. Closer and closer to the beautiful eyes that became softer and more enticing the closer she came. Abruptly she woke to the sound of his voice and the blue eyes looking nervously at her. Shaking her head slightly as if trying to distinguish between the dream and reality she heard him saying, "I didn't know if you were asleep or if you had passed out again."

On a nearby table sat a tray with an assortment of fruit, biscuits, butter, warm soup, tea and water. Sitting up she reached for the water. Reaching it before her he poured a glass. It was sweet and pure, by far the best water she had ever tasted. The water in the glass made her feel like the water in the dream. She became acutely aware of how the coolness felt in her mouth as it flowed down her throat and how it filled the emptiness in her. Holding the glass in her hand she stared at it as if it was something to be treasured.

Realizing he was intently watching her she became flushed as she put the glass down. What if there was something in the food? That was a silly thought. Why would he go through all this trouble and then poison her? Realizing what she was thinking, he said, "It's not poison. Do you want me to taste it first?" Shaking her head she reached for the bowl of soup. It was a creamy yellow squash soup. She'd never tasted it before and was amazed at the smooth texture and very slightly sweet, yet tangy flavor.

"This is really good. I've never tasted soup like this before."

"It was a recipe my grandmother used to make. I always thought it was a rich man's soup." This made her smile. Indeed it did taste like it was fit for royalty. Already she was beginning to feel better. The dizzy feeling was gone and the nausea, too. He buttered each of them a biscuit and they ate in silence. When done he took the tray and headed back into the kitchen without saying a word.

Waiting for him to return she looked around the room. Like the room she occupied upstairs, it had a clean, airy, cozy feel. The oversized furniture was inviting, not overpowering and offset with lighter more delicate furnishings. It definitively had that ranch house appeal but with a touch of richness, making it homey and relaxing. Standing quietly at a window she listened to the birds as they made their way to their nests for the evening, unaware that he had come back into the room and was watching her. He finally spoke. "Would you like to go for a walk outside? It's a beautiful evening."

"Where is your dog?"

"Probably out chasing down a jack rabbit or two. It seems to amuse him. He never goes very far. If I want him I just whistle and he comes running."

Favor didn't say a word but she was sure he'd made a point of telling her the dog never went far, because he didn't want her to get any ideas about trying to run off again.

"So do you feel up to a walk outside? I think some fresh air will do you good." He opened the door and she followed him outside onto the long porch. "The porch used to be about half this size. I lengthened it when I was doing renovations. I think it made it more inviting." An old swing hung at the far right end of the porch along with an array of slightly weathered porch furniture along the sides. Soft cushions and pillows were arranged neatly on them. Quietly taking in the vast countryside that lay spread out in front of her she noticed several wild turkeys meandered along the edge of some nearby trees. Just ahead she saw a weathered arbor with grapevines trailing up and over it. Beyond was a small lake slightly over grown with peat moss and water lilies?

"We can walk down there if you want," then led her down the path. Avoiding looking at him she followed, careful not to get too close.

"I need to clean out some of the peat moss along the edges and some of the plants. If I don't clean it out, it will eventually become completely over-grown. There are some good fish in there that comes from the streams that feed this lake. There's a larger lake in the mountains above here called Sweasy Lake. It feeds into a stream which feeds into this lake. I'll teach you how to fish sometime. You'll enjoy that."

She suddenly wanted to yell at him for assuming once again that she would like fishing, but held her tongue because she had secretly wanted to go fishing, though she wouldn't let him have the satisfaction of knowing. On either side of the grape arbor were benches.

"I meant to repaint it this year but I ran out of time. Maybe we could do it together. It is a nice comfortable place to read and sip some tea or coffee." Once again she didn't respond, and averted her eyes to avoid looking into his. They passed through the arbor and walked to the edge of the lake. Standing about two arms lengths away they avoided looking at one another, instead looking straight ahead at the water. The air was warm and balmy. Overhead several small birds flitted about and the smell of the various plants and trees heightened her senses. Off to the left she saw a movement. Two deer approached the lake to have a drink of water. Motionless they watched as Mother Nature's peacefulness settled on the evening.

How long they stood side by side watching the animals, she couldn't tell. The sun had dipped lower behind some trees and the air was beginning to turn cool. Neither had spoken for some time. He finally turned and said, "It's time we were getting back to the house. It will be getting cold soon and I'd like to get a fire started." Without another word they both turned to head back. Her eyes met his briefly and she felt like her breath was being stolen away. She'd never seen a more handsome man and it frightened her the way he could take her breath away with just a look. He had kidnapped her. What was she thinking? He was being mister nice guy right now, but in time she knew he would want more and when she said no, he'd surely escalate. "Oh, God," she silently prayed, "please help my friends find me."

To the left of the house stood a large vegetable garden and greenhouse. Farther back behind the house was a large barn and shop area and a large chicken coop. Fruit trees at the far end were surrounded by deer fencing. At the house he spoke softly, "How about I show you the rest of the house?

Favor only shrugged her shoulders. It would be good to know her way about. It would give her a better edge if she was able to make her escape. She didn't want to seem interested though. Why give him that satisfaction?

"You've seen the living and dining areas. That door leads into the downstairs bathroom," pointing to a door just off the living room. The kitchen was light and spacious with a large pantry generously stocked with dry goods and home canned fruits and vegetables.

He led her past the bathroom to the left of the staircase. A hallway led into a wonderful room filled with books. He called it the library. There was another fireplace in this room as well and large overstuffed furniture to curl up in and read to your heart's content. "I added this room a few years ago and brought a lot of books from another ranch I own since I knew I'd be spending so much more time here. A desk sat to the far right in front of a window. On it sat a computer. Hope! Computer meant the possibility of internet and communication with the outside world.

"Well, I see you have a computer. That's quite a surprise."

"I know what you're thinking. A computer is a useful tool if used right, I need it for my business but I assure you it is password protected. We'll be spending a lot of time in here when winter comes. You'll find all sorts of books to read."

"If I were going to stay here I would most certainly need the internet."

"You might need it, but you're not going to have it."

"Why?"

"You'd find a way to let someone know where we are and that would ruin everything."

"Well, finally you've got something right," she turned indignantly away from him and left the room. He followed her out and reached for her arm to stop her retreat. As he whirled her around to face him he was met with an icy glare.

"Let go of my arm this instant." He released her arm but stood ready to take action.

"I think it's time you went up to your room. I'll be up in a little bit to be sure everything is ok and bring up some of your favorite tea."

"Oh yeah, I've been a bad girl 'cause I didn't agree with you, so by all means send me to my room. That's real typical of how you operate. Are you going to give me a spanking, too?"

"I'll do that and more if you don't knock it off."

"Oh, I'm so scared."

"Favor, I'm warning you, don't push me or I'll forget I'm a gentleman." Oddly she wanted to push and make him feel her anger. The look on his face was enough to make her rethink and hold her tongue. Ascending the steps she heard the front door open as he whistled for the dog. Within seconds the dog had entered the house and she heard him say, "follow." With that she heard the dog heading up the stairs. She nearly broke into a run to get to her room.

Ten minutes later he arrived with her tea and placed it on the night stand. She was standing at the far window with her back to him refusing to acknowledge his presence. When he drew near her body shuddered at the feel of his warm breath near her cheek and the smell of his cologne made her feel that mysterious attraction as he placed his hands on her shoulders. Still she kept her eyes focused on the outside. He drew her body close to his as he gently kissed the top of her head and then her neck. This was it. He was going to make love to her. Could she resist? Hardly able to breathe she turned. Looking into his eyes for a moment she wanted him. She wanted him to touch her and make love to her. An instant later he lightly kissed her lips. She wanted him to draw her into his arms and kiss her passionately. But then he turned and quietly headed for the door. Oh yes, he'd seen the desire in her eyes and knew she wanted him. That was satisfaction enough for now.

"I'll see you at eight for breakfast." And then he closed the door. Shocked, she began to shake. How could she even have thought about making love to him? He's the enemy, the bad guy, the kidnapper. What the hell was wrong with her? She stood at the window and watched the fading light cast long shadows across the moor as the light slowly faded into darkness. Cold and alone she walked over and poured some of the tea. Her favorite, Red Zinger. It had turned slightly cold but still tasted good. Listening to the frogs and crickets she finally slipped between the sheets thinking of the man in the room across the hall as she drifted off to sleep.

Chapter 8

The next morning Favor got up and dressed for breakfast. Seeing the dog wasn't there she didn't wait for him to come to her room, but instead assertively made her way down the stairs on her own. He was standing in front of the fireplace with a cup of coffee. Pleased that she had come down he watched her graceful movement and wished he had made love to her the night before. "Did you find everything you need in your room?"

"You should know!" Her sarcasm was apparent.

"What's that supposed to mean?"

"How embarrassing, you even bought my personal things. You knew exactly what merchandise I use right down to the feminine products. How many times were you in my house and when? How dare you invade my privacy! You violated me."

"Violated? I may have intruded, but I have not violated you, nor will I ever. As for my intrusion into your house, it was easy. You made frequent trips to the city for your designs. All I had to do is walk in and write things down and take a few pictures. Brand, quantity, sizes, you name it I did my homework. You really should have locked your door."

"I live there because it is secluded and safe. We've never had to lock our doors."

"Correction, you lived there. Now you live here."

"Wrong, this is not and never will be my home."

"Favor, please don't start with the attitude. Now let's get some breakfast and then we'll have coffee on the porch afterwards."

"Damn him!" He was so condescending. Resentment and anger were on the threshold of her emotions. She kept her eyes turned downward as she ate, grateful that he didn't speak. Every-time she glanced up at him she felt feelings she didn't understand. He seemed to be studying her. What was it about him that made her so confused? Realizing he was speaking to her she looked up. "I'm going to get us some more coffee. Meet me on the porch. It's nicer out there. Go out and make yourself comfortable?"

"You trust me to go out there without you. Aren't you afraid I'll run away?"

"No! Cloud's out there."

"Cloud? That's what you call him? Not a very imaginative name. Sounds lame."

"Well he likes it," he said as he walked away.

Out on the porch Favor was deep in thought. "Favor?" Startled, she turned toward him where he had taken a seat on one of the porch chairs. "You don't have to be afraid to talk to me. The fact is we need to talk. You have questions, you're angry and confused because you're attracted to me. I see the way you look at me, and you're angry for feeling that attraction."

"Oh God this is freaky. Now he's a mind reader." Her thoughts raced through her head.

"I'm not crazy. I had to do this. Think of it as your own personal fairy-tale come true."

"What! You make a ridiculous statement like that and you expect me to think you're perfectly sane? This is not a fairy tale and this is not Fairy Land. This is the twentieth century and when a guy is interested in a girl he introduces himself, asks her out, and she decides if she wants to pursue a relationship with him. He doesn't force her to be with him *unless* he's crazy."

When he suddenly stood up she realized she had been screaming at him. "Now it's my turn to be angry and frustrated." Favor eyed him warily. "I haven't tried to rape you or violate you as you would have put it. I haven't been unnecessarily rough with you, have I? But there is nothing I want more than to take you up to that room and make love to you. I'm a patient man, but if you keep being so obstinate I'm going to lose control."

His own words surprised him as they both stood staring at each other. He was angry for losing his cool and angry that he couldn't take her right then and there. A tear slowly trickled down her cheek. "Don't look at me that way," he said.

"Damn it, I don't even know your name", she blurted realizing her own sudden thoughts.

A smile crossed his lips and then he let out a loud hearty laugh. "I was wondering when you were going to ask. My name is Steve. Steven Mitchell. Actually Steven Lawrence Mitchell IV." The gentleness had returned to his eyes with a hint of laughter. He moved close to Favor, embraced her feeling the warmth of her body pressed close to his. With deep passion he raised her face to his and kissed her passionately. For a moment she didn't resist, but then she pulled away, her heart racing. Turning away she retreated to the far end of the porch. When she looked back at him, his blue eyes pierced deep into her heart. How could he remain so calm and controlled? She wanted him and hated herself for it. She was supposed to love Adam Jennings, not Steve Mitchell. Taking a step back towards him her eyes pleaded for him to touch her, feel her and make love to her. Instead he called to the dog and headed out away from the house, leaving her standing there, puzzled and unsure of what she should do.

He had to put some distance between them or he would surely lose control. Watching him walk away, she studied the slim strong lines of his body, his long legs and muscular arms. Desire and a burning inside her was beginning to consume her and the overwhelming need to have him touch her was almost more than she could stand. How had it come to this?

"No, I won't think about it. I can't let this happen. There's got to be a way out of here, back to my Dad, friends, Adam, my life."

Picking up the coffee cups she retreated to the kitchen. The dirty dishes and cookware lay on the counter and in the sink. Mechanically she began to wash them and put them neatly away. When Steve finally returned she was folding the towel on which she had been drying her hands a faraway look on her face. He was studying the look when she realized he was standing in the doorway. An approving smile showed he was pleased with what she'd done.

"What? I was angry and I needed to vent. This is how I vent." Still smiling he crossed over to where she stood towel still in hand. Reaching out he gently touched her cheek. "Steve." His name sounded like music on her lips. She spoke softly. "You know this can't work. You can't buy love and you can't change how I feel. I already have a lovely home of my own. Surely you must realize that you've got to take me back."

"Favor, I don't think we should talk about this right now. Can we talk about it later? Let me show you the rest of the house. Please." He said it so sweetly with a soft kindness, so with a shrug of her shoulders they headed up the stairs. Turning to the left he led her around the railing walkway and opened the door that faced directly across to the room Favor was occupying. It was a nice sized bedroom, which looked to be recently upgraded. It too had a light and airy feeling with darker furniture but a similar style furniture as her room. A mint green chenille bedspread gave it an old time look, with a genuinely peaceful, relaxing atmosphere but was accessorized in a way that made it surprisingly masculine.

"This is my room." He waited trying to anticipate her reaction. His closeness was making it hard to breathe.

She softly whispered, "It's very nice and masculine."

Favor felt Steve leaning ever so slightly against her body. "'You know, since you're an interior designer, you're welcome to make any changes you would like to make."

"Thank you, but I'm sure I won't be staying that long." Her voice was barely a whisper. Not surprised, she noticed he ignored her comment.

"Come on I'd like to show you the balcony. It's my favorite part of the house." He opened the glass door that led out onto the balcony. I sometimes like to come out here on clear star covered nights. I have a telescope that I sometimes set up." It was easy to see why he liked it. The view was breathtaking.

"Ok, come on, one last room to see." He led her around the railing past the room he called her room and stopped in front of the last door. "I thought about turning this into a bathroom, but decided it would be too large for a bathroom. Instead I added the bathroom in your room so that you could have more privacy. It made your room sleeping area smaller, but more convenient. "He opened the door to a smaller yet still spacious room that was not yet furnished or decorated. The walls on two sides were partially slanted due to the ceiling peak, giving it less usable space. "I left this room empty for now. It will be our son's room. I want you to be able to help set it up when the time comes. We'll have a son to carry on the next generation of Mitchell's."

Disbelief flooded her body. Turning to face Steve her face burned like it was on fire. "You planned that there would be children? How dare you! I have a career and I am not planning on having any child with you! I want to go home! I demand that you take me home now!"

"Favor, haven't you learned anything the last few days? You tried pulling that stubborn act before and it didn't get you anywhere. I'm a patient man, but be careful how far and hard you push. If you give this relationship a chance I know you will love me as much as I love you."

"You have a lot of nerve. I'm not going to stand for this travesty." With that Favor turned and ran down the stairs and out the front door. The dog was on the porch. Speaking softly as she inched passed him and down the steps she continued to speak softly as she walked slowly away. His wolf eyes followed her movement but he didn't move or make any attempt to block her. He didn't growl like before, or follow. There was no sign of Steve so she turned and walked quickly down the road. When she felt she was far enough away she broke into a run. Then she heard the whistle. Looking back she saw Steve was standing on the balcony watching. Then she saw the dog racing after her. Turning she ran as fast as she could, but the dog was gaining on her. She could feel it coming closer so she stopped abruptly to face him hoping if she showed him she wasn't afraid it would confuse the dog. Before she knew what was happening she was on the ground, the weight of the dog on her as she screamed in fear and anger. Her voice sounded like the voice of a stranger. Still screaming she realized Steve was cradling her in his arms. The wolf dog, no longer on her, had settled down waiting for his next command.

"It's alright. You're ok. You shouldn't have run."

"Damn it, keep him away from me, and let go of me." Their eyes met and the blue of his eyes cooled the fire and fury inside her. "Please! I won't run away again, I promise. Just keep him away." Favor's eyes pleaded.

"Do you mean that?"

Hesitating, knowing she'd just made a promise, she gave a weak response, "Yes."

"I'm sorry he scared you, but I won't tolerate any more of that behavior. Let's go back home. It looks like you could use some freshening up." Her clothes were soiled and her face smudged with dirt. She wanted to cry but refused to give him that satisfaction. Steve watched her as she headed upstairs. "Are you going to be alright?" Favor ignored the question. Closing the door softly behind her and throwing herself on the bed she sobbed into the pillow.

The light in the room was growing dim when she woke up. How long had she slept? What day was it? How many days had passed since he brought her here? Two? Three? Looking in the mirror she saw a stranger with a dirty face, tangled hair and soiled clothing. Drawing a warm tub of water she poured some bubble bath into it, slipped out of the dirty clothes and eased herself into the tub. When she returned to the bedroom a half hour later she saw fresh flowers on the night stand. A note read, "I looked in on you earlier and saw you sleeping. I heard the bath water running so slipped in while you were bathing. Dinner will be at seven. I hope you'll join me." How much more could she take.

The clock on the night stand read six-forty. Food was the last thing she wanted but didn't feel like another confrontation. Slipping into a little summer dress, promptly at seven she slowly descended the stairs. Much to her surprise, the food smelled good. Steve was standing by the fireplace dressed in a western shirt and vest. He handed her a glass of wine, Red Zinfandel, her favorite. She took it but didn't speak. "The dress looks good on you. Dinners ready." Though she didn't feel like eating, she had to admit to herself, he was a damn good cook. The seasonings blended nicely enhancing the natural flavors. There wasn't much conversation and Steve didn't force it. She found him intriguing. It seemed he could do anything and everything about him fascinated her.

When they had finished she politely offered to clear the dishes. "Don't worry about it. I'll take care of it tomorrow morning."

"Thanks, the dinner was nice." Then without thinking, "Where did you learn to cook?"

"You're welcome, and to answer your question, both my parents were good cooks. They spent a lot of time cooking together. I think they were a bit competitive, but all in good fun. Dad used to say there's no such thing as a woman job and vice-versa. A couple should always work together as partners or helpmates. It makes you appreciate the other person more. Mom even went hunting with Dad sometimes."

"Where are your parents?"

"They both died on a river rafting trip when I was sixteen. My aunt raised me after that. She'd always been jealous of my mother. She and my father had been close friends while they were growing up, but he fell in love with my mother. When they married she said my mother stole him away from her. This house belonged to my parents and she tried to get it when they died, but my parents had a trust leaving everything to me. I was determined that one day I would have a wonderful wife like my mother. The first time I saw you, I knew you were the one." Favor decided not to comment on the wife statement and noticed he was smiling at her with a boyish glint in his eyes.

"Why are you smiling like that?"

"Because, I just realized we're actually talking. We're having a conversation."

A sweet sense of familiarity seemed to settle in the room and the rest of the evening they engaged in pleasant, simple conversation and listened to the crackling of the fire as it warmed the room. Why wasn't she afraid of this man who had kidnapped her? What was it that drew her to him and found talking to him so comfortable? Favor looked at some of the books in the library and sipped hot tea. Somehow the atmosphere in the room made Favor relax. Strangely, being in each other's company somehow felt right. Favor was perplexed, wondering how she could possibly feel this way. The silence was broken when Steve said, "It's late, Favor. I think we should be going to bed." She felt her body tense. He must have noticed because he said, "Don't worry, you to your room and me to mine."

At her door she turned to him, "I'm truly sorry about your folks. It sounds like they were very special. I still wish you could understand my need to choose who I want to be with and what I want to do with the rest of my life." He made no reply as he studied her eyes then leaned down and kissed her goodnight lingering longer than he should. Starting to turn away he leaned in and kissed her again, putting his arm around her, pulling her closer, then turned and walked across to his room leaving her wanting more. It occurred to Favor that he did this on purpose and though she wanted to be angry with him the sweet sense of his kiss lingered on her lips and the feel of his strong arms embracing her remained making her body tingle.

Chapter 9

F avor changed into some night wear and slipped between the cool
sheets. Snug under the covers lying back against the soft pillows
her mind went over the events of the day. It had been emotionally
exhausting and difficult. As she drifted off to sleep her sub-conscious mind
couldn't rest resulting in disturbing dreams.

A sound woke her but she wasn't sure what it was. She went to the door
and listened. It was quiet, almost too quiet. It gave her an eerie feeling.
What could the sound have been? Opening her door she looked out into
the dimly lit hallway. The dog was nowhere around. She thought about
knocking on Steve's bedroom door, but was afraid he'd get the wrong
idea, so she closed her door and slipped back into bed. Maybe it was just a
manifestation of her dream and she only thought she'd heard a sound. But
that didn't stop her from listening for any more sounds until sleep finally
overtook her again taking her back into foreign places that threw her back
into a fitful dream state.

Nearly two am Steve woke to the sound of terrifying screams coming
from Favors room. He grabbed his robe as he ran into the hallway. Her
screams shattered the night as he rushed into her room finding her
thrashing about in the bed. Pulling her into his arms the screams stopped
as she woke. Gasping for air her breath came hard and fast. Looking into
Steve's eyes the tears streamed down her face. She couldn't speak as she
continued to gasp for air.

"It's alright. I'm here. It was just a bad dream."

"It was terrible," she choked out.

"I'm sorry. It was about the dog wasn't it?"

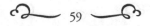

"No, partly, maybe, it was more. I don't know," she stammered as she tried to focus. His arms around her were comforting and for a moment she wanted to stay there and forget there was anything or any other place in the world. Feeling her relax he rose and said he was going back to his room. "Call me if you need me."

"Steve," her voice was almost a whisper, soft, tender and oh so beautiful. "I don't want to be alone. I'm scared. I can't handle what you're doing to me. It's confusing me. Please, stay." She didn't know why she said it. He was her kidnapper, but being near him somehow felt right, safe, secure and better than being alone.

Her eyes were pleading. "Are you sure you want me to stay?"

"No, it's ok. Oh, I don't know. I just want to go back home. I miss my friends and my work." Confused she burst into a new flood of tears.

"Favor, if I stay in the same room with you when you're dressed like that, I'm afraid I can't be accountable for my actions, if you get my drift." The embarrassment in her eyes was very moving. "I have an idea, why don't you meet me downstairs. I'll get the fire going again and we can relax, maybe have a drink." Favor nodded in agreement. When he left the room she slipped into a long lounge gown with spaghetti straps. He already had the fire going, and he was seated on the couch with a beer. The setting was so surreal, like something you would see on TV. "Hi, can I get you something?"

"No, I'm fine."

"I'm sorry. I let this thing with the dog get out of hand. He's really very gentle, and faithful. Did I tell you he's actually half wolf? Wolf dogs train really well and are exceptionally well mannered and dedicated. He knows his place and would never hurt you." Favor sat down on the bear skin rug in front of the fireplace and drew her knees up to her chest. "Are you sure I can't get you something, how about a glass of wine?" She declined knowing if she had wine she would let her guard down and she wouldn't be able to resist him. Her emotions were at an extremely vulnerable state. Steve seemed to sense this and wished she had accepted the wine. It would have made it easier to be close to her. Instead he went to get another beer. When he returned she was staring blankly into the fire. The firelight made her skin glow softly. There was a faraway look in her eyes. Turning she looked at him when he came back into the room. "May I sit by you?" Nodding to him, he sat down.

"You know, it's kind of funny, but when I was a little girl I wanted a bear skin rug and a fireplace where I could sit and read. But we never even had a fireplace." Relieved that she had spoken it opened up the conversation. Steve began telling her how they had gotten the bear skin when he was quite young and how proud his dad had been. They continued to talk for a while but in time the conversation began to lag as Favor began to doze off. Steve watched contentedly as her head dropped to her knees and she fell asleep.

Another beautiful morning on the mountain. The sounds and the sun streaming in the window woke Favor and she realized her head was resting on Steve's chest. His arms were wrapped around her as they lay outstretched on the bear-skin rug. The fire had died down and the room had become chilly. Favor shifted slightly, trying to get out of his arms. The movement woke him up and he apologized profusely, "I'm sorry," he said letting her go and pulling himself into an upright position. "You fell asleep and just sort of fell over against me. I didn't want to wake you. You looked so comfortable and well, I, well, I," it was his turn to feel embarrassed.

With both of them at a loss for words and blushing, Favor quickly excused herself and headed upstairs to get dressed. He followed and watched the graceful movement of her body as she ascended the stairs. "She's finally beginning to relax and feel more comfortable with me," he thought. When she had disappeared upstairs he added some wood to the dying embers and got the fire started again then went up to his room to get dressed.

Steve was sitting on the top step when Favor came out of her room. She wore a pink spaghetti strap top and a pair of jean shorts. The pink brought out her warm tan and gave her a fresh, healthy and very desirable look.

"Hi, you look nice. I hope you don't mind me waiting for you." He rose and they started to descend the stairs. Favor stopped suddenly. There was a door she hadn't noticed the day before. She turned and stared at the door.

"Favor, what is it?"

"I didn't see that door yesterday. Why didn't you show me that room?"

"It just leads up to an attic room. Just some old stuff stored up there."

"Can I see it?" She walked assertively toward the door and reached out to turn the knob. The door was locked. She turned and looked at Steve with a puzzled look. "Why is it locked?"

"I don't want anything disturbed up there and there is no reason for you to go up there."

"Why? I want to see it."

"Not now. Another day. Let's go downstairs."

"Just like that, you're really not going to let me see that room? Well, then I'm not going down with you until you show me?"

Steve looked at her. His eyes burned with anger. His glare was piercing. "Do we have to start every day like this with you testing me? When I'm ready to show you the room, I will, but not until I decide. Maybe when I'm sure, without a doubt, that you trust and love me. Now let's go downstairs." She could feel his anger and realized she needed to let it go and not antagonize him. He waited and she started down the stairs, turning to look back at the locked door for a moment. She didn't say another word as she headed down the stairs.

Reaching out to touch her arm, she pulled back away from him. "That's ok. I can wait. One day you'll love me with the most perfect love that two people can share. And when that time comes, the bond that we'll share won't be able to separate us, even in death." What an odd thing to say. Their eyes met and she felt a cold chills run down her spine.

"You've got a long wait. That will never happen." She turned away defiantly.

"Yes it will, Favor, it's already begun. You know it has. Don't keep fighting it."

Hot tears burned at her eyes. Frustration ate at her heart. What was happening to her? Her whole life was turned upside down. It was no longer hers. It didn't feel real. She swore no one would ever control her again and here she was, her life reeling totally out of control, feeling that even death would be more welcome than this mental anguish and the feeling she was losing the battle. It was draining her will and along with it was this strange pull, a fascination and desire for this man that made her feel terrified all at the same time. How could she fight this unknown uncertainty? Steve was speaking to her, but she wasn't really hearing him. It felt like the life was being sucked right out of her. The room was spinning and she felt strangely separated from her own body. She wanted him. The passion and desire was overwhelming. Her body cried out for him. He had kidnapped her, so how could she feel this way. The spinning continued and tears were streaming down her face. She was riveted to the spot where she stood. Everything was turning to a blur and then she was falling into sweet oblivion. Her body was floating and she didn't care. His voice was trying to bring her back, but she didn't want to listen or come back to the voice. She wanted to stay somewhere between here and nowhere. But he kept calling her name, pulling her back with a voice like music drawing her in. "Fight! Don't listen to his voice!"

His body was pressed against her as she lay on the soft carpet. He was holding her wrists, "I want to make love to you, but I know I have to wait. When I do it'll be like no other love making you have ever experienced. But I have to wait till you're ready."

"That is never going to happen!" she said with defiance as she tried to push him away.

"Favor, I saw how you were looking at me a minute ago. You want me almost as much as I want you. We're going to be good together, but you still need some time. It's too soon. Just think about how our bodies feel together. I can feel the throbbing between your legs right now. You're lips are saying one thing, but your body is telling me you want to make love. What our bodies are saying is perfectly natural. We're meant to be and we belong together." He moved his body pressing himself more tightly between her legs. Then he tried to press his mouth to hers as she tried to turn her head away. Releasing her wrists he held her head, forcing her to look at him. His eyes drew her in. Pressing her hands against his chest she tried again to push him away. "You're strong willed and spirited. I like that. It makes you even more exciting to be with."

He held her head still and pressed his lips to hers. She tried to speak, but as her lips parted slightly he began exploring her mouth. She could feel his sensuality surging through his entire body. He continued kissing her and she quivered as his hands moved down her body. What was happening? Her will to fight the desire and resist his touch and kisses were making her crazy. Never had she experienced such passion yet was determined not to respond. At least that's what her brain was trying to tell her, but she felt her body going weak and then her mouth opened as he kissed her more deeply. It was intoxicating. With every touch, every movement of his body on hers, her desire cried out for more.

She melted into the curves of his body, feeling the movement as he pressed harder. Her legs parted, inviting him closer. He slid his hand down between her tender thighs. A moan escaped her lips as his hand slid up into her shorts. Feeling his warm gentle touch her body invited him to continue as his kisses became more passionate. She moved rhythmically to his touch, feeling her warmth as her body screamed out for him, begging him to take her. And finally the feeling of exhilaration as her body reached the point of no return. She moaned as her body gave in to the sensation, as she gave herself to his touch.

Reaching up she wrapped her arms around his neck pulling him down as she kissed him passionately. "I want you." She pulled his body to her and felt him pressed against her thighs. "Please make love to me."

Unexpectedly Steve pulled away from her and got up, pulling her to her feet. "No. You're not ready and it's not the right time. Now let's get some breakfast and then I have a surprise for you. After we finish eating I'm going to take you someplace special." Shocked and embarrassed she stared at him. She couldn't draw her eyes away from his and she couldn't speak. He smiled and leaned in and kissed her. "I promise you'll love what I am going to show you." Then he headed for the kitchen. What had just happened? Was he trying to humiliate her? If so it had worked, she was completely embarrassed and confused. No man has that much control when it came to sex. She couldn't look at him.

"I'm not really hungry."

"Well, you need to eat something and we need to fix a lunch, too. We'll be gone most of the day." With that he headed for the kitchen leaving her in complete humiliation. Standing there a moment not knowing what to do, she tried to sort out her feelings, the worst being the humiliation. Entering the kitchen she stood there watching him as he was preparing breakfast.

Finally finding her voice she said, "What just happened out there?"

He turned to her and smiled, "Honey, you got your rocks off. Felt good didn't it?" Then he went back to fixing the food. "How about you come over here and help me now?"

Favor felt tears surface, ready to spill from her eyes. She blinked hard to hold them back. Her mouth felt dry while anger and frustration rushed to the surface of her emotions. She had to keep him from seeing her disappointment and embarrassment. "Don't give him the upper hand," although she'd already done that. "Best to act like it hadn't happened or at least like it was no big deal." Hard as she tried to put on as though she didn't care, her emotions got the best of her and she rushed at him screaming and pounding her fists on his back. "How could you? I hate you! I hate you!"

Steven had been cutting up vegetables. Quickly dropping the knife into the sink as he turned and grabbed her wrists. "Favor, stop it. Stop it, I said." But Favor was not ready to stop. She'd been too passive through this whole kidnapping. Why? She didn't know, but now she was ready to fight. Now she didn't care. He'd taken her from her home, made her want him and then humiliated her. She didn't care what happened anymore. At her home in Fortuna she had struggled out of fear. But now she was just plain ol' 'pissed' off. "Baby, I'm sorry. Please stop!"

"Don't call me Baby," she screamed at him as she continued to fight him with all the strength she could muster. Amazed at her strength and shear will Steven continued to ward off her blows as her fists pummeled his body. They fought for nearly ten minutes until exhausted Favor crumbled in a heap on the floor sobbing.

Steven gathered her up in his arms, "I love you, Favor. I didn't mean to hurt you. God, I love you so much." Her body shuddered as she let go of all the pent up emotions. She'd lost all control as her heart was torn and racked with emotion. How much more did she have to lose? How did this man make her want him and why did it matter? Was she on a path to self-destruction? When there seemed to be no more tears left to cry they sat quietly in the middle of the kitchen floor as Steve continued to hold her rocking her gently. In time he felt her body relax as she rested her head on his shoulder.

After a time Favor slowly drew back and Steve helped her to her feet. "I'm sorry I ruined your day, Favor. It was never my intension to make light of what you were feeling. You are so damn hard to resist and what I said was coy, rude and insensitive. If you want to stay home I'll give you some space. I'm truly sorry." With that he grabbed a couple of beers from the fridge and left the kitchen.

Favor looked around at the mess they'd made during their struggle then followed after him. She found him sitting on the porch steps his head in his hands. Strange as it seemed she wanted to be near him. Without saying a word she sat down beside him and leaned in to him, putting her head on his shoulder. Gently he slipped his arm around her. Together they sat in silence looking out at the pond. Words were not needed. She'd known him only a few short days, but there was no denying their connection was strong. The two years of him calling made her feel a kinship to him and now they were bound together by some mysterious twist of fate.

Favor finally broke the silence, "What were you planning on doing today?"

"Go on a picnic, but we can do it some other day."

"I think we should do it today. It might do us both some good."

"Are you sure?"

"Why not? I don't have any other plans." Her mind suddenly went back to Adam and the picnic they might have had, but just as quickly she dismissed it from her mind. She needed to try to keep her emotions in check or she would lose control again.

After cleaning up the mess in the kitchen and having a light breakfast, they fixed a lunch to take with them. Steve put it into a backpack along with a blanket and then they headed out on foot across the clearing on which the house stood. The house was situated in a meadow with a vast array of wild flowers. They headed North East crossing the meadow and up a gently rising slope to the top of a hill. At the top they stopped and looked back below them. The old ranch house could barely be seen between the trees. It was well sheltered and secluded and seemed small like a child's playhouse. The crisp white paint stood out from the dry summer wheat colored grasses that surrounded it. Turning they headed over the next ridge. At the top they looked down onto a small herd of cattle. The sound of their soft lowing drifted up with the summer breeze.

"Whose cattle are those?" hoping it meant there were neighbors close by.

"They're ours. See the barn over there?" pointing to the far off horizon, "I have a surprise to show you in there." Leading the way they headed towards the barn. Hearing the sound of a horse nicker her eyes grew wide with anticipation. Holding her hand he told her to close her eyes as he opened the door and led her inside. "No peaking." Once inside he told her to open her eyes. In a nearby stall stood a beautiful white horse.

"Oh, it's breathtaking."

"I call her Snow. Do you like her?"

"Yes, of course. She's magnificent. You're really not very good at picking names are you?" wrinkling up her nose at the name.

"No, I guess I'm not. She's white. It snows up here in the winter so figured it would do as good as any other name." A sound from another stall alerted her attention. There stood another horse, this one completely black. "That's Denali."

"Denali's a cool name. But who's been taking care of them? They're closed up in these stalls, but the stalls are pretty clean." Hoping this meant there were other people close by.

"I know what you're thinking. There's no one else around. They weren't in the stalls till last night. I came up here on my four-wheeler after you fell asleep and put them in, fed them and put fresh water in their buckets. And yeah, Denali is a cool name. That was his name when I bought him."

Disappointed that there had not been anyone else taking care of the horses she tried to be matter-of-fact. "Oh, so that was the sound I heard last night that woke me up. I didn't know what it was, and when I went out into the hall the dog was gone and everything was way too quiet. I was going to knock on your door, but decided not to."

"Sorry I woke you. I'm glad you didn't knock on my door because you might have been scared if you'd found I was gone."

"If you didn't answer I'd have just thought you were asleep."

"Still I'm sorry. So, do you want me to saddle them up so we can go for a ride?" Nearly forgetting the embarrassment of the morning she smiled and nodded. She hadn't ridden in years.

Exhilarated they rode across the open countryside, raced across meadows, laughing as the cool breeze turned their cheeks red, and the wind whipped through Favor's hair. For a time the warm sun, fresh mountain air and extraordinary beauty around her helped her forget about her other life, if only for a while. Slowing the horses down Steve pointed out different parts of the property of approximately 600 acres. Bordered with thickly forested land, completely secluded with no neighbors they were completely alone, in their own private world. After sometime they stopped to rest the horses and let them graze and drink at a nearby stream. Wild daisies were growing all along the creek edge. Favor gathered a bundle of them and created a daisy chain which she braided into Snow's mane as well as a band for her own hair. Steve spread out the blanket and stretched out to enjoy the sun. He watched intently in awe of her beauty as her fingers gracefully created the chain of flowers. His love for her was growing stronger with each moment and he was unsure of how much longer he could wait. There was no doubt that she would eventually love him back, with no reserve, but the wait was hard. Favor turned and saw him watching her. He smiled and she broke into a giggle like a shy little girl, warming his heart at her reaction.

"You ready for some lunch?" Nodding she went over and sat on the blanket with him while he opened the back pack and took out their lunch. Eating slowly, and relaxing back on the blanket, Favor looked up at the cumulous clouds feeling peace, joy and relaxation lift her spirit.

"I see why you love it here. The air is so clean and fresh and everything is so peaceful." She closed her eyes letting the peace and tranquility fill her.

Not wanting to spoil the moment Steve just smiled letting her relax. It wasn't long before she drifted off to sleep. He felt happier than he had in a very long time. Sometime later he gently nudged her, "We need to be heading back to the house." He spoke softly in a hushed tone, not wanting to spoil the serenity of the moment. "We'll take the horses to the house where they'll be close. I had them out with the cows so you didn't see them till I wanted you to. We'll put them up in the barn by the house on cold nights." For a moment time seemed to stand still. Slowly leaning over he found her lips. His gentle kiss made her heart beat so loudly she was sure he could hear it. Sitting motionless he kissed her again holding her spell bound. This kiss invoked love, tender and endearing. Favor's eyes pleaded with him to help her understand what was happening between them. What was happening to her heart and mind when she should be despising and hating this man?

The sweet smell of the earth and grass, the soft mountain air and the wild flowers along the streams edge drew her into another world. She could feel the passion rising up inside her again. Steve saw the look in her eyes and could feel her confusion so he refrained from kissing her for now. Without a word he rose gently pulling her to her feet. Quietly picking up the backpack and blanket he walked over to where the horses stood grazing and tied the pack onto Denali's saddle.

Her cheeks flushed as she suddenly realized her own eagerness. She was embarrassed and angry with herself. "Just typical," she thought. "He deliberately weakens me and then walks away. He's just trying to humiliate me again and he's doing a damn good job of it. Just see if I let him kiss me again. I'll show him who's in control. I'm tired of his games."

They walked along leading the horses for a while. Steve tried to make small talk but he noticed something was different and she avoided any eye contact with him. The day seemed to be ruined. Stopping he grabbed her arm. "Damn it, Favor. I know what you're thinking. I can see it in your face. Do you think it is easy for me to stop myself? Sometimes I want you so bad that I feel like forgetting your feelings and taking you any way I can. But I want your love more." Once again she felt blindsided.

"Steve, I just don't know how to take this situation and you." She stood staring at him as mixed emotions burned deep inside. He looked away. "Steve, look at me! Help me understand. I don't know what you expect of me? I," hesitating, "I've only known you for a few days." He just shook his head and said they needed to mount up.

The days that followed turned into weeks. Steve made it a point to teach her something new every day. He started by teaching her about the horses and cows and how to care for them, then about gardening and preserving food. They shared all the chores of the household and the ranch. The evenings were spent engaged in meaningful conversations and reading. Steve refrained from physical contact and for now it seemed to be the best for both of them. They laughed and talked and seemed to be building a friendship and a bond seemed to be growing between them although Favor was not completely aware of it.

The nights were still distressing for Favor. Her life with Steve was so cut off from the rest of the world, that she often felt particularly lonely at night. With no neighbors to visit and get to know, it was almost like living in the pioneer days on a prairie with no neighbors for a hundred miles. During the days they were so busy that she didn't think about it much, but when the stillness of the night came she would think about the home and friends she'd been forced to leave behind and a faraway longing would come over her. How she wished to see them, go out to dinner and dancing, to mingle with a room full of people and hear the many voices as they laughed together. And there was Adam whom she missed above the others. Fondly remembering him and his tender touch, his kiss and the promise to meet the next day, she wondered if he thought of her, if he missed her or if he had just left things to the police and moved on with his life. Did any of them miss her? How long had she been gone? Not quite sure anymore she tried not to think about it, but the nights echoed her memories and played tricks on her mind. She would fall asleep from sheer exhaustion, but always the dreams came, dreams that haunted her, tore at her soul and sometimes frightened her. Dreams mixed with real and unreal confused and tortured her mind.

Through the fading memories and the nightmares, there was one constant in her new life that she couldn't deny. It was her growing love for Steve. Yet to admit this seemed like defeat and it caused her to question her own judgment and what kind of a person she was. How could she love two men and was it love she was feeling? This constant state of confusion only put her heart in greater turmoil and she found herself feeling guarded. It was better to guard her heart from feeling anything. This was her only way to survive. If she emptied her heart of emotion it wouldn't hurt. But try as she might, every time she laid eyes on Steve she was overwhelmed with her growing love and desire for him. This just couldn't be. He had broken the law. He had kidnapped her.

Chapter 10

Weeks turned into months. The leaves of the trees began to turn yellow, orange, gold, red and brown. There was a chill in the air. Autumn had arrived. As the days got shorter and the nights longer her former life slipped deeper into her memory. Her life with Steve was becoming more and more comfortable. Was she accepting her new role in life? Was she falling in love with the tall, handsome, blue eyed man with whom she now shared her life?

Steve often left early in the mornings on his quad to go hunting. On these days Favor was permitted to go riding without him, but the wolf dog always accompanied her. She was never allowed beyond certain points. If she tried to go beyond an unseen boundary the wolf dog would block the path of the horse and not allow her to proceed. She had long since learned to respect his guardianship. It was more enjoyable when Steve went riding with her, but he seemed to prefer the quad more. At times he would take her with him but she preferred not to go when it meant killing something. Learning to help him cut up the meat when he brought game home was one of her many lessons, but she really preferred not to partake in the killing. Steve told her she needed to know what to do because it was part of surviving up here alone. He taught her about wild edible plants and how to prepare them to eat. The wealth of information that he shared with her seemed endless. There were times he would leave in the truck to get supplies and gas. He always left very early in the morning and she longed for him to return more and more each time.

Snow had become her most prized treasure and they had developed an uncanny way of communicating with each other. It seemed Snow knew her feelings and a strong bond had formed between them. She spent long hours with the horse and wolf dog when Steve was gone, and as much as she hated to admit it, she missed him greatly always eager for his return. Today was one of those days when Steve had taken the quad out. Favor had spent part of her day out riding Snow but was feeling especially lonely today. She groomed the horses fed and watered them then headed to the house with the wolf dog following close by her side. He too had become a part of her daily life and she had begun to enjoy his company as well. It was quite a sight to see Favor riding the white horse with the large white wolf dog always close by her side. They looked magnificent like something you'd see in a movie. She and the dog had developed a mutual respect and she found herself longing to pet him often playing fetch with him. When she did he turned into an overgrown puppy eagerly romping around her as he anticipated when she would toss a ball or stick. When they reached the house he would sometimes run ahead and block her from going up the stairs so that she would throw the object at least one more time.

The days and evenings were getting much cooler. Today Favor noticed the chill seemed to be more intense so decided to build a fire to warm the house before Steve came home. She then slipped out of her riding clothes into something more comfortable. Steve should be home soon so Favor decided to make an apple pie, the first one she'd ever made on her own. While it was in the oven baking she cleaned the kitchen and started dinner. Busy preparing the food she suddenly realized Steve should have been home by now. Feeling anxious she began to pace the floor going back and forth to the window numerous times to look out and listen for the quad. Darkness had come creeping in and he still had not come home. Her anxiety mounted and fear began to creep in. What if something had happened to him? He was all alone out there and she was feeling very much alone herself. Fear can play tricks on your mind and Favor was imagining all sorts of things that only fueled her fears more. Relief flooded her veins when she finally heard the quad nearing the house. Nervously she waited at the door while he put the quad away.

As soon as she saw him coming up the walk she rushed down the porch steps to meet him. "I was worried about you. It was getting late and I missed you," she blurted. She threw her arms around his waist as a stray tear escaped her eyes. Looking down at her tiny frame he saw the tear and wiped it away then leaned down to kiss her and take her into a soft embrace.

"Sorry I worried you. Went farther than I realized. Took me longer to get back. Didn't get anything today. Are you ok? How was your day?'

"It was good, better now that you're here."

"Something smells good. Apple pie? And something else. Are you cooking dinner?"

"Uh-huh! Hope you don't mind. I know you prefer we cook together."

Looking up into his adoring eyes as he wrapped his arms around her his heart melted. There had not been any physical contact between them since the first day they had gone riding. She found herself wanting to touch him. "Favor, fixing dinner was the nicest thing you've done for me and I'm starving, is it ready?" She nodded. "I'll wash up then help set the table."

"It's already done."

"Wow, ok then, I'll be right back." When Steve returned he was surprised to see the table with candles burning, setting a very romantic tone to the evening. They talked long past the dinner hour about their day. She found herself reaching out for him and touching his hand. She wanted more, but she would settle for the gentle feel of his hand in hers.

"You've never told me how you make your money and how you can afford all this."

"I inherited a good portion of it. My father was a very rich man and set up a Trust. When my parents were killed I inherited it all. The Trust was set up that everything stayed in the Trust until I was 21 years of age. During that time the interest kept multiplying. I invested most of it plus I have my own company."

"What kind of investments?"

"Honey, everything I have I came by legally, but I don't feel you need to trouble yourself worrying about money and my investments."

"I didn't mean anything by asking. I was just curious. I trust you, Steve. I wasn't thinking you did anything illegal, although kidnapping me was illegal."

"I know. But it had to be done. I couldn't take any chances that you would refuse to come with me so, yes, I took you but it was necessary." He fully expected Favor to become confrontational and was prepared for an argument to follow. But to his surprise she only got up and started clearing away the dishes. He got up to help, watching her intently, still expecting her to 'lower the boom' on him. Instead they continued on in pleasant conversation. Favor was drying her hands and then folded the towel neatly. He came up behind her and wrapped his arms around her. She leaned back into his arms, nestling close to him. Then she turned around and looked up at him. He leaned down and tenderly kissed her. "Favor, honey, I want to talk to you about something very important. Let's go into the living room."

He took her hand and led her into the living room. His expression was serious and almost sad. They sat down on the couch and he took both of her hands in his. "I'm going to be gone for a few days. The cold weather is coming and I need to pick up a few supplies and another load of hay for the animals. We'll have snow soon and won't be able to get out for supplies again till after the snow melts in the spring. We don't want to run out of anything. When the snow sets in we'll have lots of time together."

Favor listened quietly, got up and walked over to the fireplace. Tears were burning her eyes and fear was creeping in. "How long will you be gone?" The words stuck in her throat.

"About three days, maybe less, but no more than that. Favor, are you alright?"

"Sure." She began to cry. The tears fell silently as she kept her head turned away from Steve. He walked up behind her.

"Favor?" No response, so he reached out to turn her around but was met with resistance.

"Steve, please don't."

"You're crying," he said as he forced her to turn around and face him. "What is it?" She burst out in sobs and Steve held her close to his chest. His arms enveloped her and she melted into his arms as her body shook. She couldn't stop the tears from coming.

"I get so lonely. These days you're out hunting a lot and I hate being alone. I'm tired of being alone, and now you're going to be gone for several days." Frustrated and angry she drew away from him, turning so he couldn't see her face.

"Favor, please don't turn away from me."

"What if something happened to you and I was left here all alone. What would I do? I don't have any idea where I am in respect to the rest of the world. I wouldn't know how to get out and your wolf sure as hell wouldn't let me leave."

"I've taught you how to survive. I'd take you with me if it was at all possible."

"Why can't you?" She yelled

"You know why. I can't risk losing you. If someone recognized you I'd lose you for sure and I'd end up going to jail. I won't take the chance of that happening."

"I don't want to be without you. I lo…, I, oh never mind."

"No," he grabbed her. "Say it! You know you love me, so why won't you just say it?"

"Please, just leave me alone." Pulling away from him she rushed headlong up the stairs into her room slamming the door.

Steve sat alone staring into the fireplace not knowing what to feel. He hated leaving her alone. When he finally went upstairs he paused staring at Favor's door resisting the urge to knock. Instead he went to his own room. Favor heard the soft click of his door. Opening her door she entered the hall listening to muffled sounds as Steve moved around, resisting the urge to call to him or knock on his door. Instead she went back into her room closing the door quietly behind her. For hours she lay awake listening to the night sounds. An owl hooted outside and another gave its answer in the far off distant reaches of the night. Hours later with tears still flowing, she finally drifted off into a fitful sleep.

The sound of Steve's truck woke her abruptly the next morning. Running from her room to the balcony doors she threw them open just in time to see Steve pulling out towing a trailer. Shocked that he had left without saying a word she watched as his truck disappeared around the bend. Slowly the tears trickled down her face. He hadn't even said goodbye. How could he be that cruel? Maybe she deserved it after the way she treated him the night before. They had enjoyed such a nice dinner together and then it had been ruined.

Despondency overwhelmed her so much so that she didn't bother to shower or get dressed. She heard the sound of the horses and looking out towards the pasture she saw Steve had turned them out before leaving. Relieved that she didn't have to deal with them she curled up by the fire Steve had thankfully made before he left. The wretched feeling in her heart was so intense that she didn't want to eat. Who wants to eat alone? Instead she added more wood to the fire in the fireplace and then sat staring into the flames. The hours passed as she cried off and on throughout the day.

It was nearly sundown when the sound of the horses brought her back to reality. She realized she had to take care of them and also knew the dog needed to be fed as well. Reluctantly she got dressed and headed outside. A cold chill was in the air as the evening shadows began to creep across the meadow. Quickly she led the horses to the barn where she put them in their stalls and fed and watered them. "Oh, Snow, why can't I say the words he wants to hear so desperately? Why can't I tell him I love him? I'm so afraid of losing my own identity." She was an image of sheer beauty standing beside the big white horse with the white wolf dog close by.

Here in all this beauty was peace and tranquility. If there was a heaven on earth it had to be right here where there was harmony and serenity. And to think Steve had chosen her to share it with him. How could she not love him? Her heart ached for him and the desire to touch him, to feel his breath on her hair, to feel his tender kiss on her lips. She missed him more than she could ever have dreamed she would.

In the days that followed Favor spent most of her time with the horses. It kept her from feeling so alone. She talked to them incessantly. They responded by nudging her or nickering in low soft sounds. The wolf dog was always close by and seemed to take consolation in her voice. It seemed he missed Steve as well. While she was cleaning the stalls on the second day, she felt something nudge her hand. Startled she jumped back only to realize it was the wolf. "Cloud, what are you doing?" She had actually called him by name for the first time. He truly seemed excited and moved closer and nudged her hand again. Hesitantly she reached out and gently touched his head. He sat down beside her and leaned against her leg. She again touched him slowly afraid if she moved too fast it would startle him and he would retreat. A hearty laugh escaped from her lips and Cloud began to jump around excitedly. From that time on they became inseparable. As night grew near she closed the horses up in the barn and she and Cloud headed for the house. Opening the door she called him inside. The fire was almost out so she added more wood to it so it wouldn't burn out. She took to sleeping on the couch in the library with the fire going all night. Steve had left her a generous supply of firewood close by and more on the back porch so she didn't have to go out to the wood shed. Cloud lay on the floor beside the couch and occasionally pushed his nose under her hand as she rested it lightly on his head.

It was the morning of the third day and she woke with a flutter of excitement as she anticipated Steve's return. In an effort to make the time pass quickly she went for a ride. After saddling Snow she decided to pony Denali alongside so that he was not left alone. Today she'd check on the cattle and ride down by the creek for a while. Keeping herself occupied seemed to make the hours pass quicker. About three o'clock she headed back to the house. Steve might just come home earlier than she expected and she certainly didn't want to be gone when he arrived. With the thought that he might come home sooner she urged the horses to pick up the pace.

When she reached the barn she fought off the disappointment at not seeing him there waiting for her. By the time she reached the barn, unsaddled, bedded down the horses for the night and put away the tack it was already dusk. She started a fire in the fireplace and settled down in the living room feeling very tired. Night came and Steve still had not arrived. What could be keeping him? Didn't he say it would be no more than three days? Her mind drifted off to thoughts of Steve. Where would he be staying? Did he have some friends or acquaintances he stayed with or would he stay in a hotel. Would he be thinking of her? Would he go out dancing or to a movie? She thought about the morning he left. He had not even said goodbye to her. People have physical needs so was he with someone who would fulfill those needs? Was he in the arms of another woman somewhere in the solitary night? Her imaginings began to give into fear and loneliness and a great sense of longing and remorse. They had established a relationship that she had become accustomed to and having him near and hearing his voice was uplifting. How amazing he smelled and even now the scent of him lingered in the room. Closing her eyes she imagined him close by her and her desire to be in his arms overwhelmed her and she began to cry. The stillness of the night began to close in on her even though she had tried hard to stay busy so that she wouldn't feel so alone. The heat of the fire warmed her as her tired body gave in to the need to sleep.

The room was cold when she woke in the early morning hours as she listened intently for any sound that would mean Steve was home. Instead there was only silence, a cold, deafening silence. She needed to get a fire started again. Her body shook as she fumbled with the lighter trying to get it to light. The cold made her hands tremble and she wished she had not fallen asleep for so long. After several tries the embers began to crackle as the fire grew in size and warmth. Her body needed fuel as well so that she wouldn't feel so cold, but she had no appetite. When had she last eaten? Grabbing a blanket from the couch she huddled as close to the fireplace as she could in hopes that the trembling would stop. Cloud wined and drew close to her as they huddled up to the warmth of the fire. How had this happened? This enormous wolf-dog had somehow become a special companion to her. Where could Steve be? He should be home.

Favor and the dog stayed huddled close to each other on the bear skin rug right in front of the fire the rest of the long early morning, long after the light of day crept into the room. The only time she moved was to put more wood on the fire. Cloud began to wine and pace the room. He needed to be let out and she needed to let the horses out to graze. Reluctantly she left the warmth of the fire and headed outside. Once she had taken care of the horses she grabbed more firewood and headed back to the comfort of the fire. She hadn't combed her hair and she looked a fright. It was now the fourth day and no sign of Steve. Depression and fear clenched at her heart. Surely he would be home today. If only they had cell phones, at least they could call one another. "For God sake this is the 20st Century." Her depression now gave way to anger.

"Here I am living like I'm in the pioneer days, all alone and yet I live in the 20st Century. How ridiculous is this? I have no idea where I am or how to get out of here, so I sit here not doing a damn thing about it. What's wrong with me? I need to get up off my ass and try to find my way out of here. I just have to follow the damn tracks of the truck until they lead me to the road. I can climb over the gates and soon I'll be back to civilization. What the hell am I doing sitting here waiting for the man that kidnapped me? Have I lost my ever loving mind? I could have been out of here days ago. What an idiot I've been. Cloud trusts me now, so surely he won't try to stop me. Steve may never come back." She felt a twinge of remorse at her thoughts because only a few hours ago she was longing for and wanting him.

Favor ran upstairs and put on some clean clothes dressing in layers since it would probably warm up considerably as the sun rose higher into the sky. At least she would have warm clothes for later in the day in case it got late before she made her way out to a main road. Using the back pack Steve had carried on their first ride she packed some food. She thought about taking one of the horses, but remembered the locked gates. Then there was Cloud. Locking the dog in the house wasn't an option. If Steve never returned, he would need to be able to hunt for food. He was after-all half wolf, and his instincts would surely kick in for the most part.

With food, water, a blanket and warm clothes, she set off across the field in the direction she had seen Steve go when he was leaving. Cloud came bounding up to her wanting to play, but she kept on walking. "Go back home, Cloud. Take care of things there. I have to find Steve," she fibbed out loud to the dog. He cocked his head sideways as if trying to figure out what she was saying or what to do. "Be a good boy. Stay."

Immediately he sat on his haunches and watched her walk away. He began to wine so Favor stopped and said, "Go home, Cloud," as she signaled for him to go back home. He seemed confused but obediently headed back toward the house. Favor smiled to herself as she watched him go. "Looks like I won that battle. Steve will be pissed off when he realizes his 'well trained wolf-dog' is not all that well trained after-all. Never underestimate the power of a woman." With that she continued on her way.

After walking for at least forty-five minutes she suddenly became aware she had not been paying attention and had lost sight of the tire tracks she had been following. She stopped and looked around. Everything looked different when she looked back. Nothing was familiar. She couldn't be lost. She'd just back track and find them and then go on from there. So she turned around and headed back in the direction she had come. "That last gate they had come through couldn't have been that far away from the house," she thought. Of course he had used something to put her out so she had still been pretty groggy and her perception was definitely off, that and the fact that he had brought her at night. Everything looks different at night than it does in the daylight. Besides it had been so long ago. Fear was beginning to rear its head as she felt herself begin to panic. Her heart was beating fast and hard. She should have thought this out better, poor planning on her part, because now she had no idea where she was, how far she was from the safety of the house or which direction to go. Looking up at the sun high in the sky she decided to pick a direction and stick to it. Eventually it should lead her somewhere where she could find someone to help her.

Thinking the house was to the North, she decided to head toward the South. After a good hour she wished she had headed North back towards the house or maybe west. It seemed easier to keep your direction if you were looking towards the sun and letting the sun guide you. So she now turned and began walking in the direction of the west, following the sun. As the day wore on, confusion and fear began to take over. Why had she been so stubborn and stupid? Tired and thirsty, she stopped to rest, eat a sandwich and drink some water, realizing for the first time how hungry she was. Spreading out the blanket under a big tree she took out the food and ate slowly, all the while thinking how she wished she was safe at the house or better yet back home in her own house. Her eyes felt heavy so she curled up in a fetal position just to rest for a few minutes. Minutes later she fell asleep.

When she woke the late September sun was slipping behind a mountain and it was beginning to turn cold. Jumping up she began to panic. The light was fading and it would be dark soon. Lost and terrified of being alone in the dark she picked up her things. "Oh why did I change directions? Which way should I go? I don't have any idea how far I've gone or what direction to go now. If I go North, I will probably be too far west once I get to the right elevation. I should have stayed going south. At least it was taking me downhill and I do remember now that the truck was going uphill." She began running in a Southerly direction, hoping to cover as much ground as she could in as short a time as possible before darkness overtook her. Running blindly she picked up speed as she ran downhill. The shadows had deepened and it was getting hard to see as she ran in a panic, and then she tripped and felt herself falling. Thrusting her hands out in front of her to protect herself and trying to break her fall, she ended up tumbling over and over finally stopping as a bush caught on the backpack. Her breath came hard as she tried to right herself. Blood soaked the fabric of her jeans where now appeared a large tear. Nothing was broken. Aside from several cuts, abrasions and bruises, she seemed to be in one piece.

Realizing she couldn't go any further she decided to look for a tree for shelter and settle down for the night. The stinging from the cuts and abrasions made her feel almost nauseous. Her head was pounding. A coyote howled in the distance and she realized she was all alone in a vast wilderness area. She knew Steve's property was in the middle of forested land and there were bear, coyote and even mountain lions. She hadn't brought any matches to build a fire. "So this is how I'll die. Alone in the mountains and no one will ever find me, all because of my own stupidity. She wanted to scream at the top of her lungs, but she was afraid it would only attract some animal. There would be no sleep this night. Huddled tight against the shelter of a tree she looked up into the starry heaven and prayed that nothing would harm her and that she'd be allowed to live, asking also that God would forgive her for being ungrateful and arrogant. If she hadn't sent Cloud away he would have been able to lead her back or at least keep her safe and warm through the night.

Favor fought the sleep that tried to overtake her. The howling of the coyotes sent chills down her spine. She ached all over and the blanket gave little warmth. It certainly was not meant for a cold night on a mountain. Hunger too plagued her but she decided to save what little she had for the following morning. Exhaustion finally won and she fell asleep.

When the first rays of sunlight began to glow along the Eastern horizon Favor woke, stiff from the cold and the blanket was damp from the early morning frost. As she tried to get up her body revolted and she sank back down on the ground. The sound of birds waking broke through the stillness and she was grateful to hear their songs. If only she'd brought some matches or a lighter she could have built a fire for some warmth. She knew she would need to get herself moving as soon as possible to get her circulation going and warm her body. No matter how much her body ached she couldn't just sit there. Gathering up all the strength and will power she could, she got to her feet. A plan was needed, but where should she start? Steve had taught her a few things about wilderness survival, but he had only had time to teach her how to survive at the ranch so far. He certainly had not expected that she'd need the skills to survive in a harsher environment. Wishing she'd paid closer attention to the edible plants didn't help now. Surely she could find some food to eat and if she put her brain to work she could figure out the logical way to make her journey easier. The damp blanket needed to dry, but she didn't want to wait until the sun came up to lay it out. That would take too long. She needed to build a fire and remembered reading about rubbing two sticks together to create friction and thus heat and then fire. But what kind of wood and she needed a knife to cut the sticks and strip away the bark.

Oh what was the use? Again she started walking. Maybe it wouldn't be all that long to a road or trail or something. So once again she headed off in a Southerly direction, downhill. The soreness and stiffness in her body caused her to move at a much slower pace. Thinking more clearly she did her best to set a comfortable pace, knowing she needed to conserve energy and watch her steps carefully to avoid any more falls.

As she walked she began to plan on how she might build a shelter to keep her warmer just in case she was still on the mountain when nightfall came again. Thoughts of Steve invaded her mind. "How many days has it been since Steve left? Is this the fifth day? Yes, I think that's right. I left the morning of the fourth day and was here all night. Yes that's right. He's been gone five days now. Or did he return sometime on the fourth day and find me missing? Well I can't be worried about which day it is now. I just need to somehow survive and find my way out of these mountains. Boy, I must be losing it because here I am talking to myself out loud." Favor began to laugh a silly nervous laugh, but the laugh soon gave way to tears, anger and frustration.

She refused to give into the fear that was building and trying to control her, so she kept moving always in a downhill Southerly direction. The going was slow. Hunger was gnawing at her insides and she was feeling dehydrated. As the sun began to sink lower in the afternoon sky she decided to find someplace to bed down for the night and figure out a way to make a small shelter. She noticed a small cropping of rocks near a stand of small saplings. If she could somehow bend these together and secure them to form some sort of canopy and then find enough small branches with leaves, she could fashion a fairly decent shelter so that the blanket did not get wet again. Then maybe she would try her hand at a fire. If she could get two dry enough sticks she could try creating enough friction to get a spark and hopefully get a small fire started.

Favor set to work pulling the saplings and bending them down in an arch and then weaving them somewhat like a basket and securing them with some long flexible twigs. Some nearby shrubs made a perfect roof which she intertwined in between the bent saplings. It took more time and more brush then she had expected. Her hands were sore and bleeding from pulling the shrubbery and breaking it free by hand. But when she had finished she had a shelter that measured about four feet deep and about five feet wide. It was long enough that she could curl up comfortably to sleep. The tall grasses on the mountainside would make a soft mattress, so she began pulling up handfuls of the long meadow grass and laying it inside the shelter. She kept building it up until it had a nice cushiony feel.

Once done she filled the now empty backpack with grass to form a pillow of sorts. Then gathered some rocks for a fire pit. A nice size flat rock with one sharp edge she use like a shovel or hoe to dig the fire-pit down into the ground on the side facing the shelter. If it worked and if she could manage to get a fire going, it would deflect the heat into the shelter and she wouldn't lose too much warmth.

Gathering some wood, twigs and dry pine needles and a little moss to use as a fire starter she only needed to find two sticks that were strong enough, but not so dry that they would snap and break that she could rub together to create friction. After wandering around for more than forty minutes she finally found a stick she thought might work. Everything was ready. She had gathered enough wood to last through the night. Breaking the stick in two Favor began rubbing them together. For over an hour Favor rubbed and rubbed the sticks over the dry needles she had found. Her arms ached and blisters had now begun to form on her hands. About ready to give up she noticed a small puff of smoke and then a tiny little flame ignited the needles. Carefully she fed more fuel to it trying not to smother it. At long last a small fire began to take hold. She carefully added some slightly larger twigs and then more as the fire took hold. Before long a steady flame was burning. Tired and sore, her arms and hands ached. Blisters had formed and broken leaving her hands burning with pain. Tears of relief gave way to the pain but at least she had a fire. Gradually she added more wood to the fire. She pulled the wood she had gathered closer so she could reach it better during the night. Afraid she would run out she painfully gathered even more. The shelter began to warm.

The last rays of sun were slipping over the western horizon, but Favor had shelter and warmth to see her through the night. If only she had some food and some water she would be set. But there was nothing around that she could see. So she laid the blanket out onto the soft grass she had piled up and pulled half of it around herself. She was careful to keep the fire going but not too big. The shelter was now warm and toasty. The fire heated the small cropping of rocks holding the heat in. She smiled to herself and felt proud of what she had accomplished. The crackle of the fire made her think about sitting with Steve in front of the fireplace at the ranch. Oh to be nestled safely in his arms right now.

One by one the stars became visible as they twinkled brightly in the sky overhead. She marveled at their beauty and was awed at how many there were and how much brighter they seemed. Her eyes were growing heavy from much needed sleep. Afraid that the fire would go out if she fell asleep she added more wood, praying if she did drift off to sleep, that God would not let her sleep too long because the fire might go out completely. Knowing if that happened she might not be able to get it started again with her blistered hands.

Chapter 11

Balmy late August summer winds were blowing. It was another beautiful Saturday on the north coast. Adam, Cindy and Houston were sitting in the grass with several of their neighbors and friends. It was the first time all of them had been together at the same location since Favor disappeared. Their thoughts had wandered back to that day. Statistics show the longer an individual is missing, the less chance they will ever be found alive if at all. With each passing day the hope they once had of finding Favor, now had dwindled. Life must go on no matter how much it hurts to lose someone you love and care for. It is the unending cycle of life. But Adam's heart whispered that as long as you believe, your thoughts and hopes can reach beyond the unknown, beyond the uncertain and reach the soul of the one who waits and hopes you will not stop searching. In turn they will know and not give up hope. They will hold tight to the unseen forces of nature and reach out with strength of mind and in time their thoughts will reach one another giving them the faith and willpower to hold on no matter what each day brings.

"It's been over three months, Adam," Cindy was saying. "The police haven't found even one clue as to where he took her. For all we know he could have taken her out of the country. The phone call was a dead end. It came from a disposable cell phone so no way to trace it."

"The thing that gets me is there haven't been any calls, ransom notes. Kidnappers always want something. They want to be noticed so they always do something to taunt the police especially a serial killer." Houston knew Adam needed to face the facts but he could see Adam still refused to accept the probable outcome. None of them wanted to think the worst, but the harsh reality was she was in all likelihood dead. What they needed was to have closure.

Cindy went into the house and came back with a tray of snacks. Sue, Paul's wife jumped up to give her a hand. The conversation drifted on. Sue was saying, "You know, you and Adam are doing a terrific job of taking care of Favor's house and things. You two just might get a thing going." She lifted her eyebrows and winked. Cindy looked at her with surprise.

"You're kidding, right? Adam has a thing for Favor. Didn't you know that? And she's my best friend. When she comes home she'll need Adam and the rest of us to help her adjust after whatever is happening to her now. I'm just glad she has real friends who will help her adjust." Cindy made it a point to emphasize the word 'real'.

"Cindy, all of you need to face the facts, Favor is gone. Do you have any idea how many kidnapped victims are never found, ever. The numbers are staggering and the statistics for her being found are one in a million. Those are not very good odds. If I were you I'd make my move while the irons hot. Adam is one hell of a catch. I know if I were available I'd be tipping my hand." Cindy noted the sarcasm in Sue's voice. "Come on let's not just stand here holding this tray. We've got some snack loving men waiting. Besides we wouldn't want them to think we were gossiping about them." Cindy glared after Sue as she took the tray from her hands and walked towards the rest of the group.

"Say that looks good," Houston was saying, "I need a cold beer. I'm going to get one, anyone else want a beer? We've got plenty." Several replied. Adam jumped up and said he'd get them. He saw the look on Cindy's face and quietly asked, "Are you ok? You look really pissed off." She turned and headed towards the house saying she would help him with the beers.

"Hold on. I'll go with you. I've got to use the john." Houston followed. Cindy stopped and shrugged her shoulders as if to say, "Oh well." Houston caught up to them and put his arm around Cindy's shoulder, "Coming little lady?" She shook her head no. Adam gave Houston a puzzled look as he raised his eyebrow and shook his head. The two guys headed into the house together. There was quite a contrast between the two friends. Houston had a husky build, broad shoulders and spoke with a southern drawl. A little rough around the edges but with a heart of gold, Houston was always good for a practical joke and a good laugh any time, always the life of the party and full of mischief. Adam on the other hand was thin and lanky. He was the quiet sort and liked to people watch. He loved to have friends over and enjoyed Houston's way of always being entertaining.

"Say ol' boy, you and Cindy could sort of make a thing of this. She's real cute and considering all the time you two have been spending together it might develop into something."

"Ah, Houston, you never quit. Cindy is like a 'pal' to me. Sure she's a sweet gal, but there's no chemistry there. My heart belongs to Favor. I thought you were interested in Cindy."

"Well, I am, but I wasn't going to stand in the way of my best friend."

"Damn it, for a guy who's so good in a crowd of people, you sure are dense when it comes to things of the heart. I thought you had already figured out Cindy is interested in you, not me. She and I are more like the brother sister type."

"I just wanted to be sure, buddy, never wanted to be one to step on anyone's toes. Favor is the kind of girl that suits you. Most guys just feel privileged to have her as their friend. Now Cindy is the kind of girl I can see myself with. She's not as complicated as Favor."

"Well, if you don't start making some moves on her and start paying more attention to Cindy, she's going to think you're not interested and give up on you. Now let's get back out there and I want to see a few sparks between you two. Just because Favor is gone doesn't mean you can't be close to Cindy. It's what Favor would want. That last night she was here, she even mentioned it. She was watching you two, but me, I only had eyes for her. Guess women are more observant than us guys anyway. So go find a way to ask her out. There's nothing to stop you. The worst thing that could happen is she says no. I know I would." Adam just had to throw in a little dig to fire Houston up.

"You're on 'ol man."

"Hey, quit calling me old man. I'm only two months older than you." They both laughed as they headed back outside with the drinks where they rejoined their other friends and neighbors. Cindy handed each of them a sandwich. Houston smiled at her, "Thanks, Cindy, you're a jewel. You're going to make somebody a good wife someday. I hope I find someone as good as you when I'm ready to settle down."

She looked at him with a surprised and questioning look. "Thanks, I think. Nobody's ever said anything to me quite like that before." Awkward! Adam put his hand up to his forehead and shook his head. "Smooth move, Houston," he thought.

Houston was talking again. "Well I don't know why? It's true. You must have a lot of guys after you. Say, would you like to go to a movie with me some time. Maybe we could even go tonight. How about it? What do you say?"

Adam was thinking, "A little awkward, but better. But a movie you oaf. Take her to dinner. Oh well at least he asked her. Now don't blow it. Give the girl time to answer."

"Sounds nice. I'd enjoy that. Haven't been to a good movie in months."

"It's settled then. We can check to see what's playing a little later and decide."

Adam chuckled. Houston needed a few pointers before the evening was over.

The conversation drifted from one subject to another. The guys decided to play some catch while the girls watched. Cindy was thinking that if Favor were here she'd be right in the middle of the guys catching and throwing that ball and being 'one of the guys'. They'd been playing a while when Houston suddenly yelled, "I've got it!"

"No you don't," Paul chided, "I do."

"No not the ball, dummy, a possible clue."

"A possible clue to what, you're talking like an idiot?"

"Wait, I'm serious. You remember the day Favor disappeared. She was playing ball with us and Paul threw a pass. She tried to get it and ended up in Adam's arms, right?"

"So what does that have to do with anything?" Dave chided.

"Paul said to move because a truck was coming down the road."

"I for one still don't see what that has to do with anything." Paul said shaking his head.

"That could be the missing link, don't you see?"

"Damn it, Houston, you've gone off your rocker." Adam said with irritation.

"Now wait a minute, hear me out. Favor made a remark about how good-looking the driver was but we were so busy watching you two in your little comedy routine that we didn't really take any notice of the truck or the driver. But maybe it was the guy who took Favor. If we could figure out the make and year of the truck we might have something to go on. When Cindy and I were out on the deck we saw that same truck parked down the street. I think it was dark green or maybe it was black, and I think it was a Dodge Ram. It looked fairly new, maybe not brand new, but not too many years old. We both wondered about it at the time."

"So what!" Adam retorted. "The guy could have been visiting a neighbor or maybe he was just sitting there, smoking a cigarette or joint, or having a beer."

"Look I know it's a long shot, but we don't have anything else to go on and neither do the police. This guy had to be watching her place, to know just the right time to nab her. If we have the police start running every dark green Dodge Ram 4x4 that has been sold in the last few years, maybe we can narrow it down. We can ask around the neighborhood to see if anyone has a friend that drives a truck with that description. If one of the neighbors knows someone with a truck matching that description we can ask if the owner was at their house that night."

Sue leaned in to whisper to Cindy, "Why is Adam getting so defensive and confrontational? He seems really upset with Houston."

"Because that same night he told Favor how he felt about her and then he let her walk back to her place alone. She insisted he didn't need to walk her home."

"That's crazy. The guy who took her would have gotten her another day if he couldn't get her that night. If he was stalking her he was probably planning the kidnapping for a long time. And I didn't know they had a thing going."

"You're the one person who wasn't here that night, so I guess there are a lot of things you don't know." Cindy moved away from Sue as she continued to listen in on the rest of the conversation between Adam and Houston. Adam was saying he was almost afraid to hope, and it bothered him to think about what they might find. But either way he needed to know what happened to her. Maybe it was a long shot, but it couldn't hurt to have the police check out the possibility of finding the truck they had seen.

The next day Adam went to the police station to talk about the truck and the guy that had driven passed them, then later seeing the truck parked down the street. He might have been checking up on Favor and might be the guy they were looking for. At first they were not very cooperative. But Adam finally convinced them that it was the only thing that night that was out of the ordinary and what if this guy was the one who took Favor. They had nothing else to go on so why not give it a try. So the police began their search to include Humboldt, Del Norte and Mendocino counties. An extensive search was not turning up any leads so they decided to widen the search over a wider area to include Trinity, Tehama and Shasta Counties.

After checking the DMV records they found three trucks that they decided to follow up on. The first truck had been in a body shop getting repaired after an accident had damaged the front end. The second truck was owned by an elderly man who used it to tow his motor home. He and his wife were traveling at the time of the kidnapping.

But the third truck had not yet been located. It belonged to a man who owned a ranch outside of Red Bluff, about a hundred and forty two miles from where Favor lived in Fortuna. The police had gone to the ranch only to find the ranch foreman and caretaker and a few ranch hands there. The foreman said the owner had several other properties elsewhere, and was not at the ranch all that often. He had been caretaking the ranch for thirty plus years. The ranch had been handed down to the current owner by his parents, which was previously owned by his grandparents. His where-about was unknown at that time. He never knew when he would show up. "He owns his own company in the city and comes by the ranch whenever he is in the area, but he travels a lot on company business. I knew him when he was growing up here with his parents. At the age of sixteen his parents died and his aunt raised him after that."

"In accordance to their trust I was retained as the foreman to oversee all the ranch operations until the boy reached maturity. When he did he decided to keep me on permanently. He said he'd never sell the ranch because it had special meaning to his parents. For a while he'd come home every holiday and special occasion to remember them. At one point he had a falling out with his aunt, dismissed her and forbid her to ever come on the property again." The foreman said he had never been to nor did he know where any of his other properties were located. When asked if the owner had been around at the time of the kidnapping the foreman stated that he had not been around for several months and to his knowledge he had not been around during the date mentioned.

A search of local records did not reveal any other properties in the name of the owner. The police could only guess that the other properties were held in the name of another entity, such as a corporation or a partnership or even in the name of a trust. Adam felt the need to search all public records, not just the local ones. The police saw no need. The guy had no police record, not even a traffic violation. Adam felt the police did not believe this guy could be the one who took Favor and were just humoring him.

To find any other properties owned by him or previously owned by his family would mean a long title search. By searching both the parents and grandparents names they could trace the locations of any other properties that may have transferred ownership to Steven Mitchell. There was the possibility that Steven Mitchell may have other properties that he purchased on his own and not inherited. Adam pressed the police for the owner's name, but they refused.

One late fall day Adam and Houston along with a few other hunting buddies, were on their way back from a weekend hunting trip. The guys decided to stop by the little Burger Bar in Mad River, California along Highway 36. It was a favorite spot of the locals and a favorite stopping off spot for hunters or fisherman and skiers who frequented Ruth Lake. They were getting ready to leave when Adam saw a green truck go by pulling a flatbed trailer, "Houston, did you see that green truck? It looked just like that one that came down the street that day. We've got to follow it."

"Come on, Adam, how many time have we chased after green trucks just to find it a dead end? Someday you're going to get sued, beat up or shot. When are you going to give it up, man, she's gone. You two will never be together again."

"Damn it, Houston, just this one last time. I just need the license plate. I've got a feeling about this one." Houston heard the desperation in his voice.

"It's your truck, follow him if you want, but I'm not going." Adam jumped in his truck and rushed off in pursuit of the green truck. Only a couple of miles ahead he saw the truck. Grabbing a pen and scrap of paper off the dash Adam prepared to write down the plate number as he drove as close to the truck as he dared to. The trailer made it hard to see the plates but he finally got it along with the trailer license. Once he had gotten the plate number he decided to try to pull up beside him to get him to pull over. His mind was racing as he tried to think of some excuse why he wanted the guy to stop. Maybe he could say his tire looked low, that way he could get a good look at him.

Just then Adam slammed on the breaks. The driver of the green truck had stopped in the middle of the lane and was getting out of the vehicle.

"What the hell are you doing you idiot? What's with the tail-gating?"

"Sorry man," Adam stammered apologetically. "I thought you were somebody else and wanted to catch up to him." Adam lied between his teeth.

"You need to be more careful. With all the pot growers up here, you could get yourself blown away just by approaching someone in that manner."

"You're right, man. It was dumb. Say, why don't you let me buy you a beer to make up for it, names Adam Jennings." Adam held out his hand to shake. The driver glared at him ignoring the out stretched hand nor did he offer his name. Adam thought about how lame his proposal must have sounded. "I've never seen you around here before. You live here close?"

Ignoring Adam's last question he said, "No thanks on the beer, I need to get going. No harm done, but you'd better be more careful." With that Steve Mitchell climbed back into his truck and drove away an uneasy feeling in his gut. Maybe he should have taken him up on the beer. It would have given him the chance to find out about this guy and maybe what or how much he knows. He'd have to be more careful and alert.

Houston glared at Adam when he got back to the Burger Bar. "I got a good look at him and I got a picture with my cell phone before I got out of the truck."

"What do you mean you got out of the truck?"

"Well, he stopped and got out of his truck so I stopped and talked to him."

"Damn it, Adam you're going to get yourself shot if you keep doing that sort of thing. Get in. We're going home and I'm driving. This is the last time I'll be even a small part of something like this again. Man, you're obsessed. You need to chill. Leave it up to the cops."

Adam and Houston drove the remainder of the way home in silence. They went over to Cindy's when they got back. She had already planned to cook them dinner. Nothing was said about the truck or the incident that had taken place. Adam was glad Houston had kept it quiet. The evening was spent in small talk about the hunting trip. Adam was unusually quiet, claiming he was tired and full from the great meal Cindy had prepared. He used it as an excuse to leave early and let Cindy and Houston have some quiet time alone.

Houston waited until Adam was gone to fill Cindy in on the incident that had occurred.

"Houston, I'm worried about him."

"You're worried! Hell, we've been friends all of our lives, but this isn't doing our friendship any good. I've been thinking of moving out."

"Don't do that. Give him more time. I'm sure he'll come to terms with it and move on. It's just taking him a little more time than the rest of us because he feels guilty."

"Maybe you're right, but if things don't get better soon, I'm moving in with you. I'll still be close enough to keep an eye on him that way but I'll have you to keep me happy."

"Oh really so you've been thinking about us living together huh?"

"Well, yeah, it has crossed my mind a few times. What would you think of that?"

"Given the right terms and conditions, you might be able to talk me into it," she teased.

"Terms and conditions. What kind of terms and conditions, little woman?"

"If in the future we entertain the idea of you moving in, then I'll let you know what they are. But, I assure you, you'll like them all."

"You know you've turned into quite the little flirt and tease, Miss Cindy. Don't get me wrong, I'm not complaining, but keep it up and I won't leave. I think I like what I'm hearing."

They laughed and hugged each other. Houston helped Cindy clear up the food and dinner dishes after which they settled down on the couch to watch a little TV before Houston headed back to Adam's house. He could really get used to the comforts of home with Cindy by his side.

Unbeknown to Adam the police conducted a wider search through records with no leads. The police were about to get what they viewed as an unexpected break in the case. The one missing green truck was spotted at a feed store in the town of Red Bluff by a passing police cruiser. The officer called for backup and proceeded into the feed store. He approached the store owner and asked if he knew who owned the truck and trailer parked outside. "Sure I do, he's a long time customer as were his parents and grandparents before him." The owner heard them asking and approached the officer. "The truck belongs to me. Why do you ask?" Not wanting to cause a scene in the store he asked the truck owner to step outside so they could talk. Immediately he was handcuffed and told not to move. "What's this all about? I haven't done anything." The store owner rushed out, demanding the officer release the man.

"Out of the way, old man. He's a person of interest in a kidnapping I'm taking him in."

"Kidnapping?" both the truck owner and the store owner yelled at the same time.

"I don't know anything about any kidnapping? Joe, take care of my things and call my foreman. Have him call my attorney right away. He has the number."

A second police car arrived as the officer was pushing him into his squad car. The young man was taken down to the police station for questioning. He was placed in an interrogation room where he sat for nearly an hour waiting. When an officer finally came in he began with an onslaught of questions. Where has he been for the past few months? What has he been doing? The questions went on and on with the young man returning each question with a question of his own rather than answering the officers questions. "Look, I haven't done anything wrong. You're wasting your time. You can't hold me or continue to question me without my attorney present. Now I want to call my attorney and make sure he got my message and is on his way here. I'm not going to answer your questions without him present."

"If you haven't done anything, then why would you want an attorney present?"

"It's my right to have one present. You searched me and then brought me here. I'd call that illegal search and seizure."

"We have probable cause."

"Based on what?"

"We just want to ask you some questions."

"Are you charging me with something?"

"No. Like I said we just want you to answer some questions."

"If you want me to answer, I want my attorney present so you can't say I said something I didn't say. I know how some of you cops operate. You act like the tuff guy, so you can prove yourself. A little respect can go a long way. Either you let me call my attorney or I'll have your badge before this is over."

It was six hours later when his attorney arrived. He had to fly into the local airport from the city and all the while the young man, known as Steve Mitchell, was held in a holding cell with no explanation. He spent an hour in the interrogation room, an hour or so with them trying to get him to answer their questions and the next four hours waiting for his attorney to arrive. His mind was in a whirl. How could they have figured it out? What probable cause were they talking about? He'd been so careful. He covered every base possible so no one could track him or tie him to Favor's disappearance. Not even his attorney and most trusted friend knew about the mountain home. He'd made sure when he hired him that he kept that property out of his list of assets. His life and his life with Favor depended on how he played his cards.

He'd planned on getting most or all of his supplies the first day so he could head back early on the second day. He'd just arrived and was just starting to pick up the supplies he needed. This ordeal was going to keep him at least another day.

He couldn't risk going straight back to the mountains with the supplies once he was released. They'd be sure to follow him. It was time for a backup plan. Had he taught Favor enough over the past couple of months that she would be able to make it alone if he couldn't make it back to her in a reasonable length of time? Fear and uncertainty made him question his decision. But he also knew that fear could cause one to make stupid mistakes. He had to push that fear aside and focus on what had to be done to get back to her. Cloud was there to protect her and Steve was sure he would do just that. His one big mistake was letting his company business get in the way so that he had not gotten quite enough winter supplies in.

If that had not happened, he would not have had to leave her and come to town for the last of the supplies. He should have waited just a little longer, but seeing her with that other guy had just been too much for him. He had lost his patience and moved too quickly. Would he now pay the price and lose her forever? Would she survive on her own in the mountains?

That was it. He'd leave the truck and trailer at the ranch in town with old Bill then fly back to the city with his attorney and lay low for a few days. Then he'd figure out a round-about way to get back to the ranch by way of another state. He'd pay cash for another truck and trailer and come back by way of a completely different direction. He could buy supplies somewhere else. They won't be able to track him and they'd be out of their jurisdiction unless they wanted to make a federal case of it. He was glad he'd had covers over the seats when he took her. He'd since taken the covers off the seats and wiped every possible surface clean so no fingerprints remained. She'd only been in the truck the one time.

His attorney listened as the police detective explained the circumstances and why they had picked his client up. He had instructed Steve not to say a word until they knew what this was all about and they could then discuss the facts.

"So you picked up my client because someone said they thought, a vehicle they saw on the night this young lady was kidnapped, was a dark green Ram 4x4, of which you do not know the year, nor do you have a license plate. Your witness admittedly said he thought it was a Dodge, but it could easily have been a Ford, Chevy or GMC. I'd say you're grasping at straws and now you're looking for a scape goat. That's not going to bring your girl back. My client is an upstanding citizen and business owner and this is harassment. If you are going to charge him, charge him now or release him."

Another officer stepped into the room and asked the other officer to step outside into the hall. Steve and his attorney could hear muffled sounds coming from outside the door. The other officer was saying, "We've checked out the truck. At this time there is no evidence of her being in the truck. There is no sign of any blood, hair or other evidence. We can't hold him."

"Yeah, I know you're right. I hate to admit it, but the guy's attorney is right, too. We don't have anything to hold him on and we don't need to get slapped with a law suit. Let's go talk to the chief."

The chief said he wanted to talk to the suspect before they let him go so he could get a feel for the guy and see if he could get something out of him. Entering the room the chief introduced himself, "Gentleman, my name is Chief O'Reilly. My friends call me Irish."

This time Steve began by saying, "Under other circumstances I'd say I was pleased to meet you, and I know your men are doing their job, but I don't know anything about a kidnapping. I'm not in the area much of the time so I don't hear much of the local news."

The captain slid a photo of Favor across the table. "Have you ever seen this girl?" Steve and his attorney looked at the photo.

Steve looked the chief directly in the eye saying, "No, is she from around here?"

The chief eyed Steve with a scrutinizing look, "Actually she lives over a hundred miles from here, but we've widened our search to six counties. So tell me about your business?"

Steve briefly filled him in on his business and that he traveled a great deal so was rarely able to visit the ranch. "Are you sure you've never seen or met her? Due to her profession she worked out of the city as well. Maybe your paths crossed a time or two. You both travel a lot and you both work in the city, maybe you were on the same flight and you took a liking to her. Maybe she didn't return the interest so you decided to have your way with her."

"Look you ass-hole," he rose to face the chief straight on. His attorney grabbed his arm and told him to calm down.

His attorney spoke, "You'll have to excuse my client, keeping him here is keeping him from his business. He's a very punctual individual, and furthermore he does not fly commercial, he has a small fleet of his own private planes. In fact that is how I got here, in one of his planes. If I'd waited for a commercial flight, I might not have been here for another day. The city is a big place. So if the young lady flew commercial, the chances of them meeting is slim to none."

"We're going to release you in the custody of your attorney for now, but I have to ask you not to leave town for a couple of days. We have to wait for the DNA tests on your vehicle to come back."

"Damn it!" he said turning to his attorney. "Isn't there anything you can do? A DNA test could take weeks. I've got work to do. I take a few days to relax and come up to the ranch and this is what I get, some hill billy country cop accusing me of kidnapping a girl who lives a hundred plus miles from here. Why aren't they looking for her in her own home town? My family lived here for three generations with not so much as a traffic ticket."

Before his attorney could speak the chief spoke up. "I'll tell them to rush the results, but if we think you're going to leave, we'll have to lock you up."

"Fine, you can find me at my ranch, which I'm sure you will be watching like a hawk."

Together Steve and his attorney left the police station. "His attorney grabbed his arm and stopped him when they got to the car his attorney had rented. "Are you sure you've never seen that girl before?"

"Jack, don't you start on me now."

Steve was quiet as they drove to the ranch. He had to stay calm and focused. Over and over in his mind he kept replaying the time she was in the vehicle and if she had touched anything that he had not wiped down. A great dread hung over him. Was this how it was going to end? He had to figure out how to get back to her the fastest way possible. How would she be? He thought about her alone in the house, scared and angry with him for leaving her alone. Then the thought occurred to him that she could easily lock the dog up and run away, but he quickly dismissed that thought. No, he knew their bond together had grown and he was convinced she was in love with him though she wouldn't admit it. Why else would she have been so upset with him when he said he'd be gone a few days? But then again, he had left without saying good-bye. It was falling apart and he felt helpless and knew he was losing control of the situation. Jack had decided to stay at the ranch with Steve while they waited for the DNA results. He watched Steve brooding and wondered. He had been the family attorney for many years and was concerned that he had never seen this side of Steve before.

While at the ranch he made numerous phone calls to his business. Jack heard him talking to his Vice President and Advisors, instructing them on what to do on several business matters. "I know I've been away longer than I planned, but I'll be there as soon as I can to sign the paperwork. I'll most likely head back to Europe as soon as we conclude our business." He'd said that out loud to make his attorney think that was where he'd been the past couple of months.

On the morning of the fifth day while having coffee on the terrace, Steve, Jack and Billie watched as a police car drove down the lane approaching the house. Steve began to sweat and his pulse began to race. This was it. They'd arrest him and lock him up and start the interrogation into where he had taken her. There was no way he would tell them anything and take the chance of them finding his secret place. All he could do was hope she could survive on her own. In his mind he kept remembering the disappointment in Favor's eye when they last spoke. Would this be his last memory of her? He had to stay calm and in control. The car stopped in front of the house. The chief and the officer who had arrested him in the first place got out of the vehicle. His attorney stepped forward ready to take control of the situation no matter what happened next.

"Good morning, Gentleman. I called in a favor and got a rush on the DNA tests. They just came back and we found no DNA evidence that our missing girl was ever in your vehicle. Yours was the only prints or DNA we found." Steve fought to control his body and expression.

"Well that's because I'm the only person who's ever in the truck."

"At any rate, you're free to go. I just want to say I'm very sorry for the inconvenience to you and your company. You can pick up your truck at the police impound yard." The captain didn't mention the fact that they had also done a thorough search on his company and family background. Why upset the guy anymore with details he didn't need to know. "I hope there are no hard feelings." He put his hand out to shake, but Steve ignored it.

Before the officers turned to go he said, looking at Billy, "I'll have you or one of the ranch hands go pick up my truck. I've lost enough time and I need to get back to work. I know you were just doing your job, but it sucks to be arrested like that and be made to feel like a common criminal."

"Again, my apology." When the captain and officer got in the squad car and drove away, Steve sat down and put his head in his hands. Jack looked at him with a question in his eyes. "Are you ok, Steve?" Jack was watching Steve intently. "Are you sure there is not something you want to tell me? You look really nervous."

"Of course I'm nervous. How would you feel? It made me feel like trash. I could see my whole life ruined by all this. People hear things and before you know it no one looks at you the same. I just want to get out of here."

Within the hour Steve and Jack were headed to the airport. They had already alerted the pilot they were on their way and Steve had called his office with instructions for the secretary to have checks ready to pay the attorney for his fee.

Steve was quiet on the flight back. He needed to figure out his plan to get back to Favor as quickly as possible. Worse yet, he couldn't shake the uneasy feeling that all was not well with her. But keeping his composure so Jack would not be suspicious was of the utmost importance. So he hatched a plan and then made up a story telling Jack he would be out of the country for a time. He would be flying to Italy for an extended period regarding a business deal. If there were any legal issues while he was gone, his advisors would contact him. He was often gone for long periods at a time so this was not anything his attorney was not used to. Besides he had a lot of other clients besides Steve and his company and he was familiar with how Steve ran his business. No wonder the guy was single. He didn't have time to meet or date anyone. He was always on the go.

Little did he know that Steve was more interested in the simple life his parents had led at their ranch and though he had money to burn and had a hugely successful business, his heart was in the simple remote life in the mountains. It meant more to him than anything else. He was like a possessed man craving the solitude and the woman he loved.

Chapter 12

When Favor woke the next morning the fire was almost out. The smallest ray of sun was beginning to brighten the Eastern horizon. Quickly adding some twigs to the fire she blew gently on the embers praying they would take hold and the fire would start up again. The flames caught. With great care she carefully added a few small pieces of wood at a time to the fire. The early morning air was cold and there was frost on the ground just outside the shelter. But the shelter had kept the frost off the blanket and the fire had kept her warm and dry. The grass bed had given her a soft place to lie down and a chance for some much needed rest. She had slept comfortably, but now it was necessary to bring more wood close to the shelter. It was still early and not quite light enough to start her journey.

Picking up a piece of wood she dropped it. Her hands were blistered and sore and her arms ached so much that she couldn't hold onto the larger piece of wood. But she knew more wood would be needed to keep the fire going. The top pieces were damp, so she laid them aside to dry. With pain staking effort she managed to bring the wood to the shelter. Once she had enough fire wood and the fire itself was burning steady she decided to lie down and rest until the sun was fully up and the earth had begun to warm. The lack of food and water was beginning to take its toll on her body and mind. She had eaten very little in the seven days since Steve had left. Weak and tired, all that really mattered to her was to stay warm and dry and she wanted to sleep and wake up to find all of this was just an incredibly bad dream. Her mind felt muddled. Nothing seemed clear and she felt dizzy.

As the day began to dawn and the sun began its morning ascent into the sky Favor felt too weak to go on. She kept looking at the frost finally realizing it was a source of water. If she could keep her mind active and if she could figure out a way to melt the frost into the water bottle she might be able to get enough water to drink and quench her ravenous thirst. Forcing herself to get back up she gathered leaves and wood and stones covered in frost and held them over the water bottle near the fire and let the precious moisture melt and drip into the container.

It was a tedious task, but finally she had nearly a half bottle of melted frost to drink. She sipped it carefully and slowly, letting the cool liquid sit in her dry mouth a moment before swallowing. Realizing it could be as much as another day before she would have any more water, she continued gathering frost and melting it into the bottle. She worked diligently before the frost was melted away by the sun. When the container was full she rewarded herself with a bigger drink and then went back to melting more frost into the container till it was full again. This she would set aside for later. For now she needed to lie down. Adding a few more pieces of wood to the fire she felt secure that it would continue to burn long enough for her to rest awhile longer.

It had been seven days since Steve had left Favor alone. As he approached the house with his load of supplies, he had a feeling of apprehension. Cloud saw him coming and began to growl at the new truck and trailer coming down toward the house. This was not a truck he recognized so he stood on the porch teeth bared and an ominous growl coming from deep within his chest. When Steve jumped out of the truck and called to Cloud the wolf-dog seemed overjoyed to see him. "Hey boy, how are you. Where's our girl? Shall we go see her?" He felt disappointed that she hadn't greeted him at the door, but what could he expect. She had to be furious with him for being gone so long. Entering the house he called her name. The house was eerily quiet and cold as he began moving from room to room calling for her. Cloud wined as he followed Steve through the house. Noticing Cloud's uneasiness Steve spoke to the dog, "Where is she, boy? Show me where she is." Cloud rushed to the door looking back to see if Steve was following, then headed in the direction Favor had gone. Steve looked down to see a half-eaten dead rabbit on the porch. That only meant one thing. Cloud had been hunting to feed himself.

Rushing to the barn he gathered halters and tack, and then caught both horses where they were grazing nearby. Cloud kept wining and running back and forth. Once they were both saddled he gathered a few provisions and a rifle and then told Cloud, "Go boy, find Favor. Go!"

Together they headed over the countryside as Cloud led the way, stopping to sniff the ground now and then before heading off again. Leading Steve and the horses south for a ways he then turned west. With Snow in tow they moved along in as fast a pace as possible. Steve was puzzled when Cloud turned south again. "Are you sure, boy?" Cloud started wining and again turned to go south. It was getting late and Steve was afraid it would get dark and they would not find her. They had been moving on down the mountain for some time. Cloud was up ahead when Steve heard him begin to howl. As Steve caught up to where Cloud was he saw the make shift shelter Favor had made. "Good boy, Cloud." Looking around he called out for her. She was nowhere to be found. Nightfall was fast approaching and Steve's apprehension began to intensify. They had to find her before dark.

"Cloud, find her." After sniffing around the shelter and the surrounding area he finally picked up her scent once again heading downhill to the south. Sometime later in the dim light he saw ahead a figure weaving back and forth unsteadily, stumbling along. It was Favor. Steve jumped off the horse and rushed to her just in time to catch her as she tumbled to the ground. Her eyes had a faraway look and she didn't seem to realize he was there. She collapsed and he cradled her in his arms. "Cloud, you did it. You found her. Good boy." Lifting her into his arms he carried her to Denali and lifted her into the saddle. She was too weak to hold on by herself, so he swung onto the horse behind her and led them back up to where the little shelter was.

By the time they reached the shelter, darkness had overtaken them. Steve knew it was too dangerous to travel in the dark so he decided to bed down for the night at the shelter. Favor hadn't spoken a word and her eyes continued to look intently off into some distant place that he couldn't go. He sat Favor down on a nearby stump and hurried to tie the horses under a nearby tree. Watching Favor warily Steve hurried to get a fire going. Once going it gave him some light to see by. He pulled water, a one meal trail mix, jerky and some bread sticks from his saddle bag. Cradling Favor's head he held the water bottle to her lips so she could drink. Feeling the cool refreshment of the water on her lips she grabbed at the bottle trying to gulp it down. "No, Favor, just a little at a time. Go slowly or your stomach will cramp. It's ok, there's plenty more." Her eyes turned wild as she grabbed for the water jug. But he kept talking and gradually her look softened and a tear trickled down her cheek. He knew she at long last recognized him but she still didn't speak though her eyes showed relief.

Steve continued speaking softly, "I'm sorry about everything. I thought I'd lost you." Kissing her tenderly he cradled her in his arms. "We'll stay here tonight. It's not safe to try to go back in the dark. You did a really good job building this shelter." He reached out to take her hand in his but she pulled her hand back and that's when he saw the blisters. "How did this happen?" Regret and sorrow at what she had suffered because of him tore at his heart.

She hung her head not able to look into his eyes. "Favor, what happened to you?"

Much to his relief she finally spoke. Her voice was weak and she barely spoke above a whisper. With broken words she related what had happened. "...rub...sticks...long...time ...made ...fire ...hurt." The knowledge that she had actually started a fire by rubbing two sticks together was astounding. He himself didn't really believe it could be done and here she had accomplished an extremely difficult task.

"I've got some first aid stuff in one of the saddle bags." He rose and got the first aid kit. In it was a container of Bag Balm, an ointment good for horses and human. Gently he cleaned her hand with a sanitary wipe and then smoothed a thin layer of the ointment over her hands. When he had done this he put pads of clean white gauze over her palms and then wrapped each of her hands with vet wrap.

She didn't speak, but continued to watch him intently as he wrapped her hands. Once again he lifted the water bottle to her lips so she could drink, careful to drink slowly this time. When she was done Steve pulled out a bedroll from behind one of the saddles and laid it in the shelter. Here, eat one of these bread sticks. I'm going to cook up one of these trail meals for you." In a small mettle cup he heated some of the water and then opened the pouch and poured it in. "This will be good for you and will warm you inside as well." She ate slowly. It was hard holding the spoon with her hands bandaged, but she wanted to do it herself. After all she'd been through she didn't want to be treated or fed like a baby. When she was done, Steve told her to lie down in the shelter and go to sleep. The despondency in her eyes was almost more than he could stand. It was hard to look at her. After he had gathered a good supply of wood for the night and moved it close to the shelter just as Favor had done he pulled out another blanket and laid it over her. He then pulled out a second bedroll, unsaddled the horses and then laid down nearby to rest. Looking up into the night sky he saw a myriad of stars and lay gazing at them for a long while before he finally drifted off to sleep. Cloud had curled up close to him and he welcomed the warmth of his companion.

The stillness of the night was shattered when the horses began to paw restlessly, snorting and pulling at their leads. With a menacing growl Cloud was on his feet staring into the darkness. The glow of the fire cast eerie shadows. Steve jumped up and commanded Cloud to stay. Reaching for his rifle he crept slowly forward. Favor woke and sat up. "What is it?" The sound of her words expressed near panic.

"Stay still, Favor. Don't make any noise."

Unexpectedly Cloud shot forward and in the dark they heard the sound of growling as a fight ensued. Steve grabbed a stick from the fire to use as a torch. He advanced toward the noise. In the dim light of the torch he saw Cloud in a fierce battle with a large coyote. Steve tried to call him off so he could get a shot off, but Cloud continued to fight fiercely. The fight continued for nearly ten minutes. It ended with a yelp as the coyote fell to the ground. Favor had gotten to her feet and stood staring into the darkness fear gripping her heart. "Steve! Steven!" The night became eerily hushed. Moments later Steve and Cloud emerged from the shadows. He stopped to check that Cloud was not injured. After checking the wolf over he determined the blood was that of the coyote. Steve looked up and as his eyes met Favor's, she suddenly came to the realization that she had been out here alone and what happened tonight could have happened to her with no way to defend herself. Tears slowly made their way down her dirt covered cheeks as the full reality set in. What had she been thinking? She'd sent Cloud away and risked her own life and because of that, the result was the risk of Cloud's life as well.

Steve seemed to know what she was thinking. Taking hold of her shoulders he looked her in the eyes, "Don't even think about it. You proved you can survive and you're safe. None of this would have happened if it were not for me. When we get back to the house, I'm going to make plans to take you back before the winter snow." He hesitated a moment and then went to check on the horses and make sure their leads were still tight.

He walked toward the horses. She spoke in an angry, reproachful tone, "Why didn't you come back? It's been seven days! You said you would be back in no more than three! Why?"

Turning to face her he said, "I'm sorry. I didn't get back till this morning and when I found you were gone, I started looking for you right away. Cloud found you by tracking your scent. I can't understand why he ever left your side in the first place."

"It just so happened we bonded while you were gone and I stupidly sent him home. I didn't think he'd obey me! I thought I was so smart that your precious, well trained wolf did what I told him to do! Instead of keeping him with me for protection I told him to go home! He could have led me back at any time if I had kept him with me, but I was stubborn and arrogant and stupid!" She was shouting. All the pent up emotions of the ordeal were pouring out of her. Loneliness, fear, anger, remorse, hurt and shame.

"I guess we both acted stupidly." With that he turned back to the horses.

When he returned to the fire she was still standing motionless staring blankly where he'd left her. The look on her face puzzled him and made him feel strangely empty.

"You didn't answer my question, why didn't you come back?"

Feeling beaten and worn he turned to her, "Damn-it, because I got arrested! Now go back to bed! You need rest. It's better than a half days ride back and in your condition you need as much rest as possible." After putting more wood on the fire he picked up his bedroll to move closer to the horses.

"Arrested, why?"

"We'll talk about it later!" he snapped.

"Are you really going to send me back?"

"Yes. That's what you've wanted all along, isn't it?" His words were edgy, cold and distant. "Now get some rest." With that he walked away leaving her with a fresh flow of tears streaming down her face. It wasn't so much his words, but the way he said them. He'd never really snapped at her like that before, but this time was different. This time his words cut like a knife. She'd finally defeated him but now it was the opposite of what she wanted. She wondered why he'd been arrested.

Confused about the prospect of going back and the thought of losing Steve suddenly overwhelmed her. Her feelings for Steve had grown stronger than she could ever have imagined. She wanted him, but now he didn't want her anymore. What had happened to make him change his mind? If only he would take her in his arms and hold her tight. But he hadn't, instead he had walked away. She felt like she was Scarlett O'Hara and he was Rhett Butler in 'Gone with the Wind'. If she had pushed him away to the point that she'd lost him for good then she didn't want to live. She couldn't live with that. Lying down on the bedroll a fresh flood of tears burned her tired eyes finally sending her into another fitful sleep.

Day eight and the morning sun once again began stretching its rays across the Eastern sky. Favor woke to see Steve had already saddled the horses and tied his bedroll in place. He stood crouched by the fire warming his hands. He looked tired and drawn. She wondered if he'd slept at all. Steve's body ached from sleeping on the hard ground though he'd welcome it any day rather than a cold hard jail cell. The first thing was to get home, put things away and then get a nice, long, hot shower. He saw a movement from the corner of his eye and turned to see Favor crawling out of the shelter.

"Good, you're up. Get warmed up by the fire while I grab your bedroll so I can tie it on the saddle. We need to get going. It won't be long till there will be buzzards all over the place trying to get at that carcass and I don't want the horses spooked anymore." He didn't even look her in the eye. Instead he hurried about his business and then started putting out the fire. Favor watched him intently as he worked at a hurried pace doing everything he could to avoid her. "We probably should change your bandages before we go. Let me look at your hands."

Favor pulled back from him as he reached for her hands still avoiding her eyes. "No, they're fine. They don't even hurt now. Like you said we need to get going."

"Fine, but if they start to hurt let me know so we can stop and check them." She only nodded as he helped her climb into the saddle. She tried to gather up the reins but found it hard to hold them in place with the bandages.

Exasperated she started to tear them off saying, "Damn it, I need to take these wrappings off. I can't hold on to the reins with my hand all bound up like this."

Steve yelled, "Leave them on!" She stopped. They looked at each other with shock at his outburst. Feeling ashamed for yelling his voice softened, "I'll take the lead rope and pony you back so you can hold onto the saddle horn and not have to worry about guiding the horse. We'll take it slow." Reluctantly she agreed. It meant having to ride closer to him than she wanted to. He untied the lead and they began their trip back with Cloud leading the way.

Over an hour later Steve finally broke the silence. He stopped to see how Favor was doing. She had a strained look on her face as she struggled to maintain her place in the saddle. "Are you ok? We can stop and rest for a while." Keeping her eyes turned downward she shook her head no. "Favor, look at me." Her eyes shot up but for an instant as she looked at him then she dropped her eyes down again. "Are you sure?" Nodding she replied with a whispered yes. Two and a half hours into the ride, Steve stopped by a little stream that Cloud found. "We're going to stop for a while to water the horses and stretch." Favor tried to slip out of the saddle on her own, but unable to grip with her bandaged hands she fell to the ground. Steve rushed to help her up. Concern creased his brow as she shook him off and stumbled away towards the stream. Sitting under a small tree she began tearing off the bandages. "Favor, don't. I told you to leave them on. I don't want to risk you getting them infected."

"Well, I really don't care what you want! It's just some blisters and a few cuts! I can handle it!" As she torn off the bandages and the air hit them, they began to burn and throb. She winced at the pain. Staring at her hands she felt the anger give way to tears. Steve retrieved the disinfecting wipes, Bag Balm, gauze and vet wrap once again. Without a word he cleaned her hands, applied fresh salve and re-wrapped her hands. When done he kissed her forehead and went to put the first aid kit back in the saddle bag. Pulling out a metal cup from the other side he headed to the stream where he filled it with sweet fresh water and took it to Favor. She cradled it carefully between her two hands. The cool water soothed her parched throat and lips. The mountain water was like no other water she'd ever had. It was pure and sweet and oh so cold.

"We're probably about half-way back. We'll rest here a while. Here's some jerky and some nuts. The protein will help you feel better." In silence they ate a little and watched the steady flow of the stream as it wound its lonely path down the mountain. The sound of the water was peaceful. Steve stood at the edge of the stream with his back to her and she marveled at the long lean lines of his body. How good it would feel to go up to him and wrap her arms tightly around him. But his rejection had been apparent and there was no use opening her-self up to more of it. Tired, weak and defeated the ache in her heart was intensifying. She'd known far too much heart ache and sadness the last few years. He said she survived, survived for what? A lost soul wandering through oblivion who didn't know who she was anymore. Like a puppet on a string, she allowed him to help her back in the saddle as they continued on.

It was nearly two when things began to look familiar and Cloud began to dance around the horses. He knew they were close and the horses seemed to sense it as well as they picked up the pace with renewed energy. They passed through the wooded part of the land and rose up over a hill that opened up to the moor where the cattle were grazing. One more hill and they were looking down on the ranch house. They stood for a moment in silence and Favor suddenly realized this might be the last time she'd ever look down on this beautiful moor and the house that had become her home. He would be sending her back. She knew he'd take her at night, like he did when he brought her to the moor. He wouldn't want her to be able to find her way back or show anyone where she'd been. But she understood it had to be that way. Steve looked back at her to see tears streaming down her face. Her heart was breaking. She didn't know his heart was breaking too. How could he let her go? He loved her so much. They needed each other, but they were both too stubborn to give in. Somehow they needed to find their way into each other's hearts and into each other's arms. Somehow they needed to stay together.

Looking away from her tear streaked face he began a slow decent down through the moor. In silence they approached the house. Rainbow Moor was her home now. Somehow she needed to convince Steve to let her stay. There was no other place in the world she wanted to be. It was the most peaceful and serene place on the planet and she belonged here. Rainbow Moor was a part of her existence and to leave it now could destroy her.

Stopping the horses in front of the house, Steve dismounted Denali and went around to where Favor sat on Snow and helped her dismount. As he set her gently on the ground he hesitated for a moment looking at her. At first she stared down at the ground but then she raised her head up. Their eyes met with each of them seeing the pain in the other's eyes. Neither one could hold the others gaze but a moment. Favor's clothes were covered in dust and dirt, her face was streaked with dried tear stains. The bandages were unraveling and were stained and soiled.

"Go upstairs and get cleaned up. Take a nice long shower or soak in the tub. I'll take a look at those hands when you're done. I'm going to get a shower after I take care of the animals. We need a decent meal. I haven't had a good meal since I left home. I'll unload the truck later. There's not anything in it that won't keep."

Favor looked towards the truck with a puzzled look. "You got a new truck and trailer!"

"Yeah, I needed to. Now go in the house."

"What was wrong with the other one? Looked pretty new to me."

"Favor, I really don't want to answer any questions right now. That's all I've done the last few days and I really don't need to be interrogated by you, too!" He walked away with the horses in tow leaving her wondering what had happened.

Hesitating she stopped and turned toward Steve. "Steve?" she began, but Steve motioned for her not to say another word and go inside. The house felt sad as if it sensed the strain between them. Things felt very different as she climbed the stairs to her room. Her defiant, proud attitude was gone, replace with emptiness, abandonment and regret for the decision she had made and the results of that decision. Life felt like it had been sucked right out of her.

In her bathroom she dutifully undressed and started the shower. Carefully and slowly she managed to un-wrap the soiled bandages. Her hands looked better than she had expected. The salve Steve had applied to them had already started to heal the blisters and cuts. Looking in the mirror she was almost shocked at the person looking back at her. She was covered in dirt and grime and her hair was a matted mess. Disgusted at herself she entered the shower and began scrubbing furiously to remove the filth and dirt. It made her hands hurt but she didn't care. The sweet smell of the shampoo soothed her as she lathered her hair the second time. While rinsing it out she let the warm water cascade down her body relishing in its warmth. Applying conditioner she turned up the hot water and stood still while it pounded her flesh. Her body began to turn red from the heat of the water. She turned it up hotter and with the flow of the water she let the tears and pain flow from her body.

She cried out, not from the pain of the hot water, but from the pain in her heart, letting the bottled up grief escape from her spirit as she cried out loud. The water continued to pound her body as she dropped to her knees in the shower and sobbed remorsefully.

Steven, heading up to his own room heard Favor's cries. Concern swept over him and he bolted through the bedroom door and into the bathroom. Quickly grabbing a towel he pulled open the shower door and turned off the water. Wrapping the towel around her he pulled her from the shower and held her to him.

"Favor, talk to me."

"I'm so sorry for what I did. Please don't make me leave Rainbow Moor. I don't want to leave you. I don't want to go. Please let me stay here with you."

"Why do you want to stay when you hate me so much?"

"I don't hate you! I love you!" There, she'd said it. Finally the words were out. Relief flowed through her veins as she leaned against him. "I love you. I can't live without you!" The words came between sobs. "Please don't send me away! I belong with you!"

Steve was having a hard time controlling his own emotions. "I've wanted to hear those words for so long. But, I haven't been fair to you. You were right about how I went about this whole thing. I have to take you back to make this right." With that he turned and left her. She sat down on the edge of the tub and continued to sob until there were no tears left.

An hour later she made her way downstairs. Steve sat in the living room drinking. He'd pulled out the hard liquor and was staring into the fireplace. Favor walked over and sat beside him putting her arm around his back. "We've both been foolish and have made stupid mistakes, but we don't have to let it end like this. We both love each other. Can't we just forgive each other and start fresh?"

Putting his drink down he leaned back, "Favor, are you absolutely sure? I don't want any more regrets and if you stay there is no turning back."

"Let me show you how sure I am." With that she stood and began to unbutton her blouse. His lips found hers as they wrapped in a passionate embrace. Her body quivered at the touch of his hands as he began to explore her body. She guided his hand to explore her inner thigh. He felt her desire. Pulling up her top he exposed her breasts. With his hands and mouth he softly caressed her. She reached down and slid her shorts lower as he began to undo his jeans. He touched her tenderly. Her desire increased and she begged for more. He pulled his body up and covered hers with his as he kissed her with desire and passion. She felt the heat of his body and his hardness as he entered her, their bodies joined together. Intoxicated by their love they clung to one another. She couldn't get enough of him. They were molded into one as they moved in rhythm to each other, heart, soul and body. And then it came in a rush. As they gave themselves to each other. He exploded within and she felt her own body give way to her desire.

He carried her up to his room where he laid her on the bed. She watched as he slipped out of his own clothes and then he was caressing her again. He entered her as she begged for more. Their desire had no bounds. There was no need for words as their bodies said it all. Darkness overcame them and still the passion raged as the love making continued. Long into the night their bodies burned with an uncontrollable desire. It was nearly dawn when they were finally spent. Entwined in each other's arms, exhausted they fell asleep in a loving embrace where they slept long into the late morning hours. When they finally rose it was nearly noon and they were ravenously hungry. The meal they prepared was simple but tasted more wonderful than any meal either of them could remember.

Steve watched her as she slowly ate a sweet ripe strawberry. He marveled at how beautiful she was and he had to restrain himself, wanting more of her.

"Favor, will you marry me?" Shocked she didn't answer. "Favor, did you hear me?"

Their eyes met. "Steve, I never expected you to ask me that."

"What do you mean? We love each other. Last night was amazing and I want you to share my name as well. Why wouldn't we take it to the next level?"

"I never thought about getting married again. I'm not sure I want to get married again."

"It's important to me and I want to be sure if anything happens to me you get all my company holdings."

"Whoa, back up the bus. I have money. I don't need anything but your love."

"Maybe you don't but for my own peace of mind and because I need this to feel complete, I'm asking you to think about it."

So this was the bottom line. Favor stood and looked him square in the eye. "You know all about me, my business and my past. I still know nothing about you except a few stories about your parents. You say you have money, and maybe you do, but I have no way of knowing if that's true. So was all of this a ploy to get me to fall in love, marry you, then you get everything I have? Oh my God, how stupid I've been. And to think I made love to you. I let you touch me and…" Favor hesitated a moment as tears burst from her eyes, "it was the most amazing experience I have ever had in my life. Even now as angry as I feel right now, I still want you. I still love you, but I hate myself for that."

Running blindly from the room as tears streamed down her face she barely heard Steve as he yelled after her, "Favor, you're wrong. If you want proof I'll give you proof." Would he ever figure this woman out? One minute she'd be purring like a kitten and the next she was like a crazed mountain lion.

Halfway up the stairs she turned and yelled back at him. "I won't marry you and I've decided you can take me back any time, the sooner the better!"

It was Steve's turn to be angry. He rushed into the library and began pulling out files from a locked cabinet. Arms loaded he rushed up the stairs and burst into Favor's room. She jumped up from the bed where she had been sobbing as he threw the armload of files on the bed.

"Look at these. It's everything you want to know about me including my assets, companies I own free and clear and all of my properties and tax information. Take as long as you like. I won't hide any of it from you. I just needed to know you loved me for who I am, before letting you know about all of this. Now I have a truck to unload." With that he left the room, slamming the door so hard that a nearby picture fell from the wall.

Stunned Favor stared at the door and the picture lying on the floor. This was her chance to find out more about the man who had kidnapped her. After pouring through the files for hours she was almost convinced. There was still one nagging question. If all this was true, why kidnap her. Why risk so much? Why not just ask her out the way normal people do? She needed to fully trust him. The papers looked legitimate. But this could be part of his elaborate plan. Drained but wanting to see him, she stacked the files neatly, gathered them up and headed downstairs.

The kitchen was full of boxes Steve had unloaded but he wasn't there. She was just heading to look out front when Steve came in the back door, shaking hay off his clothing. She realized he had just finished unloading the hay from the trailer. Tired and sweaty he looked at her and then brushed past her saying more to himself than to her that he needed another shower.

Standing in the middle of the kitchen, not knowing what to do, she realized what she really wanted was climb in the shower with him. At the bottom of the stairs she hesitated at the bathroom listening to the sound of the shower through the closed door. Instead of entering she decided to go into his room and take off her clothes where she waited for him.

Wrapped in only a towel Steve entered his bedroom. When he turned on the light he saw her standing there in all her sheer beauty just as natural as the day she was born. Stunned, he stared at her as she pulled the towel from around his waist and let it drop to the floor. Putting her arms around him she began kissing his body. Unable to resist he gathered her in his arms and tossed her on the bed. "I want to look at you, all of you. I'm angry so this could get rough."

"Whatever you want. I'm yours for the taking." The old defiant, daring Favor was back.

With that he ran his fingers up inside her watching her as she moved her pelvis upwards in response to each inward thrust. He grabbed her breasts and squeezed tightly until she cried out in pain. Then he assertively thrust himself into her fast and hard until she screamed, "Steve, please you're hurting me." But he didn't stop until he was done. When he had finished he got up from the bed and turned his back on her and angrily told her to get out of his room. Favor left leaving her clothes behind without a word. There were no tears. She got what she asked for and she still wanted more of him. She'd just have to let him come to her now.

What had he just done? He closed the bedroom door, wrapped the towel back around his waist and sat down on the edge of the bed with his head in his hands feeling ashamed. This woman was more strong willed and defiant than he could ever have imagined. He'd sure as hell met his match. Tomorrow they'd have to figure out a way to 'mend their fences', but for now he needed to sleep.

Chapter 13

The next morning the aroma of fresh coffee brewing drifted up the staircase rousing Favor from her sleep. When she entered the kitchen Steve was drinking a cup. Looking round she saw that most of the boxes were already unpacked and the items put neatly away in the pantry. Feeling ashamed at not having helped she asked if there was anything she could do.

Avoiding eye contact he answered, "No, there's not much left. I've got it under control. Why don't you get yourself some coffee? I was just going to cook some breakfast." He was feeling embarrassed at his earlier lack of control. They needed to talk about it and clear the air and make things right between them. All of his plans depended on it. Everything he had worked so hard to accomplish depended on this. They both turned to each other and started to speak at the same time profusely apologizing.

"Steve, I'm truly sorry about everything that has happened and what I said to you. I don't know what gets into me sometimes. I do love you and I do want to be with you. And if you want me to marry you, then I will. It really doesn't matter as long as we're together. But there is one thing I want from you, after we are married you have to take me home long enough to settle my affairs and let everyone know I'm alright. I'm not going to run away or report you. We can make up some story about me getting away and lost and you saving me." Favor watched him as he stood there staring at her. She could practically see the wheels turning in his brain. He put his hands over his eyes and rubbed his temples as he turned away.

Deep in thought he finally turned back to her and spoke, "When I was in town I was detained in jail because someone at that friend of yours party had seen a green truck like mine near your house the night I kidnapped you. They had been investigating everyone with a truck that even came close to the description. They stopped me when I was at the feed store and detained me calling it probable cause. I had to call my lawyer and he flew in from LA on one of my private planes. It took some convincing that I wasn't their guy before they let me go. They even checked out my truck for blood and your DNA. I had fortunately taken all the necessary precautions and they didn't find any evidence that you had ever been in the truck. So I left the truck and trailer with my ranch foreman at another ranch I own and flew out with my attorney. I was really scared they would find some evidence and you would be left here for good to survive on your own. So your story would never work."

"Favor, you need to know that I would never have told them where you were and risk them finding this place. I would have stayed in jail instead. I was finally released and I flew back via a completely different route and purchased another truck and trailer out of state. I had the money wired to pay cash for the purchase so I could get back to you undetected. It wasn't easy and I had no choice but to be away longer than I'd planned."

"You would have left me here? You wouldn't have told anyone how to find me? Steve, what is it about this place that you have to keep it such a secret? Why is it so important that we be completely isolated? That's what scares me. Something just isn't right here and though I have for some crazy reason fallen in love with you, I can't help but feel scared."

"Please, trust me, Favor. You will know everything in time and I hope it will be clear to you when the time comes why I had to be so secretive. I will never harm you. You're completely safe with me." Changing the subject he continued speaking in a thoughtful way that seemed he was speaking more to himself than to Favor, "We really have to be prepared for when winter comes. It's expected to be a long and extremely cold one this year. We have more than enough provisions to get us through. I won't be going out anywhere without you for a long while."

"Are you hiding from some drug lords or are you one of those victim witnesses? And what does any of this have to do with me?"

"Huh? What? Oh, no it's nothing like that. I can't answer any more of your questions, but I can tell you this, our union is a very important part of this and in time it will make sense. So please trust me. My love for you is as pure and real as anything in this world."

"Does this have to do with some big money inheritance, that you have to be married by a certain time to a certain kind of girl, and she has to have certain genes or some weird thing before you get your money or inheritance or some weird thing like that?"

"Favor, look at me." She turned toward him as he reached out and held her shoulders, "I've answered all the questions I can. Please don't ask me anymore?" The look in her eyes was one of deep concern and yet filled with love and desire. "Don't look at me that way or we'll end up right back in bed. I've got too much to do around here."

"Would that be so bad? I've never felt this kind of desire and passion for a man before and I like it. I can't get enough of you. It scares the hell out of me but I can't help myself."

A broad smile crossed his lips and he laughed, "There will be plenty of time for that when winter comes and we're stuck in the house most of the day."

"But, I want you now, right now!"

"What have I created?" Teasing she pulled him towards her and towards the staircase. He let her lead him back upstairs saying, "Ok, Little Lady, but afterwards we are going to get some work done around here." She giggled as they ran up the stairs to Steve's room.

"We'll see," she teased as she began pulling off her top.

Two hours later they finally went back down to the kitchen, both hungry and in contentedly good moods. Together they cooked a savory Dutch breakfast. With each tasty morsel Favor teased and enticed Steven licking her lips and flirting. "Woman will you stop? We've got work to do around here." Favor only giggled and continued. "You're a more complicated woman than I ever realized. You always seemed all business, totally focused and organized. I like this side of you. It fascinates me." A blush flushed her cheeks as a softness filled her eyes.

That evening Favor once again brought up the subject of going 'home' to take care of things. He once again became thoughtful. Then the thought struck him that if he told her he would take her back after they were married and after the winter snows had melted she might be satisfied with that. "No, Steve, I want to go before winter sets in. I want everyone to know I'm ok. They need closure as much as I do. Why else would they still be looking for me? You got arrested because they're looking. I want them to stop worrying."

"You're right. I can't promise we can go before winter, but I'll try." He told her what she wanted to hear knowing full well it was impossible to allow it. He hoped she would be satisfied with the answer for now. Her smile said she was.

"So when should we get married and where? We could make the wedding trip and the home trip all at the same time. Then my friends could come and you could meet them and they will see how wonderful you are and how good we are together and then no one will be worried anymore, and I need to find a dress, nothing too fancy, just something kind of simple, and I need to ask Cindy to be my maid of honor." She was talking so fast that she forgot to breathe. When she finally stopped and took a breath she saw Steve was staring at her wide eyed.

"Slow down. I've already made plans for the marriage. It's very simple, but it will be unique and beautiful. You'll see. Oh, and I've already gotten a wedding dress for you to wear."

Favor turn wide eyed. Taking a deep breath and then with great control asked, "What do you mean you already got me a dress? How is it that I'm not entirely surprised by this revelation? You've planned everything else and chosen all my other clothes. I should have been allowed to choose the wedding dress. So when do you let me in on your plans?"

"We're going to be married here on the property in a really beautiful spot I picked out for us. You haven't been there yet because I wanted our wedding day to be the first day you see it."

"So everyone will be coming here instead?"

"No it's just going to be you and me."

"Somebody has to marry us and we need witnesses!"

"Don't worry I've got it all arranged. You'll see."

"And when is this perfectly planned wedding going to take place?" The sarcasm in her voice was becoming increasingly evident although she tried hard to hold it back.

"You should know by now it doesn't do you any good to question me or cop that kind of an attitude. We only end up fighting. Although, making up has its upside if you get my drift."

"You know, Steve, you're right. You're always right. I think I'm just going up to bed.'

"Favor, I thought you'd sleep in my room with me tonight."

Whirling around with fire in her eyes, she said, "I don't think so, Steven Mitchell. I'm not in the mood." With that she stomped off up the stairs while Steve laughed as she ascended the stairs. Grabbing a beer from the kitchen he headed out on the porch to look at the stars. He was feeling reassured and back in control. It would be a full moon in three days. He'd have to plan something special for that day and evening for Favor. His mind began to formulate a plan.

After a number of beers and feeling happy with himself, Steve stumbled up the stairs. Glancing at his own door he headed towards Favor's room instead. Bursting into the room he stumbled. "Hey, Favor Honey, there's going to be a full moon in three nights. We're going to do something special that afternoon and then we can watch the moon come up."

Favor jumped up into a sitting position and reached over and turned on a light. "What in heaven's name are you doing? You've been drinking. Get out of my room."

"I don't think so. I'm sleeping here with my pretty lady."

"And you couldn't wait till tomorrow to tell me about your stupid full moon? You just had to come in and wake me up to tell me all about it now?"

"That's right, Baby, had to let you know." With those last slurred words he passed out beside her. She couldn't help but smile. He was so like a little boy when he had a few too many beers. She pulled the covers out from under him. Getting out of bed she went around to his side and pulled off his shoes, socks and shirt. Unfastening his jeans she managed to tug them off of him while he let out a loud groan. Turning off the light she went back around to the other side and crawled in bed beside him. He soon rolled over and tossed his arm across Favor's middle as he cuddled up close to her and fell asleep like a baby. For a while she lay awake listening to him breathe enjoying the closeness and the warmth of his body next to hers. Sleep finally overtook her and she too fell into a quiet sleep. For the first time since she had come to Rainbow Moor she actually slept a sound sleep and did not experience any nightmares. Steve's arms around her made her feel safe. They both slept through the night in sweet comfort.

Chapter 14

The encounter with the guy in the green truck left Adam more frustrated and more determined than ever to find Favor. Throughout the night Adam tossed and turned in his bed. His mind kept going back to the guy in the green truck. He had a feeling about him. The first thing in the morning he called the Department of Motor Vehicles to see if he could find out the name of the owner. The person on the other end of the phone line told Adam she could not give out the name of the owner. It was against policy. So he contacted the police department. He was surprised to find the Red Bluff police had just picked up the driver that morning and were holding him for questioning at the Red Bluff police station.

"Mr. Jennings, he is just a person of interest at this point. We do not have any reason to suspect him, but we are covering all our bases and we are being very thorough. If anything should develop we will fill you in. We are keeping the Fortuna police apprised of what is going on and you will be informed if anything comes of the investigation." The officer was silent while listening to Adam on the other end of the line. "No I can't give you his name. If we feel he could be our man and we arrest him only then will we release his name. We are not going to jump to conclusions and risk a law suit."

An idea was formulating in Adam's brain. He decided to head back to the country and canvas the local post offices and grocery stores from Fortuna to Red Bluff. He'd show the picture he'd taken and hope someone would recognize him. Stopping at the Bridgeville Post Office first Adam met a grizzly looking older man in a USPS uniform sorting mail.

"Hi I'm trying to find an old friend of mine who moved up here a few years back but I lost his address. I was hoping you could help me find him. He drives a green truck. I've got a picture of him. Maybe you'll recognize him."

"Well, I know most all the folks who live around here. Let's have a look at the picture." Adam showed him the picture. "What did you say his name was?"

Adam looked him in the eye, "Didn't say."

"Well, that could be a problem. You need to tell me his name. I can't be giving out information to just anyone who comes around asking. Maybe you've got it out for him and you want to get even."

Once again Adam was hitting a road block. He had to think fast, "Well in college we called him Rocky cause he was always going rock climbing, but his given name was, let me think, uh, Dave I think."

"Sorry, can't help you."

"Wait, no I think it was John."

"I don't know what your game is Sonny but looks like I might need some persuading if you know what I mean."

Adam pulled out a fifty dollar bill. "Is this persuasive enough?"

"That'd be a start."

"What do you mean a start?"

"You want me to risk losing my job, you better pay up. I'll take five hundred big ones before I give you anything."

"That's extortion. What if I give you the money and you don't have any information?"

"Hell, call it what you want. That's the chance you got to take."

Adam turned to walk out then looked back at the old man. "I'll find him some other way. Just so you know, this guy could be the person who kidnapped my girlfriend and if it turns out he is the one and you could have helped me, I'm coming back to whip your sorry ass."

"Sonny, you best be moving on before I call the Sheriff." The old man shook his fist at Adam as he headed out the door. "And don't be coming back here again, you hear?"

Adam headed East on Highway 36. He'd have to think of a better tactic so he wouldn't raise suspicion. When he reached the town of Dinsmore he stopped at the local grocery and hardware store.

A cheery elderly woman greeted him, "Hi, how are you doing today, young man?"

"I'm doing well, thank you for asking."

"Are you new around here or just passing through?" She could tell he wasn't one of the locals.

"The fact is I just haven't been out this way for many years, probably before college. I used to come out here with my folks and some friends when I was in High School."

"What brings you back to these parts?"

"Actually I met this guy while I was in college who was also from here. He told me if I was ever in the area and was out this way to look him up. He owned property around here. But I don't know if he still does. I've got a picture of him if you want to see it?"

"Let's have a look at it. Maybe I'll recognize him."

Adam pulled out his phone and brought up the picture, careful to zoom in a bit on the face so she could see it better.

"Why you know that could be little Stevie Mitchell. In fact the more I look at it the more I'd have to say it's him. Looks just like his daddy. Tragic with what happened to his parents."

Adam put on an heir of surprise and said, "That's it. Steve Mitchell. He never talked about any parents. What happened to them?"

"I'm not surprised he didn't talk about them. I'm sure it was too painful. They were really a close family. Terrible accident took both of them at the same time. Steven was only sixteen. Steven and Lisa Mitchell worshiped that boy. He was his dad's namesake and the fourth generation of Mitchell's. After the funeral his mother's sister, Sadie Marks, took the boy and finished raising him at least till he went to college. She moved them to the valley somewhere. His parents had other property including a big ranch somewhere near Redding or Anderson. Could even have been Red Bluff or Cottonwood, just not sure."

Ms. Ellie had a thoughtful and almost sad look at the memory of the boy's tragic youth. "Stevie liked to hang out with his dad who liked to do carpentry work as a hobby and he was real good at it. He had enough money he didn't really have to work at all, but he enjoyed working with wood. Said the wood made him feel close to the earth. He once said every tree that is cut down gives back a hundred fold if man uses it wisely.

Always had his carpenter tools with him in his truck. If he saw someone who needed a porch repaired, a railing, fence, or if he saw someone in need of something pretty to brighten up their place, he'd fix it or fashion some pretty little wishing well or planter and just leave it for them, never asked for any pay or anything in return. Little Stevie loved to help his dad with those projects and his dad told him that you have to give to receive. Yes, sir, he taught that boy high morals and respect, loved animals, too."

The frail little woman became silent and closed her eyes. Adam thought she must have fallen asleep when she suddenly opened her eyes again and kept on talking as though there had not been a single pause. "I heard Stevie followed in his dad's footsteps and whenever he came home on summer break, he'd carry his father's tools with him and do the same good deeds. Heard he worked for a local construction company for a while not too many years ago."

"Don't know if he still owns the old homestead property they had in this area. I really doubt it though. I heard the aunt and he had a falling out. Seems she had been sweet on his dad at one time, but he married the sister instead. From what I was told the only reason she took the boy was so she could get her hands on the assets Steve and Lisa had left behind. She had it in her head that her sister stole Steve from her and all of his wealth should have been hers, not Lisa's. But Little Stevie's parents had planned wisely and very well for their only child. They were very wealthy and had a lot of valuable holdings in several companies they owned as well as a lot of real estate. It all went to Steven via a Trust. Heard the aunt tried to get some or all of the assets by some unsavory means and when Stevie figured out what she was trying to do he alerted his advisors who were also handling the trust. It wasn't long after that he gave her the boot. From what I heard she received a monthly allotment for taking care of the boy. Heard he instructed his advisors to purchase a comfortable little house for her and she continued to receive a handsome monthly allotment so she was not left destitute. But the stipulation for her to continue receiving the allotment was she was never to contact him or she would lose both the monthly allotments and the house as well. Course this is just what I heard. You can't take it as gospel."

"Do you know where the property here was located that he and his parents owned?"

"From what I know it was way up in the mountainous areas. Hard to get to and I heard there were several locked gates one had to go through to get there. I think you had to get to it by way of the old McClellan Mountain Road but I'm not really sure. These days with all the pot growers trespassing on private and forest service land to grow their pot, a lot of people sold and got out of the area. I suspect he did the same what with all his other properties, why would he want a place like that? It was so remote and isolated. Besides you'd think the memories would be too painful. His dad was a very successful business man and I wouldn't be surprised that he followed in his father's footsteps and possibly took over running the businesses once he got out of college."

"Well, I know he still had the place when we were in college, but you're probably right. He probably sold it after college. That was a lot of years ago." Adam felt bad lying to such a sweet old lady about going to college with Steve Mitchell, but he felt it was the only way to get the information he needed to try to track Mitchell down.

"Most likely he did. I've been in these parts all my life and I certainly haven't seen Stevie for a lot of years. I'm sure if he still had the old place he would have come by the store now and again. No, I imagine it's sold or gone to rubble over the years. Heard it was a real fine place at one time though. Yep, times sure have changed."

The sweet old woman's eyes took on a distant look that seemed to suddenly envelop her as she remembered the days gone by when life was simple and family ties bound households together in sweetness and harmony. Adam thought he saw a tear in her eye as she remembered and a look of longing came over her as she thought about how pure life used to be. There was a strange aura about her and Adam stood silently waiting, not wanting to disturb her thoughts. As quickly as she had drifted away into the thoughts of the past, she came back to the present. She looked at Adam giving him a sweet smile.

"Oh, my goodness, here I am rambling on while you stand here waiting. Forgive an old lady for letting her mind wander into the past for a bit. You know, my dear boy, sometimes the past is much more pleasant than the present what with all the troubles in the country these days."

"I didn't mind a bit. I'm glad you shared your thoughts with me. Nothing wrong with slowing down and thinking of the by gone days.

Memories are treasures to hold onto. Well, I'm going to buy me something to drink and then I'll be on my way."

He purchased a soda and some chips. As he was heading out the door she called after him. "Young man, you come back and see me sometime soon."

"I will."

"What is your name, young man?"

"Adam. Adam Jennings. And what may I call you?"

"Ms. Ellie. Everyone calls me Ms. Ellie."

"I will certainly stop in to see you when I can. I hope to be coming by here more often."

"Good, Adam Jennings, I will look forward to seeing you again. Oh, and whatever is plaguing you with guilt, let it go. It is not your fault. Everything happens for a reason." Adam stood staring at her a moment and she smiled an ever so sweet smile and waived him on. "Go on, Adam Jennings, you have things to do."

"Yes mam, good day, Ms. Ellie." Adam sat in his SUV for a few moments reflecting on what had just happened and what Ms. Ellie had said as he was leaving. How could she know he was riddled with guilt? What caused the strange aura that seemed to surround her? Was there some greater force at work here that he didn't understand? As he sat there pondering these questions a feeling of peace enveloped him. Had Ms. Ellie caused that to happen? Still confused but feeling a weight had been lifted from his shoulders, he started his engine and drove away. He had a name now. Steven Mitchell. It was a start. He somehow knew if he found this Steve Mitchell he would find Favor as well.

Adam felt his day had been successful. He had a name so he could start searching public records and see if he could find the old homestead. If this guy still owned the property it would be an ideal place to hide Favor. Mentally drained he arrived home later that afternoon.

Houston had been at Cindy's and came walking in the door. "Hey where were you all day? I tried calling you several times. What you're not answering your phone these days?" Adam didn't answer. Houston suddenly realized what Adam had been up to. "Oh no, you didn't try to find that truck did you?" Adam still didn't answer. "You did, didn't you? What the hell. So what did you find out? You are going to tell me aren't you?"

"I've got a name and approximate location of where he may have taken Favor."

"Oh sure, in one afternoon you do what the police haven't been able to do for months, location and all. I'm supposed to believe that?"

"As a matter of fact I did. Tomorrow I'm going to talk to the police about it. They picked up a guy in Red Bluff who could be our guy, but they wouldn't tell me his name. His folks owned property here and in Red Bluff, so it's no wonder we saw him in this area headed in the direction of Red Bluff."

"Can't you let it go? You're going to end up pissing someone off and get yourself hurt. You can't go around accusing perfect strangers of kidnapping. You have no proof."

Favor's friends had lost all hope that she would be found alive, if ever found at all. All of them except Adam believed she was deceased. Adam felt she was still alive although he feared for the situation she might be in. He knew she was strong willed and independent and she was smart and would do everything possible to stay alive.

Cindy and Houston were now in a serious dating relationship and encouraged Adam to move on with his life and enjoy dating as well. But no matter what, he couldn't get Favor out of his mind. He was obsessed with finding her and wouldn't even think about dating anyone else. The regrets he lived with haunted him daily. Demons visited him in his dreams at night. Why hadn't he insisted on walking her home and why hadn't he told her sooner how he felt about her? It was eating him up inside.

His friends tried not to mention her name around him or talk about things they all liked to do. Every time they mentioned her they could see his demeanor change and see that it upset him. His lighthearted spirit had vanished when Favor vanished. No matter where they went Adam was looking and listening for any information that might lead them to find her.

The next day the early morning light filtered through Adam's window searching out his closed eyes. He blinked hard as his eyes opened and adjusted to the soft rays. Through the open window a balmy breeze softly drifted into the room carrying with it the soft scents of the morning. The hope that he was one step closer to finding Favor lured him from his bed. Still a bit groggy he wandered into the kitchen where he put on a pot of coffee and then headed into the bathroom to get a quick shower and dress. The aroma of the freshly brewed coffee made its way through the house reaching him and alerting him to his need for a cup of the inky black substance. At the deck door he stood looking out onto the horizon as he gulped down the hot coffee. The sky was cloudless and the sun had already cleared the horizon shining brightly across the countryside. It was a new day with new discoveries to be made and new hope to hold onto.

The smell of coffee reached Houston's sleeping senses and he came wandering out of his room yawning and stretching as he tried to focus. "You're up early ol' man. Coffee smells good. Think I'll throw on some bacon and eggs. You want some?"

"Nah, I'm going to head out as soon as I have one more cup of coffee. Got things to do."

Houston eyed him warily, but decided not to say anything. He had a pretty good idea what Adam would be doing and he didn't want to get into any kind of confrontational conversation this early and on such a beautiful morning. "Ok, man, but you're really missing out. I thought I'd throw on some homemade hash browns to go along with it, but I guess that will be that much more for me. You don't know what you're missing."

Adam realized he hadn't spent much time with his best friend over the past few months and he actually missed him. A few more minutes wasn't going to make any difference and a home cooked meal sounded darn good. Looking at Houston he smiled, "Ok you twisted my arm. What can I do to help?"

After a hefty sized breakfast and a third cup of coffee Adam said he needed to get going. Houston had already offered to clean up the kitchen knowing that if he pressured Adam or tried to find a reason for him to delay leaving he would become moody and it would spoil the whole day. He was glad he'd managed to get him to stay and have some breakfast. Adam had not been eating much these days and had lost a noticeable amount of weight. He had always been on the thin side but was toned and firm. He had lost enough weight that he was beginning to look gaunt. This worried Houston and a number of their friends had made comments about it.

"So will you be around for dinner tonight?"

"I'm not sure, maybe." Adam hesitated a moment realizing how much their lives had changed and the losses that they all had suffered because of Favor's disappearance. He wished so much he could turn back the clock and recapture the happiness they all seemed to have lost. How could one person affect so many lives in such a profound way? He didn't know or understand it, but what he did know was that finding her was the only way they could possibly have a prayer of regaining any of those losses or to be able to move on with his life.

Adam drove straight to the local police station to discuss what he had found out about the guy in the green truck. He was shocked and dismayed when the police officer said, "Yes we had him in custody for a few days and we did a thorough investigation of the owner and he was cleared. We're doing everything we can to find your friend, but there just are no more leads."

"I know he's our guy, I can feel it in my gut. You've made a big mistake letting him go."

"Look, Mr. Jennings, there was nothing to hold him on. He's not our guy. The truck you saw that night could have been a dark blue or black. We were grasping at straws. It's a dead end. We tried but there's nothing more we can do. We have to look at other possibilities and hope we get some other lead. The case will remain open, but at this point it is no longer a priority case. After the first forty-eight hours if we don't find something the chances of finding her alive plummet. There are no similar cases to compare it with, so we have no idea if this is a onetime occurrence, if there are others we don't know about, or if this is just the first of more to come. I'm truly sorry. We sent out a message in a press conference asking if any women had been getting anonymous calls like Ms. Durand. We have not received a single response. Now go home, Mr. Jennings. You need to move on with your life. She would have wanted you to."

"You're talking like you think she's dead. I know she's alive. I can feel it." His voice was agitated and he was speaking in a loud tone.

"Mr. Jennings, you have to stay calm and I need you to leave now." The officer's voice had become strained and edgy. "Get some grief counseling."

"Fine, I'm leaving, but I'll prove to you how wrong you are. I'll find her myself. You just wait and see." Adam was pointing his finger at the officer and his voice had risen so he was almost shouting as he turned towards the door to leave.

"Don't be going and doing anything stupid, Jennings. I don't want to have to arrest you, so don't give me a reason." With a look of contempt Adam disappeared out the door.

Chapter 15

Remembering Ms. Ellie had said Steve Mitchell had worked for a local construction company for a while, Adam decided to start by looking up any and every company he could find along with private contractors in hopes of finding someone who knew Mitchell. He was amazed at how many construction companies there were in the region and even more independent private contractors. For days he gathered as much information as he could. The list seemed endless. Names of companies, their owners, subcontractors, addresses, phone numbers; the list went on and on. Finally when he felt he'd gathered enough information to start his search he began driving around, contacting owners and making phone calls. With the list longer than he had expected, Adam decided to take some time off work to continue his search. His boss had decidedly agreed it was a good idea for him to take some time off since he had not been focused on his work for some time.

"Good idea to take some time off. You have a lot of vacation time and it would be good for you to go do something fun, visit your family, take a nice long leisurely trip. Get back in focus. You haven't been yourself since you lost your girl."

"Yeah, I know I haven't. It all sounds good to me."

"Take as long as you need, son. I want you one hundred percent when you return. You've been with this company a long time. You're one of my best men. You deserve some time for grieving and healing. I was thinking about suggesting you take some time off myself. Keep in touch and come back when you're ready. Your job will be waiting."

"Thanks, I really appreciate it."

His boss had no idea that he would not be vacationing. Adam now had all the time he needed to devote to his search for Favor. For the next two weeks Adam spent every waking hour sifting through the information, contacting contractors, driving out to construction sites to show the picture of Mitchell to every owner, boss or foreman he could find. No one knew anything about the guy. Adam was becoming discouraged. The list had grown shorter and shorter with him no closer to finding Favor than when he started. Lack of sleep, little food and endless days of traipsing around the county had left him exhausted and discouraged. Winter would be coming soon and he sensed an urgency to find Favor but his own health and strength were now becoming an issue. He knew he needed to slow down and rest, but his mind kept pushing him on. Physical and mental exhaustion were beginning to win over his determination, but guilt kept egging him on. Adam even toyed with the idea of hiring a private detective to help him out, but he wasn't quite ready to relinquish the control to someone else who would not understand his desperate need to find her and who would probably just suck his finances dry. Discouraged and ready to head home Adam decided to make one more stop at the Anderson Construction Company.

"Sure," the head foreman was saying, "I remember him. He was one hell of a worker, talented and a real nice guy, one of the best. I could always count on him to be on time, willing to stay late and come in on the weekend if there was a deadline we needed to meet. During lunch or on breaks, he'd take scraps and make really pretty things and then give them to the other workers for their wives, girlfriends, sisters or moms. Never wanted any money for the items he made. The wood would have just been wasted or used for firewood or rotted somewhere. He made everything he touched turn into a work of art. The guy was amazing."

"So what happened to him? Did he move, or quit or what?"

"No, just never showed up one day. Didn't come by to collect his pay and we never knew what happened to him. Sure did miss him. He was a real lady-killer." Adam cringed at the foreman's choice of words. "Wish I had half his looks. He had a big white horse and a big white dog. Said it was half wolf. Had them wolf eyes. Saw them at the rodeo one time. He sat astride that big horse with the dog by his side and watched. You could see the women strut by him giggling while trying to get his attention. He'd give them an occasional smile and tip his hat, but never anything more. Believe me there were plenty of them that tried to get him to notice them. I remember him watching one girl. She didn't seem to notice him, but he sure kept watching her."

"What did she look like? What was so special about her?"

"She was real pretty, not at all like most of the girls trying to get his attention. She was graceful and moved with confidence. Had the prettiest black hair and smiling deep brown eyes."

"How long ago was this?"

"Hell, I'd say maybe four years ago."

"Do you have any idea where he might have gone?"

"Nope, I heard the only family he had left was an aunt. Find her and you might find him."

"Do you know her name or where she lives?"

"No. Never knew."

"Do you still have his address?"

"Look, if I did I wouldn't be able to give it to you."

"Thanks, I appreciate your time."

"You didn't say why you're looking for him."

"He may be the last person to have seen my girlfriend. The girl you described that he was watching fits her description. She's been missing for several months now. If I could find him I could get some answers. I believe he called her the day she disappeared."

"Are you saying you think he took her, because if you are, you're barking up the wrong tree? Mitchell was a rare breed, a true gentleman and a good man."

"No, but he may know something to help us find her."

"Well, like I said, I haven't seen him in a long time. Hope you find your girl."

In his truck, Adam leaned his head back letting out a deep sigh as he tried to sort the information in his mind and focus on his next move. Right now he was so tired. A good meal and some sleep was what he needed. Heading for home he came around a sharp bend in the road. A deer was standing in the middle of his lane. As he swerved to miss the animal his truck struck the edge of the hillside. Jerking the wheel in the opposite direction, he over-corrected and his truck went careening out of control.

Spinning the wheel he tried to straighten it out but instead the truck went into a spin and slammed into a large tree. The impact caused the vehicle to flip over onto its side. Searing pain shot through his body as he heard the terrible snap of bone, his own bone, and then everything went black.

As Adam regained consciousness he heard sirens and saw flashing lights. Trying to move he felt another searing pain shoot up his leg, and a deep throbbing in his head. Warm blood trickled down over his left eye like thick sticky syrup. Shattered glass from the windows of the truck lay all around him. Someone was shouting orders as he heard the sound of metal being ripped back. The smell of diesel, his own sweat and blood mingled together made his stomach queasy. The blood had a heavy smell hard to describe, but a smell you wouldn't forget. Struggling to stay conscious Adam tried to call out but no sound escaped his dry parched lips. The light slipped away as he again fell unconscious.

When Adam finally regained consciousness he was lying in a hospital bed, leg elevated, encased in a large cast from his lower thigh to his ankle. Gauze bandaging was wrapped around his head. His mouth was swollen and his body ached all over. A voice forced him to focus as he was greeted by a man who introduced himself as Dr. Sanders. Another voice to his left drew is attention. Cindy and Houston stood at his side.

"Hey, pal. You gave us quite a scare for a while there." Houston had taken hold of his hand in a gesture that was meant to be a handshake.

The doctor spoke again. "You're very fortunate. You sustained a concussion, a broken leg, a couple of broken ribs and a lot of cuts and bruises, but you'll be alright in a couple of months. The leg was a clean break. We're more concerned with your head injury. We'll be keeping you here for a while to monitor your condition. I want to ask you a few questions to see how coherent you are."

With that the doctor proceeded to relay a series of questions which Adam seemed to do fine answering. "Ok, you did really well. I'll be checking in on you tomorrow. In the meantime the nurses will be monitoring your vitals." The doctor turned to leave, telling Houston and Cindy not to stay too long. He wanted Adam to rest.

"Wait," Adam said. "How long have I been in here?"

"A couple of days." Then he turned and walked out the door.

"A couple of days, I've got to get out of here!"

Houston nearly laughed, "In case you haven't noticed your leg is in a cast and by that remark, I'd say you still have a few screws loose in that thick scull of yours."

Adam reached up to feel the bandages on his head and winced from the pain. "Yeah, I guess that sounded pretty dumb. So how bad is my truck?"

"Totaled. But I've got your insurance company on it. You fared better than that deer you hit. Not much left of it."

"I thought I missed it."

"Oh no, and if you were looking for a new hood ornament, I could have found you a cheaper one." That was Houston, always ribbing him about something. Cindy nudged him to quit and he smiled down at her and merely laughed. Adam smiled back at his friend and then closed his eyes a moment.

"We need to let him rest." Cindy tugged at Houston's arm as she nodded toward the door.

"Yeah, you're probably right. Besides that cute little blond nurse should be back in a bit. I'm sure Adam would rather us not be around when she does."

"Stop it! Let's go so he can rest. Adam, we'll see you in the morning." Adam nodded as they slipped out of the room leaving him to his thoughts as he tried to recollect the accident.

Leaning his head back his thoughts traveled to the memories of Favor and his need to find her before winter. It was almost September and it sounded like he'd be laid up for the better part of a month or more. A harsh early winter was expected this year. An overwhelming feeling of remorse and guilt brought tears to his eyes. "All right, Adam Jennings, you're a grown man and grown men don't cry. Buck up and face the situation. Stop sniveling," he inwardly rebuked himself. Time was no longer on his side. The guilt of losing her returned full force. He was beaten. His remorse gave way to unrelenting tears like he had never cried before. The words of his mother came back to him from his youth, "God gave men tears just like a woman. It's ok to cry or He would not have given you tears at all." When he had cried all the tears he could his feelings gave way to dismay and anger. Defeated he fell asleep. Visions of huge trees lunging at him, the sound of metal tearing apart and a spinning sensation filled his dream.

Deer were everywhere he turned as he tried to dodge them. Then he saw the face of a sweet brown eyed girl smiling at him and waving him on. He woke with a start, sweat trickling down his face and back. Those eyes and that smile, who was she? Then he remembered. It was Favor. Was she giving him a message to move on with his life as she was waving goodbye?

Adam stayed in the hospital another week. His physical condition continued to improve, but he was broken. He managed to hide his feelings from everyone, with the exception of Houston and Cindy. Adam worked for a consulting company. When he was finally released he talked his boss into letting him do some work from home to keep him occupied. Throwing all his energy into his work he pushed aside the thoughts of Favor. His boss was so impressed with his accomplishments that he promised him a huge promotion and a new office when he was able to physically return to work. Adam had found a way to move on. Work was the key to forgetting. Hard work was the key to success and a way to make amends. He was determined not to let his boss down or fail him like he had Favor. The love in his heart was replaced by bitterness and his focus was now on making money, lots of money. Why? Why not? There was nothing else and money could buy you anything you wanted, anything except the most important thing, love!

Returning to the office, true to his word, his boss had a large new office waiting for him. Life had settled down into a busy routine of work and little time to socialize. He rarely spent any time with the old group. Houston had moved in with Cindy in Favor's house and Adam found himself completely alone. The only people he saw were from work or social aquaintances his boss introduced him to, mainly to recruit business for the company.

As predicted winter came early with the high winds and cold rain so familiar to the north coast. The mountain areas were seeing unusually heavy snows. Adam didn't seem to notice or care. He had deadlines to meet and more work than he'd ever had before. No time to worry about the weather or who was doing what or where. The past was the past. He didn't have time to think or worry about it.

One evening after returning from a late night social meeting he was greeted at his door by Houston and Cindy. "Hey, what are you doing here?"

"Don't you ever answer your cell phone? I've been trying to reach you for hours."

"Sorry, the boss had me at some fancy social event for the business. Doesn't like it if we have our cell phones on when entertaining a potential client. It's not a good way to impress them. Makes them feel unimportant."

"Well, obviously we're not. Come on, Cindy, let's get out of here."

"Wait, I didn't mean anything by that. You know you're important to me and always will be. I've just been busy with work. I care about you."

"You have a really funny way of showing it. You've changed, Adam, and not for the best. I don't know who you are anymore and frankly I don't like the new you."

"Come on, Cindy."

"Houston, maybe we should tell him."

"Tell me what?"

"You don't give a damn. Just forget we were here. Forget we ever knew each other."

The anger in Houston's voice cut through his heart like a knife. Had he been that shallow? Had he lost sight of what really mattered? Houston was leading Cindy away and the sight of them leaving felt so final that it scared him. A profound feeling of rejection and loss held him in place. He'd felt alone when he lost Favor, but this was different. This was so final and cold that he suddenly felt like ending his own life. As the thought momentarily crossed his mind it terrified him as he realized what his life had become. Worthless, empty, without meaning.

Cindy turned to look back at Adam and saw something in his eyes she couldn't describe. Her heart went out to him and she stopped. Looking at Houston she said, "We have to tell him!" Then turning back to Adam she blurted out, "They found a body."

"Cindy, damn it! Get in the car!"

"No, Houston! Look at him. He needs to know just as much as we do."

Houston looked back at Adam who stood motionless, tears streaming down his face. "Oh, man, we came to tell you, but you pissed me off." With that he approached Adam's side and gave him one of his big ol' bear hugs. Adam nearly crumbled. "Let's go inside." They gathered in Adam's living room.

Adam finally choked out the words. "Is it Favor?"

"We don't know. The body fits her description. We've been asked to come and identify the body. We thought you should know."

"When?"

"We were heading over to see the coroner now."

"I want to go with you."

"If it is her it could be hard on you. Do you think you can handle it?"

"I have to know and if it is her I have to see for myself. It will give us the closure we need if it is her. I need to know. I've been trying so hard to forget by diving into my work. I didn't realize how shallow I've become. I'm sorry. I can't lose you two as well."

"It's settled. We all go."

At the coroner's office the three stood silently waiting for the medical examiner to come out and talk to them. When he finally came out he addressed them by saying, "The young woman we found has not been dead for long. Her body is still in fairly decent shape, so not as bad as if she had been gone a long time. She fit the description, height and approximate weight of your missing friend. There appear to be some broken bones and bruising. Do any of you need a few moments before we go in?"

They all shook their heads no.

They were led down a hall to what appeared to be an examination room. On a cold hard examination table was the covered body of a young woman. Slowly they approached as the examiner pulled back the white sheet covering the woman, revealing her body.

Houston gave out a great groan and turned away. Cindy gasped as she turned toward Houston and he wrapped his arms around her. Only Adam stood staring at the body without moving. His eyes focused on the lovely face before him. Tears streamed down his face. Finally the examiner spoke. "I have to ask you, is it your friend, Favor Durand?"

Adam turned to him, "I am so sorry for this young lady, but thank God it's not Favor."

Chapter 16

Three days passed. Tonight would be a full moon. Steve had planned to make this day special. He'd already been up for hours when Favor woke. Hearing him moving about the house, she got up and groggily headed to her bedroom door. What was he up to so early? Reaching for the door she turned the knob. The door wouldn't open. Puzzled and thinking it was stuck she tugged on the door handle twisting the cold, shiny knob back and forth. It wouldn't open.

"Damn, what's wrong with this thing?" Again she tried. She stood staring at the door knob as if with a bit of staring, and wishing, it would open like in Alice in Wonderland. A little chuckle escaped her at her own silly thoughts of the beloved fairy tale. What would Alice do? Of course there would be a convenient tasty little cake of sorts of which Alice would take a bite, grow smaller and then crawl conveniently under the door. But this wasn't Alice in Wonderland. It was Favor Durand, stuck in her own wonderland with nothing being as it seemed. There are no magic cakes, no mysterious bottle filled with a strangely bitter sweet liquid and no magic wand to wave. Decidedly she began to pound on the door. Steve finally heard her pounding and calls. Soon he was outside her door asking her what was the matter. "The door is stuck. I can't get the knob to turn. I seem to be locked in. Can you try from that side to get it open?"

"Favor, it's not stuck. I locked it. I've got something really special planned for the day and I don't want you to come out until I'm ready for you to."

"What? Steven, is this some kind of joke? Because if it is I'm not laughing. Now please open the door." Favor stood expectantly staring at the door with her hands on her hips.

"Sorry, Babe, look around your room. There is a tray with some really nice treats for you. Didn't you see it? I knew you'd need something to eat."

Favor turned and her eyes swept around the room finally resting on a tray on a corner table near the settee. It was beautifully laden with vibrant colored fresh strawberries, raspberries, blueberries, tart apples and breakfast pastries, a coffee carafe' as well as tea. A single red rose stood in a bud vase and a crisp white linen napkin all set on top of a white doily, finished off the tray. Eyes wide with wonder her thoughts mysteriously returned to the Alice in Wonderland story. This was a little freaky. Here she was thinking of delicate pastries that made Alice grow or shrink and here she was staring at a tray heavily laden with sweet and savory delights like in a tea party so much like in the classic tale. Blinking hard, she shook her head, looked away towards the door and then back to where the tray stood. It was still there. She hadn't imagined it. Steve's voice jarred her back to the present reality.

"Did you see it? Is everything ok? I'm sure there is plenty." Favor didn't answer. Stunned she just stood motionless as if waiting for the white rabbit to suddenly appear checking his pocket watch. Again Steve called her name.

"Yes, Steve, I see it. It's very nice, but how long are you going to make me stay in here?" There was no answer, only the sound of Steve's footsteps as he retreated down the hall and descended the stairs leaving Favor to her own imaginings.

"Ok, get a grip here. You should be used to his mysterious ways and sometimes weird ideas." Just when she thought she knew him and was feeling comfortable and relaxed with him, he pulled another strange episode that left her wondering about his sanity and her own for that matter. Surprises could be nice at times, but for now she felt she'd had enough surprises to last a lifetime. So here she was stuck in this room, locked up like the prisoner she really was and not too happy about any of it. She had to throw up her hands in submission. Here for the duration, she ate some of the fruit and a delicate blueberry scone that was so fresh she swore it had to have been prepared by a fairy. She then curled up on the bed with a warm cup of tea. Once again the almost forgotten sense of longing for days gone by began to creep into her memory. The need for other companions traveled into the here and now, bringing with it a feeling of melancholy and tears. When would all this end and how? She felt an overwhelming need to sleep and not think about it for now. Setting the tea cup aside her eyes felt heavy and before slipping off into the land of dreams she thought, "There must have been something in the tea. What was Steve up to?" Unable to fight the groggy feeling her body relaxed and sleep took over.

Dreams are a strange thing. Reveries born of unanswered questions, aspirations, wishes, mysteries, desires, fear, uncertainties and so much more. Our minds sometimes play tricks on us. In many cultures dreams are believed to be a manifestation with a greater meaning. Are they pieces of a puzzle put together from the subconscious? Or are they merely fragments of an overactive imagination? Whatever they are a dream can leave the dreamer searching to make some tiny bit of sense out of it.

Thoughts, fragmented pictures and twisted emotions, swirled around in Favor's head as she slept. Images emerged from her past mixed up with the present. City lights, country roads, vehicles she'd driven or ridden in, places she'd traveled to, faces from the past, some vaguely familiar, some sharp and intensely clear, some obscure with no distinctive features at all swirled aimlessly about in her brain.

Unseen hands reached out to touch her. She could feel them but could not see from where they came or whose hands they belonged to. Twisting to and fro trying to avoid their touches, she felt with each touch some sort of sensation. Some were harsh, dry and rough feeling. Some burned her skin, while others felt icy cold. A gentle touch that felt like velvet, or a soft feather brushing tenderly against her skin. Some touches were followed by a gentle breeze like springtime, or the balmy cold of autumn with a certain impending chill in the air. Others held the warm feel of summer sun while others a bitter stinging cold like those from a winter storm.

Then there were the smells. The smells of exhaust fumes in the city, mountains of rotting trash down a dark alley, the putrid smell of burning flesh, sweaty unclean bodies, vomit from a drunken derelict, manure, and rotting fish on an old fishing dock. But there were also the smell of an exquisite dinner at her favorite restaurant, sweet orange blossoms and tangy lemons, pine needles and roses, the smell of sweet savory pastries from a corner bakery, hot coffee and tangy barbeque and the smell of fresh cut hay.

Sounds mixed with the images, feelings and smells. The screeching of tires and of cars crashing into one another as the twisted metal scraped and tangled into each body of steel, horns honking, the sound of tires on a gravel driveway, a dripping faucet, a plane taking off and mounting to the sky over a Chicago runway, a baby crying, a dogs bark and a cats yowl as it warned another to stay the distance, the sound of a broom swishing across a dusty floor and the pounding of a hammer, the sound of an axe as it connected with wood, making a ripping sound as it split through the firewood. She heard the familiar beat of a country music song, the words enveloping her mind, the soft lilting sounds of a steel guitar playing a Hawaiian love song, a bird's morning twitter and a frog croaking near the pond. From far off she heard the soft rhythmic sound of a stream, the soft lowing of cattle, the neigh of a horse and the sound of a mellow voice saying "I love you."

With the sound of the voice she woke with a start. Her body shaken she looked about to see where the voice came from. She knew that voice, but couldn't quite remember who it belonged to. It was a gentle, sweet, calming voice and she clung to the feeling of love and security it gave her. Whose voice was it, Conrad, Adams, Steve's? She was unsure. Was it all of their voices blended together? It was as if the voice itself had wrapped around her to keep her feeling safe and secure, reassured, peaceful and most of all loved.

Looking over at the clock she saw it was three o'clock in the afternoon. Had she really slept that long? Hungry she looked over at the corner table. The tray of food was gone and in its place sat two gifts, neatly wrapped. A card nearby read "open last". The larger box she opened first. It contained a pair of ladies white platform sandals. Next picking up the smaller gift box Favor slowly opened it. Inside was an exquisite diamond and emerald ring. She drew the ring from its velvet lined box and slipped it on the ring finger of her right hand. It fit perfectly just as everything Steve picked out fit perfectly. Sitting back down on the edge of the bed she gazed at the simple, yet elegant ring. Hesitantly picking up the card she opened it and read, "A small token of my love. Meet me downstairs at four. Love always, Steven. P.S. There's a dress hanging in the dressing room I hope you will see fit to wear. She was feeling strangely confused and the thoughts of the dream, though not so vivid now, still haunted the boundaries of her mind. With a deep breath she rose and walked into the dressing room. There hanging neatly from a hanger was a beautiful, yet simple white dress. It had a strapless fitted bodice which enhanced a classical, elegant sweetheart neckline. The tiered organza design over silk was delicately offset by a rose detail on the left front of the slightly A-lined knee length skirt.

Favor's breath caught in her throat as she stood staring at the dainty lines of the dress. The words on the paper echoed in her brain "see fit to wear". The dress though simple with elegant lines was of a fabric that screamed semi-formal or afternoon wedding dress. If not for the white, it could certainly be a cocktail dress but she had an unsure feeling about this.

Ok maybe she shouldn't jump to conclusions. Take it at face value and don't over think this. But then again he had locked her in her room and then obviously laced her food with something to make her sleep. Then leaves an obviously expensive ring and a dress he wants her to "see fit to wear". Something inside her said the battle was already won and not by her. She quickly showered, put on a little makeup and then slipped into the dress. It fit as though it had been personally tailored for her. The shoes were a bit simpler than she would have chosen to go with the dress, but they fit comfortably.

At four o'clock she reached for the door knob and turned. It opened with ease. She wondered if it had been open at three when she first woke up. She had not thought to try the door at that time, probably due to the grogginess after waking up. Quietly she slipped from the room. For some reason she felt like she should tip toe. The house was too quiet. At the top of the stairs she hesitated for a moment and then began descending the staircase. She was a picture of beauty and grace as she made her way down. Her body seemed to glide gently with each step. Suddenly Steve was there, standing at the bottom of the stairs. She stopped a moment enthralled by the man she saw standing below. He wore a pair of gray pants and a gray vest over a white shirt and a light blue tie with black boots. In his hand he held a white cowboy hat. He motioned for her to continue as he smiled up at her. Her body began to shake and she could barely move. What was this all about? Why was he dressed like that? Then he spoke.

"You look more beautiful than I have ever seen you. We're going on a date to a special place. I told you on the night of the full moon we would do something special." Leading her out onto the porch Steve held her hand. "Your chariot awaits." His eyes twinkled with the look of mischief and he smiled as he leaned over and kissed her cheek. Opening the door of the truck he held her hand as she slipped in. Favor began to feel excitement rising up inside her. Looking at him she began to feel that urge and need to make love to him. Once again he took her breath away and no amount of logic could explain how being near him made her feel so out of control.

Steve climbed in beside her and started the engine, heading down the road leaving the house behind. Favor felt ecstatic. She was finally getting to go out like a real couple. She could hardly contain herself. She was overjoyed. Ahead was the gate with the Rainbow Moor sign hanging over it.

"So where are you taking me? Are we going out to dinner someplace? I'm so excited."

"You'll see, beautiful."

Just before the gate Steve shifted into four wheel drive and turned off the road, proceeding across the open fields. Favor, confused, became progressively upset. "What's going on? Why did we leave the road? I thought we were going someplace nice to eat and maybe do some dancing."

"We'll have something to eat and if you want to dance, we can dance as well."

"Where are we going? Steve, I want to go to a nice restaurant and enjoy being out around other people. I need a social life. Why do we have to live like this?"

"Favor, I'm really trying to make this a special and memorable day. Please let me. I've really put a lot into this day."

The look on Steve's face was puzzling. He had an unmistakable need and no matter what she felt he had his own agenda. Tears welled up in Favor's eyes and threatened to spill down her cheeks, but she held them back. Somehow she sensed this day was unlike any other day and a feeling of urgency hung heavy in the air. Why was this day so important to him? A sudden overwhelming need to run from him was coupled by an incredible desire for him. Her soul silently screamed. Tired of this emotional roller coaster, her life racing out of control like a train about to de-rail, like a bad dream she couldn't wake from, she held tight to the small amount of sanity she still possessed. The feelings were agonizing and her heart cried out for relief.

Steve stopped the truck and his eyes pleaded with her to trust and accept him and everything around her suddenly felt like she was in a glass bubble looking out, trapped forever. With a defeated sinking feeling she nodded her head trying to find her voice again. The pleading in his eyes seemed to be replaced with relief and he leaned in and gently kissed her. He withdrew for a moment and then leaned over and kissed her passionately as his hand tenderly caressed her breast for a moment. Slowly he turned his attention back to the truck and began driving again.

They made their way over the grassy terrain towards a low mountainous region where Steve stopped and parked the truck. He got out and walked around to Favor's door, opened it and reached out for her hand. Reluctantly she placed her hand in his and stepped out. Walking along a narrow path in a slightly wooded area, the path wound around through an outcropping of trees and rocks which opened up into a lush green area with a tropical atmosphere. This part of the path was abundant with beautiful flowers and ferns lining the pathway. Favor heard the sound of water and looking up ahead she saw a magnificent little waterfall which spilled into a small pond with crystal clear water. Every few feet Steve had placed a tiki torch on each side of the path leading up to and around the pond. At the forefront of the pond he had assembled a small archway. Cloud was there, standing guard over everything. Steve greeted him patting his head telling him what a good boy he was. Then he said, "Truck. Go to the truck, Cloud."

Between the arch and the pond was what looked like a small bed blanketed in white. At one side of the arch was a small table. Steve uncovered the table to reveal two trays with strawberries, kiwi, pineapple, more delicate pastries and truffles. A second table held a vase of flowers, two glasses and a bottle of champagne. The area was like an emerald isle and breathtaking. Favor looked around in disbelief. "Do you like it?" She turned to him with an astonished look of awe and wonder. Too amazed to speak she only nodded. A smile of approval creased Steve's lips. Reaching behind some ferns he pushed a button on a portable CD player and the most beautiful Costa Rican music began to play. The music filled the air wrapping them in unseen arms as it enveloped them. It reverberated off the rock walls and waterfall, bouncing back as it surrounded them. Leaning down his lips found hers as he slipped his arms around her in a tight embrace. The sweetness and tenderness of his kiss made her feel drunk. Releasing her he turned and opened the bottle of champagne, poured it into the two glasses and handed one to her. Taking the other in his hand he raised his glass and made a toast to the two of them. Steve took her hand and led her to sit on the edge of the bed. Together they drank champagne and ate the sweet delicacies.

"Tonight will be a full moon. I thought it would be romantic to lay here under the stars and watch the moon come up. Does our date meet your approval?"

Like a kid in a candy store, Steve's eyes twinkled and she couldn't help but smile. "You planned all of this for me. That's why you locked me in my room so you could get it all ready."

"So it meets your approval?"

"Yes, of course it does."

"I wanted it to be special and memorable. I started planning this a long time ago." Steve stopped a moment reaching for the bottle of champagne he poured Favor another glass watching her intently as she sipped from her glass. After she drank the second glass he poured yet another. "Steve, slow down. I'm beginning to feel a little tipsy."

"Nothing wrong with that," he said as he stood. "Come over here." Taking her hand he led her to stand under the archway. "I thought this would be a perfect time and place to exchange our wedding vows."

Did she hear him correctly, wedding vows? "Steve, you have to have a minister to get married legally, and witnesses. You don't have any of that so it wouldn't be a real marriage."

"I arranged for the marriage license and a marriage by proxy with two witnesses. I had to use a little trickery and a bit of monetary persuasion, but I was able to get signatures. Even though I did it a little on the shady side, I managed to make it legal."

"When you say shady, what do you mean?"

"You really don't want to know. Now why don't we get started with the ceremony?"

Without waiting for a response he withdrew a piece of paper from his pocket and handed it to Favor. On it he had written 'her' wedding vows to him. "Read these vows to me."

Her hands were trembling so much that the paper in her hands shook and made a funny crackling sound. Tears blurred her eyes so she couldn't see the words. Steve reached down and held both of her hands tight. "Favor, you need to say them." Still unable to see or speak the words Steve spoke again. "Favor I'm waiting." His voice was stern and commanding.

"I can't see the words."

"Then you can repeat them after me." With that he took the page and began.

"Before God, His angels and all of nature, I Favor Durand, take you Steven Mitchell to be my lawful husband and companion from this day forward unto death and for all eternity. I will be your devoted soul mate and love you all the days of my life. I do so pledge to you this day."

The words were repeated in but a whisper. She agonized and barely recognized her own voice as she struggled with each and every word. Her body trembled as she struggled to keep her composure. Why was she even saying these words? She should have refused to say them, but instead here she was repeating what he told her to say. Was it fear of his reaction if she didn't? Was it the champagne? Had he put something in it?

And then it was his turn. He raised her chin up with his hand forcing her to look in his eyes as he spoke. "I Steven Mitchell, before God, His Angels and all of nature, take you Favor Durand, to be my lawful wife and companion from this day forward unto death and for all eternity. I will be your devoted soul mate and love you all the days of my life. I do so pledge to you this day." Favor noticed a slight hesitation when he said the part, about death. For a moment a slight look of sadness crossed his brow and clouded his eyes. From his pocket he pulled a set of wedding rings and put one on her left hand, instructing her to do the same for him. It was September 23, 1991, the eve of the full moon.

There was a pause and then he said, "Favor, you're my wife now." Favor barely heard his words, unable to look at him any longer, her eyes closed and as he released her chin her head dropped down. As she fought to hold back the tears Steven once again reached down and raised her chin up. Trying not to look at him the allure of his presence forced her to raise her eyes to his. Leaning down he took her into a firm embrace and kissed her. She suddenly realized he had reached around her and unzipped her dress. Trying to pull away, he held her tight as he let the dress slip to the ground. All the while he kept kissing her passionately. Her bra came loose and dropped to the ground. His hands were all over her and she felt him pulling at her slip. She pushed against his chest trying to move away as he struggled to slide it down her hips. Their lips parted and gasping she turned her head away. Through blurred eyes she reached down for her dress as she tried to turn and stumbled in a hurried retreat. Grabbing her from behind, holding her with one arm around her waist he pulled the slip the rest of the way down and it too fell to the ground. Now with only a tiny pair of white satin and lace panties on, he lifted her up, swung her around and dropped her onto the bed. Leaning over her body he quickly pulled her shoes and her panties off of her body, leaving her naked, as she struggled to free herself.

"It's our wedding night Favor, don't spoil it." What was he saying, don't spoil it. How dare he? This wasn't the way it was supposed to be. Of course they'd made love, but this was different. She was supposed to feel happy. She'd said she would marry him, but not like this. Why had she said the vows? She stopped struggling as her body stiffened. The effects of the champagne made her head spin. She stared at him and with eyes locked on each other he quickly took off his own clothes. Feeling overpowered and lightheaded she struggled to stay focused. Running a hand down her body he probed her inner thigh finding the delicate, sensitive place that set her body on fire. Feeling her begin to respond he climbed onto the bed and entering her body with his. She moaned as she responded to the desire. Night came bathing them in soft moonlight and the glow of the tiki torches.

When they had fulfilled their need Steve rose, picked her up and carried her towards the waterfall. Slowly he stepped into the cold clear water and lowered himself into the pond with Favor still in his arms. He set her on her feet and pulled her towards the waterfall. Together they stood under its flow as it tumbled over their bodies, all the while Steve explored every curve and tender spot on her body, making her beg for more. She could hear his voice as he encouraged her to go with it and let her body reach that magnificent ecstasy that only love making can bring.

When she was done he kissed her and led her out of the pond. Behind a large flat rock he reached down and pulled out a plastic bag from which he pulled two large white towels. He'd thought of everything. Wrapping one around Favor, another around himself he led her to lie back down on the bed. Steven cradled Favor in his arms as they watched the bright silvery moon rise higher into the night sky.

The CD player had long since stopped playing, replaced by the soft sounds of the night. An owl hooted and the repetitive sound of crickets echoed as they played their night songs. Their song became reminiscent of something long ago. As sleep began to pull its veil over Favor, pictures in her mind, recollections of the past began to drift through her memories. Like sheer draperies seemingly unattached and blowing in the summer breeze and fluffy white clouds slowly stretching out across the sky until they broke apart and become so thin that they disappear, so were Favor's memories becoming. Though they were fading, she tried hard to hold onto the emotions and senses they brought to her. It felt like they were becoming buried and she somehow knew she needed to hold onto them at all cost or lose her mind and will forever. Her mind was telling her, "Hold onto the feelings, hold onto the senses. You mustn't lose them. They are your lifeline." Favor had drifted off to sleep. The familiar memories were becoming faded and dim. There was no logic or sensible order to the visions in her brain and her tethered heart called out to the memories begging them not to go as they drifted farther and farther off into the distance like the mournful sound of a coyote so far away it could barely be heard. If you didn't dare to breathe you might still be able to hear its lonesome call. But if you breathed, the sound of your own breathing would drown out the faint sound. And so Favor's night passed with its disquieting requiem.

The familiar sounds of morning and the soft particles of radiant energy from a beam of the early morning sun fell across Favor's cheek as the gentle light warmed her face. She stirred as the nearby sound of movement alerted her. Opening her eyes she began to focus on her surroundings and slowly she began to gather her senses. Looking around she discovered she was in her own room and was wearing a tiny white negligee. She'd never seen it before and realized Steve had to have dressed her in it. Her body began to tremble as she began to recall the events of the previous day. But then doubts began to creep into her mind. Was it just a dream or had the events surfacing in her memory actually occurred. Was part of it real and part of it a dream? As she sat upright in the bed the door to her room opened and Steve walked in carrying a tray with a bud vase holding a single red rose, hot tea, toast, bacon, eggs and sautéed asparagus. The tray also held silver utensils and a crisp white linen napkin. Steve smiled and said, "Good morning, Mrs. Mitchell."

Chapter 17

Had she heard him right? Did he just call her Mrs. Mitchell? "What did you call me?"

"Mrs. Mitchell, I called you Mrs. Mitchell, of course. Don't tell me you don't remember our wedding day? That would crush me." His eyes were teasing. "However, you did have a few drinks last night. But you performed very well, just as I expected you would. You couldn't get enough of me and you just about wore me out."

Favor's cheeks flushed with embarrassment even though she could not recall the entire evening. Trying to keep her composure she said, "I remember falling asleep in your arms on a white couch like bed. So how did I get back here and dressed in this?" She pointed to the tiny negligee she was wearing.

"Baby Doll, I had to put something on you since you were stark naked."

Infuriated she could feel the anger begin to burn. How dare he insinuate she had taken her own clothes off, she remembered him unzipping her dress and pulling off her clothes. It was all coming back and she looked at him with fiery eyes. "You took my clothes off and I'd be willing to bet you drugged me as well."

"Favor, Sweetheart, yesterday was our wedding day, the most beautiful day of our lives together and here you are speaking in that tone and acting angry. It got cold out there so I carried you to the truck and brought you back to the house. You cuddled in my arms the rest of the night. Now please, let's enjoy our day." With that he turned and climbed onto the bed where he straddled her body. She drew back, but his lips found hers and he kissed her passionately. Then he drew back and with a twinkle in his eye he looked at her and in a teasing manner said, "We'll make love later, for now let's eat before it gets cold."

Though her anger made her not want to eat, she had to admit she was hungry. Not knowing what to say to Steve they ate in silence. When they were done, Steve set the dishes aside and gathered her in his arms. "Now, Mrs. Mitchell, what shall we do today?" With the smell of his skin and the warmth of his body as he held her, she began to relax against him. He spoke in soft tones as he talked of their future together, all the while he stroked her hair, her cheek and down her body. She melted into him as he slid the night gown up. Yes she knew they were about to make love and she could not resist him.

They spent most of the day in bed. He made her laugh as he told her silly stories of his childhood. In the evening they took a walk and watched the sunset. He held her hand and they walked side by side like two people in love. Could it be that they were in love and by getting married they had sealed that love? The past was gradually slipping away along with the memories. But how could that be? How long had she been at Rainbow Moor? It seemed so long but she knew even though she'd lost track of time it couldn't have been so long that the memories had faded. They were becoming vague and distant. Sitting on the porch loveseat, Steve spoke of the fast approaching winter months.

"This winter is expected to come early and it is expected to be a harsh winter. We'll want to be completely prepared for it. The winters up here can be very beautiful and fun. It's like a wonderland when the snows come and everything is white, but if you're not prepared, it can be miserable. I think we have enough of everything we need and then some. We should be just fine. But I do want to go over all our provisions with you and make sure you know where everything is and how to use the generator and everything you need to know about how to take care of ourselves. Then we can settle down to having some winter fun."

Just as Steven had said, winter was fast approaching. It was now mid-October. The past few months had pasted quickly. They'd spent the last couple of months canning and preserving everything imaginable. Corn, green beans, peas and more filled the jars that lined the pantry shelves. They'd made strawberry, blackberry, loganberry, raspberry, Marian berry and gooseberry preserves. They'd dug up enough potatoes to feed a small army and canned peaches, apricots, pears, apples and applesauce lined the shelves along with tomatoes, homemade spaghetti sauce and salsa, all of which had come from their garden and fruit trees. In the cold storage hung onions and garlic braided together by their stalks. Large baskets were filled with potatoes, carrots and squash. Smoked fish and jerky had been sealed in air tight bags, as well as walnuts and almonds. The freezer was filled with beef and venison, carrots and more corn and other vegetables. There was plenty of flour, sugar, oatmeal, cornmeal, yeast for baking bread and a numerous assortment of spices and other staples. They had worked hard to get prepared for the winter and had everything they needed.

Favor had just finished making her first butternut squash soup and Steve was quite pleased with the results. She beamed with pride as he took her in his arms and told her how good it tasted and how proud he was of her. It was amazing how much she had learned to do in such a short period of time.

The firewood was stacked neatly in the wood shed and the barn was full of hay, and grain for the animals. They had moved the cattle down to the fenced in pasture near the corrals close to the house where they would be safe from hungry predators and where they had a large shelter enclosed along one side allowing them room to move around but a way to get out of the inclement weather. The horses spent the nights in the barn and would be kept in if a storm approached. Cloud slept in the barn most nights now, but at times would venture in to lay in front of the fireplace beside Favor. Steve smiled at the way the two of them had become so close. He remembered how fearful she was of Cloud when he first brought her to Rainbow Moor. They had kept one cow for milk and butter, plenty for just the two of them. He had taught Favor how to make butter. She had been fascinated the first time she watched him make it. He wouldn't tell her what he was making, but kept telling her to "just watch". The longer he whipped it the thicker it became and the color began to turn a light yellow.

A large oversized, very secure, heated chicken coop had been constructed which housed 16 chickens. They had been laying eggs for a while now so they had plenty of eggs for cooking and eating. Steve said by heating it, they would lay eggs all winter.

Favor was becoming used to the simple self-sufficient life they had established for themselves and listened intently to everything Steve told her. She laughed at his stories and reveled in his adventures, hanging on his every word. Each night after the animals were bedded down in the barn they would cook dinner together and then spend the evenings talking, reading or playing table games. Some nights they would go for a short walk, but the days were growing so much shorter and colder that more time was spent in front of a crackling fire instead.

By November the first snow had already come. Favor woke one morning to a strange eerie quiet. At first she couldn't figure out what was so different about that morning. She rose slowly from the bed to see Steve standing at the bedroom window.

"What is it, Steve? Everything is so quiet. It feels scary."

"Come here, Baby. Come look out the window. We have our first snow. That's the quiet you feel." Favor slipped out of the bed and over to him where he pulled her in front of him and wrapped his arms around her as they looked out onto the first snow of the season, their first snow together. The scene before her was like something you'd seen in a greeting card. Fresh, soft fluffs of snow covered the ground while more snowflakes continued to drift slowly down.

"Oh, it's so beautiful!" She spoke in a whisper. It was so quiet that it felt like you had to speak in a whisper, like a reverence or respect for the awe of what nature had brought to them.

"It is beautiful, isn't it? It's almost as beautiful as you." Turning her gently to face him he looked down at her. "Favor, I love you so much."

His words, so simply put, for the first time felt intensely sincere. Looking into his eyes her heart felt full. "Steven, I love you, too. I really do." Steven knew this time she meant it with all her heart. At that moment they both knew their lives were now one. The love they both felt was as pure as the newly fallen snow. Nothing else mattered but being together. Softly their lips met. This kiss was not passionate and sexual. Instead it was a kiss of love, contentment and commitment. Her heart felt at peace as she allowed the past to fade away. All she cared about was being with him, sharing his love and his life.

It seemed they had managed to slip back in time, to separate themselves from the rat race of the modern world and had learned how to live off the land. Most people would say they were living in the dark ages, but they felt safe and content. They were oblivious to whatever was happening in the outside world. Steve said when springtime arrived he would go to the city and catch up on the news. He would have to check on his businesses and get supplies. He had told her that he had informed his CEO that he would be on a sabbatical and would not be in contact with them for several months, but that he would return in the spring and go over the business records. And he had promised Favor she would accompany him on at least one of his trips. She was excited about traveling with him. But for now they would stay on the mountain and ride out the winter in their safe haven.

Though the long hours of gardening, canning and preserving were done, there was still a great deal to do each day. With the days being shorter it meant getting things done in less time. Steve walked the fence line on a regular basis to check that there were no damaged posts or broken fence lines. Cattle have a tendency to be hard on fencing and since the cattle were used to roaming the open fields and meadows it was necessary to keep a close eye on them and the fencing. Due to the colder nights the horses and the one milk cow spent more time in the barn making it necessary to clean the stalls each day. With the days becoming increasingly colder, firewood had to be brought in several times each day as well to have enough to keep them warm through the night. Favor found herself spending more time cooking and baking. She'd never done many of these domestic things before, but was becoming quite proficient at each new task. When Steven left her alone while he worked outside she would get out one of the many recipe books he had on hand and try something new. He was never sure what she would come up with but found she had quite a knack for cooking and managed some very sophisticated dishes. Sometimes she talked of a meal she had eaten at some little Italian or French restaurant and would go searching for that recipe. At times she had to improvise, but Steve was always pleased with the results. It sometimes worried him that talking about those faraway places would make her homesick and sad, but if it did, she never let on. She seemed content and his most favorite part of the day were the evenings when she would cuddle up close to him while reading or talking. The more time spent together the closer they became.

Even more surprising to him was her knack for creating beautiful things out of almost nothing. The table was always decorated and set in a welcome way. It was no wonder that she had become an interior designer. At times she would casually state something like, "I could have done it better if I had a glue gun or some soft burgundy velvet fabric would have been nice." Then she would smile at him and say, "But that's ok. It was more of a challenge this way and I think it turned out ok."

It was those times when taking her away from her old life tugged at his heart strings and he wondered if he had done the wrong thing when he took her away, yes kidnapped her. What if he had gotten to know her in a conventional way? Would she have been willing to go away with him and still love him? Did she love him because she had no other choice and had just resigned herself to this life, hard as it was? He had a destiny to fulfill and taking her had been necessary.

There were days when he became angry with himself doubting his decisions. At those times he would go off somewhere outside and work on the property leaving her alone sometimes for hours. On one of those days, Favor needed him to help her move some furniture so that she could clean behind it and she was in the mood for rearranging as well. Favor noticed he was acting moody and not wanting to talk. She wondered if he was not feeling well and told him it was ok and that she would do it some other time. This made him angry. Why did she have to be so agreeable and nice? In the past she'd challenge him or be insistent, which often lead to a bit of a standoff which he normally won.

"Damn it, Favor, I'm here now so let's just get it done." The moment the words left his mouth he felt extremely remorseful for what he had said and how he had spoken to her. Worse yet was the shock, dismay and hurt he saw in her eyes. She didn't speak at first and then softly said, "Excuse me, I need a moment alone," and then hurried out the front door into the cold morning air. She didn't even take a jacket with her. Steve just stood in the middle of the room staring at the closed door expecting her to be gone for 'only a moment or two'. But first five minutes, then ten minutes passed. Twenty and then thirty minutes and she still had not come back into the house. It was time to swallow his pride and go out, find her and apologize. Donning his jacket and grabbing one of her jackets as well he stepped out into the brisk air. He thought he would find her sitting on the front porch but she wasn't there. A steady snow had been falling all morning and had covered her foot prints. Not sure of which way she had gone, he assumed she would head out to the horses where he expected he would find her talking openly out loud and grooming them as she often did. Cloud would be laying nearby watching and all would be well. To his surprise she was nowhere to be found. "Cloud, where's Favor? Where'd she go, boy?" He cocked his head to one side as if to say, "Why are you asking me? I've been here guarding the horses, doing my job." Then he plopped down and laid his head between his front paws, let out a sigh and closed his eyes.

"I get it, you're going to take her side and ignore me. Fine. I deserve it, but it's cold out here and snowing harder and she doesn't have a coat on." With no choice he headed back to the house to see if she'd headed back inside. Wandering through the house he called her name and searched each room. Back outside he checked the chicken coop and other out buildings. Each place he looked for her footprints but found none. The snow was falling heavier now and the wind had picked up. In the distance he heard the cattle lowing as they moved up from the lower pasture towards the shelter where they would be safe from the increasing wind and snow. Maybe Favor was herding them up this direction. That had to be it.

He headed back to the barn to get the tractor and load up a good supply of hay to put in the shelter and some straw to lay on the ground for warmth. When he reached the shelter the cattle had already arrived and were anxious to eat and bed down under the covered area out of the wind and snow. He put the hay in the feeders and spread the straw on the ground. Favor wasn't there. He looked for her footprints among the cattle's prints, but did not see any. It was now approaching two hours since she had walked out the front door. The jacket he had grabbed was not one of his heavier coats and the cold was turning bitter. He was not wearing boots for the snow and his feet were getting wet and cold. He needed to go back to the house and put on some warmer clothing. Surely she would be back in the house by now.

Back at the house an eerie quiet seemed to emanate throughout. The fire in the fire place was burning low so he added more wood to the fire to get it going again and warm up the house. Maybe she'd gone upstairs to rest? Taking the steps two at a time he rushed up only to find she wasn't in either bedroom. Concern creased his brow as he once again hurried down the steps. Removing his damp shoes and socks he put on a dry pair and warm boots feeling guilty all the while that she was out in the cold with no jacket or even a sweater. He put on a heavy warm jacket and grabbed one for Favor as well.

Out on the porch he hesitated for a moment, trying to figure out which way to go and where she might have gone. Suddenly he looked off in the distance toward the arbor near the pond. He strained to see through the falling snow. Was that Favor huddled up on the bench under the arbor? How was it that he had not looked in that direction before? Had she been there earlier? And why wouldn't she come back into the house instead of holing up there. Damn that woman was stubborn sometimes.

Hurrying down the path to the arbor he found her curled up, shivering with her eyes closed. When he touched her shoulder her eyes opened, but didn't seem to focus. "Favor, you need to get up and get in the house. You'll freeze out here. I'm sorry for what I said."

Trying to focus she looked at him. "Can't."

"This is no time for you to be stubborn. Now get up and let's get you inside."

"No, I really can't. I tried to. I fell and hurt my ankle. I crawled this far, but it hurt so bad I couldn't go any farther, and I was too cold."

"Why didn't you call me?"

"I tried but the wind, the wind carried my voice away."

Carefully he looked over her ankle. It was swollen and bruising. He hoped it was not broken. Wrapping the jacket around her he lifted her into his arms and trudged carefully back to the house. Inside he set to work, getting her warmed up and checking her ankle. It appeared to be sprained. Keeping it elevated he put an ice pack on it making her as comfortable as he could. Frustrated he looked at her, "Favor, I don't know what I'm going to do with you. Every time we have a disagreement you run off and then things happen. I need to know that you are going to be ok if I am not here to take care of you."

Sitting upright she glared at Steve. "How dare you act like this is my fault! You started this so maybe we should finish it here and now. I wouldn't have gone off outside if you hadn't been such a jerk. What did I do to deserve being yelled at like that? I worked so hard for you all summer long. I never complained and I did everything you told me to do and then some. It's always about you, Steven. What about me? You act like a damn dictator and I have no choice in the matter, yet I love you and do whatever you teach me without complaining."

"I'm sorry, Baby. I was having a bad day."

"No, Steven Mitchell, you don't get to use that excuse. That is not a legitimate reason or acceptable excuse. What was so bad about your day that it gave you the right to unload on me and be so cruel and rude? And damn you, your answer better be good!"

"Ok, but you have to hear me out without interrupting."

"Always your way, Steven. Always your way." Her sarcasm cut deep, but he knew he deserved every word.

"Not this time, Favor. Honest. It's just that if you don't hear me out without interrupting I won't have the guts to explain it to you and finish what you deserve to know."

Still in pain it made her anger more intense and she braced herself to keep her mouth shut till he had a chance to say what he wanted to. But then she was prepared to unload on him like she was holding two guns. "Fine, you'd better start talking and fast." She could see the pain in his eyes but at this point she really didn't care if he felt bad or not.

"When I see how you can take the littlest thing that looks totally worthless and make it into something elegant and beautiful, I get to feeling extremely guilty for taking you away from your Interior Design career and your friends and happy life. I had planned all this for so long and I was so obsessed with my own destiny and making it happen that I never thought about the effect it was having on you, yet you have become everything I dreamed you would be and more. You are fulfilling my destiny and I have taken your destiny away from you."

His words were anything but what she had expected to hear. She was stunned beyond belief and felt the pain he was feeling. "Steven, I don't understand this destiny thing you keep talking about, but I do know that you are my destiny and yes I didn't want to come here and I wish you had done things differently, but the fact is I am madly in love with you and I believe in our love. So stop letting this guilt eat you up. Someday we can go back and visit everyone. Maybe this could be our summer home and the rest of the time we could have a place in town close to people. Our lives won't and can't ever be the same, but we will always be together. Don't ever doubt my love for you again and don't be afraid to talk to me. I need you.

I don't want to live without you." Relief flooded his body as he wrapped his arms around her and tears flowed down his face. The fear of losing her no longer a threat.

"Steven, what is this destiny you referred to?"

She felt his body stiffen, "Could we talk about that another time, I am so worn out and tired and I just want to lay down beside you and rest awhile. I don't think I can talk anymore."

Favor sensed something like a dark cloud hanging over Steven. Yet somehow she also realized she needed to trust him and let it go for now. Whatever it was, it seemed to make him tense. She felt it in his body the way he stiffened when she asked the question. Something or someone had a strange hold over him and it was greater than anything else in his life. She decided not to press him. Besides she too was much too tired and the pain in her ankle made her feel a bit nauseated. Best to let it go for now. They both needed to relax and get some rest before the evening chores had to be done.

Chapter 18

After viewing the body of the young deceased woman Adam realized he had been running from everything near and dear to his heart to avoid any more hurt. He'd gotten lost in his work to avoid his own feelings instead of dealing with it and had pushed everyone and everything familiar away so he would not be reminded of his failure. He now recalled the words of Ms. Ellie. She'd told him to let go of the guilt. He hadn't let go of the guilt, but instead had buried it deeper and in turn buried his feelings. Seeing the girl made him realize what he'd done. Instead of letting go of the guilt he had become bitter using work as an excuse rather than facing his feelings and getting on with life, he got lost in his work so he could avoid life.

Houston, Cindy and Adam walked out of the coroner's office together. When they reached the car, Houston turned to Adam, "That was a pretty intense moment in there. You know for Cindy and I, living in Favor's house has not been easy but her dad really wants someone in there who cares about Favor. He doesn't believe she's dead and wants to be sure her place is in the hands of people who care about her. It's been a really long time since the three of us have been together. Favor brought us together as friends and once again it is because of her we are standing here now. How about the three of us going to dinner together? We could talk about old times and maybe sort out our feelings about all of this. We've never done that. It seems like after she disappeared we all avoided saying what we really needed to say to protect one another's feelings. But instead it just separated us."

Adam stood there, hesitating. It wasn't because he needed to get back to his work, but because he knew he needed to be honest with his old friends and not be afraid to say how he felt and what he believed. Seeing his hesitation Cindy spoke up. "Adam, please come with us. We all need to talk about it and how we feel rather than avoiding the subject and judging each other. We may feel differently, but it doesn't change the fact that we all love Favor and each other."

"Yeah, I think you're right. We've avoided and skirted around our feelings rather than allowing each other to be our support even if we don't think the same."

They decided to head on over to the local Eel River Brewery. It was a place they had all like to go as a group. Adam hadn't been there since before Favor disappeared. They were able to get a corner table away from the hub of things. The brewery was a sports bar and could be pretty noisy, but it still was a place you could go and not feel like you had to eat and get out of the way for someone else to take your place. A lot of regulars would hang out there for a couple of hours or more watching sports and shooting the breeze. They took a little time to order and then Houston decided to initiate the conversation.

"Adam, I need to apologize to you. I wasn't very supportive of you when you were looking for Favor. I thought you were nuts and obsessed and when you were in that accident I realized we could have lost you as well. I knew you'd been out looking for a lead to what happened to her the day of your accident. You were really a true friend to Favor to keep looking against all odds. You're the best kind of friend anyone could want. Cindy and I could have chosen to live someplace else together rather than in Favor's house. Her dad really want us there and for a long time I hated the daily reminder that it is really Favor's house and not ours. But as the months have passed I've become comfortable there and somehow I've known in my heart it is where we belong."

Cindy nodded and agreed with Houston. "I've felt very peaceful there and somehow I feel she is alive. I've not felt anything more than that. In my heart I know there is a reason why she hasn't found her way back to us, but someday she will. Maybe she has amnesia or just can't get away, but somehow I sense through her home, that she is alive somewhere."

Houston looked at Cindy with surprise. Adam looked relieved. "Cindy, how come all this time we've been living there together you've never told me that?"

"Because I figured because you believe she's dead you'd think I was nuts and treat me the way you treated Adam. I didn't want to lose you. So I respected how you felt and kept my thought to myself."

"Go figure, I was afraid to believe she could be alive, because then we might find out she wasn't and that would make accepting her death even harder."

It was Adam's turn to speak, "We all handle loss in our own ways. For you, Houston, accepting her to be dead was the best way for you to handle the loss and you may well someday be proven to be right. But for me, like Cindy, I believe she is alive. I only hope this guy who took her has not abused her or if he has that she has figured out a way to survive the abuse. I believe I have the name of her kidnapper. I felt I was getting close before the accident, but after the accident and the winter weather coming on, I got really discouraged and felt I had let her down. Everything I've heard about this guy is that he's a really good guy, that he's talented and artistic and a really hard worker. If that's the case, he has either fooled a lot of people or there is something very unusual about him. I met a little old lady named Ms. Ellie at the Dinsmore store who recognized the photo of that guy I took a picture of in that green truck. I learned a few things about him and got really discouraged after the accident so immerse myself in work to avoid dealing with the discouragement. After tonight I think I'm ready to start back on the search. And Houston, I respect what you feel even if I don't agree."

"Well, if there is anything I or Cindy can do to help you just ask. Sooner or later we hopefully will have some answers and we can all be at peace."

"Actually I could use some help doing some research on this guy." Adam proceeded to tell Houston and Cindy what he had learned and what he needed to find leads on.

They talked for a couple of hours finding peace in sharing their feelings and as the time passed the old bonds between them began to grow strong again. It felt good to be laughing and reminiscing about old times, the things they'd done together and the feelings they had experienced during those times. They talked of places they'd gone and what they'd like to do in the future, and of personal relationships and the bonds that joined them together as friends. For the first time they were able to be completely open with their feelings and not be afraid of being judged. It was a time of awakening for them and a time of healing and renewal. Adam decided it would be good to drive out soon and see Ms. Ellie. The weather had been really bad of late, but as soon as possible Cindy and Houston agreed to accompany him on a drive out to see her. After all, Adam had promised Ms. Ellie he would stop by from time to time.

A week later, the three of them decided to take the drive out to Dinsmore and the Dinsmore Store to see Ms. Ellie. When they arrived and walked into the store, Adam was surprised to see it looked different. It looked more modern and had a different feel about it. A gentleman who looked to be in his early fifties was tending the store. He greeted them and seemingly expected them to go about shopping for whatever they came into the store to buy. Adam stood there looking around so the man asked him what he might be needing today. Adam looked at him with a puzzled look on his face. Then he said to the man, "I was here a few months back and I met Ms. Ellie. I promised her I'd stop back by and see her next time I was in the area. Is she here today?"

"Ms. Ellie? Is this some kind of joke? Ms. Ellie was my mother and she's been gone for several years now."

"What do you mean gone? Did she move away? I spoke to her only a few months ago."

"Look man that's not possible. You must be mistaken about the name. My mother was the founder and owner of this store till the day she died, but like I said, she's been gone, dead, for several years."

"No I'm not mistaken and what did you do to this place. It looks different and it feels different. It doesn't feel the same as when Ms. Ellie was talking to me."

"Look. See that picture on the wall? That's my mother Ms. Ellie standing here in the store when she was alive. Wouldn't let me make any upgrades as long as she was 'in charge', was the way she put it." He pointed respectfully to a picture hanging nearby. "She was a real firecracker and the way she ran the store worked for her. I respected that."

Adam stood staring at the picture. He turned to Houston and Cindy, "I don't know what's going on here or what this means, but that's the woman I spoke to and that's what the store looked like."

At that moment, the front door to the store opened and shut, but there was no one there. Then they heard the door lock latch and the open sign suddenly flipped over to the closed side without anyone touching it. The four of them stood for a moment staring at the door and sign and then at each other. The store owner suddenly felt a tug on his sleeve. No one was there and then he felt someone or something pulling his head down and felt a soft kiss on his cheek. The three looked at him as his head went down and then back up and wondered what the hell he was doing. He looked pale and in shock. A moment later Adam felt a gentle hand on his arm and distinctly heard the voice of Ms. Ellie whisper in his ear, "You're doing just fine, young Adam Jennings." And then the closed sign flipped back to the open, the door unlatched and once again the door opened and closed gently. The distinct smell of lilac permeated the air as they stood motionless not sure whether to move or not.

"Mother said I should be polite." Then choked, "What just happened here?"

Adam stood smiling as a peace enveloped him. "Do you smell the lilac?" They all looked at one another then back at him. "I remember Ms. Ellie smelled of sweet lilacs."

Houston looked at him, "What the hell are you smiling about? Whatever just happened here is really creeping me out." Cindy stood clinging to Houston unable to speak.

"Damn it, that's true. Lilac was her favorite scent. Mother is probably trying to punish me for modernizing her store, but why wait till now to do it?" He stood looking ashamed, bewildered and scared.

Then they heard the clear distinct voice of Ms. Ellie say, "The store looks very nice, Son. Your dad would have been proud. Now you be nice to this young man. He'll be needing your services in the future. I'll be moving on now. My work is finally done here." A soft gentle breeze swept through the store and with it the smell of lilac. The scent lingered a while and then softly faded away.

As the four of them stood afraid to move, a woman entered the store and as she passed by them she said, "Oo-oo! I smell fresh lilac. Reminds me of your mother, Jake." Turning to Cindy she said, "I'm sure it must be you, none of these gentlemen would be wearing lilac. Jake's mother always wore lilac."

Stunned, and not knowing what to say Cindy managed to meekly say, "Yes, mam."

Houston and Cindy wanted to leave. No, they wanted to run out of the store, but for some strange reason they found themselves unable to move, grounded where they stood. Jake managed to act like he was busy checking something for them and when the lady had made her purchase and left he decided to close the store early and lock everything up. He looked at his three visitors who were as confused as he was and said, "There's a little burger bar not far from here with a bar next door. I think I need a drink. Anyone care to join me?" They agreed they could all use a cold one and Jake let them out of the store while he took care of the register and locked up. Jake really didn't expect them to be waiting for him when he came out, but they had waited. It seemed they all needed answers or at least they needed to clear the air about what had happened.

"If we tell anyone about this they'll think we've lost our minds." Houston was saying.

"Houston, I know you heard the voice too. You can't deny it. She told me, 'You're doing just fine, Adam Jennings!'."

"What did she mean by that?"

"She knows I've been searching for Favor. I think she was saying to keep looking, and I was doing fine. Maybe she was saying I'm on the right track. Maybe she meant I was even getting close."

"Favor? Who's Favor?"

Cindy turned to Jake. "She's a friend of ours who was kidnapped in June. Adam has been searching for her and he said he'd found a possible lead, after he spoke to your mom, or what he thought was your mom. He was in an accident that same day and was laid up for some time. He has just gotten back to picking up where he left off in the search."

"I believe her disappearance is connected to a man with the name of Steven Mitchell. Ms. Ellie kept referring to him as Little Stevie."

"Hell, I remember Steve Mitchell. Nice kid. Lost his parents when he was just a teenager. Let me think." He was silent a moment as he thought. "Yeah I remember, his full name was Steven Lawrence Mitchell IV. Yep that was it. His mother was Lisa Mitchell. He was a fourth generation Mitchell. But he hasn't been around here for a number of years. I don't see how he could be linked to the disappearance of your friend."

"So you think my mother was a messenger to help you find this girl? Man I've never believed in this stuff, but tonight, well tonight made me feel like a scared little boy who'd had such a bad night mare that he wet the bed. It made me a believer even though I don't want to believe. My gut tells me my mother was sent to give you and I both a message and it came in loud and clear. I don't think I will ever be the same again. Part of me doesn't ever want to go into my store again and wants to sell the store, but somehow I think that would be a huge mistake and I would regret it later on. I sure as hell won't be telling anyone about this. It would be bad for business. Her message was damn clear to me. I just hope her 'work here' really is done. I don't think I could take another encounter like that."

The four of them had headed to the bar and had seated themselves at a table in a far corner and were talking in low voices so no one in the room could hear them. Adam filled Jake in on what had happened thus far and his encounter with Ms. Ellie. It was the first time he trusted an 'outsider' to know the story of his search.

They sat silent for a while thinking about what Jake had said and what had happened. It was like a dream they were all sharing or some movie they had all watched together, but instead of watching it they were part of it. They were the actors who were playing a part in a mystery but none of them had asked to play the part. Somehow they all knew they were bound to each other for life because of this experience. As terrified as they all felt, there was an awe about the whole incident. For Adam it was more. He felt a degree of peace knowing he was on the right track, but he also felt a degree of urgency that he couldn't put into words. He just knew time was of the essence and it was running out. Finding Favor would once again become his priority even if it meant his job.

"Ms. Ellie told me the Mitchell's used to have a place somewhere up in the mountains above Bridgeville or somewhere in between there and here. She said something about the old McClellan Mountain Road. Do you know anything about this place?"

"Yeah, I've heard quite a bit about it actually. I have an old mountain man friend who could tell you a lot more and knows that part of the country pretty well."

"Can you get me in contact with him?"

"Not likely till spring. He holds up in the mountains all winter and most likely won't be back down till the winter snow's thaw and he needs supplies. He gets his supplies, doesn't hang around long and then he heads back to the mountains where he has a cabin. Comes back down just before winter and then he's gone all winter long. Chances are he's gotten all his supplies for this year. There's a remote chance he might make another trip down the mountain before the heavy snows, being this is expected to be one of the coldest winters in years. He's a 'real' mountain man if you get my drift. Not just a want-to-be mountain man, he's the real deal. Spent a lot of time in the Alaska Wilderness, Canada, High Sierra's, Marble Mountains and the Alps. Took to staying in these parts because he's getting on in years and the winters are milder than they are in some of those other places. But he's the real deal alright. If anyone can help you find this place, he can. We call him Ol' "Smokey""

"Do you think he'd be willing to help?"

"He's a good man, bit of a loner. But if he decides he likes you and you win his trust he may be willing to help you. I got to tell you, he's pretty rough and if he decides he doesn't like you for even the smallest reason, then nothing will change his mind. In the meantime, I'd suggest you try to find out exactly where this place is. Go to the recorder's office and do some research. He's not going to do all your work for you, so you'd better have something to give him. He knows his way around, but he also respects other peoples land and around here, if you trespass on the wrong land, it could get you shot at or killed. Lot of pot growers around here now if you know what I mean."

"Look maybe if you show me on a map this McClellan Mountain Road and how to get to it, I could just go on up there and try to find this place myself without bothering anyone else."

"Are you crazy? You can't just go traipsing around in these mountains when you don't know where you're going and you don't know private land from Forest Service or Public Lands. People around here are not very tolerant about that kind of thing. There's been plenty of people who did and ended up on a missing person's list. You're going to have to wait the winter out. Besides from the look of you, you're not experience in wilderness survival of any sort."

"Speaking about winter, we really need to be heading back," Houston was saying. "There's supposed to be another heavy rain storm coming in tonight."

Jake stood up. "Yeah and that means snow in the higher elevations. We're expecting to get some more of the white stuff here tonight. Give me your name and number and I'll let you know when Smokey comes back down the mountain. He usually stays a couple of days before heading back. All the old timers around here know him and he usually stops in to pay them a visit before heading back and some of them get together to trade stories. I don't expect I'll see him any sooner than late March or as late as May."

Adam looked disappointed as they traded information. Jake noticed and told him to remember what Ms. Ellie had said and not to get discouraged. The three of them left Jake and headed back to Fortuna. Jake had been frank and straight forward. Adam liked that about him. He could see he was a good man and the experience they had all had that day was definitely one they wouldn't forget. He knew he had no choice but to wait until he was able to meet Smokey and hopefully he would help him.

Until then Adam needed to search the public records and see what he could find on Steven and Lisa Mitchell and their son as well as try to track down the aunt, Sadie Marks. He would search out what companies they owned, properties or anything else that might lead to Steven Mitchell, knowing there was a possibility the property might be held in the name of one of the companies or in the name of a Trust. By finding out this information he could possibly find out the exact location of the house in the mountains.

The three were quiet as they headed back towards the coast. Cindy couldn't keep quiet any longer. "What do you think about what happened back at that store and what it was? Adam, you didn't even seem to be scared. I was petrified."

"As much as I hate to admit it, I was. Adam, you were so calm? Have you had this happen before?"

"Hell no!! Damn, if I hadn't met her when I was there before I would have been more scared. But you have to understand, I carried on a conversation with her for a decent amount of time. I purchased a soft drink and some chips from her. I saw her in the flesh. At least it sure seemed like it was. There was nothing with my encounter with her that day that would have led me to believe it was anything more than a 'live' sweet little old lady I was talking to. When she touched my arm today and said I was doing just fine I was too shocked to be afraid. She remembered and called me by name and her touch wasn't like some cold, clammy, dead thing. It was soft and gentle and the smell of the lilacs was sweet and refreshing and it made me feel reassured and comforted."

"Man, I've heard of people having things like that happen, but never in my wildest imaginings did I believe them nor would I have ever expected to have anything like this happen to me. The things you see on TV always seem so fake and sensationalized. The encounters are never nice. They are always mean, ugly and annoying." Houston pulled off the side of the road and turned to look at Adam and Cindy. "It's got me really freaked out. I don't think I could ever go back there again."

"I want to." Cindy's words shocked Houston. "I need to, if only to reassure myself that it was a onetime thing and that she is gone. She said her 'work is done here'. I've heard of people's spirits not 'crossing over' to the other side because they still had something they had to do or they had a message they had to convey to a loved one and until they were able to do that they couldn't cross over."

"I think you're right. She had a message for me and Jake and now she can cross over."

Chapter 19

The brilliant gold, yellow and red colors of autumn had faded into the cold gray days of winter and the clean crisp white of the snow. Fruit and other deciduous trees were bare and empty. Tall redwoods and pines were heavily laden with snow. The once bright green and yellow grasses were buried under a blanket of white, and the birds were quiet and no longer sang their morning songs. Favor missed waking to their trill and chirpings. A sometimes eerie quiet invaded the landscape and Favor longed for the bright colors of spring. Warm puffs of smoke rose from the chimney their only source of heat. The sweet hickory smell drifted over the countryside giving the old ranch house a warm and welcoming feel.

Favor woke early one October morning. She had just gone down to put some coffee on. Steven woke to find her missing. He quickly headed down the stairs when he smelled the fresh coffee. In the kitchen he found Favor bent over the downstairs bathroom toilet vomiting. For the next month or more each and every morning she suffered the same fate of disgusting vomiting. Certain foods made her feel ill. Favor was newly pregnant and experiencing morning sickness. "I don't want to take nine months of this. I'm tired of being sick every day. We never talked about having kids. I'm not sure I want one and I don't know anything about babies." To her surprise he presented her with a book on pregnancy. In the evening cuddled together in front of the fireplace Steven read to her.

"Listen to this, 'in most cases morning sickness only lasts for a few weeks. In some rare cases it may last for the duration of the pregnancy.' See, you'll probably be over this in a matter of weeks."

"I wish I could feel as optimistic as you, but it's not you puking your guts out every morning. Did God do this to punish women or did He see it as some kind of joke?"

True to the book, a few short weeks later and the morning sickness had dissipated and Favor was feeling her normal energetic self again. Steven was so overjoyed at the prospect of a child that he doted over Favor constantly. She enjoyed the attention and pampering to a degree but sometimes it felt like he was smothering her. At times she would go to her room just to have some space and time to think. Steve realized she needed this time alone though he'd rather spend every moment with her.

When he went out to feed or do barn chores Steven would insist she stay inside. It made her feel anxious and bored. She missed the horses, the smell of hay, the sweat of their coats, the dry heavy smell of leather and the sweet smell of grain. Favor longed for the feel of their warm bodies and the softness of their noses, the gentle feel of their warm breath as they nuzzled close and blew into her hair, their unconditional trust and their massive yet gentle strength. Steven tried not to be gone long, but there were stalls to clean and horses to feed. The one milk cow had to be milked and the cattle had to be fed and the fencing checked regularly. There were eggs to gather and the chickens to feed. Occasionally after the main chores were done he would come back to the house and have her go with him to check the fencing. But he didn't like her out in the cold too much. One day after he left for the barn she quickly put on her snow gear and boots and followed him out to the barn. When he saw her standing there he started to tell her to get back in the house.

She looked at him with defiance and said, "I am not a baby. I am a grown, healthy woman who just happens to be pregnant. I miss my horses and I hate being cooped up inside all the time. It is not fair that you get to go out into the fresh air and I have to stay inside all the time. So for now on we do this together until I am not able to and then I will stay in. Until then, deal with it!" Her voice was unyielding and powerful.

From then on they were back to working as a team. Favor felt more content and enjoyed grooming the horses each day. Steven chided, "They don't need to be brushed every day. We didn't groom them every day before."

"I know they don't but since they have to be stuck in this barn and since I like doing it, I see no harm in it. Besides they enjoy it, too. Listen to how they talk to me when I come in."

"You spoil them too much."

"Oh, are you jealous?" She enjoyed teasing him. He could see she was right so there was no more mention of it. He rightly enjoyed her being there and watched how she interacted with the animals. To his surprise she even brushed the milk cow a little and the crazy cow seemed to like it. She never failed to amaze him. The simple pleasure of these moments filled Favor with a sweet contentment. Caring for these incredible animals filled her with amazement. The days of winter seemed less oppressive and smothering. To most of the world this life would be mundane, boring, commonplace, too routine and much too ordinary. It was anything but.

One winter day after coming out of the barn Favor stood quietly looking at the softness of a newly fallen snow. She marveled at how the snow sparkled and changed the countryside. Even the sounds and feel of their surroundings changed. The stillness and quiet could be felt deep inside the depth of your soul. Sounds that normally carried for a quarter mile now sounded strangely muffled and traveled only a few short yards away. She longed to hear the birds and the laughter that seemed to fill their little voices.

"That's it!" she suddenly thought. "We need to laugh and be silly. We need to do something fun and crazy." She bent down to gather snow in her gloved hands and began forming snow balls. The coldness could be felt through her gloves and the snow crunched as she squeezed it hard to form each ball. She'd formed a small pile of more than a dozen snowballs when Steve emerged from the barn, his head down with his cowboy hat pulled low over his brow. His shoulders were hunched forward as if to keep the cold away. With one swift move Favor fired the first snowball at him hitting him square in the shoulder. Before he knew what hit him she fired a second hitting him in the stomach. Her laughter rang out over the stillness as she watched the expression on his face when he finally realized what had hit him.

It only took him a moment to gather his own snow into a ball and fire back. Favor was ready and his snowball sailed past as she dodged out of the way. Before he could send another in her direction she once again pelted him with yet another well assemble ball. His hat fell off his head and into the snow. Game on! They began a volley of snowballs back and forth as their laughter rang out breaking the silence of the countryside. After about ten minutes of continuous volleying back and forth Steven rushed in for the tackle. Favor dodged out of his grasp. Spinning around he lunged toward her again. This time he successfully grabbed her around the waist and they tumbled into the snow laughing. Favor squealed as Steven held her down and tickled her relentlessly, pleading for him to stop all the while squealing and giggling. Falling into the snow side by side they laughed till they could laugh no more. Breathing hard they watched as the warmth of their breath escaped and turned into tiny clouds as it hit the cold air.

Finally Favor got up and moved to an area where the snow had not been disturbed. Steven watched her with amusement. She had a look in her eyes as if he was supposed to guess what she was going to do next. To his surprise she spread her arms out to her side and let her body fall straight back into the snow as she then made a snow angel all the while laughing. Steven chose a spot near her and did the same as his deep hearty laugh filled the air. Pulling her to her feet they noticed Cloud watching them intently, his head cocked peculiarly off to one side as if to say, "What are you crazy humans doing?" He looked unsure as to what he should or shouldn't do.

"Come on, boy!" Favor patted her knees for him to come and in one swift bound he was at her feet playing like a puppy. She formed a snowball and tossed it to him. As he caught it the snowball broke and spattered at his feet. The cold on his tongue made him shake his head with an inquisitive look as if to say, "What kind of ball is that?" They laughed at the expression on his face. The three wrestled and romped in the snow until Favor finally said she'd had enough.

Shaking the snow off his hat Steve placed it back on his head, all the while watching to be sure she didn't attack again. Then he wrapped his arms around her and looked lovingly into her eyes. "Woman, you're crazy and I'm crazy in love with you. Now let's get inside and make something warm to drink, besides I'm starving now. You made me work up an appetite."

Her smile and the renewed twinkle in her eyes warmed him deep inside. Her look was enticing and he was beginning to feel the need to touch her body. It was like a hunger. She knew what he was thinking and with a giggle and tease she ran to the porch, turned and gave him that come on look she knew would tempt him into the bedroom. Rushing inside they pulled off their jackets and gloves hanging them to dry on the coat rack. Steve added some wood to the fire place and turned to see Favor had taken all but her underclothes off. With yet another giggle she bound up the stairs with Steve close behind.

Steven loved these moments of spontaneity. Favor was intriguing and exciting. Her every move made him want her more. To Favor, Steven was her only reality now. Every move, every touch and every word he spoke breathed renewed life into her body. She melted into him intoxicated by his love. Once again in the soft light of their room their bodies became one as they entwined in each other's arms, caressing one another as they melted into the feeling of ecstasy that only comes from lovemaking. As he held her he thought about the new life that was growing within her. He wondered if the child would have her brown or his blue eyes. He thought about what it would be like to hold his child for the first time.

Favor noticed the look on his face, "What are you thinking about?"

"I was just thinking about our baby and whether he might have your eyes or mine. I was trying to imagine you holding him in your arms nursing him."

"First of all, Steven, it could very well be a girl and second, I don't plan on nursing."

"Favor, the child you are carrying is a boy, of that I have no doubt. And you most certainly will be nursing our son. That is not an option."

"Wait one cotton picking minute, you do not get to say if I nurse or not."

"He will be nursed! Besides we don't have any bottles and he will need nourishment."

"So we will go to town and buy some."

"No, you will nurse him. End of discussion."

With that Steven got out of bed, dressed and left the room. Favor was infuriated. She loved Steven, but she had not wanted nor planned on having children. Or had she? Something deep in her memory stirred, reminding her of a time that seemed like a lifetime ago. A time when she and Conrad had talked about starting a family. She tried to remember the face of the man who once was her husband. It was hard to see his face in her mind anymore. All she could see was Steven's face. The past had slipped farther away from her. She didn't want to be angry with Steven. It had been a wonderful day. She wanted to lay in his arms longer. Why did he always have to be in control? She slipped into some other clothes and went downstairs. Steven was standing in the kitchen with a cup of coffee sulking, and turned to look out the kitchen window when she entered the room. It was warm and toasty in the lower rooms of the house.

Drawing close to him she wrapped her arms around his waist. "Steven, I'm sorry. I didn't mean to spoil our day. Please hold me. Don't be angry with me."

There was no resisting when she asked him that way. Setting the cup on the counter he turned and wrapped his arms tightly around her. "I'm sorry, too. I shouldn't have spoken to you so harshly. We'll work through all this. I promise you. You're going to be a wonderful mother." He kissed her softly and once again she felt secure and content in his arms. Before long they were talking, laughing and working side by side preparing something to eat. It was good, it was all good. This life was good, happy, simple and peaceful.

"Steven, what are we going to do about baby clothes and all the stuff a baby needs? We don't have anything for a baby."

Steven smiled at her. "Favor, do you really think I didn't prepare for that as well? I planned everything else, didn't I?"

Her eyes grew wide and she stood rooted to the spot where she stood. Of course he would have planned this as well. Her clothes, the food to survive, the wedding, right down to her dress had been meticulously planned. Of course he would have planned for the next natural order of things. It was so like Steven. It was moments like this that she felt that eerie wave of uneasiness in her gut. It was a strange feeling of uncertainty that she was not able to understand. She knew this intriguing, mysterious man that she was so totally bound to, controlled everything, yet she was so drawn to him that she couldn't resist anything he did no matter how hard she might try. It always ended up with her unable to resist him and her body and mind begging for him to touch her and possess her.

"Can I see what you have?"

"Not just yet. All in due time. When I think you're ready."

"I'm ready now."

"No you're not. What you said proves that to me. When you feel the unmistakable movement of our son inside of you, and completely accept this pregnancy, then I'll show you."

"Please, Steven. Please show me."

"Favor, you know what happens when you push me. I don't want to fight. I've done well by you so far haven't I? I've never done anything to hurt you and I've taken good care of you. I will do the same for our baby."

What could she say or do? Nothing. She simply nodded and didn't say anymore. Her life was planned right down to the smallest detail. The most joyous occasions in other people's lives would have been planned together, but hers was planned for her and she had no voice in those plans. "I think I'll go upstairs and lie down for a while."

"Are you feeling ok?"

"Yeah, I'm fine. Just a little tired."

"Are you sure?"

"Yes, of course." What she really wanted was to be alone and have a good cry. It was one of those moments when the faded memories from her past tried to reach her again and she needed to reach out for them. She needed to be alone.

Steve watched as she climbed the stairs, a look of concern creased his brow. He didn't feel like being alone today, but the conversation had turned to such that it drew them away from each other. A feeling of loneliness and sadness seemed to ebb into the room. Favor was right about his need to control, plan, organize and be certain everything was perfect. She was right. It was perfect for him, but not necessarily for her. If she only knew how important this child was and how much he needed to be sure the two of them would be alright if he was not there to take care of them.

He decided to get the baby things out and surprise Favor with them. As quietly as possible he went to the locked attic room and began bringing out box after box and taking it to the room which would be the baby's. Each time he entered he was careful to lock the door from the inside and again when he came out. He had other things in the room she was not to see yet. With each trip to the room he listened intently but no sound came from Favor's room. Finally all the baby things were brought out and placed in the baby's room. It would have filled the truck and then some. He smiled at himself remembering what it had been like shopping for all the baby things. The store clerk had asked why "the mother" was not picking out the baby things. He simply lied, telling her she was bed ridden, "troubles with the pregnancy" and that made the clerk go out of her way to help him. It was amazing how much a baby cost even in the beginning.

The excitement of showing Favor was making him feel like a child anticipating a wonderful surprise. He couldn't wait any longer so knocked on Favor's door. When she didn't answer, he slowly opened the door and peeked inside. She was laying on the bed curled up in a fetal position. In her hand was a bundle of Kleenex. She'd been crying and had in all likelihood cried herself to sleep. Why did he always seem to hurt her? If only she knew how important she was to him. He hesitated and then turned to leave the room when he heard her voice.

"Steven? What are you doing?"

"I was just checking on you. Actually I was hoping you were awake. I miss you and I have a surprise for you." Favor sat up. He missed her. That was so sweet and a surprise? Whatever could it be? Thinking maybe he had fixed something special to eat she smiled and told him she'd be right down.

"I just need to freshen up a little first."

"You look fine to me."

"I'd feel better if I took a few minutes to wash my face and brush my hair."

Smiling he said, "Ok, but please don't be long."

When Favor finally emerged from the room she was surprised to see Steven sitting on the top step of the staircase waiting for her. He rose quickly as she approached. "I'm sorry about earlier today. I upset you and made you cry. I saw the tissues and your eyes were swollen."

"Don't worry about it. It's probably just hormones. I seem to cry quite easily these days."

"If you say so, but I think it's more than that and I'm really sorry." Her eyes dropped and she stared at the floor. He knew it would not be a good idea to pursue a conversation about it so he blurted, "So do you want to see the surprise?"

"Sure, of course. What did you do? Cook something special?"

"Better than that." Reaching for her hand he led her to the baby's room. "Open the door." Hesitating a moment, she fully expected to find he had completely decorated the room. It's certainly what she'd expect from him. But to her surprise when she opened the door she found a mountain of boxes and what looked to be some furniture crates.

"How in heavens name did you get all this in here and when?"

"Just did while you were sleeping. Go ahead. See what you think."

For the next couple of hours she opened and unpacked boxes. A kid in a candy store couldn't have been more overjoyed. It was fun and she was delighted with the choices he had made. They laughed and talked about where they could put things and suddenly the reality of the baby began to take hold. Almost simultaneously they stopped and looked at each other. Somehow they both realized it at the same time and for the first time they felt like a family. "Let's get something to eat. I'm hungry. Afterwards if you feel up to it we can start putting the crib together."

"It's getting late. By the time we eat and feed the animals it will be dark. We can do it tomorrow. I'm a bit overwhelmed by all this. I think I've had enough excitement for one day. You really out did yourself. Actually you went a bit overboard."

"Hey that sales clerk was pretty convincing. I practically bought out the whole damn baby department by the time I was done. She showed me things I never even dreamed existed. We finally narrowed it down and what you saw isn't even half the things she showed me. I hope we have enough diapers and other essentials. She was pretty good at calculating how many a baby would need in a day, times seven days, times a month and so on. She figured on growth and weight and you name it. The gal knew her stuff. I was there for several hours and boy was I exhausted by the end. If she gets paid by commission, she made a hauling on me."

Favor began to laugh so hard listening to Steve that she couldn't stand up.

"Hey, why are you laughing at me? This was hard work. How many guys would do something like this? And the sales clerk kept talking about a baby shower. So we did this registry thing they do these days. Later I just ordered everything else through the registry from my office so she wouldn't get suspicious. That was pretty cool and I got everything a little at a time because it was shipped from different places. I really didn't realize how much I'd ordered till it all came. It was like a crazy game."

The more he told her the harder she laughed. She was rolling on the floor in the living room and couldn't stop laughing. "I'm sorry. I can't help it! Just imagining you, big, tall, sexy, blue eyes buying baby stuff. That girl was probably having the time of her life. She's probably still talking about it to all her friends and co-workers to this day. What a site that must have been!" Then she broke out in another burst of uncontrollable laughter. Steve stared at her with a bewildered look.

Chapter 20

Monday morning came and Adam told his boss he needed to take the afternoon off for routine checkup after the accident and run some errands. "That's fine. We'll see you in the morning then."

Adam headed for the recorder's office in Eureka, about 20 miles away where he began searching the Mitchell name in or near the township of Bridgeville and Dinsmore. Hours of searching lead to one dead end after another. Anything leading to the Mitchell family and the house in the mountains ended up the wrong Mitchell family in the wrong direction.

Closing time came and a young woman approached him. "I'm sorry, but you will have to leave now, we're about to close."

"Look, I just need a little more time."

"I can't. You've been here for hours. Come back tomorrow. I have to close now."

"You don't understand, this information could be a link to finding a girl who's been missing for months. You've got to let me keep looking."

"I'm sorry. Everyone else is gone and I have to lock up."

"Just give me another half hour. I'll pay you twice what you get paid for your time."

"I can't. It could mean my job. You'll have to come back tomorrow. Is she your wife?"

"No, but she's very special. She was kidnapped and I have reason to believe she's still alive. I believe this guy I'm looking for is the one person that can lead me to her."

"Why not go to the police about it?"

"I already have. They've reached a dead end. The case is no longer a priority. It's considered a cold case. There are no other cases that match the same scenario."

"Come back tomorrow and I'll try to help you, but you have to leave now."

"Ok, but I'm going to hold you to helping me."

"Deal. Names Katie she said holding out her hand."

"Adam, Adam Jennings. Pleased to meet you."

"See you tomorrow," she let him out and locked the door. On the ride down in the elevator she told him a lot of public records can be found on the Internet.

"I've tried, but they all want to sucker you into paying and it leads you on a wild goose chase from one site after another. All these sites want a fee and before you know it you've paid all these fees and you're back where you originally started with only more questions. And then the fee turns into a monthly fee and if you don't cancel within a certain time you're stuck."

"She must be special. Tomorrow we'll see what we can find but I'd recommend you don't get your hopes up."

"Hope's all I have."

Adam left an early message for his boss that he wouldn't be in again and headed straight to the recorder's office. Katie was just opening the office when he arrived. She let him in and told him she had a few things to do and would help him between customers. This time he began his search with the name of Sadie Marks. Five hits came up. One in Northern California in the town of Redding caught his attention. He'd start from here. An address that he hoped was current, led him to call information for Redding. He was able to secure a phone number and jotted it down. Not wanting to be heard he left to go out into the hallway to make the call. A woman answered and he said, "Hello, I am trying to locate Sadie Marks, the aunt of Steven Lawrence Mitchell IV. Have I called the right number?"

A pleasant voice on the other end said, "Yes, but..." Before she could say another word, Adam went on, "Thank, God! I've got to talk to her as soon as possible. I'm in Eureka headed for Redding, I'll call you when I arrive. I must speak to her today. It's an urgent matter."

Katie had noticed Adam was no longer at the records table and had left one of the books lying there. A bit frustrated she picked it up and looked around. Just outside the office she saw Adam in the hall talking on the phone. He saw her just as he hung up and waived. "Got to run, may have found something." Then he was heading for his truck to make the drive to Redding.

Three and a half hours later he arrived in Redding. With his GPS he located the address. He found a modest home located on the South end of Redding in a beautiful setting at the end of a paved road. The home was surrounded by wrought iron fencing with well-groomed gardens. Feeling like an intruder he drove through the gate and approached the house. Exiting his truck he walked hesitantly to the front door. Knocking he waited nervously for an answer. A woman who appeared to be in her mid-forties answered the door opening it only part way.

"Yes, what do you want?"

"My name is Adam Jennings. I spoke to you on the phone a few hours ago. I'm here to see Ms. Sadie Marks. May I come in? I have ID if you would like to see it first," he said handing her his license.

"What's this urgent matter? How do I know you are not here to harm us?"

"If I was here to harm anyone, do you think I would have told you I was coming? I must speak to her regarding her nephew."

"What's this got to do with Steven?"

"Please, please let me come in and talk to her?"

The woman opened the door wider. She could see the look of urgency on his face. "If you had given me a chance to speak on the phone, I could have saved you a trip all the way out here."

"I guess I should have first asked if she was home."

"It's not that, Ms. Sadie passed away two weeks ago."

Adam stumbled back, his hand went to his chest as he felt the emotion begin to overwhelm him. He had been so hopeful. Grief struck him and he buried his face in his hands. "This can't be. It just can't."

He felt a gentle hand on his arm and the soft voice of the woman as she said, "I'm sorry. Do you want to come in? You look like you need to sit down. I'll get you something cold to drink." With that she gently guided him into the well lit room. Sitting on the sofa with his head hung low, his face look drawn and tired. The woman spoke softly. "My name is Sarah. Sadie was a long-time friend of my family and a member of our church. I've been living with her for the past eight years helping her keep up this place and keeping her company. You said you needed to speak to her regarding an urgent matter."

"It was regarding her nephew, Steven Mitchell."

"Yes you mentioned his name on the phone. Like I said you hung up so quickly."

"We've been trying to locate him but can't find him."

"We? Who do you mean?"

"Some friends, and the police have been trying to help as well."

"That makes no sense. Steven died in 1988. When we got word he had died, a copy of his Trust and Will were delivered to Sadie. Steven had left a sizeable amount of assets to his aunt. He had not had any contact with her for many years due to a disagreement, but he had continued to take care of her financially as long as she kept her promise not to try and contact him for any reason. He told her if she did, she would lose everything and he would leave her destitute. It broke her heart. He was the only family she had left. But she had no choice. The instruction in the Trust were very clear as to where Steven was to be laid to rest and Sadie was careful to follow every instruction to the letter. His attorney's contacted her and made sure everything was done according to his instructions. When his trust and will were read we found everything, absolutely everything he owned including his company holdings was left to his wife except for the few provisions he left to Sadie. We've tried for some time to locate his wife. But, no one has been able to locate her. Sadie hadn't even known he'd gotten married and his wife has not come forward. She wasn't present for the burial because she couldn't be located."

"Do you know where he was buried?"

"Yes, of course. He was buried on their old homestead in the Mitchell family plot. As far as I know no one has been to the place since then. When we went up there to have him buried it felt kind of creepy. Both of us kept feeling like we were being watched the whole time. We left as soon as possible after the burial. Sadie intended to go back and sort through the things in the house but somehow it didn't seem right knowing there was supposed to be a wife out there. We made certain the house was securely locked. We never went back. As far as I know it was entirely deserted from then on unless the wife came back. Chances are the local pot growers have taken over the place."

"You say, the family plot?"

"Yes. There are now four generations of Mitchell's buried there."

"Where is this house located?"

"In the mountains between the towns of Dinsmore and Bridgeville off of Highway 36." Adam felt his heart jump, but he tried not to let on how important this information was to him.

"How did he die?"

"Horseback riding accident. He had this big white horse that he was very fond of. I guess he was riding one day and took a nasty fall. He was able to contact emergency services with a Satellite phone he carried. By using the GPS on his phone they were able to pin-point his location, but by the time they reached him there really wasn't much they could do. He had internal bleeding and succumbed to his injuries soon after they arrived. The horse had broken a leg and had to be put down. It was so terrible. It's too bad he and his wife didn't have a child. The one thing Steven wanted was to have a son to carry on his family name. At least we don't know of a child. Then again we can't find his wife either."

Adam hesitated before asking the next question. "Do you know what his wife's name is?"

"Why yes. It is a rather unusual name. Her name is Favor. It's all in the Trust and Will."

The color left Adam's face. He looked like he'd seen a ghost and he could feel his heart racing. Sarah rose and looked at him realizing this news was of great importance. She saw pure disbelief in his eyes. "What is it? You're scaring me! I think you need to leave."

Adam regained his composure, "Please, I didn't mean to scare you. Let me explain."

"Alright, but you better stop scaring me like that."

"You see I've been searching for a very dear friend who disappeared some time ago. Her name is Favor Durand. We think she was connected to Steven Mitchell, but we haven't been able to find her." Adam was careful not to tell Sarah that Favor had only been missing since June of that year, 1991. "The police ruled it a cold case and stopped looking for her. I just haven't been able to give up looking."

"Well, it seems to make sense then. This friend Favor has to be the same Favor that Steven married. After all it's an uncommon name and it makes perfect sense. We know she has got to be alive or else she passed after he died, because if she died before him, he would have had her buried in the family plot like all the other wives of the four generations of Mitchells."

"No, I believe she's alive. Do you still have the copy of the Trust and Will?"

"Yes, it's in with Sadie's important papers. I haven't gotten rid of anything."

"May I see the documents?"

"Alright, I'll get them. Wait right here." She returned within minutes with the papers. Adam read over them. He knew that whoever this guy was in the green truck had to be the person who had taken Favor. But if Steven Mitchell had died in 1988, then someone else was using his name and identity for their own means to get the fortune belonging to Favor Mitchell.

"Do you have a photo of Steve?"

"Yes, even though Sadie was not to have any contact with Steven herself, it did not mean I couldn't have any contact. I had a friend who was a client of Steven's. He kindly used his friendship with Steven to get a photo of him each year at my request. It was our little secret and I gave it to Sadie every Christmas as a gift. She treasured getting the photo each year. We suspected he knew it was for Sadie even though it was at my request. She never tried to contact him herself. Look there behind you in the corner. That was the last photo taken in 1988 not long before he died. The one beside it is of her and Steven not long after his parents passed away."

Adam walked over and picked up each photo looking them over carefully. It looked exactly like the guy in the green truck. He was petrified out of his mind. Not wanting to alarm Sarah he said, "Would it be possible for me to take this photo of Mr. Mitchell for a while? I promise to get it back to you."

"Why? He's dead. What good could it possibly do you in finding this woman?"

"I don't want to alarm you, but there is a slight possibility that there is someone trying to impersonate the real Steven Mitchell." He felt like he was lying, but what else could he say? "I'd like to take this photo to the police so they can have a photo for their records. Then if this other person shows up using his name or claiming to be him they'll be able to see it's not the true Steven Mitchell. If you have a copy of the death certificate it would help with the investigation as well. We believe Favor could or is being held against her will by this other person. That would explain why she has not come forward and why she wasn't present for his burial. I promise to get them back to you."

"One other thing, would you have a record of the property where Steve Mitchell is buried? The police will want to be sure no one is using the property for illegal means and they will probably want to be sure Mrs. Mitchell is not being held there against her will. You did say it felt like someone was watching you when you were there to bury her husband. It's possible she is being held there by someone and that person was watching everything that was going on that day. Did the police ever investigate as to whether his accident really was an accident? Maybe this person caused him to have an accident."

"Do you really think that is possible? That poor woman. If she is still alive she must be terrified. But it's been three years since Steven died. Do you think there is a chance she is alive? And course you can take them. I'll get the Deed and Legal Description for you. It's in the name of The Steven Lawrence Mitchell IV and Favor Mitchell Family Trust. There are several originals of the death certificate, I am sure it would be no problem and an original would probably be best. Please don't lose any of the other items. They are the only ones I have and are the originals. If it helps the police to find her, by all means please take them."

"I promise to get these back to you as quickly as possible."

"Do keep me apprised of any developments in the case won't you?"

"You have my word. Here's my business card in case you want to contact me. It's easiest to reach me on the cell phone."

With the photo, death certificate and Deed in hand, Adam left and began heading back toward Fortuna. The events of the day and the information had been overwhelming. Exhaustion was beginning to overtake him. He recalled his accident and decided it would be best to get a hotel and stay overnight in Redding rather than drive back in his current state of mind. At first he wasn't going to tell anyone where he was but decided to call Houston instead and let him know.

"I have some compelling evidence regarding Favor, but I need to show you rather than tell you on the phone. I'm just too tired and I need to get some food in my stomach, so I'm going to stay here tonight. Could you call my boss for me? I really don't want to have to talk to him or try to explain why I'm here instead of at work."

Houston thanked Adam for letting him know where he was and promised to make the call for him. There was definitely an edge in Adam's voice and he could tell he was exhausted. It made him feel better knowing he had learned his lesson from his accident not to push himself too far and was taking measures to keep himself safe and healthy while looking for Favor.

Adam ordered some food to be sent to his room. In the quiet of his hotel room he looked over the documents and stared at the photo of Steven Mitchell. It was the face of the man he had stood face to face with. There was no mistake about that. But how could this be? The man had been dead for three years.

Something kept gnawing at his gut. For some reason the idea of taking the information to the police didn't feel like the thing to do. His thoughts kept going back to what Jake had said about the old man in the mountains. For some reason he felt like he'd rather take his chances with him rather than the police. If he went to the police they would take the information and it would take months, who knows, maybe even years to process and then it would end up in a box filed away under unsolved cold case files. In his opinion the local police were not well trained in the field of finding missing persons. It felt like they had an attitude of "Oh well! Too bad, so sad!" He didn't have a lot of confidence in them. Maybe he was just being impatient, but he couldn't shake the feeling that Favor needed to be found soon.

Another thing caught his eye as he read over the trust agreement again. It was the Social Security numbers. He noted the number for Steven Mitchell IV and that of his wife Favor Mitchell. When he got back he would have Cindy and Houston see if there were any old tax records in Favor's house that would show her Social Security number. If not they could contact her father and see if he had her records. One way or another if the numbers matched they would be certain that the woman mentioned in the trust is one and the same person. Hopefully it would put them that much closer to an answer.

Adam found it hard to sleep. He was restless and wanted to get back to Fortuna. He finally fell asleep sometime after midnight to the drone of the TV. When he woke again about five thirty the next morning he took a hurried shower, donned the clothes he'd been wearing since yesterday and hurried to check out. He took advantage of some coffee and a pastry in the dining area where a Continental Breakfast was being served. A kindly older lady noticed what he was having and commented that he really needed more nourishment than that. There was something strangely familiar about the face of the woman, but he dismissed it as he thanked her for her concern and said, "I really must be going. I just don't have time."

"Oh but you do, young man. You do!" Something about the way she said it made him stop and turn to look back at the woman. She was nowhere to be found. Looking down the corridor he saw the woman entering the elevator. Running to stop the elevator he reached it just as the doors were closing. The woman looked him right in the eye giving him a sweet smile as the doors closed. Pushing on the button several times he glanced up to see what floor it was going to. The door didn't reopen. Frustrated he waited. The elevator stopped at the fifth floor. The doors to the adjoining elevator opened and he rushed inside. Looking down at the buttons he realized there was not a button for a fifth floor. This couldn't be. He was sure it said a "5". Pushing the "1" the doors reopened and he excited the elevator. Looking up at the numbers overhead he saw only four numbers. The doors opened and he entered. The doors closed and he turned to the numbered keypad. There was a "5". His hand was shaking as he pushed the number 5 button. Once again his eyes went to the numbers above the door as it began to ascend upward. When he reached the fourth floor the elevator stopped and several people entered carrying their luggage. The door closed. "First floor, please." Adam looked down at the keypad to hit the number one when he noticed there was no "5".

Hesitating and looking bewildered he said, "Where's the 5th floor?"

A man that had entered looked at Adam with an annoyed questioning look and reached in front of him to push the number one. "There is no fifth floor. This hotel only has four floors. It's a little early to be drinking, buddy."

Adam stepped back into the corner, beads of sweat forming on his brow. When they once again reached the first floor the other passengers stepped out. The man looked back at him and shook his head. Unable or willing to move the doors closed again and Adam stood staring at the key pad. The two lit up and the elevator once again ascended upward. At the second floor the door opened and a family with three children entered. The father pushed the first floor button the elevator started back down. When the doors once again opened on the first floor Adam rushed out nearly knocking over one of the three kids. Apologizing he turned and looked at the numbers from outside the door. Only four numbers. Feeling sick he rushed out of the hotel to his truck. He needed air and he needed it now.

Chapter 21

Steven and Favor spent the better part of the next day putting together the baby crib and other furniture. They unpacked and put baby clothes and various baby necessities away. The closet was stacked with diapers and clothes of various sizes. In the dresser they placed the items needed for a new born. All the while Favor kept noticing there were no clothes for a girl.

Hesitantly Favor finally asked, "Steven, what if we just happened to have a girl instead of a boy? You've purchased everything for a boy. Nothing for a girl. You could have bought yellow or green for a girl or boy and some outfits for a girl and some for a boy."

Looking over at her with no uncertainty he confidently said, "Trust me, Favor, it's a boy." With that he went back to the task at hand. Why rock the boat. Nothing she could do about it now. If the baby turns out to be a girl he will have to come to terms with it and do something about it. She hoped he had saved all his receipts and they had not expired.

None-the-less she was having fun and there was no sense worrying about it till later. Besides it made her much too tired these days.

It was now mid-November. Favor wasn't sure how long she'd been pregnant. She'd first made love to Steven in August and they married in September. Was she two or three months into her pregnancy? She had no way of knowing since she had not seen a doctor. It worried her a bit not knowing what to expect, but every time she expressed a concern, Steven would produce a book which conveniently had the answer to her concerns or questions.

At times it scared her when she really thought about how he had planned every detail of their lives. How could any one person do that? But when she was near him and felt his gentleness and love she would push the thoughts away. He had never threatened her nor hurt her in any way. All of his efforts and plans were executed with the deepest thoughtful tenderness. And how she loved his touch and making love to him. It always made her feel intoxicated and she never tired of having him close.

"Favor, guess what it will be in a few days?"

"Our second month anniversary is already past. I don't know. What?"

"Thanksgiving! We need to do something special and I need to get us a turkey. I saw some wild turkeys the other day at the edge of the lower meadow. I'm going to get us one for Thanksgiving Dinner."

"I don't want you going far just for a turkey. It's so cold these days and the weather has been getting worse every day. It's not safe."

"I won't go any farther than the lower meadow and maybe I'll bring back two so we can have one for Christmas, too."

"I know I can't talk you out of this. When you decide you're going to do something you do it no matter what. Just be sure you take Cloud with you."

"No, I want him here with you."

"I'm safe here and I have everything I need. If anything happened I want to know you have Cloud with you and are not alone. Please do that for me." His blue eyes twinkled and he got that school boy look in his eyes. Kissing her forehead he agreed, then his lips found hers and he kissed her first tenderly and then she felt his passion as he kissed her long and hard. She knew he'd try to leave Cloud behind but she'd send Cloud after him knowing Cloud would track him from a distance if he tried to send him back. A few days later Steven set out to find the wild turkeys with Cloud close behind.

It wasn't far to the lower meadow where Steven set up a blind so he could watch and wait for the turkeys to appear. He'd sat quietly most of the day. It had begun to turn bitterly cold. Steven kept his eye on the northern sky. The clouds were turning darker as the day wore on. It was late afternoon and he had just decided to pack it in for the day when he heard the familiar "gobble, gobble" sound of the wild turkeys. Patiently he watched as they wandered closer to the blind. Two swift precise shots and he had his two turkeys. He watched as the others scattered before approaching. Both were nice big birds, not too old, not too young. They were both Tom's and looked plump and healthy. To pack them back he would need to strap them onto his back in the large sacks he had brought along. Together they weighed in excess of forty pounds.

It was slow going in the snow, carrying the weight of the two carcasses. Steven kept an ever watchful eye on the sky as dark clouds approached carrying with them bitter cold snow. Cloud stayed close sensing the impending weather. Steve needed to get back quickly and take care of the animals before the snow storm hit. He'd stayed longer than he planned and was beginning to feel concern.

Back at the house Favor too had noticed the sky was becoming darker and she kept going to the window to look out for Steven. Butterfly feelings in her stomach and the jitters had returned the way she always felt when she was alone. The clock on the wall read four pm. It would be dark by five and Steven could not be seen. She'd already begun preparing the evening meal. It was in the oven and would not be done for at least forty-five minutes. Grabbing her winter coat and pulling on her snow boots, gloves and hat, she headed to the barn to take care of the animals. One less thing for Steve to worry about when he returned. A half hour or so she'd be done, before the dinner was finished cooking.

She took care of the chickens then headed to the main barn to load hay on the wagon for the cattle. She hoped she'd meet up with Steven. If not he should see the tracks from the tractor and know they'd been fed. Once back she'd care for the horses. The bales seemed heavier than usual so she flipped them end over end so she could get them onto the trailer. Six bales would have to do. If she had time she'd take a few more down later. Steve had been planning on building a small hay barn closer to where the cattle were, but had not had time. The big barn out at the far pasture was well stocked, but with the cattle closer to the house due to predators, it meant hauling hay almost every day down to them.

Once she returned with the tractor and trailer she parked them in the breezeway of the barn out of the weather, then set about taking care of the horses. All that was left was milking the darn cow. This she really hated doing and had only done it a couple of times. She knew dinner had to be just about ready so decided to check on it first. Everything was looking good. Now for the cow. Grabbing the milk pail and lid she started to head back to the barn when peering into the fading daylight she could barely make out the figure of Steven as he trudged wearily across the moor. His steps were slow and she could tell he was tired from carrying his heavy load. Relieved that he was home she dropped the pail and ran to meet him.

Breathless she reached him with a smile on her face. "Woman what are you doing out here in this cold?" He tried to sound gruff, but his eyes told her he was glad to see her. Hugging her close he kissed her cold lips. "We are going to have to warm those lips up." She laughed her approval as they trudged the rest of the way back hand in hand.

"The cows, horses and chickens are all fed. I just need to milk the cow and dinner is nearly ready. So you got two turkeys I see."

"Yep, and they're nice ones. I'll take care of the milking while you finish dinner, then I need to get these birds prepped and cleaned after we eat. I'm starving." Steve headed to the barn with Cloud while Favor headed back to the house."

The savory smell of fresh baked bread filled the house and the smell of thick homemade vegetable beef soup simmering made Favor's mouth water. The bread was just ready to come out. Favor had made a fresh batch of butter just that morning and she knew Steve would be cutting into the bread first chance he got. From the pantry she pulled a fresh jar of her apple butter and some blackberry jam. The peach pie she'd baked earlier with its golden brown crust was cool and ready to eat. Something about fresh baked bread and pies and homemade soup made a cold winter night feel just right. She was pleased and happy with what she'd prepared and was anxious for Steve to return to the house.

Cloud had come back to the house and was laying contentedly by the fire, having eaten a hearty helping of his own food and nearly emptied his water dish. The wind had begun to pick up outside and had turned from a whistling wind to a loud rumbling wind. Snow had already begun to fall and Favor wished Steve would hurry up. She heard the tractor and realized he was taking more hay down to the cattle and wished he would wait till morning. The daylight was fading and it would be completely dark by the time Steve made it back.

A few moments later Cloud jumped up and began to growl. His growl grew louder like a rumble deep down in his chest. "It's ok Cloud. It's just the wind. It's going to be a nasty storm tonight. Settle down." But he kept growling, no matter how hard she tried to calm him he wouldn't stop. He stood staring at the door. Maybe something had happened to Steve. She knew she should let him out to check, but for some reason she hesitated. Then she heard it.

A voice from outside called out, "Hello, inside. Is anyone there?"

"Who are you? What do you want? What are you doing on our property?"

"Please," the voices were closer, right outside the door. "Please, let us in!" Favor froze. The voice she heard now was that of a woman. "Please, we're lost and so cold. We don't mean any harm."

"Back away from the door." Favor yelled as she grabbed the 357 revolver on the shelf above the coat rack. She told Cloud to heel as she cautiously opened the door. She knew whoever they were, they could rush her and attack and kill her, but she would be ready with the revolver and Cloud. Carefully she opened the door. At the bottom of the porch steps stood a young man and woman. They were obviously cold and shaking so hard that she instantly knew they were in need of help. But Steve had taught her well.

"How do I know this is not a trick and there are more of you out there? What are you doing up here, trespassing and probably growing pot on other peoples land. Am I right?" She held the gun firmly in her hands pointing it at the two.

Then the man spoke again. "We saw the smoke from your fireplace and your light from the window. We've been lost in the mountains for over a week. We've run out of food and supplies. We thought we were going to die out here till we saw your house."

With that the girl burst into tears and fell to her knees. "Please, there's no one else. I'm so cold and tired. We're lost and haven't eaten in two days." The hikers could smell the aroma of the fresh cooked food coming from the inside of the house. The young man stooped down to help the girl to her feet. "We'd be happy to sleep in your barn if we could just get out of the cold. We never dreamed there would be a house this far up in the mountains let alone someone being here this time of the year. Please don't turn us away. We won't make it in this storm."

Just then Favor saw the lights of the tractor and the hum of its motor as Steve approached the barn. "That's my husband. He won't be happy about this."

"Look we understand. But we don't know what else to do. Maybe your husband could show us the way out of here and we won't bother you anymore. But we at least need someplace out of this storm to sleep tonight." Then Favor saw Steve approaching from the barn. He had broken into a run seeing the two strangers at his porch steps and Favor holding the gun.

Grabbing the gun from Favor he pointed it at them. "Who the hell are you? You're trespassing. What are you doing scoping out our property for your next pot garden?"

"Honey, look at them. Look at her! Do they look like two people out to get us?" She quickly explained what they had told her. The girl was sobbing uncontrollably now and her tears were nearly freezing on her face. The young man was holding onto her tightly trying to keep her warm. She could see sandy colored hair under the hood of his jacket and a strong square jawline. He obviously had a strong build and his eyes were intense as he tried his best to be polite and stay calm. But he was obviously becoming agitated and concerned for the woman at his side.

"Look if you're not going to let us come in, then just shoot us here and now. There is no way we are going to make it if we have to spend the night out in this storm."

Favor turned to Steve. "Remember when I got lost a few months ago? That was summer. Think of what it would have been like for me if it had been winter!" Steve suddenly softened remembering what Favor had gone through all alone

"All right, get inside before you freeze to death." Favor rolled her eyes at him. He was still using his tough, mean voice.

The two moved quickly into the house, but stood waiting for further instructions, hesitant as to what to do next or what to expect. They both looked longingly at the fire burning in the fireplace. Favor gently helped the girl remove her backpack and outer clothing and boots. She was still crying, but gratefully accepted Favor's assistance. The young man slipped the pack he was carrying off and let it slip to the floor. Once they had removed their wet outer clothing Favor hung them to dry on the coat rack. Steve still holding the gun, nodded towards the fire and they both hurried over to it to warm themselves. Outside the wind had picked up and begun to howl like the fury of a child and with it came the snow. The big old house seemed to moan its discontentment at the change in the weather. Gone were the sunny days and moon lit nights. Old man winter was here to stay for a while.

"We really appreciate your letting us come in. We will be happy to sleep in your barn after we get a chance to warm up. We won't be any trouble and we'll leave at first light. I'm going to reach into my pocket now and pull out my ID so you can see who we are. My name is Mike Conley and this is my wife Jan. You are welcome to go through our packs to see we don't have anything out of the ordinary for a backpacker. We're not into marijuana and it's just the two of us." He handed Favor his ID and Jan pulled hers out of her pocket as well. "We took a late packing trip this year because we wanted to experience some of the country in the fall. The colors are so bright and we felt it would be a great experience. The weather turned cold earlier than usual and we both came down with something. We tried to go on, but the fevers we were both experiencing got us disoriented and we ended up lost. We've been wandering for about a week now with no idea where we are or where we've been."

Jan who had been taking in her surroundings now spoke, "We haven't eaten in two days. Could we trouble you for a bit of bread and some fresh water?" Favor sensed she was not used to asking for help let alone asking someone for food. She was clearly embarrassed about it. Large brown eyes looked at Favor with worry and pleading. Her features were small and though she showed strength, she seemed beaten and so tired that her shoulders slumped over. Short blond, slightly curly hair surrounded her face with graceful softness. Though her figure was slight and thin it was obvious she had strong legs and arms from backpacking. Her skin was bronze from long hours in the sun and there was a wholesomeness about the two visitors that Favor immediately liked.

"We haven't had our supper yet and were just getting ready to eat. I've made some fresh homemade soup and bread. We have peach pie for desert made from our own canned peaches. It will only take me a few minutes to set the table. You just get yourself warmed up."

"Is there someplace I could wash? I feel pretty messy."

"Of course come this way."

Favor noticed Steve bristle like a porcupine. He was not sure about the two intruders, but that was what Favor expected. "We'll let the boys talk while I show you to the bathroom."

"Wait," Steve sounded off abruptly. "We haven't properly introduced ourselves. I'm Clint and this is my wife Kathy. Last name's Williams." Favor glared at Steve. What the hell was that all about, giving false names?

"Pleased to meet you and thank you again for letting us in."

Favor guided Jan towards the bathroom showing her where things were. While she waited for Jan she wondered why Steve had told them their name were Clint and Kathy. She hated the name Kathy. It was too common and she didn't like being given a common name. It simply did not fit her at all.

Jan emerged from the bathroom, her face shiny and clean and a smile on her face. "You really have a nice home. That soap smells nice and the warm water felt really good on my skin." Favor laughed and directed her back to the living room to wait until dinner.

Within ten minutes the table was set and Favor was calling them to sit down. Steve immediately began to serve his plate while the two looked back and forth between themselves. Then they took each other's hand, bow their heads and said a soft little prayer between the two of them. When they were done they looked up to see both Steve and Favor staring at them. "I hope you don't mind. We were raised to say grace before every meal. We hope it didn't offend you."

"I think that is wonderful. Would you like to say a blessing for all of us?" The two smiled and Mike then gave a blessing for the four of them, thanking God for this safe haven and a warm fire, good food and a special blessing for 'Clint' and 'Kathy' for sheltering them during the storm that was now raging outside. Steve never closed his eyes surprised that Favor had asked them to include them in their prayer. Then something in his past surfaced. He remembered his parents had prayed at their meals. They had also taken him to church. That had been such a long time ago and so much had happened that he had forgotten those long ago childhood days of going to church and singing songs and reading the Bible. Shame made his cheeks suddenly turn red and his eyes looked far away. He suddenly realized Favor's hand was on his arm and she was asking him if he was ok.

"I remember my parents used to do that. After they died I never went to church again. No one took me and I didn't think about it or ask."

"We didn't mean to bring up any bad memories."

"On the contrary, they were good memories." From then on the conversation was happy and laughter rang out as they shared stories and adventures among themselves. All of a sudden Steve stopped, "Babe, I forgot the turkeys outside. I need to take care of them."

"Say if you need a hand, I'd be glad to. I used to go pheasant and wild turkey hunting with my dad. I've cleaned my share of them growing up. It would sure make me feel better after eating your food and sharing the warmth of your home." Together they put on their coats and headed outside to get the turkey and take them to the barn to clean.

"I'm afraid my wife would skin my hide if I took them into the house to clean. We have a shed outside with water and everything we need to clean them properly."

"Ok let's get it done. Between the two of us we can get it done in half the time and get back inside where it is warm. So how did you come to live way up here and why do you live here instead of someplace close to a town?"

"This house has been in my family for four generations, soon to be five. I've always loved it here and I want my family to enjoy living self-sufficiently as well. The world is only getting worse and I want my family to know how to take care of themselves."

"That's part of the reason Jan and I learned to backpack. We want to know how to survive in harsh conditions, although we didn't do too well this trip. So you said 'soon to be five'. Is your wife expecting?"

"She is. The baby is due in May."

The conversation went from one topic to another and before long the turkeys were cleaned and the men carried them proudly to the house for Favor to wrap for the freezer. The snow was coming down harder now and the wind was bitterly cold.

Mike and Jan thanked them again for their hospitality, "We really should be getting to the barn before it gets much colder out there. Could you direct us as to where would be the best place to sleep?"

Favor jumped up. "I won't hear of it. We have this big old house and I will not have you sleeping in the barn. That is out of the question." All three of them looked at her, stunned by her outburst. She figured Steve would be mad at her, but she really didn't care.

"Well, now, I think my little woman has spoken her mind. We have an extra room all set up."

"Actually, you'll be sleeping in my room. Well, we still call it my room, because I came to live here before we were married and I had my own room until we got married. Now we share whichever room we feel like sleeping in. I like my room because it has its own bathroom. St...err Clint," she stammered, "made it really special for me. It will be more comfortable for you two since it has a private bathroom." Jan didn't seem to notice Favor's stammer, or at least if she noticed, she didn't give any indication.

"I'm sure it will be more than we could ever have expected. It sure will feel good to sleep in a real bed for a change." Together they changed the bed and hung fresh towels in the bathroom. They laughed and talked like two school girls who were spending a weekend together. When they were done Favor showed her the baby's room. Looking over the baby things they chattered about how cute everything was. Then they heard Steve calling up the stairs.

"Did you two get lost up there? We're going to eat all the pie if you don't come down."

"We're coming." They closed the door to the baby's room and headed down stairs where they all had pie and sat around the fireplace telling stories about each of their childhoods. It was as if they had been longtime friends. They felt comfortable in each other's presence although Favor noticed Steve was still being cautious. He picked his words carefully and let Mike and Jan tell most of the stories.

"Well it's getting late and I think we all need to get some rest. You folks go on upstairs. You'll probably need your packs for your personal items, but if you need anything I'm sure we have what you may need. Honey you go on upstairs too. I'll put some more wood on the fire and turn out the lights down here."

When Steven came upstairs he had the gun in his hand. He'd told Cloud to stay outside their door so he could warn them if the couple left the room for any reason until morning.

Alone in their room, Favor spoke in hushed tones. "You were really rude, Steven. You really acted stupid. But, thanks for letting them stay."

"Yeah, but I'm not entirely comfortable about it. What if it is a trick? What if they recognize you from the paper or something? They could even be someone hired to find you."

"In the dead of winter? Really, Steve. By now everyone will have quit looking for me. Besides would that be so bad if they found me? I'm your wife now. I'm going to have your baby. I wouldn't leave here without you. Don't you know that by now? This is your chance to show me you trust me and have some faith in me that I will stand by you no matter what. And what's with the names. Kathy doesn't fit me in the least. I don't like it. It's too common for me, Clint. You sure picked a better name for yourself."

"Will you take a breath? Gee whiz, Honey, I'm sorry. It was the first name that popped into my head. And you're right, it doesn't suit you, but we can't do anything about it now. I'd go to jail if they found you with me. What if they were to tell someone about staying with us? And what if that person remembered the name Favor? They would come looking for you. I can't risk losing you."

"I'd just tell them you found me wandering around the hills and I had amnesia."

"Then they'd want to know why I didn't bring you in and try to find out who you were."

"Guess you've got a valid point there. But no matter what, I wouldn't let them put you in jail. You know you could take me back for a visit in the spring."

"I can't take the chance on you seeing that guy and not wanting to come back with me."

"So that's it. You're jealous. I didn't have any commitment to him."

"Favor, I've heard you call out for him when you were having one of your nightmares."

"When? How long ago? When I first came here? I don't *have* the dreams anymore." She was crying softly. Steve could see genuine pain in her eyes. "I had no idea, Steven. I love you and I don't want to leave you *ever!*" Steve drew her close.

"I shouldn't have said anything. It wasn't fair of me." A smile crossed her lips and he felt relief flood over him. Then he saw the mischief in her eyes. "What are you thinking? You've got that look in your eyes."

"So, Clint, how would you like to make love to me, aka Kathy, for the first time?"

"Knock it off, Favor. We can't do that. They might hear us."

"Give me a break, they're clear across the other side behind closed doors. They're not going to hear us and I want to."

"What am I going to do with you, Favor? Get in bed." Wrapping his arms tightly around her he drew her close to his body feeling her warmth. The room would be especially cold tonight so being close felt exceptionally good.

Outside the winds had picked up even more. It sounded like a hundred wolves howling mournfully at the night sky. Favor shuddered and drew in closer to Steve. "Are the animals going to be alright? It sounds so scary out there. Just think how horrible it would have been for them if they had not found us."

"I know you're right about letting them stay, and I hope the animals will be ok. The horses, milk cow and the chickens are safe. I hope the cattle will be alright. They were all bedded down in the big shelter. I counted them and they were all there. I took the extra hay just in case I can't get down there tomorrow. They seemed comfortable and the troughs were working well as long as they don't freeze over. I've done everything possible to keep them safe. I'm just afraid we're in for a really hard winter. We've got plenty, and I took in almost twice as much hay this year so we don't run out. It won't be easy, but we'll be ok."

They lay quietly in each other's arms listening to the howling of the wind outside, while across the hall their guests prepared for bed as well.

"Mike, listen to that wind. It makes me shudder to think of how horrible it would have been for us if we had not stumbled onto this house and met this couple."

"I know, Jan. The thought of being out there scares me to death. But you know God led us here. He knew what we needed and where to send us."

"You know something, I don't think they gave us their real names, do you?"

"Why do you say that?"

"Because when we were making the bed, she started to say a different name that started with an S and then caught herself and said 'Clint'."

"You may be right, but we can't question them. God led us here for our protection and we have to respect them. They have their reasons if they've given us bogus names. They are probably doing it to protect themselves and maybe even us in a round-a-bout way. Now let's get some sleep if we can. That wind is really blowing out there."

"You're right. Oh by the way, did you know they're expecting a baby in May?"

"Yeah, he told me. Sounds really happy about it. Say's it'll be the fifth generation."

"She's only a couple months along and they already bought everything imaginable for the baby. And get this, everything is for a boy. She showed me the baby's room. There's no way they could know this soon if it is a boy or a girl. They must have been planning on having a baby for a long time to have everything set up already."

"It's possible they already had the room set up for another child, lost that one, and are now hoping to have a successful pregnancy with this child."

"Mike, you always seem to have a logical answer for everything. You're probably right."

"I try. I'm just glad to be in this nice warm bed and safe from that wind and snow out there. I don't want to get into their personal lives or business. Now let's try to get some sleep. This storm should be blown over by morning and we can be on our way. Hopefully Clint can direct us out of here by way of the shortest route possible. I'm more than ready to get home."

The wind outside continued to howl throughout the night. Steve went downstairs a couple of times to put more wood in the fire so the main house would stay warm. The upstairs didn't get a lot of heat, but since heat rises, some of the heat made its way upstairs. Each time he told Cloud to stay at their bedroom door. This early storm would last for many more days and make it impossible for their guests to leave the mountain. With the storm came a greater trust and love for Steve and Favor. When the first gray light of morning began to filter into the house Favor woke to hear the wind still howling angrily outside. "Steve, listen to the wind. It sounds terrible. I thought it would have blown past by now."

"I know. This is worse than I expected. I'm going to get up as soon as it gets a little lighter outside so I can check on everything. I hope there isn't any damage. It hasn't let up all night. You were right to insist we have them stay. There is no way they would have made it in this weather."

"I'm glad you said that. I was scared for them. They can't leave in this storm"

"I know what you're thinking. They can't leave till it's absolutely safe. We may have company for Thanksgiving! What would you think of that?"

"Steven, serious! That would be so fun!"

"Don't get your hopes up. They're probably anxious to get home to their families."

"I know. I know. But, it's nice that you said it either way."

Holding onto each other they listened to the rumbling that at times made the old house quiver. Favor clung tighter to Steven every time she felt it. He kissed her tenderly as if to comfort her fears and make her feel safe. When it was light enough outside Steve rose from the bed and dressed. "I've got to check on the animals. You stay in bed awhile longer."

"No, I'm coming downstairs. I'll start some coffee and some breakfast. If you need me for anything I'll be ready."

"Ok, but I don't want you to even think about going outside."

"You may need help."

As they were leaving their room, Mike stepped out of the bedroom across the hall. "Storms still going. Thought you might need some help with your animals and checking things."

"I probably could use the help and I am concerned about my stock."

"Jan's just getting dressed. She'll be out in a few minutes. I'm sure she'd be willing to help with anything she can." Just then she appeared at the bedroom door.

"Good morning, Jan. Did you sleep ok?"

"All I could think of, was how thankful I was to be here and not out there."

Together the four of them descended the stairs. The fire Steve had kept going throughout the night had kept the downstairs at a comfortable temperature. Steve added more wood to the fire and then bundled up to go outside. Mike followed suit and they headed out to the barn. When they left Jan turned to Favor, "Do you really like living way up here alone?

Aren't you afraid? I like to go backpacking but I still get awfully scared sometimes. You don't really seem to be the type to be here. You've got a quality about you. Like a real lady. I don't think your husband's too happy to have us here."

Favor stood smiling at Jan. "At first I didn't want to live here. I fought S…Clint," there she did it again. She needed to be more careful. "I fought Clint about it, but as time went on I came to love it here and the peacefulness. He makes me feel safe. And don't worry about him. He likes to act the tough guy to show me he can protect me. He doesn't really mean anything by it. The only time I get a little scared is when Clint goes down the mountain for supplies or to check on his company."

"Don't you go with him?"

Favor realized she'd already said too much. "Not if he's going to be gone overnight. Someone has to stay and take care of the animals. Mainly the cow and the chickens. In the spring and summer the horses and cattle have plenty of pasture to graze on." She hoped Jan would be satisfied with her explanation and promptly changed the subject suggesting they should get started with breakfast and hoping she had not noticed her slip up. Jan didn't seem to notice her hesitancy or if she did she was careful not to let on.

Throughout the day the winds moaned and whistled around the house as the snow continued to fall. By mid-day Steve was becoming concerned about the cattle. So with the tractor he began to blade his way down to the lower pasture with the trailer hooked up behind carrying more hay. Much to his relief the cattle were still huddled close together under the shelter. Steve unhooked the trailer and bladed the snow away from the shelter's open side, leaving the snow at the back and sides to create a barricade and windbreak, thus holding the heat inside. The cattle seemed comfortable. The far trough outside of the shelter had a thin layer of ice on it, but the trough under the sheltered area was not frozen over, much to his relief. The automatic water valves were working well. Fresh water was still pumping in from the underground pipe he had laid. He put the hay in the small storage area at the end of the shelter and together he and Mike fed the cattle a generous helping of hay.

"You've got a nice setup here. Never knew people did this sort of thing for their cattle."

"Bigger ranchers drive their cattle to lower pastures during the winter. I don't have that luxury so I keep a small herd. I have to do whatever I can to keep them protected and safe. This is going to be one of the roughest winters I've ever seen up here. I've tried to be prepared. By keeping the cattle here instead of on the open range I can better protect them from predators and I can get feed to them more easily."

The wind was so loud that the two men had to shout at each other to be heard. When Steve was satisfied that the animals were going to be ok till the next day when he could check on them, he motioned Mike to hop on the tractor so they could head back. At the house the girls were preparing a warm meal for the men when they came back. Jan was amazed at the skill in which Favor planned and prepared everything from scratch and her timing was amazing. Everything was ready at once and she knew just how long to plan before cooking each item, from the time she heard the tractor coming back to the barn.

The storm continued for the next two days, dumping several feet of new snow on Rainbow Moor. It was like no other storm that Steve could remember. This was highly unusual. Winters were not normally very bad in this region, but this was severe. It made him nervous. He was constantly watching and caring for the stock making sure they were safe. Mike and Jan pitched in cleaning stalls, gathering eggs and even trying their hand at milking the cow. At times you could barely see your way to the barn.

On the morning of the third day the storm finally broke. Mike and Jan planned to leave and asked Steve if he could help them get started off in the right direction. "Look, the snow is too fresh. It needs time to pack down and harden. You won't be able to tell what's under the snow. That could be dangerous. We'd like you to stay a while longer. It's not that long till Thanksgiving and I know Kathy would love for you to stay and spend the holiday with us."

Shocked they looked at Steve with mouths open. "We don't want to wear out our welcome, but we'd really like to stay a while longer. The thought of trying to get out through the snow isn't something we're really prepared for. Are you sure?"

"I'm sure."

"Clint, I don't know what to say?"

"Just say yes. Fa...uh, Kathy already said she'd hoped you would stay." Both girls looked at each other, squealed and hugged each other like two school girls. The guys just shook their heads and Steve pulled out a couple of beers from the fridge and motioned Mike to head into the living room.

Favor ran into the living room throwing her arms around Steve. "I love you so much. Thank you." The admiration and love he saw in her eyes warmed him all over. There was no doubt that she truly wanted to be with him. It was a new beginning, and a new trust that was growing ever stronger between Steve and Favor. And now they had new friends to enjoy.

When Favor left the room Mike noticed the look of love and happiness on Steve's face. "I can see you two have something really special between you. Jan and I have a great relationship, but there's something unique and almost reverent between you and your wife. Maybe it's because of where you live but I think it's more."

Steve looked at Mike. "You're right. You have no idea. Our love even amazes me at times. I can hardly wait till our son is born, then I'll feel complete. I'll have my heir to carry on the next generation."

Steve's words made Mike feel enigmatically aware of something remarkably unusual when Steve spoke, but felt puzzled by this perception. Somehow he knew it was best not to say anything more out of a peculiar sense of respect. Steve felt relaxed and content. He fully trusted Favor and knew in his heart she would be careful with her words so they would not raise any questions or suspicions about them.

The girls were laughing in the other room and Steven felt proud hearing Favor's laugh. His own emotions surprised him. "We need to plan our Thanksgiving dinner." Favor was saying. "Let's make some decorations for the table so it will look really festive. What do you think?"

"Sounds like fun. But what can we make? We don't have anything do we?"

"Of course we do. I have some pinecones I gathered earlier this fall that I thought I could use for Christmas, but we could use some of them to make little miniature turkeys as decorations at each place settings on the table. We can get some feathers from the chicken coop to use for the tails and wings. There are always a bunch of feathers in there. We can draw the heads on paper, paint them and cut them out. I dried some marigolds from the garden that we can use to make a floral centerpiece and I pressed some fall leaves that we can spread around on the table. Clint got me a bunch of ribbon and I'm sure I can find some fall colors. It will be fun. I used to be a designer so he bought me a lot of things to keep me busy." For a moment her mind flickered back to some remote part of her memory, but she promptly dismissed it.

The girls set to work later that afternoon making their crafts. They instructed the guys to keep their noses out of the kitchen where they were working on their project. They made miniature bales of hay for the center of the table hiding them in a box not to be revealed until Thanksgiving Day.

When the day finally arrived the men were up early taking care of the animals while the girls began baking and cooking in the kitchen. Steve had taken one of the turkeys out the day before so it could thaw. Favor had seasoned and dried bread earlier to use for dressing. By the time the pies and cakes were finished cooking the turkey was ready for the oven. When it was time to decorate the table the men were banished from the dining room to the library so as not to ruin the surprise.

"Come on, Babe, just let me get a couple of beers."

"Oh no you don't. I'll bring them to you. You are not coming in here till we say."

"We're getting hungry. And don't tell me you two haven't been sampling the food. It smells so good it's driving us crazy."

"We'll bring you a snack to tide you over, but you can't come in here!"

Steve and Mike were amazed when they walked into the dining room to find it festively decorated and laden with more food than they expected. The girls had prepared the turkey, dressing, mashed potatoes, gravy, and green-bean casserole, corn on the cob, sweet potatoes and biscuits. For dessert they had baked apple pie and mini chocolate bunt cakes, as well as apple juice that Favor and Steve had pressed in late October and some wine. Favor said she wanted her guests to enjoy the wine though she would only be drinking apple juice because of the baby.

It was the best Thanksgiving any of them could remember. Mike and Jan felt especially thankful because had they not stumbled onto Rainbow Moor they surely would have frozen to death in the storm. But even more they were grateful for their new friends and the bond that now tied them together. It was a day of new memories, thankfulness, peace and trust.

Chapter 22

A dam had begun the drive back to Fortuna. As he drove over the winding road of Hwy 299 he kept replaying the events over and over in this mind. As he thought over what had transpired in the last 24 hours he kept trying to place the face of the elderly woman. Then it hit him. He recalled the photo of Sadie Marks with her nephew Steven Mitchell when he was sixteen. The old woman in the elevator had all the features of Sadie Marks only older. Two strange encounters with people who had passed on un-nerved him to the point he had to pull off the side of the road. What was happening here? Were these women guiding him to Favor? This just couldn't be. He didn't believe in the super natural or messengers, angels or demons or whatever it seemed to be. It had to be some freak coincidence. What else could it be?

"Who's to say what is real and what is not real. Who am I to decide, question, dismiss or accept? And why is this happening to me?" He had gotten out of his truck and was pacing along the roadside. Looking up towards the sky he shouted, "What do you want from me? Why can't you leave me alone? Haven't I done enough to find her?" He was terrified but driven to continue his search. But at what cost? His own sanity? His job? His friends? It was too much to bare. Then he sat down on the side of the road, buried his face in his hands and sobbed like a child.

He didn't know how long he sat there, but in the end he got to his feet, took a big gulp of air and squared his shoulders. He would see this through no matter what the cost. If he didn't he knew he would spend the rest of his life regretting his decision. Not knowing was worse than knowing. Somehow, deep inside he felt stronger and accepting of whatever this all meant. Be it fate, destiny or his damnation he knew this was his cross and he would carry it to hell and back if that was what it took. He cut off onto Highway 3, a connecting road from Highway 299 to Highway 36. First stop, the Dinsmore Store to inquire about Ol' Smokey.

"Hey! Adam Jennings, I've been trying to call you on that cell phone of yours for the last few hours. It's your lucky day. Smokey came down the mountain for one last load of supplies. Said he had a feeling he was going to need more supplies because there's a big storm brewing. Said he could feel it in his bones that this was going to be a big one. I told him about you and your lady friend. Said he'd be heading back day after tomorrow and if you wanted to go back with him you'd best be here tonight to talk it out and then he'd decide by tomorrow if he'd be willing to take you now or in the spring or if at all."

"I've been out of cell phone range. But this is perfect, because I got all kinds of information that can help us find that house. We're getting closer. I can feel it."

"Ok, be here at five when I close the store. You two can talk it out, then you let him decide. Don't pressure him and don't go off on a tangent or he'll tell you to go to hell. Give him the facts and then let him chew on it awhile. He's a good man but doesn't take well to people pressuring him or arguing or 'begging' neither. He's good at reading people so don't try any funny stuff. Just be honest and factual and be yourself. He may say you have to wait till spring. Don't argue if he does. Accept it and learn anything he tells you to learn."

"Thanks, Jake. I'll do exactly as you say. This could be my last chance and I'm not going to blow it. I've gone through a lot the last couple of days that you would hardly believe."

"If it's more of that weird crap we experienced then I damn well don't want to hear about it. I'm still freaked out."

"Hey it was your mother. And you sure as hell don't want me to tell you. I'll be back in a couple of hours. Got to make a few phone calls."

He needed to call Houston to see if they had any papers around with Favor's social security number on it so he could compare it to the one in the trust papers, then he needed to call his boss and tell him he wouldn't be in tomorrow either (and maybe not all winter) depending on what the old mountain man decided. Somehow, he felt peaceful about whatever decision the old guy decided to make about him. He had begun to believe there was a higher power at work in his search and he had to trust that he was being guided and come what may, it would all work out in the end the way it is meant to.

He put in the call to Houston and gave him the social security number for Favor Mitchell. Houston said he'd call him back as soon as possible but that he might have to get the number from Favor's dad. Within an hour Houston called back.

"Adam, you'd best be sitting down," there was a slight hesitation on the other end of the line as he waited for Adam to say something. "That number you gave me? Well, it matches the one I found in some old records in the bedroom. They are one and the same. This Favor Mitchell is our Favor Durand. I'm just glad I found information here. I would have hated to have to call her dad and not know what to tell him about why I was asking. What are you going to do now?"

"Will let you know by tomorrow. I have someone I need to talk to first and depending on how that conversation goes, will depend on my next move. I'll let you know as soon as possible. And Houston, can you keep this under your hat for now? I don't want to cause any problems that could blow this whole thing. I need to keep it quiet for now. Can you do that for me, please?"

"You've got my word. I just hope you know what you're doing."

"Trust me. I do. I have no doubt."

"All right man, just keep me informed as much as you can." With that Houston heard the click of the phone as Adam hung up.

The call to Adam's boss was uncomfortable to say the least, but for some reason his boss took it quite well that he wouldn't be in again the next day.

Almost five o'clock. Adam was sitting in the store waiting. Jake proceeded to close up shop as if Adam wasn't there. Promptly at five in walked an old bearded gentleman. Though somewhat roughly clad, he had a stately manner with gentle eyes and weathered skin. Jake and the old man shook hands. "Well I see Miss Rosie got her mitts on you and gave you a haircut." He proceeded to lock the door behind him and turn the open sign around to the closed side.

"Dang woman just cain't keep her hands offn me when I come in." Jake responded with a big roaring laugh. "Got's ta admit, she does a right fine job of it. Cain't really complain none. I think she's still sweet on me."

"Damn it, Smokey, you know she is. She'll probably wait for you till one of you die."

"Ya probly right." Then Smokey looked in the direction of Adam who was waiting patiently and quietly on a stool. Smokey looked at Jake and nodded towards Adam. "So that be him? The one ya told me 'bout?"

"That's him." The two spoke as if Adam wasn't there or able to hear them. Then Ol' Smokey approached Adam. Adam stood to his feet out of respect and waited politely.

Smokey turned back to Jake and said, "Bring a couple of stools and join us over here, but first off how 'bout you get us all a drink." Then he turned back to Adam and reached out a hand to him. "Folks round these parts call me Smokey. Used to smoke too much. Dun give it up some years back. Name stuck. Guess it be a reminder not to do it no more. What might yer name be?"

"Adam, sir, Adam Jennings. I'm pleased to meet you."

"Likewise, I'm please ta make yer acquaintance as well, Adam Jennings. Jake dun filled me in on yer story. Since ya be here, I gather yer little lady's still a missin'."

"Yes, sir, she is." Adam was careful to let the old gentleman ask the questions and go at his own pace. Jake joined them and handed each of them a soda. "Gave up smoking, drinkin, mainly whiskey, but don't think I'd be fool enough ta give up women." Then he threw back his head and let out a loud hearty laugh that echoed throughout the store. Adam smiled and laughed along with him. "Wouldn't expect any man in his right mind to give up women. Now tell me a bit 'bout yerself and yer little lady."

Jake looked at Adam with a knowing eye reminding Adam the instructions he'd given him. Stick to the facts. So Adam briefly told him about himself and Favor, keeping it simple.

Smokey listened, then turned to Jake, "You bin coaxing this boy on what ta say, Jake?"

Jake smiled and nodded. "Just a bit, Smoke."

Once again Smokey threw his head back and let out another loud peel of laughter. Then he smacked Adam on the shoulder and looking at Jake said, "I like this boy. He kin foller instructions pretty good. Hear ya got some info fer me and some things fer me ta look at." Adam nodded. "Well, let's git down ta business and have a look see."

After looking over an old forest service map Adam had managed to acquire, the Deed and a very old Plat Map, Smokey sat back with a thoughtful look on his face. "Ifn thet thirs where the ol' homestead is located thir ain't no way yer gonna git up thir this time a year. I hear snows a comin' in a few days. Gonna be a bad win'er this year I'd be sayin'. But come spring we kin make our way up. I know the area. Ev'ry time I get close to that area I get a feelin' I don't belong. Like it's a special place. Thir be an ol' road leadin' in, but thir be gates and fences so we gonna have ta go up and around the long way and come back down. Hope ta be able ta find it. Won't be easy and sumthin' up thir that don't let nobody git too close. I've herd tell of a legend in them parts."

He sat back thoughtful like and took a big gulp of coke. Abruptly changing the subject he continued, "Yep, I hear tell o' some young couple bin a missin' in them hills fer nigh on a week now. They's bin a packin on foot. Durn green-horns. They got no bisness traipsing around them mountains when they's don't know thir way."

"So what are you saying?"

"Son, ya bin pretty good on the patient end a things so fer. Ya don't want to be spoilin' things. Yer green. Need sum learnin. I'll be havin' ta teach ya a thing or two before we attempt to go in. Got me sum mules up in the hills, I speck I'll be needin' ta take um along with us." In his eyes was a sparkle Adam hadn't seen a moment ago.

"So you will help me!" Adam's eyes lit up.

"I like ya son. I ain't had a good adventure in a while. But we do it my way. Ya listen, ya learn and in the end we'll find yer girl."

"Yes, sir."

"Let's git to plannin'."

For the next several hours Smokey planned what they would need for the trip. They would only go part way up the mountain, to his lower, main cabin with the jeep. Here he would take the time during the hard cold winter months to teach Adam the ways of the mountain men and how to survive its harsh elements. He'd teach him how to pack on a mule so their trip from the lower cabin upward would be much easier and quicker. Adam would learn how to cook and survive off the land.

"If ya don't know these things ya ain't gonna be bringin' no one including yer self outa them mountains. I ain't havin' ya git me hurt or killt jist cuz ya don't know what ya doin'."

Smokey knew he needed to plan for more than his normal supplies since he'd be taking Adam along. He liked the determination he saw in Adam and his willingness to listen and learn although he could also see he was anxious. But the experiences Adam had gone through in the past few months had in their own way helped to prepare him for the next step in his search. Together they purchased the needed supplies and packed the jeep. Adam had to make the dreaded phone call to his boss and then he let Houston know he'd be gone for an extended period of time. He'd need him to take care of his home and personal affairs. Smokey made sure he had what was absolutely necessary with only the barest of personal necessities. "If ya cain't carry it on yer back or on a mule ya don't need it. Now go git some rest. Be here 6:30 sharp."

"Tell me more about this legend you were talking about."

"Did ya hear me? 6:30 sharp!" Then turned his back on Adam who left without a word.

At first light Adam arrived back at the store. "Pour yerself a cup a coffee," he said nodding towards the coffee pot. Smokey was sitting in the same spot as the night before as if he hadn't even left at all. "'Bout that legend, thir was this wealthy family s'posed to have settled up thir yers ago and some tragedy occurred. Heard tell thir be some phantom ghost runnin' round up thir thet keeps intruders out. Yep, a rider and a white hoss. Land there's protected they say." Was Smokey trying to get a reaction out of him? Was he trying to test him to see if he'd be scared? After what had happened to him recently he'd believe just about anything. Some old legend wasn't going to stop him from looking for Favor.

Smokey and Adam finished packing up the jeep and headed up into the mountains for the lower cabin. It was late afternoon when they arrived and unpacked the jeep. Adam 'introduced' him to the mules that would eventually be their method of transportation to the upper cabin. "Tomorrow ya start learnin'. So ya needs ta git plenty a rest tonight."

"Will we be taking all four of them up the mountain?" Stupid question.

"If we don't whose gonna care fer the one's we leave behind? Mules gotta pack yer supplies and unless ya want to walk, ya needs one ta ride. These here be my main saddle mules, them twos are my main packin' mules."

Adam needed to learn how to handle and saddle a mule, and most of all learn to ride, something he'd never done. Smokey started by teaching him about the animals, their care, how to catch and halter them. Then he taught him the parts of the saddle and how to put on their headstalls. "Why do I need to know the parts of a saddle? A saddles a saddle."

"Wrong. There be all kinds of saddles. Ya needs ta know the parts and ya needs to know how to look fer wear in the leather. Ya never know when ya might have to do a quick repair to a broken lashing or belt." Smokey patiently explained the parts of the saddle and how other saddles differ. He had several worn books with pictures he showed Adam. After a day of learning the equipment and how to put it on and off and properly take care of the equipment he said Adam was ready to learn to ride. That would be the next day lesson.

The following day he sent Adam out to saddle up both saddle mules while he fixed breakfast. Adam was a bit apprehensive about handling the animals on his own, but did as he was told. Animals are smart. They know when someone is a 'greenhorn' and will enjoy testing them. The mules didn't make it easy. It took less than five minutes for Smokey to catch the mules the day before. A full half hour went by before Adam could catch the first one. They'd run away from him put up their nose and bray at him as if laughing. He was about to give up when the oldest mule finally let himself be caught. By this time breakfast was ready and Smokey was standing on the porch of the cabin laughing at Adam.

"Tie 'im up and git in here and eat. Ta other will be easier."

Frustrated Adam obeyed and went in to eat. Nothing was said till they'd finished eating then Smokey sent him back out to finish catching and saddling the mules. Nearly another hour went by before he had both mules caught and saddled. Smokey had taken to sitting on the porch watching and drinking coffee. When Adam was done Smokey went to the corral and checked to see if Adam had saddled them correctly and put their headstalls on properly. When he had inspected them he looked at

Adam and asked if he was sure everything was right. Adam looked them over and said yes. "Ya sure now?"

"Yeah, I think so. I don't think I forgot anything."

"Ok then. Git on and I'll be showin' ya how ta ride."

Thinking about what he'd seen in the movies he mounted from the correct side and slipped easily and comfortably into the saddle. Smokey instructed him on how to use his feet and how to rein, then they set out to ride. They'd ridden for about an hour when Adam noticed something didn't feel quite right. The saddle was slipping and no amount of trying to get it centered would keep it in place. They had just started up a small hill when the entire saddle slipped to the side and off went Adam hitting the ground with a thud as Smokey and the two mules moved on ahead. His mule began bucking and kicking trying to get the saddle off. "Hey!"

Smoke stopped and looked back. The mule Adam had been riding stopped as well. Smokey laughed as Adam scrambled to his feet. At the same time the mules did the same, or so it seemed. "Ya did right good ta git this fer. I knowed that cinch was too loose. Git on up here and fix it. This time be sure it be tight enough." Adam obeyed. The rest of the day went without incident. By the time they returned to the cabin every muscle in his body ached and his derriere felt so sore he could barely move.

"Ya'll git used to it," was all Smokey said as he walked off laughing. "Now unsaddle, brush and feed 'em, then clean and put the gear away. I'm going ta start supper." Supper was ready when Smokey came out to check on Adam as he was just hanging up the last headstall. Smoke looked over the equipment, smiled, slapped Adam on the back and said, "Quick learner." Adam nearly fell over from the slap and staggered to keep his balance. He was almost too tired and sore to eat, but the smell of beef stew and pan fried biscuits were too good to pass up.

Outfitters, backcountry horsemen, and others have developed some ingenious techniques and equipment to reduce their impact on the environment and save them time when traveling in the wilderness with pack and saddle stock. Traveling by horse or mule requires planning, preparation and the right equipment. Matching stock to the terrain you wish to travel in and considering the weather plays a big part in wilderness travel and a successful, safe trip.

For the next four days Smokey had Adam saddle the mules and ride the better part of the day, getting Adam more and more conditioned to being in the saddle. All the while Smokey taught him about the vegetation along the trails, trees and how to watch for signs of bear. He told him story after story of his mountain adventures, each story with a lesson that would help Adam to have a keener awareness of his surroundings and be a better and safer rider and packer. Adam became more and more comfortable and he looked forward to the lessons each day.

Smokey kept an ever watchful eye on the weather and showed Adam what to look for in the sky as well as how to listen to the animals of the forest. On the sixth day Smokey pointed out the greying skies and said there would be no riding for a while. They'd have to stay hold up at the cabin for a time. The weather was changing and snow was coming. Instead Adam's lessons would take on a new twist. Adam thought it would be easy days ahead, but much to his surprise they were just as hard if not harder than the previous days had been. Smokey set him to work chopping more firewood to stockpile. Adams arms ached from chopping and stacking wood. "How much wood does one man need? We won't be here the whole time."

"Keep chopping. Ya cain't ever have too much firewood." When he felt Adam had chopped enough for the day he'd set to teaching him other lessons on wilderness survival and equipment used in the back country. He learned how to highline the mules without damaging the tree bark, to make a makeshift feeder and a tent with just a tarp, how to make a temporary corral and to safely stake out a horse if no highline or corral was available. Knot tying became a nightly event. Each night Smokey taught him a different knot and the importance and use for the various knots. The most useful of these was the Bowline. Other knots he learned were the Hitch knot, the Sheepshank, Dutchman, Clove and Timber Hitch, your basic Square knot and the quick release Square Bow knot. He even learned how to make a rope halter. All this helped to pass the time and Adam became more and more fascinated with the simplicity of the life of a mountain man as well as the importance of knowing the right things to do at the right time.

Smokey taught him fire building skills and different methods of starting a fire. He learned how to prepare food over an open fire and how to protect your equipment and animals during a snow storm. The food they prepared was some of the best he had ever tasted. Not only did he learn how to use the resources that nature abundantly provided, but he learned to respect nature and care for her as if she was a delicate, beautiful woman.

Adam learned what to look for in a good pack animal like prominent withers to keep a saddle and pack from slipping and a good strong back, not too flat. He learned that a strong neck and deep chest (not too broad) a well-rounded barrel and straight powerful hind quarters were important in a good pack and saddle animal. Smokey taught Adam how to watch for injuries such as how resting a foot on the front of the hoof or toe could mean a shoulder injury or soreness. Pointing a front foot could mean a sore foot or possible bruised frog or sole.

"How did you learn all this?"

"Took years of learnin'. Started out when I was 'bout ten. Plenty of mistakes. Lots of trial and error. Had me some good teachers like me pappy and grand pappy, an uncle and some good friends. Most of 'em have passed on now. Yu be gettin' a crash course, so's it be real important ya listen good and learn the first time round."

"So why mules and not horses?'

"Mules don't need shoein' like hosses does. They be a bit more stubborn, but they be real tough and sure footed on the trails. I've had some good hosses though."

What fascinated Adam the most were the pack saddles. He was surprised at how many different kinds there were. He decided he liked the Decker pack saddle the best. While Smokey liked the Sawbuck. Learning the different methods of tying on and balancing a load was amazing. Smokey taught him the basket sling, barrel sling, crowfoot sling and the best knots to secure them. There are all types of panniers for transporting supplies, both soft and hard as well as canvas wraps. The way to fold and secure the canvas is crucial to making sure the load won't slip or come apart. Adam found that the Squaw Hitch was one of the easiest and quickest for him to learn and use, but his favorites was the Box Hitch and Diamond Hitch. Smokey taught him how to repair a fraying rope and how to make Tandem hitches and ties.

Smokey's favorite tricks was to pack eggs inside the animal grain to keep them from breaking. By first putting two at a time in a plastic bag, twisting the bag and then placing it back in the carton ensured that if an egg broke it was still usable because it was inside the plastic and wouldn't leak all over the carton and grain. Dehydrated foods and dry goods such as dry milk, biscuit and pancake mix, instant potatoes, and corn meal are lighter and more cost effective.

First aid for both horse and rider was another valuable set of lessons. Smokey had him practice different bandages and quizzed him on what to do in the event a certain injury occurred. Even more important was keeping tools and first aid supplies handy. "Ya don't want to be havin' ta unpack the whole load to git to the most important things in the event ya need 'em in a hurry. Always pack them last near the top or on the out sides so's ya kin git to um fast."

Preparation and awareness of wildlife such as bear, cougar or coyote that could spook a pack animal and knowing the best and safest way to lead a pack string could mean the difference in one animal's nervousness spooking the whole pack string. Careful preparation and constant alertness could make the difference in keeping your stock safe and healthy as well as yourself.

Adam practiced making camp outside the cabin. "Camp is what ya make it! Always pack out what ya pack in. Everyone shares in the chores," were just a few of the things Smokey taught him. How to make different types of shelters and different uses for tarps as well as where to set up a tent to be sure you don't get runoff if it were to rain, were valuable lessons as well.

The days slipped by as Adam continued to learn and grow in confidence as he learned the necessary skills to survive and be a good packer. He would have been surprised to know that the road to get into the property where Favor lived was not that many miles away from the road they had come in on, though its access was blocked by several locked gates. Smokey knew this, but he also knew the only possible way into that property was to go high up above and work down through the forest. Besides, it gave him a chance to teach a "young buck" the ways of the mountains, patience and respect for the wilderness. He'd been in the area before and knew it was an area well protected from intruders. If the girl was there he knew her captor had planned well and was knowledgeable of the forest and its boundaries.

The holidays would come and go and Adam would not even know it. He would lose track of time save for the changing of the seasons. But he would be prepared and he would be a changed man by the time the winter snows passed. They would soon leave for the upper cabin so Smokey could put Adam's new skills to the test. He was a little concerned because of the unusually early heavy snows this year. It would be better to stay at the lower cabin, but he knew the way well and his many years of packing were no match for this area. He'd packed in areas far more rugged and remote. To Smokey this area was child's play and would be good practice for Adam. It would also keep him from feeling he was wasting time and feel like he was getting closer to finding Favor.

Chapter 23

Thanksgiving was over and only a month till Christmas. Though it continued to snow lightly the snow was not menacing like the strange storm that had come through earlier that month. Mike and Jan were making plans to leave. Favor was feeling dread at having them go. She wanted them to stay through Christmas, but knew they needed to be on their way. They had families that would be worried about them. Favor thought with sadness about her own Dad and family and her old friends who must have worried about her when she disappeared.

Thinking of them preparing for the festivities and the bright Christmas lights, the Christmas Carols, Nativities, dinners and celebrations made her miss them. She tried to picture their faces, but they seemed so distant and remote and unfamiliar now. She tried to remember their voices but couldn't. It was going on seven months since she'd come to Rainbow Moor. Somehow it seemed longer. How could she forget so soon? If she'd forgotten them, they must by now have forgotten her and moved on with their lives. A deep melancholy within overshadowed her entire countenance. Trying hard not to let it show was almost more than she could bare.

Steve noticed she was quiet and not her usually jovial self. "Are you feeling all right?"

"I'm fine. I just hate to see them leave." Finding it hard to look Steven in the eye she looked away. Noticing her aloofness, he realized there was more than their leaving troubling Favor. So he came up with an idea that hopefully would make her feel better.

"I know. It's been nice having them here. Maybe we could have an early Christmas with them before they go. How would you like that? We could decorate a tree and make presents for each other. After we exchange gifts we could have a Christmas breakfast before they leave. That way it would feel more like Christmas. What do you think? We'd have to ask them and start planning right away. But they may rather get going and to be on their way today."

Favor tearfully looked hopefully at Steve. "Would you please ask them?"

Steve headed up the stairs and knocked on the door of the bedroom Mike and Jan were staying in. Mike opened the door, "Is something wrong?"

"No, but I do have something to ask you. Kathy is really feeling down that you are leaving so I came up with an idea to hopefully cheer her up. How would you feel about staying over at least one more day to do an early Christmas? I thought we could get a tree and decorate it, then we can make each other some simple little gift to exchange. We could have Christmas the next morning and then have a real special breakfast before you leave."

Mike and Jan looked shocked. "I don't know? Jan, what do you think?"

"I think it's a beautiful idea and if it will help Kathy then what's one more day?" Jan still felt there was something unusual about Clint and Kathy's living situation. In the back of her mind she felt like she'd seen Kathy somewhere before, but couldn't remember. She just didn't feel like she fit the lifestyle and she had felt all along they were hiding something. "I'd love to myself. But it's ultimately up to you. We could still be home to spend Christmas with our families. It's still two weeks away."

"It would mean so much to Kathy."

Looking at each other they both smiled and began to laugh. "Let's do it!" The three of them rushed down the stairs to tell her the good news. Favor was so happy that she burst into tears. Jan hugged her tightly. Awhile later the men bundled up and headed out to find the perfect Christmas tree while the girls began popping popcorn and stringing it for garland.

For ornaments they made colored popcorn balls, wrapped them in cellophane, tied with red ribbon to hang. White construction paper was cut into the shape of candy canes using red paper for the stripes. Yellow paper made stars with a touch of glitter to make them twinkled. White paper was folded and cut to make snowflakes and iridescent glitter to make them glistened. Brown paper was made into gingerbread men. While they worked at making the ornaments they planned what they would make for Christmas Eve dinner and tomorrow's Christmas Breakfast. "This is the kind of Christmas you might read about in an old pioneer story book or like the 'Little House on the Prairie' series books."

"Jan, I'm so glad we're doing this. It will make a wonderful memory."

Jan sat back thoughtful for a moment, "Yeah, Kathy, it will make a wonderful memory. Kathy, I'd like to ask you a question. You don't have to answer, but I have to ask." Kathy felt apprehensive waiting for the question. "I feel like there is more to you than meets the eye. You and Clint really seem to love each other, but it doesn't seem like you belong here. In fact you both seem out of place somehow. Kathy listened and then chose her words carefully.

"This house has been in his family for generations. I think he may have been born here. His parents used it as a summer home at first and later as a weekend and holiday retreat. He loved coming here more than anything when he was young. His fondest memories of his parents are here. They died when he was only sixteen. This place is very special and this is where he wanted his child to be born. So he made the decision to live here year round."

"You said 'he made the decision'. You didn't say 'we'."

"Did I? Well, I meant 'we' made the decision."

Just then they heard the men coming so they donned hats, coats, gloves and boots to go out and see the Christmas tree they'd chosen. It was a beautiful tree which they placed in a bucket after fashioning a small stand. Rocks were used to weigh it down. Then they filled it with water to keep it fresh. It was decided they would all decorate the tree together in the evening, but for now they would make their gifts. The guys went to the shop to make their Christmas gifts. They had the look of mischief in their eyes like two school boys. "Honey you know that old trunk in our room? You might find some things in there that you could use to make something." he winked. "If you know what I mean."

Favor looked at him with laughing eyes and rushed upstairs. The trunk held an array of old keepsakes, some fabric, yarn, embroidery thread and an old fur stole. Favor decided she'd make Mike a warm hat and Jan a soft muff to keep her hands extra warm. It would be their gifts to Mike and Jan. For Steve she took a blue shirt from his closet and embroidered a white horse on the back.

Steve decided to give each of the girls a piece of heirloom jewelry from his family keepsakes and for Mike he chose a knife his father had given him many years before.

Mike busied himself in the shop carving a set of wooden bookends for Steve. For Jan he carved two candle sticks. And with Steve's help they fashioned a baby cradle for Favor.

Jan found some beautiful green fabric and she made a set of four placemats for the table which she edged in lace for Favor. For each of the men she quickly wove two scarves. Favor watched in amazement as the knitting needles and yarn she found in the trunk seemed to fly through her fingers.

"Where did you learn to knit so fast? I've never seen anyone do that before."

"It's really simple. I'd teach you if I had more time, but I saw a knitting book in the trunk that you might be able to learn from. My grandmother taught me when I was only nine years old." In no time she had both scarves completed.

"I wish we had some pretty wrapping paper."

"We could use some brown paper bags and decorate them."

It was well into the late afternoon before the gifts were complete. They'd worked hard and fast to get them done, not even stopping to eat. When finished the girls began cooking dinner. After dinner they would all trim the tree together. The guys were still out in the shop. The girls were getting excited wondering what they were making. It was already dark when they finally came in from feeding. Dinner was waiting and they sat down to enjoy their last evening meal together. When they were done they trimmed the tree together and then stood back to admire it. No store bought glass bulbs and no tinsel, but it was beautiful in a most simplistic way. One thing Steve said was a must and that was that there be sixteen candles on the tree. When he told them it had been a family tradition he had a faraway look in his eyes. When they were done Mike excused himself for a moment and stepped out onto the porch. When he returned he held out a beautiful hand carved star to Favor. The finely crafted star portrayed the nativity neatly carved into one side.

"Kathy, Clint told me this will be your first Christmas together and we are honored to be able to share it with you. I made this for the tree so that you will always remember Jan and me. Our names and the year are carved on the back side." Favor took it in her hands and held it reverently as a tear silently fell. Admiring the intricate details he had carved into the star, a tiny manger with the baby Jesus at the lower part of the star and at the peak of the star an angel looking down. Her eyes met Steve's and without thinking she spoke, "Steve, look at it!"

The room became silent as they looked from one to the other. Surprisingly, it was Mike who spoke first. "It's ok, we pretty much knew you had not given us your real names. But, we figured you had your reasons. You saved our lives and we've been blessed in more ways than you know. Your secret is safe with us."

"My real name is Steven Lawrence Mitchell IV. My wife's name is Favor."

They all began to laugh. Favor joked out a tearful request, "Mike will you do the honors of putting it on the tree?"

They each felt the importance of the moment as they watched in silence as Mike placed it on the tree. A bond of friendship had grown between them. Though their lives were destined to part and maybe never cross paths again, they knew they had built a friendship that would never be forgotten, a friendship that would carry them through a lifetime.

Jan broke the silence, "I think this calls for some hot cider and pie."

"Pie? When did you girls have time to make pie?"

"We were multi-tasking all day."

The fire crackled in the fireplace and the cider warmed them inside. Steve found a Christmas CD which he put in the CD player. The voice of Clint Black filled the room and they sang along to the Christmas tunes. In time they all retired to bed, the girls hugging each other outside their rooms as they said their goodnights.

In the morning the guys were heading down the stairs for the gift exchange before the girls were barely awake. They were like four little kids on Christmas morning, barely able to contain themselves. The girls laughed and rushed to catch up to them. Cloud sensed their excitement and jumped up and down wanting to romp around. "We need to go feed before we open our gifts, we'll be back in a bit."

Favor and Jan stood looking at each other. "Now what do you suppose they're up to?"

"Don't know, but they're not just going out to feed. They're up to something."

It wasn't long before they returned carrying a large object covered with a blanket, which they set beside the tree. Favor eyed it curiously. "Ok, I'm ready to open presents!"

Laughing and carrying on they each exchanged the gifts they had made or chosen for each other. It was such fun. Then Steve said, "Favor, this one is for you from Mike and me. We made it together." With the shyness of a school girl she pulled the blanket back to reveal the most beautiful handmade cradle with delicate carvings along the sides and ends. Favor was shocked and amazed at its beauty.

"This is so beautiful. I don't know what to say. It's amazing."

"I believe you saved our lives by taking us in. I am honored by both of you," Mike was saying. "This is a real old fashioned Christmas and one I will always cherish. It will be remembered as the best Christmas I've ever had."

Though they tried to keep the breakfast light hearted, it was difficult knowing in less than an hour Mike and Jan would be on their way home.

Steve prepared to guide Mike and Jan part way down the mountain. There was too much snow on the road to drive them to the main road. Favor would have to stay behind. He wouldn't risk the baby by having her go. They had given Steve and Favor their address in the event they were ever in their area they could look them up. He would take the horses. Jan would ride Snow with Steve leading. Denali would carry their packing gear while Mike led him. The snow had packed down considerably and was fairly easy going. Favor had insisted Cloud go with them as well. It was a tearful goodbye. The women hugged each other several times before Jan got on Snow and they started down the mountain. Favor was uneasy as she watched them go. "Please, God, keep them safe."

Once again the old memories somewhere in her past tugged at her heart strings. A time of family, friends and freedom. Dismissing it from her mind she lay down on the couch to look at the tree and soon fell asleep. Several hours passed before Steven returned. When he came in she woke, jumped up and rushed into his arms. "Did you miss me that much?"

"Yes. Do you think they'll make it alright?"

"As long as this weather stays clear they will be down the mountain in no time."

"Are you sure?"

"Of course I'm sure. I wouldn't have let them leave if I wasn't." At that moment Favor burst into tears. "Hey, what's going on? What's wrong?"

"I didn't want them to leave." She buried her face in his chest and sobbed. Steven felt helpless and all he could do was hold her.

That night Steve and Favor woke to the familiar sound of wind howling. Favor sat bolt upright in bed. They both looked at each other knowing this unexpected storm was not good for their friends. There had not been any signs of another storm coming and Steve knew this wasn't good. He was hoping they got far enough down the mountain to where they would only get a light snow. Maybe it wouldn't be as bad farther down.

Down the mountain, Mike and Jan were making good time as they were careful to stay on course the way Steve had directed them. They decided to make camp and get an early start in the morning. After setting up their tent they cooked a light supper then turned in early. It was dark by five and walking through the snow was more tiring and difficult than when there was no snow. During the night the winds picked up and whipped the tiny tent threatening to tear it apart. Fear gripped their hearts. The wind brought with it an intense cold. Fearing for the worst they clung to each other for warmth. Somehow the tent managed to hold together through the night, but the wind kept blowing. They decided to hold up in the tent hoping the storm would pass and not be like the last one. By the next morning the storm had only let up slightly. "We can't just stay here. We've got to try to make our way farther down."

"Mike, we can't!"

"We have to try." With that they managed to roll up the tent enough to get it on their pack and started making their way down. The going was rough and they were not able to see very far ahead of them. Little did they know but they were going in a lateral position westerly instead of in the downward path they should have been going. They'd lost their way in the storm.

The light was growing dim. They knew they needed to find a place to set up the tent or find some sort of shelter. The cold was getting to be too much. "I wish we'd never left Steve and Favor's house. We're going to freeze out here."

Mike felt completely helpless. "I'm sorry, Jan. I'm really sorry. Let's just see if we can find someplace with a little shelter from the wind and set up the tent. We don't have any other choice." They moved on, heads bent against the wind and cold. Unexpectedly they came out onto a small clearing. In the fading light through the snow they saw what appeared to be a small structure. They looked at each other with surprise as they both turned and rushed towards it. It was a small cabin of sorts.

A heavy door was latched securely shut but was not locked. They lifted the latch and pushed the door open. It was very small, not more than ten by twelve feet. The tiny windows were covered by shutters making it hard to see. Mike located a lamp and some matches in a tin can nearby as Jan held a flashlight. Lighting the lantern they could see a small wood stove in the far back left corner and a small supply of firewood stacked nearby. In the front left corner was a sizable cupboard. Mike opened it to find a supply of dry goods, canned foods, cooking and eating utensils. To the right were two small cots. In the center of the room stood a small handmade table with two chairs. They couldn't believe their eyes.

Mike set to work building a fire to get the little cabin warmed up. "I've got to see if there is any other firewood. This won't last through the night."

"It's getting dark out. You won't be able to see. I'll go with you so I can hold the flashlight if you find some." Together they made their way outside and began walking around the cabin. To their relief they found a lean-to against the cabin which contained a generous supply of firewood. There appeared to be another smaller structure that looked like it might be an outhouse. Sure enough it was. Mike was so surprised and excited that he burst out laughing. "Does that beat all? Never thought I'd be so happy to see a privy in my entire life."

Gathering up as much fire wood as possible he took it into the cabin, then went out for more, wanting to be sure there was enough for the long night ahead and not wanting to have to go out again once they were settled inside, they both used the outhouse before settling in. The sound of running water drew their attention. A small creek just beyond the outhouse, though partially frozen over, would give them a source of water to cook with and use to clean their utensils. In the fading light they could see a small corral. "Must be a miner's cabin. Whoever owns this must pack in with horses or mules."

It wasn't long before the cabin began to warm. It was made up of sturdy logs and had been made airtight. It felt like a luxury to be out of the storm in such a strong, well-constructed shelter. "Mike, I can't believe we stumbled onto this place."

"You and me both. God is watching out for us." They found a bucket to carry water in. Before long they were eating some canned stew and hot coffee from an old coffee pot. It tasted amazing. "We'll have to try not to use too much of their supply and we'll be sure and leave them some money and a note thanking them and let them know we had no other choice." The cabin soon was warm and toasty. Their stomachs were full and they were safe. Pulling out their sleeping bags they rolled them out onto each cot and settled in for the night. In the morning they'd look around and see if they could find a trail and head out again.

The storm didn't let up for another day and a half. When the weather seemed to clear enough they decided to secure the cabin and leave. The going was rough and extremely slow. The snow had not packed down making it more difficult to make their way. They'd traveled about two miles when Jan suddenly slipped off the edge of the trail into the snow tumbled down a small embankment. She felt her foot hit a log or something in the snow and felt a sharp pain. Removing his pack Mike scrambled down to where she lay as she grabbed at her ankle. Fearing it was broken Mike gently felt her ankle. It seemed to be a sprain. Looking up he had to figure out a way to get Jan back up to the trail. It was steeper than he'd thought. He took her pack off her and carried it up to the trail returning with a rope from his pack to help pull her up by wrapping it around a tree and then around her and billeting her up like rock climbing. It took nearly an hour to get her back up.

Knowing they couldn't go on they decided their best chance was to return to the cabin. Barely able to walk Mike found a stick she could use as a crutch. He tried to carry both packs but wasn't able to. "Mike I can carry mine. I have to. We need the supplies." He supported her weight the best he could, but they had to stop frequently. It took so long that by the time they returned to the cabin it was already starting to get dark and it was snowing again. The cold helped to keep the ankle from swelling too much, but they were hungry and near exhaustion once they reached the cabin.

Mike's first priority was to make Jan as comfortable as possible, get her foot elevated and get a fire started. He worked as fast as possible, then brought in more wood and water for cooking. Jan's hiking boot had helped to protect her foot but when Mike removed her boot it began to throb worse than before. Tears stung her eyes. He decided to fill his Boda bag with snow instead of water and place it like an ice pack on her ankle. It helped some and Jan finally fell asleep while he fixed them something to eat.

They made the decision to stay until they got sunshine. "Mike, its December now. Winter has just begun. If this keeps up we will be here for a lot longer than just a few days. We need to figure out how much food we have and how much is here so we can calculate how long we can make it last. I'm scared."

"I know you are. So am I. We've made it this far, we'll make it the rest of the way. God will take care of us and provide our needs. He has so far." They pushed the two cots together so they could be closer to each other then went to sleep.

A week past. Jan's ankle was doing well, but the weather outside had not improved much. It continued to snow everyday but at least it wasn't a blizzard. They tried to conserve as much food as possible feeling guilty for using someone else's food. After calculating what was there they figured there was at least a two month supply. Mike spent his days carving wooden spoons and a set of wooden bowls to be left as a gift to the owner of the cabin.

Two weeks had passed. The cabin had begun to feel like home. They sang songs, read from a few books Jan had found in a small trunk under one of the cots and Mike chopped wood during the daylight hours with an ax he'd discovered by the woodpile doing his best to replace what they had used being sure to keep the wet new wood separate from the dry seasoned wood.

Even before the cabin was in site Smokey became cautiously aware something was not right. Smokey stopped the mules. Grabbing his rifle he told Adam to stay with the animals while he went ahead on foot. "What is it?"

"Cain't ya smell it boy? Someone be a usin' my cabin. I smells smoke from the wood stove. You sit tight while I check it out. Could be trouble. If I ain't back in ten minutes you hightail it outa here and git my team back down the mountain. They'll know where to go. They'll take ya right to the other cabin."

"But."

"Ya do as I say boy. No arguin'." Adam nodded then watched as Smokey disappeared around a bend in the trail.

Mike was out chopping wood when he heard a voice yell at him. Startled he looked up to find himself staring down the barrel of old Smokey's rifle. Jan heard the voice and ran outside. Seeing Jan Smokey yelled, "Damn, you nuts bringin' yer woman up here this time a year. Must be the two been missin' awhile." Then he turned and yelled back at Adam. "Git the team up here. Got compny. Couple greenhorns."

Jan was trembling as Mike went to her side putting his arm around her. They stared at Smokey not daring to move and watched as Adam came around the bend leading the string of mules. "Who might ya be?" Smokey bellowed. "Seems ya two has made yerselves at home."

"We didn't mean any harm. We got caught up in a snow storm and got lost. We stumbled onto your cabin. We tried to leave but my wife sprained her ankle so we had to come back. We didn't know what else to do."

"That be all well and good but it dun't tell me who ya be."

"Names Mike Conley and this is my wife Jan. We'll pay you for the food we ate." Here they were again in another situation begging for mercy.

"Nonsense," he said putting the rifle down. "Ya had ta eat dint ya?" Mike nodded. "Read about ya in the newspaper. Been missin' awhile now. Backpackers. Thought ya two'd be dead." Then turning to Adam he said, "Let's be getting' them mules unloaded. It be gittin' late." Then turning back to Mike he said, "Git on over an help him. He'll be showin' ya what ta do. I gotta hit the head." He disappeared around the cabin heading for the outhouse.

Mike rushed over to help Adam as they introduced themselves. "Don't worry about Smokey. His barks worse than his bite."

"Coulda fooled me."

"He's harmless. Don't let it bother you. You'll see. He'll be telling you stories and talking your ear off before you know it. You'll be his captive audience." Then he laughed at his own joke. The two set to work getting the mules unloaded by the cabin door. By the time Smokey returned they had the two pack mules unloaded and Adam was proudly showing Mike how to properly put up the pack saddles. Smoke walked past them being careful not to let them see his smile, as he entered the cabin leaving Adam to show Mike how to unsaddle the mules. Jan stood staring at the entrance visibly shaken as he walked in. Smokey introduced himself with a soft gentle voice putting her at ease. "Why dun't I git ya ta help me put some of them there supplies away. Then we kin git some grub on. I'm feelin' powerful hungry." He smiled at Jan and she instantly relaxed.

It took the better part of an hour to get everything put away and the mules taken care of and fed. The cabin was crowded with the gear and supplies, plus two more bodies. Mike said he and Jan would set up their tent outside. Smokey wouldn't hear of it. "We'll make do. There's plenty a room. We'll jist move the table and chairs back a bit ta make room for our bedrolls and we'll all be nice and warm. No one need be sleepin' out in the cold."

Mike turned to Adam, "What got you started mule packing and this way of life?"

"Actually I'm looking for someone. She was kidnapped and I have reason to believe she's somewhere in these mountains. I've been looking for her since June." He reached in his pocket and pulled out a picture of Favor. "Here's a picture of her taken not long before she disappeared. Her name's Favor Durand." He handed the photo to Mike. He took one look and handed it to Jan who suddenly spilled her cup of coffee. Apologetically she rushed to clean up the coffee as she handed the photo back exchanging surprised looking glances at each other. Recovering from the shock Jan looked at Adam and with little expression said, "She's very lovely. What makes you think she'd be up here or even that she'd be alive after all this time?"

"She's alive. I know she is. She's important to me. I'm in love with her and I won't give up till I find her. You didn't by any chance run into anyone while you were backpacking? You two have been missing for some time. How'd you manage up here all this time?"

Smokey was eyeing Mike. "Ya couldn't have bin here long by the looks of the provisions. Ya would've used up more of it." He looked directly at him as if daring him to lie.

Avoiding the part of the question about whether they had run into anyone in the mountains Mike explained, "We didn't want to use all your provisions. It just didn't feel right. We used our own provisions sparingly until we had no choice but to use the food stored here. We caught fish and I managed to get a wild turkey and a rabbit or two. I kept chopping wood to replace what we used." Mike felt pangs of guilt as he built his lie to sound as credible as possible. What else could he do? These men were now helping them much in the same way Steve and Favor had, but somehow he felt they had to keep quiet if not for the sake of the baby that would be born in the spring.

Changing the subject Jan said, "I'm going to the creek for some more water and to freshen up a bit. Anyone want to come?" The question was actually directed at Mike.

"I'll go with you. I don't want you to carry that heavy water. We'll be back in a bit." The two hurriedly left the cabin carrying the water bucket. When they were far enough away from the cabin and without looking back or in either direction, Mike spoke. "Did you take a good look at that photo? It was Favor."

"Yeah, and he said he's in love with her. You saw how Steve and Favor were together. They are so much in love and they're going to have a baby. How do we know this guy isn't just obsessed with her and Steve had to take her to their mountain home to keep her safe from this guy? If Favor is happy, no one has any right to interfere with her happiness."

"You're right. We need to keep this between the two of us. They saved our lives. They're our friends. We owe it to them to keep this to ourselves."

"We better hurry and get back. I don't want them to get suspicious of us."

Back at the cabin Smokey was talking in hushed tones, "Them two knows somethin'. Whether they seen or heard somethin', I dun't know, but they be knowin' somethin'."

"What makes you think that?"

"She spilt that coffee as soon as she seen that photo. When ya gits to be my age, and ya bin around a while, ya git so's ya kin read folks. They's be a bit uncertain 'bout what they know, but my guess is they'll come round when they be ready. Don't rush things, be patient and it will git you results. Ifn they know somethin' that means we be gittin' close."

That evening Smokey showed Jan how to make pan biscuits and cooked up some more stew, but this stew was from some venison meat he'd brought up the mountain. The flavor was incredible and heartier than the canned stew they'd eaten. Just as Adam had said Smokey enjoyed making them his captive audience by telling one tale after another.

Mike and Jan decided to move the cots back to their original places and share one cot while Smokey slept on the other. Jan felt more secure huddled close to Mike. She felt unsure of their situation but knew they had no choice. She prayed they were safe with these men and found it hard to sleep. Adam had doubled up his bed roll with Smokey's to make it thicker and softer. They were all comfortable, safe from the cold and full from their meal. It wasn't long before they had all drifted off to sleep.

In the early hours of the morning another storm began to blow and continued on through the better part of the next day and on into the night. Smokey seemed uneasy and went down to check on the mules as soon as it was light. He checked to be sure the shelter he'd built several seasons past was safe and secure for the animals. His small feed storage concerned him. The early storms were unusual this time of year and more and more he realized they needed to go back down the mountain as soon as possible or the animals would not have enough feed to get them through for very long. They would leave the provisions at the cabin and pack back in more feed for the animals. He'd bring more provisions back as well. He also felt he needed to help this young couple get down the mountain and home by Christmas. Adam would be upset and maybe even angry, but he hoped he had taught him enough that he would not question the importance of making these decisions.

When he got back to the cabin he informed the three of his change in plan. "I've spent yers in these here mountains. I know the weather patterns. This yer is a bad one and I cain't be riskin the lives of my animals or others. As soon as this here storm passes we be headed back down the mountain. We kin git ya young folks home fer Christmas." Turning to Adam, "I know ya not happy with this decision, but ya got's ta know it be the right one. Ya got's ta trust me on this one. Who knows maybe our first purpose was ta find these young'uns and git um home safe. The good Lord has a plan. We jist gots to trust His leadin."

Adam looked directly into Smokey's eyes and without hesitation, "I know you're right, Smokey. I do trust your judgment and I believe you're right about the good Lord's plan. I won't be arguing about your decision."

Mike and Jan looked at each other with surprise. All they could think was what was said about 'the Lord's plan' and they were grateful for the decision that had been made.

The next morning the snow had stopped and though it was bitter cold they began their trip down the mountain. It would be faster going down with no provisions to carry. Since Mike nor Jan had ever ridden a mule he put each on one of the pack mules padding the pack saddles with the tarps making them as comfortable as possible so they could lead the pack mules the normal way. Being an experience packer, Smokey did a pretty good job of making it comfortable for them both. Mike and Jan would be home for Christmas.

High up in the mountains, Steve and Favor felt safe from intruders, happy in each other's love, and at peace in their cozy home. Somehow they knew Mike and Jan were safe and everything would be alright.

They arrived back at the main cabin by the middle of the afternoon. The snow wasn't nearly as deep as at the smaller cabin. They'd spend the night and then take Mike and Jan down to Dinsmore where they would be able to pick up the vehicle they left nearby at a friend's home, call their family to let them know they were safe and then head home.

"Well, ya all be meetin' up with yer family by tomorrow night. Be home for Christmas in a few days. Yer kin will be real happy to see ya."

"We really appreciate what you've done for us. We'll always be grateful."

"Jist promise me if ya do any more packin', ya don't do it in the winter months."

"It's a deal. We don't want to go through another experience like that again."

Adam stood by the corral looking up at the snow covered mountain. He could feel Favor's presence there. There was no doubt in his mind he was close.

"Is he going to be alright?" Jan felt concern for Adam.

"Truth be told, I don't know. Love can make a person do some crazy things. I don't know if she felt the same 'bout him. Love is a powerful thing. I only know he needs some answers and he be learnin' a lot about his self before this ordeal be over. I'll be thir to help him pick up the pieces ifn it don't go well." Smokey looked over at Adam, sighed and slowly shook his head.

"If it's ok we'd like to give you our information so you can let us know how things go."

"That be right fine with me."

"Will you be going back up the mountain after you take us back?"

"No, we'll be waiting till spring now. Too risky and too hard to take provisions through the snow. We'll hole up here till spring, unless he wants to go see his friends and family. Then I'll go down for him come spring."

"Well, I've got a feeling he'll want to stay here instead."

The next day they headed down the mountain. The good byes between them were brief unlike the farewell they'd had with Steve and Favor. One moment they were there and the next they were gone. Smokey left them at the store in Jake's company and he and Adam headed back to the main cabin.

Chapter 24

Early April, and spring had finally reached their mountain home. It had been one of the longest and harshest winters the mountain had ever seen. Most of the winter snow had finally melted away. Gone was the great blanket of white as if some unseen hand had taken a paintbrush and swept the countryside with new brilliant colors. Only small patches of the fluffy white remained in some shaded areas, a subtle reminder of the long cold winter passed. Everywhere small creatures were venturing out to explore the fresh newness of spring. The birds were returning, their beautiful songs filling the air. The new green grasses looked like the emerald isles Favor had read about in some of Steven's books. New life was stirring everywhere. Favor could feel the life of the child stirring within her and she marveled at the feeling as she felt the strange movement within. The certain joy of motherhood was nearing. Steven doted over Favor, being over protective of her and his future heir.

Though the days slipped by rapidly, they seemed endless to Favor. She tired easily and was finding herself limited to the things she could do. At the bedroom mirror she eyed herself critically. Her once thin waistline was now miss-shaped by the child she carried. "Damn, why does a woman have to look so disgustingly ugly when she's pregnant?" she blurted out loud, unaware Steven was watching her.

"That's not so! You are just as beautiful as before only in a different way."

"Easy for you to say, you're not the one who's all pushed out of shape. You get all the fun. I'm sick and tired of looking this way."

"I know how you feel, but it's important for this son to carry on the family name."

"No you don't know how I feel. All you care about is your precious family name. As long as it is healthy who cares if it's a boy or girl?!"

Glaring at Favor he yelled, "This child will be a boy. I know it will. It has to be."

Whether hormones or just plain shock at his outburst she began to cry. "I'm sorry, Babe. I love you. You and this child are what *give* me life. You *are* my life. You're what *keeps* me alive." Strange words for a tall, strong, jock.

Watching him intently she sensed a fear of the unknown. Recently she'd heard him call out in his sleep. "Not now, I'm not ready. It's too soon!" She figured he was dreaming about an early birth and not being ready to be a father. Hell, she should be having that sort of dream instead of him. When she asked about the dreams he'd say with an embarrassed look that he didn't remember.

The time had come to plant the new spring garden. Steven would turn the soil several times to allow the warmth of the sun to warm the ground before finally planting the seeds. There was so much to do. Steven was also preparing to take a much needed trip to attend to his business and get supplies. He wanted to be sure he was not gone long. He didn't want it to get too close to Favor's due date which he hoped wouldn't be till at least early June, but could very well be a May birth. Favor was afraid of him going but knew he had to. When he did finally go, he was only gone four days and returned with a truck and trailer load of hay and supplies. The animals had all been turned out to pasture now where feed was plentiful, but Steve needed to stock pile hay for the next winter. It was a never ending cycle of preparation. Prepare for winter to survive the winter and then start all over again in the spring.

By the first of May the garden was all planted and by the end of May the garden was beginning to produce. It seemed almost magical to see the little sprouts as they pushed their way up through the warm soil reaching ever upwards to the sun. Each day they grew from little sprouts into strong healthy vegetables. The fruit trees would soon produce an abundance of fruit and then the canning and preserving would start all over again. This was the cycle of life for Steve and Favor. It was their means of survival.

Now late May, nearly a year had passed since Favor had come to the mountain and Rainbow Moor. She'd become accustomed to her life on the mountain. Favor sat contentedly on the front porch watching Steve working in the garden. It had become too difficult for her to bend over in the garden to help with the daily weeding, so she had to be content to watch.

Standing up she stretched and made her way down to the garden. Steve smiled as she approached. "Pretty isn't it?"

"What?"

"The garden, silly."

"It is isn't it?"

"And, Mrs. Mitchell, you are the most beautiful flower in the whole garden."

"Why thank you, Mr. Mitchell. I'm glad you called me a flower and not a vegetable."

"Hmmm! Vegetables are very tasty and you my dear."

"Don't you dare say it, Steven, I'm in no condition for your mischief." With a pretentious toss of her head and a giggle, she wandered down the rows of vegetables. Steve laughed and went back to his weeding. Bending over to pluck a weed from the garden she felt a sudden pain in her abdomen. She drew in a deep breath and straightened up. Hesitating a moment she contemplated that it must have been from bending over. Walking on down several rows she again felt a twinge of pain and then a slight cramping. Once again she stopped. Thinking it best, she turned to walk back toward Steve. Again she felt a shooting pain the intensity so strong that a cry escaped her tightly clenched lips. Startled by the sound Steve looked up just as another spasm of pain made Favor drop to her knees.

"Favor, what is it?"

"I don't know. Sharp pain." Lifting her gently he quickly carried her to the house.

"I'm alright now. The pain is gone. It must have been a cramp when I bent over to pull a few weeds. I think I'll go lay down awhile. I feel kind of tired."

"Are you sure?"

"Yes. I'll call you if I need you." Steve walked her upstairs and helped her onto the bed, gently drawing a comforter up over her.

"I'm going to put the garden tools up and then be right back in."

When he returned and looked in on Favor, she was sleeping soundly.

How long she slept she didn't know, but a sharp pain woke her and she cried out. Hearing her scream Steve rushed up the stairs to find her doubled up in a ball, tears streaming down her face. "It hurts, it hurts. Steven help me!"

"You've got to relax. Don't fight it or it will hurt more."

"How would you know?" She screamed as another shooting pain wrenched at her body.

"Baby, you've got to try."

"I can't!"

"Yes you can. Remember what we read about. You can do this. I'm here to help you. Try to remember the breathing thing."

"Easy for you to say, damn it! You don't..." stopping mid-sentence, "Oh, no! My water just broke all over the bed."

"It's ok, we'll take care of it."

For ten hours Favor labored. Soaked with perspiration, her hair clinging to her neck from the moisture, and aching from head to toe, on May 28, 1992 she finally delivered. She heard a tiny cry as Steve lifted the tiny bundle and wrapped him in a soft towel. "What is it?" Raising up trying to see the tiny bundle. Tears of emotion were streaming down Steve's face as he spoke.

"It's a boy, a wonderful boy, just like I said it would be. Meet your new son, Steven Lawrence Mitchell, the V." Cradling little Steven he gently laid him in Favor's arms as he wrote down his time of birth and when Favor began to drift off to sleep, he took baby Steven from her arms and weighed him on the scale he had purchased along with all the other baby things. Six pounds, five ounces. Then he bathed and dressed their tiny miracle and sat down in a nearby rocking chair holding him and watching over Favor and Steven as they slept. He needed to put him down and help Favor get cleaned up and change the bed again, but he wanted to relish these first few moments as he thought about his parents, wishing they were there to see their grandson. Strangely he even missed his aunt. Life had been full of losses and many lonely days. His work had taken him to great heights in the corporate world, but nothing could begin to compare to the love he felt for Favor and this new little life he held in his arms. It was the most peaceful he'd ever felt. Steven had it all, wealth, success and notoriety. He'd traveled all over the world and had properties of sizeable value. But his heart had always and still was here in his mountain retreat. This was the place with his fondest memories of his childhood and his parents. Of all his assets, it was the most precious and dear to his heart. Here he was content and at peace.

His attention was jarred back to the present when he heard Favor give out a little moan. Laying little Steven gently in the cradle he went to her side. Her eyes met his, "Where is he?"

"I just put him in his cradle. He's sleeping. How about we get you cleaned up. You can soak in the tub while I get the bedding changed."

It was after midnight, nearly an hour later, when she finally climb back into her bed. They were both tired, but little Steven was now waking up and needed to be tended to. Sleep would have to wait a while longer. In the wee hours of the morning Steven climbed into bed beside Favor. The baby was now fast asleep and his new mom and dad could now get a little rest of their own. Steve wrapped his arms tightly around Favor. She snuggled close relishing in the feel of his body next to hers. "Thank you, Favor. You were wonderful. Thank you for our wonderful son. My life is complete. I could never be happier or more content than I am at this moment. I have the love of my life and the son I always wanted to carry on my legacy. What more could I ever want. I can rest in peace." Then he fell asleep.

Favor lay awake thinking about his words and how her life had radically changed in the past year. She was still apprehensive about this motherhood thing. She'd never even spent time around small children and except for a brief time with Conrad the thought of children had never crossed her mind. Not many of her friends had them. Conrad! She tried to remember his face. Friends. What had become of them and did they ever think of her anymore? How good a mother would she be? Would she even know what to do? Questions swirled in her head, but there were no answers to put her mind at ease. Shouldn't she be blissfully happy at this moment? Something was tugging at her emotions and heart. Why would Steven say he could now rest in peace? Did he mean he could fall asleep and sleep peacefully now that the baby was born and seemed to be totally healthy? Or was he talking about the bigger picture. How do parents rest in peace when they have the next eighteen plus years to worry about a child? Finally out of sheer exhaustion she fell asleep in the arms of the man who had a year ago been a complete stranger. The man who had kidnapped her was now the father of her child.

Time has a way of slipping by all too quickly, like water through your fingers. Steven and Favor were learning that being new parents was not all that easy, but they were adjusting and having fun learning the unending needs of a new baby. Scheduling became crucial when before they had none. Favor happily was getting her slim figure back and was getting the hang of this mother thing. What really amazed her was how Steven took a very active role in parenting and how organized he was, more so than she. Used to dealing with organization and deadlines and being creative with her time, this new role was more than she expected. Steven on the other hand seemed to relish in the whole thing. He juggled the garden, going to "town" to take care of business and the baby. He even set aside time for Favor to take a ride on Snow at least three times a week.

One brilliantly sunny morning Favor entered the kitchen to find Steven busy making breakfast and a picnic basket set out. "What are you doing?"

"I am fixing a special breakfast and then we're going to go for a ride and a picnic."

"We are? What brought this on?"

"Little Steven is one month old today so we're going to celebrate by spending the entire day together as a family. No work today. Just fun in the sun and time together enjoying the day."

"He's a month old already? I hadn't realized how quickly the time has gone."

They rode the horses through the moor to the spot where they had their first picnic. Steven carried Little Steven with him on Denali. When they arrived alongside the stream, Steven spread out a blanket and fixed a spot to lay the baby. Cloud lay down at the edge of the blanket as close to little Steven as he could. He seemed to be intrigued by this little person and seemed to sense he was someone special. The soft rays of the sun and a gentle breeze drifted softly down through the meadow as the stream meandered aimlessly down the little canyon. The sound of the water as it tumbled over the rocks was soothing and sounded like a melody, enchanting as it stirred their senses and new memories formed in their hearts and mind.

For the next couple of months Steve and Favor worked in the garden and canned the vegetables they grew. Like the previous year they prepared for the upcoming winter. Steve kept reminding Favor how important it was to be prepared. "Steve, why are you talking so much about this? We were more than prepared last winter and had a lot of reserves. You seem anxious even though you have a perfect system set up for everything."

"I just need to be sure. You need to know what to do if I'm not here to take care of you and Stevie and I need you to know how much I have loved you. You are what has kept me living. And no matter what I will always be with you in your heart and mind. Don't ever let go of that."

"Of course. But why are you talking this way? A body would think you were getting post-partum blues. That's for me." Favor laughed at the thought of a man getting post-partum.

"I'm sorry. Didn't mean to sound depressing. Just want you to know how much you mean to me." Steve drew her body close and she felt him shudder. "Steve, are you alright?"

"Just concerned about you two. Does it feel a little cold?"

"I think you have a sickness commonly known as 'fatherhood'. First child and all that."

"Don't make fun of me. I'm serious."

"I know you are. You're so sweet and it makes me love you even more."

The months passed quickly. Summer was slipping away and it seemed like it had only just begun. Steve and Favor cherishing every minute together, their love growing stronger and greater with each passing day. They celebrated their first anniversary with a campout at their wedding site. Little Stevie was growing fast and had begun to find his own little voice. Laughter filled their home as they watched his ever changing antics and expressions. Steve spent more time holding and coddling him then Favor did, marveling at the wonder of this little person they had brought into the world together. Evenings were their favorite time of day when the chores were done and supper was over they would play with Stevie and relax in each other's arms. A chill filled the night time air as once again the days were becoming shorter. Favor hated the winter and dreaded its coming. But secure in her love for Steven and once again completely prepared for the coming cold she reveled in their time together.

An unusually early snow greeted them one morning. Steven stood looking out the window as the soft snowflakes floated down softly from the gray sky. The light was fading fast. "Favor, do you forgive me for bringing you here?"

"What? Why do you ask and especially now?"

"I just need to know and that you know I have never loved anyone more than I love you."

"Steven, there is nothing to forgive. I love you more than life itself. I'm happy in this life with you and I'm glad you chose me to be your wife. I have unfinished business that you need to let me take care of one day, but please believe me and never doubt it again. We have something special and extraordinary and we're good together. Why do I sense an unrest in you? Are you regretting bringing me to Rainbow Moor?"

"Never! No never! Is that what you think? I just know I wasn't entirely fair and need to know you don't hold it against me."

"You've always been one to surprise me and our lives are anything but ordinary, but I'm truly happy with you. I just wish you had given me the benefit of the doubt and trusted me. I wouldn't trade my life with you for anything. We have a child together. Everything happens for a reason, so people say. A higher power guides our lives, whether good or bad. I believe the power guiding us is on the side of good. So stop worrying!"

Taking her in his arms, Steven kissed her passionately. Again she felt his body shudder. She teased him, "Hmmm! Stevie is asleep. I think we should take advantage of it and have some fun before he wakes up."

"Woman, you're amazing." His hands caressing her and she melted into him. They made love with a passion that was tenfold what it had ever been before.

It was October 14, 1992, the night of a full moon. Favor woke with a strange eerie feeling. The early morning light was just beginning to creep over the Eastern horizon. The room had become cold. Steve was not in their bed. She rose and went to Little Steven's room who now slept in his crib instead of the cradle in their room. Thinking Steve would be there tending to the baby she found Little Steven was sleeping soundly and Steve was not there. Tiptoeing out of the room she started down the stairs when she heard a long mournful howl. The house was much too quiet. Taking another step she again heard the howl. Hurriedly she made her way the rest of the way down the stairs. The whinny of a horse drew her to a nearby window. Looking out in the early morning light she could see Steven bareback on the back of Snow with Cloud nearby. They stood motionless facing the house. Favor ran outside calling to him but he did not answer. Instead he held his hand up high and gave a slow wave as Cloud once again threw back his head and howled another long mournful howl sending shivers up her spine. She called out to him again, "Steve, what are you doing?" He didn't answer. "Steve!" she screamed, but to her shocked amazement he didn't answer. Instead he turned and rode slowly away. Running after him she began screaming his name but he just kept going. An unexplainable terror gripped her heart.

A fresh snow had fallen making it hard to run. She wore a light pair of slippers and the moisture from the new snow began to seep into them making her feet nearly numb from the cold. They began to ache. Hurriedly she returned to the house where she quickly put on warm clothes and snow boots. Running back outside she made her way to the spot she had last seen Steven. Snow's hoof prints led in the direction of the woods. Favor followed them thankful that it was not snowing or it would have covered the prints.

The tracks lead to the place where they had been married. She'd come here with Steve a number of times since to picnic with Little Steven. The waterfall was not flowing as freely as it did in the spring. Steve was not there, but the tracks lead beyond the pond and waterfall. She'd never been past this point before. Off in the distance she heard Cloud's howl once again. The fresh snow slowed her pace as she followed the tracks.

Panic set in as she continued. Screaming at the top of her lungs for Steve made her hyperventilate and breathing became increasingly difficult. Was she losing her mind? This couldn't be happening. It had to be a dream and she had to wake up. Adrenaline kept her moving. Where were the tracks leading and why was Steven doing this? She was so panicky that she had completely forgotten that baby Steven was alone at the house in his crib. In a state of confusion she finally remembered. Tears burned her face and crystalized on her cheeks. Stumbling, she fell to her knees. The cold snow felt like it was burning her hands as she crawled a short distance. Struggling to her feet she realized she needed to return for the baby. Agony tore at her heart. Why would Steve do such a thing and act so strangely.

There was a path that wound around in an uphill direction, making it even more difficult to walk. As she rounded a bend she came out on a beautiful little clearing, In the middle of the clearing was a large oak tree with a beautiful picket fence encompassing the tree. An opening was just in front of her and at the opening the hoof prints stopped. Staring down at the tracks she noticed canine tracks as well. There were no tracks leading into, away or around the opening. They just stopped right there. How could this be? It was impossible. Terrified and confused, looking beyond the opening she saw several headstones. A tremble began from deep within her body and she was soon shaking so badly that she was unable to move. Trying to focus and make some sense of what was going on, she willed her body to move forward.

The first headstone read Martha Mary Mitchell, Born November 12, 1874 Died June 9, 1940, age 66. The second was Steven Lawrence Mitchell, Born January 17, 1873 Died March 3, 1943, age 70. Next was Steven Lawrence Mitchell II, Born May 22, 1898, Died October 1, 1968, age 70, followed by Anna Lee Mitchell, Born February 15, 1898, Died April 28, 1971, age 73. Favor realized she was in the family cemetery. She felt a strange peacefulness about this place as she moved on to the next set of headstones. Steven Lawrence Mitchell III, Born August 19, 1929, Died July 4, 1972, age 43, followed by Lisa Marie Mitchell, Born June 10, 1931, Died July 4, 1972, age 41. These were her Steven's parents who had died in the auto accident when Steve was only sixteen years old. It had been on the fourth of July. The next read Steven Lawrence Mitchell IV, Born February 6, 1959 Died August 14, 1988 age 32. Favor let out a gasp as she stumbled back away from the headstone. This couldn't be.

She'd married Steven Lawrence Mitchell IV on September 23, 1991.

If he died in 1988 who was the man she'd just spent the last year and nearly five months with? Whose baby had she born? Overcome, she fell to her knees burying her head in her hands she wept bitterly. Anger began to manifest its ugly head as she finally rose to her feet. Had the man she'd spent all this time with stolen the Mitchell name and identity? Was he a criminal who had used her and now left to pursue some other identity? She had lived with and loved him. He had always taken care of her. This didn't make any sense at all.

Turning to leave she wondered about the hoof and paw prints that had stopped right at the entrance to the little cemetery. Near this entrances she stood once again staring down at the prints when she felt a hand placed firmly, yet gently on her shoulder. Whirling around, in her haste to see who had touched her, she almost fell. No one was there, but a set of footprints larger than her own lead directly to the headstone of Steven Lawrence Mitchell IV. How could any of this be? What was happening? She cried out in anguish as the tears fell from her eyes. Again the whinny of a horse made her turn. There stood Snow and Cloud standing in their own prints at the opening. She was losing her mind. But then a voice so soft and sweet whispered her name. Turning she saw Steven standing at his own headstone, or the headstone of the real Steven.

"Steven!" She started to move towards him but he motioned for her to stop. Again Snow let off one of the soft gentle sounds horses make. Favor glanced in her direction just as the horse lay down on the cold snowy ground. Looking back, Steven was gone. "No! No! You can't be gone! Please! Don't leave me!" she wailed as she stumbled forward. At the base of the headstone now lay a single red rose. It felt as though her heart were being torn from her chest as she dug her fingers into the snow and ground beneath the stone. Bitter tears fell on the rose and right before her unbelieving eyes they multiplied into a bouquet of white roses. One rose for every month they had spent together. Her eyes fell upon a note, written in Steven's own hand.

"Though death came too soon
I bridged the divide.
Finding favor in my eyes,
I took you to be my bride.
Forever in your love I'll live
And with the child you bore within.
One day upon this hallowed ground,
Our love will join and peace be found.
Go my love and hold me dear
Within your heart I'm forever near.
Your beloved husband,
Steven Lawrence Mitchell IV."

Hugging the cold marble headstone her cries echoed throughout the canyon. Nothing could take away this agony and pain. Her thoughts finally took her back to the child she'd left alone several hours ago. Rising she gathered up the roses and carried them to where Snow still lay waiting. She climbed on her back as the horse rose gently to her feet. In silence and without guidance Snow turned down the trail. Favor turned to look back at the little cemetery. She saw the form of a man dressed all in white, waving goodbye, and then he was gone. She heard a long mournful howl and she knew in her heart this was Cloud. Tears continued to fall from her swollen eyes as Snow made her way down the trail to their home.

Several hours had passed since Favor first left the house. When Snow stopped at the front porch Favor could hear the terrifying cries of her son. Sliding off the horse she started up the porch steps, Snow turned and kicked up her heels, then rose on her hind quarters pawing at the air. Landing back on all fours she turned and ran back to the edge of the woods where Cloud stood waiting. As they disappeared into the forest, Favor somehow knew it was the last she'd see of them, taking with them what was left of the beautiful world she and Steven had created. For a moment she stood watching the place they had stood. The loneliness and emptiness she felt was more than anyone should ever have to bear. Slowly she entered the house and climbed the stairs. Steven's cries only made her feel more agonized. He was soaking wet and undoubtedly hungry. Emotionally numb, she methodically set about tending to his needs.

The remainder of the day Favor held little Steven as she stared out the window hoping to see Steven returning. Hearing Denali's call from the corral she hurried outside, hoping to see Snow as well. He stood with the milk cow nearby. Angry and sullen that she even had to tend to them at a time like this, once again she set about methodically taking care of the evening chores.

For the next few weeks Favor carried out the daily chores, feeding, clothing and bathing little Steven with little or no emotion. She barely ate and her clothing became soiled and dingy. The house became dusty and dirty dishes filled the sink. She had turned off all emotion. Little Steven's cries often went unnoticed. Just as there was no way to console Favor, little Steven was suffering right along with her. It hadn't snowed since the day

Steven disappeared. Favor knew the winter snows would come, but she couldn't get motivated to prepare for its coming.

One morning when she came down with Steven in her arms she had a strange sensation. When she turned towards the dining area a familiar scent filled the room and on the table she saw a red rose and something shiny. Beside the rose lay a note, "I know and feel your grief. Please don't give up the life we built. Love forever, Steven." The shiny object was Steven's wedding ring. Beside it was a note that read, "For the day our little Steven finds his true love."

Favor's spirit lifted, realizing something extraordinary had happened on this mountain. Though her mind couldn't grasp everything her heart knew the man she had spent all this time with had somehow transcended death so that he could bring an heir into the world. He had chosen her to be his wife because she found favor in his eyes.

Favor decided to take Little Steven on a picnic. Saddling Denali she rode to the gravesite. Even Denali seemed excited. At the grave she told little Stevie about the things she and his daddy had done. The child seemed intrigued with the softness in her voice so much that he cooed and giggled the whole time. Favor laughed at his joyous little squeals of delight. A gentle peacefulness settled over her and she noticed it seemed to affect little Steven. When they were leaving she placed her hand on Steven's headstone and whispered, "We miss you, my love." The cold stone beneath her hand became warm and she smiled knowing his spirit was near.

Chapter 25

Old Smokey and Adam had weathered the harsh winter storms at the lower cabin. Spring had arrived and the snow was slowly melting. Flowers were miraculously pushing their way through even the tiniest crevices adding color and brilliance to the stark countryside. The familiar chattering of squirrels and Stellar Jays could once again be heard in the early morning. The intense quiet of the winter months slipped away. Morning woke up to fresh new smells and new sounds and the sudden realization that spring had returned to the mountain.

Mother Earth had finally awakened from her deep winter sleep. Everything felt new again. Life had renewed vitality and the air filled with magical energy. Like a bear waking from a long winter nap of hibernating, so it seemed the earth was waking up from its own long nap.

Adam had been patient through the winter, learning all he could about the ways of a mountain man, the rules and respect for the mountains and its inhabitants. Most of all he had adopted the 'Leave No Trace' philosophy. Even more he had attained a reverence for the wilderness. A feeling of anticipation was eminent at spring's rebirth. Adam stood at the base of the mountain looking up. How does one describe the feeling of the mountains and the smells of nature? It's more of a sense or impression.

Smokey approached him, "Still be a lot of snow up thir. We be leavin' for the upper cabin soon. Be needin' to take a good bunch of supplies along with us. Thir be a vast amount of land up thir. Too bad we can't git in from the road side, but that all be private land. Libel to git shot. Goin' in from the wilderness side will be harder. Then we got to figure out how far to drop down. She may not even be thir now. Could be gone or dead."

Adam slowly turned to look at the old pioneer as if studying him. Noticing the look on Adam's face he simply said, "I says it like I sees it."

Adam turned back towards the vast mountain region and spoke in a hushed whisper as if it would have been irreverent to speak too loudly. "She's there. I know she is. I can feel her."

"Son, I hope yer right." Turning away from Adam, Smokey left him alone with his thoughts. He had done everything he could to prepare Adam both physically and mentally for his trip up the mountain. He saw the determination and yes maybe obsession in his student, and that obsession could very well destroy him if not handled in the right way. Yet that determination and obsession is what made Adam special. In some ways he saw himself in this young man and it gave him a sense of satisfaction and purpose in teaching him the old ways, the ways of a mountain man and how to survive and respect Mother Nature and all she has to offer. He felt the Man upstairs had a bigger purpose for Adam.

A few days later they set out for the upper cabin and the high country. It was already the middle of June. When they reached the cabin they found there was still a great deal of snow. The unusually cold winter had caused several trees to snap and fall near the cabin and corral. These needed to be cleared and cut. Firewood had to be cut for the next season and supplies replenished. Adam was becoming anxious, feeling it was taking far too long and they were wasting precious time. Smokey cautioned him, reminding him that the Good Lord was in control and everything happens for a reason and all in His time. "Ya need to wait on the Good Lord's leading and everything will fall into place according to His plan." Adam tried to be patient but as the days past he felt more and more agitated. It was a huge relief when Smokey told him they would be heading on up the following day.

It wasn't till the middle of August they finally left the upper cabin and headed into the high country. Adam was beginning to doubt Smokey knew where he was going or if he really knew this part of the country like he thought he did. It was to the point he wanted to go back down to the lower cabin and get the jeep and go over the private road areas. Locked gates or not he was ready to take bolt cutters and cut every lock off every gate he came to till he found the place where this house was supposed to be. Smokey wouldn't hear of it and kept reminding him of God's leading and told him the story of Moses in the Bible and how the Israelites wandered the wilderness for forty years while the Lord taught them the lessons they needed to learn before reaching the Promised Land.

"So what are you saying? You really believe all that Bible stuff? So are you trying to tell me God is making me wait for a reason? Or is He trying to tell me something else? Is He saying to give it up?"

"Hey, don't be shootin' the messenger. I ain't saying nuthin'. That be for you to decide."

"Well at least tell me what you think!"

"I spends most all my time in these here mountains. I be jist along as a guide. Where ever the good Lord leads, I be a followin'. Plain and simple."

"Damn it, Smoke! Sometimes you infuriate me. For your information I'm not ready to give up." Then he softened a bit. "Besides, I like it here and what you've been teaching me."

"It be settled then. We keep searchin'.

They wandered the mountains in search of the place they had learned about. It seemed as if something didn't want them in that area and things kept happening to make them have to find another way. The mountain seemed to be protecting someone or something. You could sense it. They got a strange feeling every time they thought they had found the right place. Something always hindered their progress. It felt like they were not wanted there and like something was watching them every time they approached a certain area of the mountain. Smokey said it was probably Big Foot and then he'd throw back his head and laugh. Adam would look at him and wonder if he really believe the legend or if he just liked to scare him. It "creeped him out".

All the while the search went on Adam learned the ways of survival and how to fish and hunt. They encountered their fair share of deer, bear, mountain lions, coyote and other small game. The weeks turned into months.

One late October morning Adam turned to Smokey and with a beaten, dejected look spoke the words he thought he'd never say. "Smokey, I've been searching for Favor for over a year. I couldn't have done it without you. We've been back and forth through these mountains. I've learned so much from you and I'm glad I did. The biggest thing I've learned is patience and I've learned something about the harsh realities of life and its cycle. For some reason I lost the one person I really loved and wanted to spend the rest of my life with. I've never felt that way before. I guess it's time for me to accept it wasn't meant to be. I still believe she's up here. I can feel something about this place unlike anything I've ever felt before on my search. You said to wait on the Lord and He'd teach me what He wants me to learn. Smoke, I'm done waiting."

"Watcha sayin', son? Ya ain't givin' up now is ya? Thirs still a fair many days a good weather and we be doin' ok on supplies. Plenty a time befir the heavy snows come."

Adam hung his head. "You wanted me to learn patience and acceptance but you let me learn it on my own terms, with you guiding me so I could make peace with myself."

"It was the good Lord doin' the guiding. I just be His tool. I ain't sayin what be reality and what ain't. Not me. When ya live in these here mountains as long as I been here, ya git a respect for certain things even ifn ya can't explain 'em. But if yer sure 'bout this, we be headin' down the mountain come mornin'. We'll head due south and then cut to the west further down. If ya changes yir mind come mornin' we kin always keep lookin'."

"My mind's made up. I need to get on with my life and figure out what I want to do with it now. Who knows maybe I'll buy me some pack mules so all this teaching doesn't go to waste."

"Ya absolutely sure 'bout this?"

"It's time to let go. Now if you'll excuse me I think I'll go down to the creek and wash."

Smokey watched him head down to the creek. He knew Adam didn't need to wash, but needed some time alone. For the first time in his life Adam prayed. He finally let the tears go as he let go of Favor. From the depth of his heart he wept and let out the grief he had so stringently held inside and asked for peace to go on. Tomorrow he'd leave the mountain behind and with it the memory of a beautiful woman he once knew. He'd leave behind her laughter and song. Favor would be another cold case in the police files, a secret well-guarded by some mysterious hand.

That night Adam's dreams were of a sleek young woman running gracefully across a meadow her long dark hair cascading over her shoulders. Wearing a sheer white dress and with bare feet it looked like she was floating over the ground as she approached. In one hand she clutched a handful of wild daisies, the other hand was outstretched in a beckoning motion reaching forward as she ran. With excitement and joy he called out to her as he began to run towards her, but she passed right by him, her eyes fixed on a tall dark haired figure at the other end of the meadow. The look on her face was pure and full of love. But just as she reached the figure he suddenly disappeared.

Adam woke with a start, sweat pouring down his brow. It was nearly dawn and from a distance could be heard the sound of pounding hooves vibrating on the ground and then he heard a long blood chilling howl. Was something or someone being chased by coyotes or wolves? Smokey heard the sound as well and they both jumped up from their sleeping bags and rushed out of the tent.

"Lordy, what be goin' on!" He was clearly shaken.

"There! Look!"

"I see it, but I don't be believin' it! The legend be true!"

One moment there stood a white horse and wolf like dog with a lone rider and the next moment they were gone. Only a misty cloud hung low over the area. The two men ran to the spot where they had seen them. There were no hoof prints, but a small patch of snow covered the ground where they had been standing.

"Snow! Tain't bin no snow. How'd it git here?"

Adam slapped Smokey gently on the shoulder, "We've been in these mountains far too long. The early morning light's just playing tricks on us."

Smokey reached down and picked up a handful of snow and held it out to Adam. "Do this look like yir eyes be playin' tricks on ya? Look pretty dang real ta me and damn cold, too. But I agree we bin here too long. Let's be gittin' some coffee and then git on down the mountain. We can eat a bit later. I'm just wantin' to git gone. Never seen anything like that before."

"You said something about a legend. What were you talking about?"

"I hear tell, few years back a young man was kilt when he and his horse went down. Heard tell he had one of them solar phones and was able to call out. They tracked him by some GPS thing-a-ma-jig on the phone. Found him too, but his injuries were bad. Died right there. Big white horse he rode had broken its leg and fallen on top of him. Horse had to be put down right on the spot. They was both buried up here somewhere. Legend is he rides these mountains still. His spirit never settled. Must have had some unfinished business."

"How long ago?"

"Not long. Round 1988 I think." The news of the legend left Adam shaken and mystified.

They packed their gear quickly and loaded the mules. Neither of them wanted to talk about what they'd seen. It's the twentieth century. Adam kept telling himself things like that only happens in the movies. But the events that had occurred during his search for Favor disturbed him.

Adam and Smokey had been riding in a southerly direction through the woods since early morning. It was around two in the afternoon, judging by the suns position in the sky. Weaving through a cropping of trees they found themselves in a beautiful meadow. Stopping suddenly they looked at each other. They had come out on a rise and were looking down.

"Smoke, tell me you're seeing what I'm seeing." Smokey nodded yes as he continued to stare ahead of him. "You don't suppose this is the place do you?"

"Well, son, we still be pretty high up on the mountain. Could be. Looks out of place like it be too nice a place for these parts. Somethin' don't feel right."

Before them stood a stately old ranch house not like anything you would expect. As they approached the house they noticed a corral just beyond. "Let's see if someone's about."

They knocked on the door, but no one answered. Adam tried the door. It was unlocked. He called out thinking the inhabitants had not heard their knock. The house was silent. Though the fire had gone out, there was still some warmth from the coals, letting him know someone had been there earlier and was most likely somewhere close.

They decided to tie up the pack mules by the corral. While Smokey tended to the animals Adam walked around to the other side calling out to see if someone would answer. He had just come back around the front of the house when he saw someone coming from the woods riding a black horse. It was a woman with long dark hair. Her head was bent low and she seemed to be carrying something. She was unaware of the two men watching her as she approached the house.

"Hello there!" Adam called out as he moved in her direction. Her head shot up and she saw Adam approaching. A smile crossed her face, her eyes wide with hope that Steven had returned. In an instant her expression changed as she realized it was not Steven but two strangers.

"Who are you and what are you doing here? You're trespassing."

Adam stopped in his tracks. His search was ended. Before him stood his beloved Favor.

"Favor, it's me Adam! I've been searching for you!"

"I don't know you. How do you know my name? My husband won't like you being here. He doesn't like strangers. Down Denali." At her command Denali dropped down on his front knee so she could dismount with little Steven strapped securely to her front.

Adam stood frozen to the spot where he stood staring at the bundle she carried. He felt angry knowing the man who kidnapped her had also gotten her pregnant. Trying to control his emotions he spoke gently, "Favor, you must remember me. I'm your friend, Adam. You disappeared in June of 1991. I've been searching for you ever since. Tell me you remember!"

Smokey stepped up before Adam could say another word. "Scuse me mam, but we bin packin' a long time. Would it be ok to let our animals rest in yer corral a while? And could we be trublin' you fer a cool drink of water? We don't mean to trouble you none. We could take care of yer horse for ya, seeing you got a little one there in your arms that might need tending to."

"I guess it would be alright. Steven doesn't like other people hanging around. But, once we had house guests for a whole week." Just then little Steven begin to cry. "I've got to take care of little Steven." Then she rushed into the house. Adam and Smokey headed over to put the team in the corral and take care of Denali.

"Did you hear that? She said husband and she called him Steven and the baby is little Steven. How much you want to bet the last name is Mitchell?"

"Look here, Adam. Ya gots to take this slow. It's a delicate situation. She don't seem to remember you so ya cain't be rushin' things. Give the little lady time to remember. We don't know what has gone on here for the past year."

"It's only been a little over a year. How could she forget me? We've known each other the better part of our lives."

"Maybe she was traumatized. Like I say, it looks delicate to me. When her man comes home we can learn a bit more. Remember to be patient. Don't be throwin' all the good Lord's teachings out."

"If it's the same guy in the picture, then he may remember and recognize me from the day I followed him out at Dinsmore."

"Chance ya got to take."

The two headed to the house. Favor had left the door open, but out of respect they knocked on the door. She appeared holding the baby. Adam noticed her clothes were soiled and her hair uncombed. There was a smudge of dirt on her cheek. "Come in. I'll put Steven in his play pen and get you some water."

"I see your fire is almost out and it's getting cold in here. Would you like me to get it going for you again? I also saw you have a cow out there. Does she need tending to? I'd, I mean, we'd be happy to tend to your animals and restock your wood pile. Looks like it's a bit low."

Favor looked at him with surprise. "Cow's dry. I haven't been good about milking her. Baby's still nursing." She blushed at her own simple disclosure. "Steven usually takes care of the animals since the baby came. He." Stopping her sentence a puzzled look came over her and she seemed confused for a moment. "The cow and the horse go in the barn at night. Snow and Cloud are gone. I need to find Steven." With that she wandered outside calling to Steven. Several minutes went by before she came back into the house. The baby had begun to cry so Adam picked him up. The child seemed to like Adam and began to coo and giggle. Adam found himself laughing at his cuteness. "What are you doing with my baby?" Rushing over she grabbed him from Adam.

"I didn't mean any harm. He was crying. It seemed like he needed to be held."

With that Favor shoved the child back into his arms. "I forgot to get you your water."

Smokey averted the conversation and set about getting the fire started as she rushed into the kitchen. Head down he muttered under his breath, "Well don't that beat all."

When she returned with two glasses of water Adam was sitting on the couch holding Steven and the two of them seemed to be carrying on a childlike conversation with little Steven making all sorts of baby sounds and Adam laughing. He'd never held a baby that he could remember and was surprised at how endearing the child was. Smokey reached out for one of the glasses, "Thank you." Adam took his and set it on a nearby end table.

"Your husband wouldn't be Steven Mitchell, would he?"

"Why yes, Steven Lawrence Mitchell IV. Do you know each other?" Adam had the answer he was looking for. Mitchell was the one who had taken Favor.

"We met some time ago. So is it safe to assume this little fellow is Steven Lawrence Mitchell V?"

"Indeed it is! How did you meet my husband?"

"I had been hunting with some friends. We had all stopped at the Mad River Burger Bar to get something to eat and we happened to meet. I have a picture of your husband. Would you like to see it?"

Favor looked at the photo. "That's my Steven." A sweet smile crossed her lips and a softness came into her eyes. She ran her fingers over the photo. It looked as though she was about to cry. "Can I keep this? I don't have any photos to remember him by and it is such a nice one." Adam nodded and said she could keep it. He had made several other copies and scanned it into his computer. The original he had tucked safely away to return to Sarah. Somehow he wished he had the original with him. He would have gladly given her the original. What did she mean 'to remember him by'?

Looking around the room she said, "It wasn't always like this. It was lovely and clean and dusted. I just haven't felt like doing much. Maybe when Steven gets back I'll feel more up to it. We always did everything together."

"Has he been away long? When do you expect him back?" He wondered if he had abandoned her since there was a baby now. But that just didn't seem like the case.

"Stevie and I went to visit Steven today. We rode Denali and we had a picnic. We do that a lot you know. We won't be able to go visit him when the snows come." Adam noticed she was crying now. Tears were slowly trickling down her cheek. As she reached up to wipe one away their eyes met. "I miss him so much. I don't understand what happened."

"Where is Steven now? Can you take me to him?" Her eyes perked up and she became excited. "You want to visit Steven, too? You did say he was your friend didn't you?"

"Yes, I would really like to go visit him. When could we go?"

"No you're trying to confuse me. Wait a minute, don't I know you?" Her mind kept jumping from one thought to another and Adam was afraid he was going to say the wrong thing and cause some sort of episode, but he had to try to get her to remember even the slightest thing.

"We went to school together and we were neighbors before you came here. Your best friend was Cindy. Do you remember Cindy?"

"No, I remember Mike and Jan Conley. They stayed with us for a whole week."

Another piece of the puzzle. The young couple that he and Smokey had helped were Mike and Jan Conley. They hadn't said a word about staying with a Steve and Favor Mitchell, but both he and Smokey had felt they were hiding something. The two men exchanged glances. Smokey spoke up. "We know Mike and Jan Conley. They stayed with us in one of my cabins part of the winter."

"They did? So did they make it home ok? Did they make it home in time for Christmas? We celebrated an early Christmas here." She became excited and told them about the presents they made each other and the cradle Mike and Steven made. Smokey remembered the matching hat and scarf each of them had worn just as Favor described it.

"Yes they made it home safe and sound and in time for Christmas." Favor was so happy that she got up and danced around the room. Then she stopped and once again the puzzled look and sadness returned and again she became quiet and distant. "Look, why don't you two young'uns visit awhile. I kin bring in some more firewood for ya so's you have plenty for the night and tomorrow too. If you like I can put yer animals up and feed 'em before we leave. We don't want to wear out our welcome. Besides we needs to find us a camp spot for the night." Adam gave Smokey a disgusted look. What was he talking about? He had no intention of leaving. He finally found Favor and he sure as hell wasn't going to leave her here alone.

"Oh, you don't have to leave. At least not right now. You've been very kind and you know my friends. If you want you can sleep in the barn tonight and I can fix you a nice dinner."

"Well, Mrs. Mitchell, that's right kind of you. You sure it wouldn't be any trouble?"

"No, not at all." Adam realized what Smokey was doing and gave him a nod to let him know he understood. Favor looked about the house and a look of shame and dismay came over her. "I'm sorry the house is so dusty and dirty. I'm afraid the kitchen is even worse."

Adam gently placed a hand on her arm. "Would you like me to help you clean it?"

"Oh, yes. Then it will look nice for when Steven comes home."

"That's right. He'd like that wouldn't he?"

Little Steven had fallen asleep so Favor let Adam carry him to his crib. Together they cleaned the kitchen and dining room. By that time Smokey had finished bringing in the wood and went back outside to tend to the animals and set up a place to sleep for the night. He thought it best to leave the two of them alone in hopes that Adam could get her to remember something from her past. Besides he wasn't one for indoor chores. He'd much rather leave that to someone else. That's why he preferred to live in the mountains with as little indoor stuff as possible.

Adam was amazed at how much food Favor had preserved and how much meat there was. "Where did you get all this food?"

"Steven and I grew it ourselves and preserved it for the winter. It was our second year doing it. The first year…." Again she paused, then slowly continued, "We always can our own food. We have to so we can survive the cold winters here. Steven did the hunting. Oh dear, I need to bring the cattle down to the lower pasture soon. We have to feed them hay in the winter because the snow covers the grasses and they can't get enough feed." The puzzled look returned as she continued, "Where's Steven? I can't do this all alone. I don't know how to hunt. He needs to come home to help me."

"I'll stay and help you."

"Steven doesn't like strangers. I told you that before."

"But, I'm not a stranger. I've met Steven and besides you and I used to know each other. I called you by name as soon as I saw you. I wouldn't have known that if I didn't already know you. Remember? Steven would be glad to have someone helping you."

"Do you really think so?"

"Yes I do, and I will stay and help you as long as you like and need me to. Maybe you could teach me some of this stuff."

Favor smiled. "Ok, but when Steven comes home he'll expect you to leave."

"Of course. I understand." Adam felt he was making some headway. At least she seemed to feel comfortable in his presence and trusted him. He hoped someday she'd find the answers that were locked up in her memory somewhere. It was hard to listen to her talk about this man and he wanted so badly to take her in his arms and kiss her. He could see by the situation it would take time. Adam set about helping Favor clean the kitchen and dining room after which they prepared a delicious meal from some of the home canned goods and other food she'd preserved. She talked about how she didn't know anything before but Steven had taught her everything she needed to know to survive. Once again she became quiet and thoughtful. Puzzlement again crossed her face as she tried to figure out her situation.

"Steven kept saying he needed to be sure I knew and could survive if he wasn't here to take care of little Steven and me. One time he was gone seven days, four days longer than he expected. It was awful. Then I did something stupid. I took off by myself trying to find my way. But he found me in time." Then she turned to Adam. "When is he coming back?"

"Favor, sit down a minute. Steven won't be coming back. He died."

"No. You're wrong. He loves us. He wouldn't do that. He wouldn't leave us alone."

"You're not alone. I'm here. I came looking for you. I found you just like you said he did. I'm going to take care of you and little Steven now."

"No. You think you can take his place? I don't know you. You're trying to trick me. You can't make me go with you!" Again she stopped. Familiar words rang in her own ears. She'd spoken those words to someone before, a long time ago. But who? She tried to think back. "You're trying to confuse me. I don't understand why you're here and Steven isn't."

"I'm just here to take care of you. That's all. I want to take care of you. We already talked about this. You said it was ok."

It was clear to Adam that Favor was having trouble making sense of the present and remembering the past. There was something she wasn't telling him. Something that was making it difficult for her to move on. He didn't want to push her too hard or she might fall apart.

Late that night around midnight, from the barn Adam and Smokey heard a voice calling out into the night. Rushing from the barn they saw Favor in nothing but a thin night gown, barefooted, calling out Steven's name. Alarmed for her health, safety and state of mind Adam rushed to her and drew her tight whispering, "Favor, I'm here. It's ok. I'm here."

"Steven! Oh my darling Steven. I've missed you so." But in another moment she realized he wasn't Steven. "You are trying to trick me! You did something to my Steven. Get away." Sobbing she rushed back into the house leaving the door wide open. Adam feared she was losing her mind. She wasn't able to deal with the grief of Steven being gone and was bewildered by it. Feeling totally helpless, he glanced over at Smokey who motioned for him to follow. Entering the open door he heard her sobbing. She sat with her knees tucked up tight against her body huddling near the fireplace for warmth. The fire had gone out and she shivered from the cold. Adam cautiously closed the door to keep out the cold, then he took a lap blanket from the back of the couch and placed it around her. Without saying a word he began making a fire. Not a word was spoken as she stared into the flames crying quietly. Adam slipped into the kitchen and drew a cold glass of water and brought it to her. Without looking up she took the glass and drank.

How long had she been alone before he found her? Was it a day, weeks or months? "Favor, I'm sorry." She slowly lifted her eyes to his. He needed to know. He needed to ask the question. "When did Steven disappear?"

"October 11, 1992, the morning of the full moon. We were married on the eve of the full moon September 23, 1991. We celebrated our first anniversary on September 23, 1992." She spoke in a matter-of fact expressionless voice, her voice trailed off as she went back to staring into the fire.

How much had she fabricated in her own mind? How much was real? Did she make up the dates as a way of surviving the tragedy of being abandoned after being kidnapped? He thought about the preserves. The tops were dated. A few had the year 1991 while the others had 1992. He knew Favor did not know how to can prior to her kidnapping. Someone would have had to teach her. So many questions needed answers, but this grieving woman had the answers locked up in her mind. Those lessons of patience were going to be needed now to get through to Favor. Noticing she was beginning to nod off he picked her up and laid her on the couch, then added more wood to the fire. He thought about the child in the crib upstairs and was glad he was sleeping. Tired he settled in a big overstuffed easy chair and watched Favor as she slept, finally drifting off to sleep himself.

The next day he and Smokey discussed what they should do about Favor. "I want to take her back to Fortuna, back to her home there. I'm hoping if she sees her residence there she'll remember what it was like, and hopefully remembers her friends and her previous life."

"I agree she needs to go back, but you gots to be sure it be for the right reasons. You want her to remember you and then fall back in love with you. It may not happen the way you want. Maybe she did make up a story 'bout what happened here just to survive. But if it be true and she really had a good life with this Steven, then she may not be happy goin' back to her old life. You gonna be able to handle that?"

"No matter which way it goes I'm in it for the long haul and I know it's a package deal. I want to take care of her, and her baby. That girl has always had a fiercely independent streak, but I want to be with her or at least be there for her. I know it won't be easy."

"Dude, you be ok. Don't want ya to git hurt. How ya plan on gitten her to go back?"

"Don't know yet. It may be too soon but I'd like to take her back before the heavy snows. If she won't go then I'm going to stay here with her and try to get her to go back in the spring."

"Son, ya got guts. Ifn she won't leave and you stay, I be comin' back in the spring to check on all a ya."

"Ok, we agree. Try to get her to go back now or I stay whether she wants me to or not."

"You be puttin' it that way, son, and she's liable to kick some butt. Best choose your words wisely. Best be askin' the good Lord for the right words."

"You're right, Smokey. Could you kind of help me out on that one? Prayer isn't something I really know how to do."

"Yeah as I recall you wernt much of a believer before. Ain't nothin' to it, you jist talk to Him like we be talking. He be listenin'."

"Sounds weird. I feel stupid."

"It be that damn pride of yours gittin' in the way, boy. Bible say, 'Pride goeth before a fall.' Don't be lettin' pride git in your way or you gonna fall flat on your face. She'll see right through you if you don't do this right. Only one way to do that is by askin' fer His help. I be askin' Him to help you to ask Him."

"Say what? That's crazy! You confuse the hell out of me sometimes. If you're going to do that, then why not ask Him for me?"

"Cuz He want you to do the askin'. That way He knows you be on the same page."

"That's crazy talk."

"Fine. Have it your way, but when things go south don't be blamin' Him. Folks always be blamin Him, never that ol' devil guy or themselves. That be all I gots to say on the matter. End of discussion." Smokey walked away leaving Adam to think things out. In the end Adam put aside his pride and simply asked, "Ok, Big Man upstairs, Smokey swears by You, I don't mean swears, like the bad kind of swearing, I mean he says you listen to people if they talk to you, so I'm asking for the right words so I can get Favor to go back with me. That's all."

Adam was concentrating on how to do the asking so hadn't heard Smokey approaching. Smokey overheard the prayer and smiled to himself. "Yep, not too bad, he be learnin'."

Both Smokey and Adam agreed to stay on a few more days till they felt Favor trusted them. Then they were both going to leave, but their plan was to camp a short distance away and watch her without her knowing it. Then they'd show back up a week or so later as if they were just stopping by for a visit. They'd test her and then decide their next move depending on her reaction. She seemed to grow more comfortable in their presence. A few days later they announced they were leaving and thanked her profusely for her kind hospitality.

"I was hoping you'd stay till Steven came back. I know he'd like to meet you and thank you personally for your help around here. Will you be back?"

"We still want to get some more hunting in before the snows come, but if we find ourselves in the area we might stop to visit."

"Are you sure you have to leave? I've really enjoyed the company. You've both been very kind."

"You have your life and we have ours to get back to. I have a job and friends back home that I want to get back to and you and little Steven have your life here." He was deliberate in pointing out those facts, hoping it would hit a cord or trigger a memory.

She held Stevie in her arms watching on with tears in her eyes as they loaded the mules. Before leaving Adam walked over to her and gently kissed her cheek. "You take care. Good luck and take good care of the little guy." She didn't say a word so Adam mounted his mule and they rode away. He forced himself not to look back until they were entering the woods. Favor was standing in the same spot watching them disappear into the forest.

For over a week Adam and Smokey pastured the mules in a portable corral while they hiked back to where they could see the house from a distance and watch each day. During this time they watched her struggle with the animals, the firewood and other chores. A great deal of the time she spent indoors so they couldn't tell what was going on inside. It bothered Adam that she left the baby alone a lot. Not knowing much about babies he had to assume he was sleeping. One morning they heard the lowing of cattle and a small herd appeared. Favor saddled Denali and herded them to a lower pasture where Favor closed them in. There was a large supply of hay already in a covered area. "How do you suppose that all got there?" Adam whispered to Smokey. "That's not something she could have done herself. That guy she was with had quite an operation here. Everything was very systematically well organized."

Another day about an hour after feeding she emerged from the house and once again saddled Denali. She went back into the house and returned with the child strapped to her front and a bag she tied to the back of the saddle. They heard her telling the child they were going to visit Daddy and have a picnic with him. The mules were at least a quarter mile away and if they went back for them they might not be able to find her tracks and follow her. So they decided to follow on foot. Though the horse moved at a fairly fast pace, an early morning frost had made the ground soft enough to hold the tracks making it fairly easy to follow. The tracks led to the waterfall where Steve and Favor had married. They were both surprised at what a beautiful place it was. But the tracks did not stop here. Proceeding on they followed the tracks around a bend in the trail, upwards, finally coming upon the opening where the gravesites stood. They had to quickly duck behind a bush. There just ahead was the horse grazing and a short distance away sat Favor holding her child. She was talking. At first they thought she was talking to the child but then they realized she was talking as if another person were present. Carefully they skirted around to a more hidden area away from the trail. Here they could see and hear her more clearly.

"Oh, Steven, it's so hard without you. My heart aches for you. We had some visitors again. They were two very kind gentlemen. One of them had met you before and he knew me and greeted me by name. One was a much older man and he kind of talked with an accent. They helped me quite a bit, but they had to leave. They had packing mules. I think you would have liked them. Oh and the cattle came down from the high pasture so I didn't have to go get them. I already put them in the lower pasture. Stevie is getting so big. He misses your voice. I can tell."

"Sometimes I get really scared by myself, like when you used to go to town, but I'm trying to remember all the things you taught me. I dread when the snow comes because I may not be able to come up and visit with you so often. I wish you could come back. I'm lonely without you. Why did you do this to me? How could you? You never even said goodbye. You brought me here and made me fall in love with you. We were married and I had your baby. How could you make all these plans, teach me so much and then go away and leave me to raise him alone? I don't understand, I'm not happy without you. How am I going to go on? I want to be with you."

Favor continued to talk to the headstone as if an unseen person was standing there. She had spread out a blanket where she laid Steven who was fast asleep. She finally fell asleep curled up in a ball with her head resting against the headstone. Steven woke and she gathered him up and began nursing him. When he was done, and with him strapped securely to her chest, she gathered up her belongings, tied them to the saddle, kissed the headstone, said goodbye, and slowly rode away. The two men waited until they were sure she was gone and then walked over to the headstone and read the inscription. It was just as Sarah had said. The name and dates on the headstone matched the date on the copy of the Death Certificate he carried in his belongings. How could any of this be? The guy in the photo he'd taken and the guy in Sarah's photo were the same guy and Favor identified him as her husband, yet here was a headstone confirming all the information about his date of death. He began to wonder if there really was a body in the grave. If so was the body really the guy they said was supposed to be in there. And what about the rider he and Smokey saw? Was this part of an elaborate hoax, and if so, why? He wanted some answers, but more than that he wanted to get Favor away from this place.

Adam and Smokey made their way down the trail. There were too many questions and not enough answers to this mystery. As they found themselves nearing the house, they skirted around it carefully so Favor would not know they were near. She had arrived back long before them and had already put the horse up in the barn and had fed the animals. She was already heading into the house with a basket of eggs she had gathered from the chicken coop. Adam wanted to run to her.

He and Smokey stayed away for the next two days. It was too emotional to see the woman he had searched so hard to find, knowing she did not remember him.

"Son, the weather be turnin' colder and a decision has to be made. You gots to decide to leave or stay." They loaded up the team and headed towards the house, acting like they were just passing through again on their way back before winter set in.

When Favor heard them approaching she came out to greet them excited that they had come. "I didn't really think I'd ever see you again. I'm so glad you stopped. How did the hunting go? Can you stay a while? Would you like me to fix some dinner? You can tell me about your hunting?"

"Whoa, Missy, slow down a bit. One question at a time. Ketch yer breath and give us time to answer." Favor flushed with embarrassment but seeing Smokey's smile realized he was teasing.

"Hi, Favor. You look beautiful today. Don't mind Smokey. How's that little fella of yours?"

"He's fine."

"We really didn't get much hunting in, and I suppose we could stay a few days if you need some help around the place."

"I didn't mean it like that. I just enjoyed the company. It was nice having visitors."

"Well, Smokey, what do you say?"

"I be willing to stay, and I may even make myself useful, but only ifn I get some more of your tasty apple pie. That be one way of twistin' my arm."

Favor smiled from ear to ear, "Oh, Smokey, you're just a big ol' softy at heart. You've got a deal, but this time you two can sleep in the house. It's too cold in the barn."

"I'm used to the cold. But this young chap aint so used to it. I'll take my place in the barn, but I think this greenhorn might be better off with a place on yer couch."

"Since Steven hasn't come back yet, I'm sure it will be ok. Smokey there's no heat of any kind in the barn. Just promise me you'll come in by the fire if it gets too cold out there."

"It's a deal."

Adam and Smokey exchanged glances. Was she just trying to make them think he was just away for a while or did she somehow in her mind believe he was coming back? Adam thought about her reaction when he had told her Steven had passed away and the fact that she visited his grave.

For several days Adam and Smokey stayed on. Favor had them playing games in the evening and laughing and singing songs. During the day the men made themselves useful checking fences and the livestock as well as making sure everything was in good working order before the end of fall. On one of these days Favor told them to take Steven's truck down the road to check on things. It was on this day that they discovered the first locked gate and the sign above reading Rainbow Moor. When they returned Adam asked Favor about the gate and how far the property went?

"I don't know. I've never really left the property since I came here. I've been riding up above the moor and I know there are several locked gates on the lower property, but I was never allowed to go into that area. I left once on foot when Steven was gone for seven days, but I got lost and was going the wrong way. When he came back and found me gone he and Cloud, our wolf dog tracked and found me."

"You're kidding me!"

"No I'm not."

"How often do you have company?"

"You're only the second guests we've had. Mike and Jan Conley were the only other visitors. I really hated to see them leave. It's been so lonely here since Steven had to leave."

Watching her intently Adam spoke very carefully knowing she was feeling some intensely strong emotions at this moment. "Favor, why did Steven have to leave?"

"I'm not sure. I think it was his time."

"What do you mean by 'his time'?"

"Why are you asking me all these questions? I don't want to talk about it. Stop asking me questions!" With that she turned away.

"Wait, please don't go! I'm sorry! It's just that I'm concerned about you. I don't want to leave you here alone. I'd like to take you with me. Or I could stay and keep you company if you don't want to leave just yet." He watched her intently hoping she wouldn't get upset with him. She seemed thoughtful at first and then her expression changed to one of perplexity. "You can think about it. You don't have to answer or say anything right now. You could think of it as a vacation. I'd bring you back when you were ready to come back."

"I can't leave. I have my animals to take care of, but a vacation sounds nice. Do you think Steven would mind?"

"Under the circumstances I think he would approve. He'd want you and little Steven to be taken care of, don't you think? We could take the horse with us and put the milk cow in with the other cattle. I'm not sure about your chickens though."

"No, I can't go. The animals need hay in the winter. They depend on me."

"Then would you let me stay and help you with them? Steven is so little. It would be too hard when the weather is bad for you to take care of the animals and him too."

"I can't pay you."

"I'm not asking for pay. I just wouldn't feel right leaving you alone. I won't do anything inappropriate, I promise. Gentleman's honor."

A slight hesitation and then she interjected, "Well I guess at least until Steven returns."

"Of course. I understand." Adam thought about the papers he carried in his gear, the death certificate, the marriage license, the deed which had Favor's name on it, and the photos. These would have to be the key to convincing her to leave with him, but he'd have to ease into it. One step at a time. He had to first gain her complete trust.

A few days later Smokey packed up the mules and headed out for the cabin, promising to return in the spring. In the meantime Favor found another set of keys in the truck and a key they found unlocked the gates to the property. Adam told her it was important that they had them in case of an emergency and they needed to get off the property. One evening after eating and putting little Steven to bed he asked her, "Favor, why didn't Steven take his truck when he left?"

"Because he took Snow." Once again that puzzled look crossed her brow. "I wonder why he took Snow and not Denali. Snow was the horse I usually rode. She was more my horse."

"Do you know where he went?"

"Of course I do."

"Where?"

"To be with his parents."

"Where do his parents live and why didn't he take the two of you?" Adam knew the parents were dead, but he wanted Favor to accept it and say it herself. He needed to make her think about her situation.

"He couldn't."

"Why, Favor? A man doesn't just up and leave his family like that."

"He did what he had to do. He'll be back. You just wait and see."

"What if he can't come back?"

"That's not," she hesitated, "going to happen, so I don't want to talk about it anymore."

"At least tell me where his parents live."

"Stop asking me these questions! If you keep asking me, then you'll have to leave." Her words were full of frustration and close to anger. Adam knew he had given her something to think about so dropped the subject for now.

The days were growing shorter and colder. One morning when Adam went down to tend to the cattle Favor quickly saddled Denali and left with the baby to 'visit' Steven. When Adam returned and found her missing he figured she had gone to the grave site. He noticed fresh hoof prints leading in that direction. Knowing she needed the time alone to grieve he chose not to follow this time. When she returned he helped her with the baby and Denali, careful not to ask her where she went he simply said, "Did you have a nice ride?"

Surprised she said, "Aren't you going to ask me where I went?"

"No. I'm not your keeper or prison guard. This is your home and property and you don't need to ask my permission to go, nor do you have to tell me. Although it might be kind of nice, if as a courtesy you were to say you are going riding. But that is entirely up to you."

Embarrassed, her face became flushed and she avoided any eye contact, "I'll get supper ready," then turned and hurried into the house.

From then on she would tell Adam, "I'm going riding today." He would simply say ok, or say to have a nice ride. Some days she would be gone a couple of hours, other days she would be gone all day. On those days she began leaving little Steven with Adam. He had grown quite fond of the little guy and found he wasn't that hard to watch. As long as he followed a simple routine each day the little guy seemed happy and content. Some days she rode to the high meadow and ran Denali over the moor. Feeling the cool air on her face and breathing the fresh mountain air seemed to calm her. She never talked about going to the grave site, but on occasion she would talk about her ride through the moor.

One day while riding she noticed the cold had become more intense and clouds had caused the sky to turn a milky gray color. Then it began to snow. Favor seemed troubled when she returned earlier than she wanted to. Adam noticed she was nervous and fidgety. "Favor, what's wrong?"

"I don't want the snows to come. I won't be able to go out riding." What she was really thinking was that she wouldn't be able to visit the grave site.

Adam knew this and said, "It will all still be there when spring arrives again." This seemed to calm her slightly for a while. Favor stood at the window watching the snowflakes drifting down as a soft blanket of white began to cover the once green landscape. As the day wore on and the snow came faster and thicker she began to pace and talk to herself. Little Steven was crying but she took no notice. Adam watched her intently peering out into the fading light. "Favor, Steven is crying. You need to tend to him." There was no response. The crying grew more intense, but Favor didn't move from the window. It was as if no one else was there. "Favor, did you hear me. You need to take care of Steven."

With that she rushed towards the door yelling, "Steven! Steven! Oh, Steven, you're home!" Out into the cold gray day she rushed barefooted as she continued to scream Steven's name. Adam was shocked and didn't know what to do. Should he tend to the baby or go after Favor? The latter seemed more important at the moment. As he followed Favor out into the fading light he saw her stop abruptly and fall to her knees. When he reached her she had burst into tears. "He was standing here. I know he was. Where did he go?" Then she began calling out for Steve as Adam pulled her to her feet.

"It's just the fading light playing tricks on your eyes. Come inside. You don't have any shoes on and Steven is crying."

Reluctantly she let Adam lead her inside. "Sit down by the fire. I'll go check on the baby." When Adam came back downstairs with Steven she was sitting close to the fire warming her cold feet. She didn't look up when he entered the room. He tried to hand her the baby and she waved him away. "Favor, we need to talk."

"I don't want to talk."

"If you don't want to talk, that's your choice, but you damn well are going to listen to me and what I have to say." His frustration was apparent in his voice, which made Favor look up with wide eyes.

"You dare to speak to me like that when you are a guest in this house?"

"You're damn right I do, and you will listen! You are the mother of this beautiful child, and you need to make him your most important priority. You ignore him and expect me to take care of him. I don't mind helping you with him, but you can't continue to ignore him. I know you are grieving for his father, but do you think his father would want you to ignore his son and not take proper care of him? Now take him and be a mother to him. And furthermore has he ever seen a doctor? I'm assuming he was born here since you said you haven't left the mountain since you came here."

Shock at the blatant truth of his word Favor turned to Adam and with weary tear filled eyes reached out for Steven. Finding it hard to look at Adam she softly apologized. "Neither of us have seen a doctor. But we've both been just fine."

"Well, as soon as spring comes both of you are going to see a doctor." That plan would be put into action much sooner than Adam or Favor expected.

Winter's great white blanket once again covered the mountain. Adam and Favor were getting along much better since their little 'talk'. The three of them were beginning to look like a family. Favor was attentive to little Steven's needs and even found herself fussing over Adam a bit. Laughter had once again come to her home. She continued her visual over Steven's grave whenever she could get out to ride up to the gravesite. Adam never spoke to her about where she went, but as long as it was cold out he would not let her take the baby.

One early morning after caring for Steven, Favor announced she would be going riding. Steven hadn't wanted to eat much and fell back to sleep almost immediately. Adam didn't think she should go and this time told her so. "Favor, I don't think you should go. It's dangerous. I worry about you when you're out there alone." Favor only looked at Adam with a sad longing.

There was a light snow falling and he was afraid it might increase while she was out in the cold. She assured him she'd try not to be gone long. By mid-afternoon Favor had not returned from her ride. It was still just a light snow out, but Adam's concern switched to Steven. He had been sleeping nearly all day and had not woken up even for his normal lunch time feeding. Concerned Adam went to check on the little guy. When he touched his little head and face he noticed he was unusually hot. Looking around the room he found an infant thermometer and discovered he was running a temperature of 102. His lack of knowledge about infants lead him to search for a book on infant care among the many books in the Library. Finding one he read up on fevers. Reading that temperatures can spike in the night time hours made him concerned that it was too high for this time of day. Checking Steven's temperature an hour later he became more concerned. It had increased to 103 and Favor was not back yet. Steven was listless and refused to eat. Adam tried to get him to at least take some fluids, but he only fussed and cried. Becoming irritated at Favor and frustrated that he didn't know how to help the crying child he cradled him in his arms as he searched for an answer in the books he had pulled from the library shelves. It was nearly four o'clock when Favor returned. When she had put the horse up in the barn she entered the house looking tired and cold. "Adam," she called out. "I'm home. I'm going to draw a warm bath."

Adam rushed into the room carrying Steven, "Something's wrong with him. He's running a temperature. You need to check him and figure out what to do."

Scared and bewildered, she stared at Adam holding the child. "I don't have a clue. What is his temperature?"

"103, too high."

"Let's try putting him in a cool bath to bring the temperature down and I think Steven got some liquid baby aspirin stuff in his room. We can give him some of that and see what happens." Through the night they stayed up checking on little Steven. When his temperature didn't improve by the early morning Adam told Favor they needed to get him to a doctor. "What? We can't! We don't have one. We've never left the mountain. How could he get sick like this? They're going to ask questions and I won't know what to say."

"We'll worry about that later, but for now we have to get him medical care. Now where are the keys to the truck and the gates?" Finding the keys he went out to get the truck warmed up instructing Favor to get whatever they might need for Steven. When she returned with a diaper bag stuffed full of clothes, diapers and whatever else he might need Adam told her to put it in the truck and bundle Steven up. "I turned the horse and cow out and put out extra feed for all the animals. There's enough for at least 3 days. We'll stop by the cattle and put out extra feed. We may be gone a few days."

"What do you mean, a few days?" Fear gripped her heart as the unknown circumstances began to sink in. She was leaving her beautiful mountain and she didn't want to go. How could she trust this stranger? What if he never brought her back? "You take him! I'll stay and care for the animals."

"If it is longer than we expect, I will come back and check on the animals, but you are going and you will stay with Steven if that becomes an issue. So get some clothes together for yourself as well and any personal items you might need. Now where is his car seat?"

"We don't have one."

Adam stared at her in disbelief. "You have clothes for all sizes and everything else one can imagine, and you don't have a car seat?"

"Steven bought everything before I ever got pregnant! What do you want from me? My whole world feels like it's falling apart and all you can do is criticize me about a stupid car seat!"

"I'm sorry. I'm just concerned about him and his safety. I don't know what to do any more than you do. Let's just get going before it gets any later." With the necessary essentials loaded in the truck Adam put it in four wheel drive and slowly headed down the snow covered road. Favor began to shake as they drove away. Looking back she watched the house disappear as they rounded a curve. Tears trickled down her cheeks and she began to sob. Adam looked helplessly in her direction. He had no idea leaving the mountain would be so difficult for her. He only hoped she would begin to remember things when she returned to Fortuna.

The going was slow because of the snow. As they came to each gate he unlocked it and relocked it after they passed through. There were three gates in all each several miles apart. No wonder she couldn't be found. Steve Mitchell had made sure they were securely hidden from intruders and prying eyes. Once reaching the main road he wrote down the mileage so he would know just how far to the first gate and entrance as well as a note of the mile marker on Highway 36. He wanted to be sure he could find his way back. All the months he spent searching for Favor he expected she would be thrilled to see him and they would pick up their lives where they had left off. This whole nightmare would be but a memory and they would be happy together.

He always believed he would find her, but never in his wildest imaginings did he expect to find her with a child and little or no memory of her past life. Maybe she had been brainwashed. Whatever happened he hated Steven Mitchell for taking her life from her. As if she could read his mind she said.

"I know you think he abused me, but the truth of the matter is he never did nor did he lie to me. Steven loved me with all of his heart and soul and I loved him the same. I am glad he chose me to be his wife.

I can't explain it but we were connected in a way even I can't understand. I know you and I knew each other in the past. I don't understand why I can't seem to remember but I do feel something familiar about you. I'm sorry. I believe you when you say you'd been searching for me for a long time. I can't explain any of this. You've been so kind."

"It's ok, Favor. We'll figure it out in time. We just have to take it slow. The most important thing is to get little Steven healthy again." Adam wanted to tell her how much he loved her, how she was his life and Steven Mitchell had stolen their lives from them, but what good would that do. All he could do is love her quietly for now and hope to win her back. Favor continued to cry silently. She couldn't stop the tears. Losing Steven had been devastating enough, but leaving the mountain only added to her pain.

Adam had turned on his cell phone and had been checking it every so often. He finally got a signal. Knowing it would be brief he pulled over to the side of the road and dialed a number. Someone answered, "Cindy, its Adam. Is Houston there with you?" Favor could hear a girl on the other end squeal and call out to someone in the background. "Put me on speaker." There was a slight pause. "I've found Favor and we're on our way to the hospital. We're probably an hour out. I'm bringing her and her year old son. He's been running a high fever." Favor could hear excited talking on the other end, but was unable to make out what was being said. Adam answered back, "I can't talk now, I'll fill you in the best I can when we get there. It's very complicated." Then he hung up.

"Who's Cindy? Your sister?"

"No, but she is like a sister. She was your best friend and is engaged to my best friend."

Favor didn't reply. Turning her head away more tears fell from her already swollen eyes. Steven lay listlessly in her arms, hot to the touch. Favor was beginning to think he might die. He was all she had left of Steven. Regretting she had not been more attentive to him and realizing if Adam had not been there she would not have noticed he was ill and the thought of what would have happened only added to her agony. On top of her grief and fear she felt overwhelming shame. She did not deserve this child and she certainly did not deserve to be loved by Steven or Adam or anyone. Pulling him closer and cradling him tighter she whispered softly to him. "Forgive me my beautiful child. I am so sorry. I've been so sad that I didn't pay attention to you. You must live to carry on your father's name. Please be alright!"

They rode in silence the remainder of the drive down the winding road. Adam concentrated on his driving and Favor finally dozed off from shear emotional exhaustion. An hour later they arrived in Fortuna. Adam drove straight to the emergency room of the local Redwood Memorial Hospital. Houston and Cindy were waiting. Cindy threw her arms around Favor overjoyed at seeing her. Getting no response from Favor she pulled back and saw a puzzled look on Favor's face. Catching Adam's eye and a shake of his head she softly apologized for her enthusiasm. Cindy and Houston had alerted the hospital so they were rushed into the emergency where an emergency room doctor was waiting for them. Favor began to shake profusely as the doctor took the baby from her arms and laid him on the examining table.

Noticing her condition Adam gently guided her to a chair nearby to sit down. The doctor was asking her something, but she was unable to respond as her body went limp. Favor had fainted and now needed attention as well. More medical help was called for as her limp body was lifted onto another emergency room bed nearby. Adam was beside himself, but having Houston and Cindy there helped. The doctor was asking him questions so many of which he couldn't answer. Houston saw a man who was worn and beat. He'd found his beautiful Favor, but at a price. Only time would tell how great a price he had paid.

Chapter 26

News of Favor's return reached the local newspaper. Once again the town was buzzing with the story about the young woman's return and the child she now carried. Friends and family flocked to the hospital to see her bringing cards, gifts and well wishes. Her room was filled with colorful flowers. Except for having lost a considerable amount of weight, Favor was in good physical condition. Their greatest concern was for her emotional and mental state. She was withdrawn and depressed. Adam filled the doctors and police in about what he knew, but there were so many unanswered questions that only Favor could answer.

The buzz was that she had been brainwashed and made up a story to deal with her situation, but Adam was sure they were wrong. He'd seen enough in the mountains to make him believe there was a higher power at work in Favor's life and as unusual and unbelievable as it seemed, he believed Favor.

Mike and Jan Conley saw Favor's picture in the local newspaper, read the news story about her being a kidnap victim and being found. Rushing to the hospital, they hoped she'd remember them. Slowly peeking into her hospital room they hesitated. They were thrilled when her reaction was pure joy and excitement at seeing them. "You came. I'm so glad." Jan and Favor hugged each other and tears flowed freely.

"Favor, they're saying you were kidnapped."

"You can't believe everything you hear. Steven and I loved each other deeply."

"We figured you were hiding from someone. When we read the story about you being kidnapped, we had to come and see for ourselves."

"We truly loved each other. I didn't want to leave the mountain. If our baby had not gotten sick I would still be there. No one believes me and no one understands. Steven is my husband and I love him more than life itself."

"So he didn't kidnap you! We're so glad to hear that. We believed you two were truly happy together so we kept your secret even when we knew they were looking for you. You two saved our lives and we couldn't betray your trust no matter what."

"You are true friends. Truth is he did kidnap me, but he was a true gentleman and I fell in love with him. I just want to go home but they keep saying they have to do an evaluation of my mental condition. I heard them saying he must have brainwashed me. That is the farthest thing from the truth. I know they mean well, but I don't need all this. I just need my baby to be ok and to get back home as soon as possible. Can you help me? Could you please tell them how wonderful Steven and I were together and how much we loved each other? Please, please help me. I have to get back to Rainbow Moor."

"Favor, whatever you do, don't say anymore than you have to. Maybe you could tell them it was someone else who kidnapped you and he saved you. And why do you keep saying everything in the past tense? Did something happen to Clint, I mean Steven?"

Favor's eyes grew sad as she tried hard to hold back the tears. In almost a whisper, she said, "He had to go away. He's with his parents now. I know he didn't want to leave and he tried his best to prepare me, but one can never be completely prepared to lose the love of their life. My whole world stopped. I just want to go home." She began to sob and both Mike and Jan wrapped their arms around her.

"We'll tell them. We'll do everything we can to get them to let you out of here."

Several days past with Favor growing increasingly depressed. The police were investigating Steven's death and were making plans to have Adam guide them to the mountain home so they could investigate. Adam had not yet heard of their plan but when he did he blew.

"That is her home. It would tear her apart if I took anyone there and she'd hate me."

"She doesn't have to know. A crime was committed so we need to investigate."

"No you don't. She said she loved him. There are no charges being filed so you need to let it go and let her get on with her life in whatever way she wants."

"Sorry, we can't do that. A crime has been committed and someone has to pay."

"You can't or won't? Sounds like you just want a story and you want to sensationalize the story to meet your own agenda."

"You'd better be careful or we will charge you with obstruction of justice."

"What justice? Her husband is dead. Who are you going to go after? What crime has been committed? Ask her. She'll tell you they were simply two people in love who like their privacy."

"We need to take her back to the scene of the crime and see what she can tell us."

"No, you need to let it go and let her get on with her life. She has a child to care for. Think of that and drop it. She's no longer a missing person, ere a happy ending. Go investigate something else or I'll hire the best lawyer in the world and make you look like fools before this is over."

"We could arrest you right now for threatening a peace officer, so you better watch what you say from here on out." The two officers left the waiting room where Adam stood furious at the conversation he'd just had. He would protect Favor in any way he could, but how could he do that without ending up in jail. Favor's father had been contacted and was soon to arrive. He hoped he'd know what to do.

Upon the advice of Mike and Jan, Favor was contemplating denying Steven kidnapped her. Just in case, they came up with a plausible story to get them to release her and somehow get her home again. These two friends were the only ones she felt she could trust. Everyone else seemed determined to tarnish Steven's name and keep her there instead of letting her go back to the moor. She was beginning to remember her old friends and her father but it was still complicated. The doctors seemed determined to keep her in the hospital.

In the meantime little Steven recovered, had been circumcised, given his shots and given a clean bill of health. They told Favor these things needed to be done when she began to protest and then threatened to charge her with child abuse if she didn't sign the papers. Hearing Steven's tiny screams broke her heart and Adam's as well. All he could think of is if he had not kept looking for her she might still be happy in her home on the moor. Yet, if he had not been there, Favor in her grief would have continued to ignore the child and he might be dead by now. No matter how he looked at it, there was no happy answer. He wished Smokey were there. He'd know the right thing to say. The old mountain man was solid as a rock and Adam wished he were there to help him know what to do. His own words came back to him, "I'm in it for the long haul." And what a long haul it was turning out to be.

Favor gave Houston and Cindy permission to take care of Steven until they let her out of the hospital. She was surprised to learn from her father that they were living in her house and taking care of her things and personal affairs on her behalf. Though he was overjoyed to have his daughter back he could see she was a changed woman and wasn't sure how to approach her.

It was Adam who finally convinced the doctors to let her go to her home in Fortuna. But they refused to release her from the doctor's care and wanted her to come in for weekly evaluations. Winter was fast approaching. Adam wanted to steal her away back to the moor but there always seemed to be someone watching and prying. He wanted to be sure no one could follow them. He couldn't risk someone stopping them. Favor tried her best to act like everything was alright, but the longer she was away from the mountain the sadder she became. In time she began to remember everything, but somehow none of it meant anything to her anymore. The only thing she cared about was going home to Rainbow Moor. She wondered what had become of her animals. Adam had managed to sneak away to check on them and each time told her they were ok except he'd had to bring the chickens back to town with him and had someone keeping them for her. This gave her a small sense of relief.

Adam and her father accompanied her to each of her doctor visits. On one visit to the doctor's office she was met by the doctor, and the two police officers that Adam had gotten into the confrontation with. The three of them were taken aback at the fact they had not been forewarned that they would be there. The doctor explained they needed to ask her some questions in order to decide if they were going to close the investigation or pursue it. And to determine if she was mentally stable. The doctor began by asking Favor if she understood.

"Of course I understand. But do you understand I did not ask for anyone's help and that I am being forced to do this against my will?"

"We'll be asking the questions," one of the arrogant SOB police officers piped up.

The doctor stopped him and said, "No I will be asking the questions. Favor is my patient and I am the expert in this field. If you have a question you want asked, write it down and I will decide if it is appropriate at this time. You are only here to listen and observe. Do I make myself clear?" There were no comments, only an exchange of disgusted glances.

"Now, Favor, would you tell me your complete name and date of birth?"

"Favor Jasmine Mitchell, Born February 17, 1967, wife of Steven Lawrence Mitchell IV, mother of Steven Lawrence Mitchell V. Is that a satisfactory answer?"

"Favor, I have your name as being, Favor Jasmine Durand, widow of Conrad Durand. Isn't that your real name?"

Favor began to shake at the mention of Conrad's name and being his widow. "That used to be my name. I remarried Steven Lawrence Mitchell IV and had his child Steven Lawrence Mitchell V." The doctor made note of her emotions.

"Isn't it true that Steven Mitchell kidnapped you and held you prisoner and forced you to have sex with him, got you pregnant and then left you to bear the child of that rape alone in some mountain hideaway?" One of the police officers had jumped up and was yelling at her.

"That's not true. Stop saying those terrible things about him. Stop! Stop it right now!" The room had become chaotic. Everyone was yelling. Favor was sobbing in her father's arms. He was yelling at the doctor. Get him out of here or I will be filing harassment charges against him and the police department. The officer was ordered out of the room and order was restored.

"Favor," Dr. Salter was saying, "I'm sorry about that. We can continue this later."

But her father and Adam spoke up almost in unison, "There won't be another time."

"I can do this, Dad. I'm not crazy. I am Mrs. Steven Lawrence Mitchell and my husband taught me to be strong." In his eyes he saw a delicate, strong woman with a soft countenance. He marveled at the beauty she had become and the strength that came from somewhere within.

"Ok, baby girl, but if at any time you want to stop or don't want to answer a question, you just say the word and we'll leave." Then looking at the remaining officer and investigator he said. "What I said to that other jerk stands for you too." Looking back at the doctor he nodded.

"Ok, so tell us about your marriage to Steven Mitchell."

"Alleged marriage!" the other officer piped up. Dr. Salter gave him a look and the officer apologized for his interruption. Favor told them briefly that they were married in a private ceremony on the mountain above Rainbow Moor.

"Just because two people say they were married in a mock ceremony doesn't mean they are legally married."

"We have a license and everything."

"Who were the witnesses?" Favor didn't know what to say, then Adam spoke up.

"Doctor, I obtained a copy of their marriage license before I found Favor. I have it here in this folder. It has the names of the witnesses on it." Adam pulled out the license and handed it to the doctor. Relief flooded Favor's face. Adam decided not to mention Sarah or Sadie and how he got the license. Seeing how poorly this whole thing was being handled, he certainly didn't want them questioning Sarah.

"So it was you, Steven, the witnesses and affiant, correct?"

"The names are all on the license. No one else."

The doctor exchanged glances with the officer and then moved on to more questions. "Tell me about your home." Favor's eyes lit up as she told them about her home, about their garden, the canning, the animals and everything they did together. Her body physically seemed to become lighter. "So you never left the mountain all the time you were there. Not even once."

Adam knew this was a trick question and knew it was very important that she answer it correctly. He saw the lightness leave her body and she looked towards him with a pleading look. Then she stiffened and look directly at the doctor.

"Well we did have to get the license." And then she smiled and went on as if he had not interrupted the flow of her story. She had not lied, but she had answered what Adam thought was satisfactory. The officer did not seem satisfied and glared at the doctor with a look that told him to ask more questions.

"After the baby was born, why didn't you bring him to a hospital and get his birth recorded?"

Adam interrupted again. "There is a birth certificate on record. Here is a copy of the record." Handing the doctor the record, he hoped this would stop this line of questions.

After looking it over he handed it back to Adam. "It looks to be in order, but why wasn't he circumcised?" Another question that threw Favor for a moment.

"Not everyone believes in that and it's not against the law."

"You say that, and yet you allowed it to take place since you had to bring him in."

"I was told if I didn't allow you to, I would be charged with child abuse, and I didn't say I didn't believe in it, I said some people don't believe in it."

"So you're saying your alleged husband didn't believe in it, and where is he now?"

With this question Favor burst into tears. Looking at her father he saw the anguish in her eyes. With that he rose, drew Favor to her feet and said, "We're done here. There will be no more questions. I'll thank you to leave my daughter alone."

The investigating officer jumped up. "There are still a lot of unanswered questions to answer."

"The only thing that matters is that my daughter was found. You no longer have a case."

"Yes we do. Steven Mitchell kidnapped her."

"Father please make them stop saying bad things about Steven."

"This is over. If you so much as come near my daughter again, I will call my attorney's and it will be the end of your career. This case is closed. Now leave my family alone."

Dr. Salter told the officer to leave. He turned and asked the others to stay briefly. When the officer had left he turned to the others. "There are a few things that don't add up here. I didn't want to bring it up with the officers present. I'm not going to go into them now, but I would like to continue seeing Favor alone, on a weekly basis for now. Favor, I know you want to go home to your moor, but with the bad weather don't you think it would be better to stay here for a while?"

"No, I know how to survive winter on the moor. We prepare all spring and summer for the bad weather and are able to live very comfortably there. Besides I have animals to care for."

"But you didn't have a child before."

"Please, don't do this!"

"I can't release you yet. Let's give it a little more time." Tears were flowing down her cheeks as her father asked Adam to take her to the car. He then asked the doctor, "What are you really trying to figure out? Favor seems completely competent to me. What is it you want?"

"Something just doesn't add up. I think she's holding some information back. Why was she found alone, and why isn't Steven here with her if he loved her as much as she says? Why is Adam the one here with her? She's very protective of Steven and his name. I think she's in denial. I think he left her alone and she can't deal with that reality. She needs to face that fact that he basically dumped her."

"I think you're wrong. She pretty much remembers everything about her life here but nothing seems to have any meaning to her anymore. I feel like I've lost her even though I've gained a grandson."

"I don't think she is bad enough to have her committed, and that would only be a last resort, but I am concerned about her emotional state of mind."

"Are you seriously thinking of having my daughter committed? That will never happen! I don't care what you say! If at any time I think you are not acting in my daughter's best interest I will have these visits stopped. I want my daughter to be ok, but I will make any final decisions even if you don't agree. If at any time I think these sessions are not helping Favor they will end."

"People often go into denial when something traumatic happens. We just need to be sure Favor can handle life from here on out and hopefully enjoy her child and move on to a new fulfilling life."

The winter months were damp and cold. Favor had moved back into her Fortuna house. With the help of her friends they'd set up a nursery for Stevie. Income from Conrad's estate was more than enough to live comfortably. Houston and Cindy moved back in with Adam on the adjoining property. Favor's father flew up every weekend to be with Favor and enjoy his grandson.

Houston had enlisted the help of some of his cowboy buddies and together they had followed Adam to the property in the mountains secretly to move the cattle to the lowest pasture where there was more area to graze and there was much less snow. Houston never told them anything about the 'owner' of the cattle and Adam never let them go beyond the farther most gate where the Rainbow Moor sign stood. He said it was at the owner's request for their privacy. Instead he went alone and loaded up Denali and brought him down to run with the cattle. He had checked on things at the house and made sure it was closed up tight for the winter. A heavy feeling of guilt made him anxious to get away as soon as he could.

Favor made it through the holidays and was her usual gracious self. A number of Conrad's friends and her in-laws had come to visit and on New Year's they all celebrated a New Year's Eve dinner party at the historic Scotia Inn. Her father had arranged it so that there would be room for her many friends and family from the past and present. They had found a young high school girl who would attend to Little Steven during the event and when it was time for him to sleep she took him to a suite in the inn where they would spend the night. Favor's father bought the young babysitter a lovely dress as well, appropriate for her age and her duties. Little Steven, who was now seven months old, was dressed in a tiny tuxedo.

Her father had taken her to a local bridal and formal wear store and had purchased a beautiful gown. Favor felt like he was getting her ready for a prom but went along with it so she didn't hurt him. It actually felt more like a coming out party then a New Year's party. She knew it was all for her and she felt as though she was being put on display, the way Conrad used to do. The memory of Conrad left her with mixed emotions. She'd loved

Conrad, but never like she loved Steven. It was a spectacular event and the turnout was short of phenomenal. Adam and her father escorted her.

The buzz was what a lovely couple Favor and Adam were. Adam acted like he was the groom at a wedding and when the clock struck twelve he had gathered her in his arms and kissed her. Favor had pushed back from him with a look of shock and hoped nobody had noticed. He was still holding onto her while others wished her a happy new year. All she wanted to do was get away from everyone. They were all laughing, cheering, hugging each other and wishing them a happy new year and all Favor wanted to do was run away. As soon as a moment presented itself she quickly excused herself and went up to the suite where Steven and the babysitter were fast asleep. Adam tried to follow her but she was too quick.

Entering the room where Steven lay sleeping she closed the door and lifted him from the crib that had been set up for him. Sitting in a nearby rocker she poured out her heart as she cried for the man she loved and cradled the child they had brought into the world. Agony filled her heart and long after the music downstairs had stopped she continued to cry in agonizing despair.

The weekly visits to Dr. Salter continued. He acknowledged she had made progress. But felt something wasn't quite right and he couldn't get Favor to work passed whatever it was. Favor took the visits as matter of fact and tried to shrug them off. She knew spring was coming and with its approach she became agitated at the continued visits. Dr. Salter noticed the change.

Everyone seemed to think she was doing fine because she had 'settled' in her Fortuna house, but he could see she was becoming increasingly depressed though she tried her best to hide it from her family and friends. With each day it was becoming harder to keep up appearances. She was grateful for everyone's help and appreciated it but she was losing weight and every day she had to force herself to 'act' happy. She needed to get back to Rainbow Moor and to Steven.

Little Steven was thriving and had become an important part of their daily lives. Visits to the zoo and parks, new toys and constant attention were helping him develop into a healthy happy child. He was especially fond of Adam and would squeal when he came in the house.

No one ever mentioned his father. It was as if it was a taboo subject. Favor noticed it but kept it to herself along with her deepest memories of Steven. After one of her visits to Dr. Salter he asked, "If you could have anything in the world, what would it be?" Tears filled her eyes but she didn't speak. "Favor, whatever you say here is confidential. I'm concerned about you. You have been losing a lot of weight and I can tell you are trying to please everyone around you. I know you care about how they feel, but what about how you feel? You're here to talk about what matters to you. I'm not here to judge you."

"Then why are these visits mandatory. I might have come anyway, but I'm being forced to come. I feel like a prisoner again."

"Again? Favor what do you mean by again?"

"Nothing." She hesitated knowing Dr. Salter was thinking about the kidnapping. But she was quick to recover. "Sometimes Conrad made me feel that way." Dr. Salter knew this was a half-truth.

"Are you sure about that? Isn't it true that at first Steven made you feel that way as well? You've had two men in your life 'control' you. Both of them you say you fell in love with. I'm concerned that this is a pattern with you. You fall in love with men who control you. It doesn't seem as though your father was a controlling person or I would think this actually had something to do with your childhood. But I don't think that is the case here. Adam is in love with you, but you are not in love with him. Is it because he doesn't try to control you? Although it sounded like you were falling in love with him before Steven." Dr. Salter chose his words very carefully. He knew Adam didn't fit the pattern he was describing but he needed to see her reaction.

"It's truly not like that. And don't tell me I'm in denial. Yes, Steven was the man on the phone who called me for two years. Yes, he did kidnap me, but even before he took me from my home I was falling in love with him. When I looked into his eyes I saw something amazing and even though I fought him, I still felt something strangely intriguing and wonderful about him. I was already attracted to him. I never made it easy for Steven, but my love for him transcends time and space and we built an incredible life together. I will never love another man as long as I live. I know that with every part of my being."

Dr. Salter looked at Favor with deep admiration and respect. "Favor, I believe you. So back to my question, if you could have anything you wish what would that be?"

"To turn back the hands of time and be with Steven at Rainbow Moor. I want only to take little Steven and go home. There is nothing more important to me."

"I understand. But you need to answer one more question for me. Why isn't Steven with you now and why were you and Little Steven found alone?"

"I can't tell you that, but I can tell you he didn't want to go away, of that I am sure."

"I think this session has been a good one. We're done here today."

Wiping the tears from her eyes she rose from her chair. She looked weak and shaky. He asked her if she wanted to stay and relax for just a bit. "I can get you some tea before you go."

"No, Steven taught me to be strong. I will be strong for him till I can be with him again."

When she had left he placed a conference call to Favor's father and Adam and told them he'd like to meet with both of them as soon as possible. They both agreed they could meet with him in his office the next day. He asked them not to let Favor know about the meeting. Both of them were nervous about what the conversation would entail when Dr. Salter refused to be specific on the phone. The next day the three men met. "I'll give it to you straight."

"This doesn't sound like good news."

"Have you noticed Favor is losing weight?"

"Yes, but she's a young mother, and she's had a lot of adjusting to do."

"When I am able to get Favor to talk, it's always about the mountain and Rainbow Moor. She talks about the visit with Mike and Jan Conley. I've spoken to them at an earlier time to find out more about Steven and their story collaborates her story to the tee. I think Favor and little Steven need to go back to the mountain. I'd like to make it a special day. Spring is March 20th. I'd like to arrange for her to go back that day. Spring is a time of new beginnings and Favor needs a new beginning. If she agrees, I'd like to have Mike and Jan Conley there, you two, Houston and Cindy. If Favor agrees I'd like to make her return a celebration."

"In the end, she will decide who she wants to accompany her. Either way I will be there to help her settle back in. I want to be sure she is able to physically and emotionally handle going back. I called and asked her to come back in today. She's due here in about ten minutes."

"How long would you let her stay?"

"As long as she wants. Permanently if that's what she wants. But I truly think she needs someone to be with her and take care of little Steven in case she doesn't get better."

"You see, Favor is mourning and for no apparent reason is dying a slow death. I believe the only chance to save her is for her to return to Rainbow Moor."

The words came as a shock to both of them. Her father began to choke up. "I thought she was doing better. I can't lose my daughter again. I just can't."

"She's been trying to hide it, but if she stays you will lose her. Something happened on that mountain. The answer is there. The moor holds a secret that we may never know or understand, but I believe it holds Favor's life as well."

There was a knock on the door and the receptionist poked her head in to announce Favor was there. When Favor walked in seeing her father and Adam she thought only the worst. They had all agreed to have her committed. She turned to flee, but the doctor had anticipated her response and quickly blocked the door. "Favor, it's ok. I have some good news for you today."

When the doctor had concluded with the plan they had discussed Favor began laughing and crying at the same time. It was the first time her father had seen the light come into her eyes. Before long they were all laughing and sharing in her joy. She was going *home* to *stay*. She was going back to Steven and Rainbow Moor. She agreed to the original idea and was overjoyed at the prospect and excited about sharing her home with her father and friends. Looking at Dr. Salter with tears streaming down her face she thanked him profusely.

The day finally came. Saturday, March 20, 1993. It was as beautiful a day as you could imagine with the warm spring air and anticipation. Cindy and Jan made potato and macaroni salads, green salad and pies. They would barbecue steaks and corn on the cob, have some wine, beer and soda. The girls noticed Favor was weak, but none the less extremely happy. "I'll get my strength back once I'm back on the moor. You'll see. There's a cute little white dress Steven bought me. I've never worn it, but it's the first thing I'm going to put on when I get home. The air up there is so clean and healthy and Steven will be there waiting for me." They exchanged glances but didn't say anything.

They set out early with Adam driving Steven's truck. The caravan of friends finally reached the last gate entering the moor. The colors of spring had returned and the moor was teaming with life. The countryside was alive with birds and theirs songs filled the air. They were all amazed to see how beautiful it was. It looked like someone had taken a paint brush and painted Rainbow Moor with all the colors of the rainbow. Adam managed to get word to Smokey and when they reached the last gate with the sign that announced you were entering Rainbow Moor he was waiting with Denali and his pack string to escort Favor the remainder of the way.

"We gonna have to put some meat back on them bones of yers. The mountain will make you strong agin." She smiled and gave him a great big bear hug. Favor then told Denali to kneel. They had all exited the vehicles and watched on in wonder as she mounted the great black horse. Mike and Jan greeted Smokey and they all laughed at the happy occasion. They let Favor ride on ahead alone with Smokey not far behind. The vehicles came next with Adam locking the gate respectfully behind them.

Nothing else mattered to Favor. She had finally come home to her beautiful moor. She heard the cattle and saw them grazing just above the house. Adam had brought the chickens back the previous day and had aired out the house. Everything was cleaned and ready for her return. It had been nearly five months since she'd been home. Favor was excited about showing everyone her beautiful home.

The picnic table outside was laden with food. Everyone was laughing and talking. Dr. Salter, her dad, Cindy and Houston were intrigued at how organized everything was. They were full of questions about how they were so self-sufficient and how they lived so remotely. Favor felt like they were accepting Steven's role in her life just by the excited questions and words of admiration for their home. Outside, Adam and Smokey noticed she kept looking in the direction of the trail leading to their wedding site and beyond. When they'd all eaten and the food was cleared away into the kitchen she went out onto the porch. Dr. Salter and her father followed.

"Steven and I used to spend a lot of time out here." She pointed out the arbor and the pond. "Sometimes we'd sit there," pointing to the seats in the arbor, "but most of the time we'd sit here in the swing and sometimes sing songs." With that the swing began to move gently. Dr. Salter and her father froze. Their eyes grew wide. Favor gave a little laugh, "It's just Steven having some fun at your expense. Don't mind him. He approves of this gathering. I can feel it." With that she walked down the steps to the arbor. It seemed as though someone was walking beside her the way she held her hand out at her side.

"Let's not say anything about this to the others. I'm a doctor who isn't too sure of what to think at this moment. I'd much rather keep this to myself."

"I agree."

A few moments later they noticed Favor looking in the direction of the path. The others had come back outside and were lounging around on the porch. Adam and Smokey knew what she was thinking.

"Favor, do you want to go for a ride? We can saddle Denali for you."

Her response shocked them all. "I'd like it if everyone could go. It's a bit of a hike though. Steven said it would be ok to let everyone come for a visit just this one time. It's his way of saying thank you for bringing me back."

"Ain't no problem little lady. We gots four mules and Denali. We kin double up. We got five of us that knows how to ride so we kin all git there."

They all agreed. It didn't take them long before they were all saddled up. Favor, on Denali, led the way with little Steven securely strapped in front of her.

They heard her saying, "We are going to visit Daddy again, Stevie. Isn't that wonderful and we have guests who want to visit him. I'm so excited." Without hesitation she started off towards the woods at a fairly good pace. When they had ridden a ways she stopped. She seemed to be hesitating. They were near the waterfall, the place she and Steven had been married. She wasn't sure if she should allow them to go through this place. It was hers and Steven's. "We can't go in there."

"What?"

"You can't go in here. It's our place. We were married here and no one else has a right to go in there. It's special just for Steven and me."

"I hear a waterfall."

"That's our waterfall."

"Ok. So we'll go around. Do you know which way to go?"

"No, we have to go back." Then she began to cry.

"Little Lady, I bin a mountain man for many a year. Why don't you let me guide us around yer special place? You kin let me know if I'm too close. Is there another trail?"

"I only know the trail that goes from our wedding place and it leads through and past to where." She suddenly stopped speaking and looked confused.

"To where Steven is waiting, isn't that right?" Dr. Salter spoke up. "We really want to visit Steven before we have to go back."

She began to cry irrepressibly. "Steven, I don't know what to do. Tell me what to do?"

Adam felt an overwhelming sense of sadness, not knowing what to do or how to console her he looked to Smokey for help. Smokey had no idea what to do. From out of nowhere a mist rose up, like the mist Adam and Smokey had seen the year before when they saw the white horse and rider. Favor suddenly became calm and softly said, "Thank you, Steven." Then she began to ride on following the mist. It lead them just on the outskirt of their wedding place. They could see through the trees the upper portion of the waterfall. Then they dropped down over the edge and then came out again above the fall and back onto the trail. The mist disappeared here and they proceeded on. A short ways farther and they reached the gravesite.

Favor told Denali to kneel got off and headed straight to Steven's headstone. "Steven, I guess you know by now some friends wanted to visit you. They're here with me now. Isn't it wonderful?" She turned to look at the group. The men wearing hats had removed them and stood respectfully waiting.

"Can we come closer?" Dr. Salter interjected.

"Yes, please do." She proceeded to talk to the headstone as if it Steven were sitting there before her. They watched on in silence for a while and then left her to her one sided conversation as they went from headstone to headstone reading the names and dates. Favor noticed and got up quietly and told them a little about each of the family members buried there. She spoke each word with a sense of pride and reverence. When she reached her Steven's grave she became silent a moment. Then she spoke more to herself than to them. "Steven, we miss you so much. I love you and always will. I couldn't have asked for a more wonderful, loving husband. We have to go now but Stevie and I will be back soon." Adam and Smokey had managed to quietly fill the group in on the date of death on the headstone so they could be somewhat prepared and let them know she was completely unaware that the two of them had followed her there once before. They thanked her for bringing them and respectfully left her alone to say her goodbye.

The group rode back to the house in silence. Favor's father hugged her tightly. He knew she was where she needed to be and knew communication with her would be difficult from here on out. They made a plan for the next date to come and visit. It would be in a couple of months on Little Steven's first birthday, Friday, May 28th. Everyone made plans to spend Memorial Day weekend on the mountain. Adam would meet them at the road and bring them up. When everyone had left and she and Adam were alone she turned to him and thanked him for all he had done for her and for helping make it possible for her to come home.

"I belong here. No place else. I am Mrs. Steven Lawrence Mitchell. I know you are my friend and I know you love me. I'm sorry I don't feel the same. I will always be grateful for all you have done for me and you are not obligated to stay. You can go back whenever you want to, but I will never leave the mountain again."

Adam felt his heart breaking. But if he couldn't have her for his own, he would at least be there for her through the cold of winter and the warmth of summer. He would treat Steven as if he were his own child. He was in it for the long haul no matter what. That had not changed.

Adam helped with running Rainbow Moor and raising Steven. He'd grown particularly fond of the little tyke and Steven toddled after him where ever he went. Favor kept a daily vigil over Steven's grave. She left each afternoon after most of the chores of the day were complete. Normally she'd be gone only a couple of hours. But, for some reason, even though she was happy to be home she continued to lose weight and at times could barely get on Denali.

One day noticing she was especially weak, Adam begged her not to go. "Favor, don't you see what you're doing to yourself and to me and little Steven? I know you don't feel the same about me as I do you, but at least think about Little Steven. He needs his mommy to be healthy and happy and so do I. I don't believe this is what his father would want. I'm begging you not to go to the grave today." She just smiled a sweet smile. "Adam, my dear Adam. I must go. He's expecting me. Don't worry I'll be ok."

It was growing dark and she still had not returned. Adam feared for the worst. He bundled Steven up warmly. The evening mountain air could turn bitterly cold at times. He had just started up the four wheeler when Denali came in to view. Slumped on his back was Favor, barely hanging on. He pulled her down from his back and carried her into the house and laid her on the couch. Then rushed back out for Steven. He was beside himself. Favor smiled at him, "I'm afraid I fell off Denali once. It was hard to get back on. I'm so very tired, Adam."

Tears ran down his face as he pulled her into his arms. "Favor, I love you so much. I want you to live, really live. Please don't give up on the living. Let the dead rest in peace. You'll see Steven someday again, but it's not your time. Let go of the grief and live again and maybe one day you will love again. I need you, Favor. Little Steven needs you."

Favor didn't go back to the gravesite. It seemed Adam's words had set in and she was giving life a chance again. Her health began to improve and she laughed and played with Steven and Adam. They enjoyed the garden and the bounty it produced. It almost felt like they were a family. On Labor Day the whole group came up again for another barbecue before the colder weather set in. Even Dr. Salter and Smokey made the trip. They were impressed with how well Favor was doing and how she had improved.

"Adam, tell me how she's doing. She looks good but how is she emotionally?"

"Doc, she has her moments. But, when she's having a bad day or feeling down we talk about it. We have an agreement to be open about her feelings. Sometimes she has a good cry but it's getting better all the time. I'm hoping to get her to take a vacation next summer. She seems open to the idea. It's knowing she will be coming back that makes her think about doing something fun for little Steven."

"That's a good sign. You're good for her, Adam. In time she will come around."

"I hope so. I searched for her so long and almost lost her. I said I was in it for the long haul. She knows that I won't leave no matter what and she knows I love that little guy of hers as if he were my own. He's my little pal."

"She's lucky to have you. You're a very special man. I'm sure she knows that."

"She's a loveable woman."

"Yes, and look at the men who have loved her. All of them totally devoted. She has a commanding presence that draws people to her, yet she has a purity and innocence about her like that of a young child. Her laugh is contagious and her voice like a melody. No it is like a song. Favor's song, a song all her own. I was in awe of her the first time I met her at the hospital. That's why I took a special interest in her case. It was one I had to see through. I think the outcome is good and will continue to be."

"Thanks, Doc. I needed to hear something like that."

A year passed. They enjoyed the bounty of the garden as Favor now taught Adam how to can and preserve the fruits and vegetables. The winter that followed was somewhat mild compared to the winter of 1991. Having spent 1992 in Fortuna, Favor had decided she preferred a white winter over a wet winter. March and a new spring came and before they knew it Little Steven had turned two with an amazing vocabulary. Adam took him riding on the four wheeler when Favor went out riding Denali. Life was good but still Favor kept her distance from Adam. Their friendship was as good as any friendship could be. Their friends came to visit often. Adam had gotten Favor a cell phone and they were able to get reasonable service at certain points on the property, allowing them to call out as often as they liked. Life on the mountain was good.

It was late September. Favor was in an exceptionally good mood. She even took a little stroll with Adam and Little Steven. The moon was coming up and lit up the countryside like a big bright light. Favor pointed out the full moon and Little Steven looked up and to their surprise pointed to the moon and said, "Daddy moon." Then he giggled and reached for both of their hands. Favor and Adam looked at each other with shocked surprise.

"Did he just call you Daddy?"

"I don't know?"

"It sounded like he was calling you Daddy and telling you to look at the moon."

"Favor, I've never called myself Daddy to him. Please don't let this upset you."

"I'm not. It just caught me off guard."

"Me, too!"

"I guess it would be kind of natural for him to call you Daddy. You are after all the only father figure he has known for quite some time."

The morning sun was just creeping up over the mountain throwing a glistening sprinkle of light on the early morning frost. The birds were waking and calling out to one another. Autumn had just arrived and the leaves were beginning to turn. Favor occupied her old room since it had the private bath. She had finally allowed Adam to occupy the room that had been Steven's. It was a big step for her, but she was so grateful for Adam being there and making her feel safe.

Adam woke and stretched listening to the sweet sounds of morning. He thought he heard Favor moving around downstairs so got up to see what she might be cooking for breakfast. He was surprised to see her bedroom door wide open. She never left it open before. He peeked in to see little Steven was still fast asleep. His curiosity drew him to the open door of her room. The bed was made and in the middle of the bed he saw something that drew him inside. There on the bed was a fresh bouquet of red and white roses. He moved in closer to read a note that lay beside it. "Love, Steven" was all it read. At the foot of the bed lay one single yellow rose. Beside it was a note written in Favor's hand, It read, "Dearest Adam, forgive me. Take care of Steven for me. Affectionately, Favor."

At that very moment he heard a horses whinny. He bounded down the stairs two at a time calling out to Favor. Denali was in the corral pacing and snorting and looking off in the distance. Adam turned just in time to see Favor on a white horse wearing what appeared to be a wedding gown. She paused a moment, smiled and waved at him. Then she disappeared into the woods. Where had the white horse come from? It looked like the horse he and Smokey had seen with the man dressed in white on his back. Snow! The horse Favor had talked about. Adam called out to her. He had a bad feeling about this. Rushing he saddled Denali, then ran into the house to get Steven. He had to get to her as quickly as possible before it was too late.

Adam rode as fast as he could not even hesitating when he reached the area of the waterfall. There were freshly lit torches and candles. He had an eerie feeling like he was intruding on a sacred place, but there was no time to waste. He could see fresh hoof prints on the still damp ground from the morning dew. Up ahead, there! He could see the white horse and what was that. A dog? No, a white wolf standing at the entrance of the little cemetery. Favor had to be at the gravesite. The wolf raised its head to the sky and gave out one long mournful howl and then he and the horse ran off together.

Adam reached the entrance. Where was Favor? Adam approached what he thought was Steven's gravesite, but suddenly realized there was a new headstone. Fear and dismay overtook him. Inscribed on the headstone was Favor Jasmine Mitchell Born February 17, 1967, Died September 23, 1994 and an inscription Beloved Wife, Beloved Mother. Today was September 23, 1994. Upon the headstone lay a fresh wreath of daisies and a single red rose.

Finding Favor and the secret of Rainbow Moor drove young Adam Jennings mad. He bought a mule team and wanders the mountains in search of his lost love. Houston and Cindy became the guardians of the orphaned child to raise as their own. The house at Rainbow Moor stands abandoned, its empty rooms silent and lonely awaiting the next heir to the moor.

Legend says if you should wander into the wilderness above McClellan Mountain near the place known as Rainbow Moor, on a clear summer morning you might chance to see a young man and a young woman dressed in white riding a white horse. Close beside them runs a great white wolf. They can be seen running freely across the moor, the sound of horse's hooves pounding the ground echoes across the mountain and the sound of their laughter dances on the wind.

Printed in the United States
By Bookmasters